TWISTED

Marcus and Lena Fulford are the envy of their friends. Wealthy and successful, the couple, with their beautiful teenage daughter, Amy, seem content. But appearances mask a relationship almost at breaking point. Marcus's latest business venture has failed and Amy is sent to boarding school while Lena strives to get her own career back. She remains alone in the luxurious family house as the couple divorce and they arrange joint custody of their only child. Then Amy is reported missing from school and her friend's mother reveals that Amy was visiting her father – a fact denied by Marcus. Lena contacts the police, but DI Victor Reid fears the worst...

TWISTED

TWISTED

by

Lynda La Plante

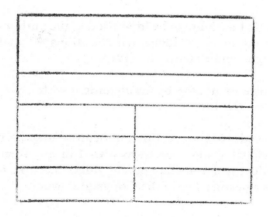

Magna Large Print Books
Long Preston, North Yorkshire,
BD23 4ND, England.

British Library Cataloguing in Publication Data.

La Plante, Lynda
    Twisted.

    A catalogue record of this book is
    available from the British Library

    ISBN   978-0-7505-4284-5

First published in Great Britain in 2014 by Simon & Schuster UK Ltd.

Published in Large Print 2016 by arrangement with
Simon & Schuster UK Ltd.

Magna Large Print is an imprint of Library Magna Books Ltd.

Printed and bound in Great Britain by
T.J. (International) Ltd., Cornwall, PL28 8RW

This novel is for a caring, dedicated doctor, a wonderful husband and father. His three sons and five grandchildren will always remember his generous, loving spirit and wonderful humour.

My last memory is seeing him surrounded by his beloved family in his new panama hat. My proud, brave brother, Michael Reid Titchmarsh, may you rest in peace.

Acknowledgements

Twisted was a difficult journey and one that required in-depth research from psychologists, who guided me through the various medical issues. My thanks and respect to the doctors and specialists who gave me their time and expertise. To Gillian Gordon for lending me volumes of medical journals and for giving me great insight into the specific medical conditions depicted in the novel. I would also like to express my sincere thanks to Callum Sutherland for his constant support and research, both in the police procedures and the editing. He is such a dedicated man with a genuine, thorough patience and an ability to ensure that I get the facts correct. I have been fortunate to have Susan Opie again to do the final edit, and as always I thank her for her enthusiasm and brilliant notes and suggestions.

I have a terrific team at Simon & Schuster, and would like to thank in particular Suzanne Baboneau and Ian Chapman; James Horobin and his amazing sales team; Dawn Burnett and Jamie Groves for marketing; Simon & Schuster International sales team, all my friends at S&S Australia; Jonathan Ball in South Africa; Simon and Gill Hess in Ireland – I look forward to seeing you all soon. My gratitude to all other departments, who work so hard to design my book jackets and produce the finished books.

Thank you to my dear literary agent, Gill Coleridge, who has guided and advised my career for so many years, and to Cara Jones of RCW; and to Stephen Ross, Dan Ross and Andrew Bennet-Smith at Ross, Bennet-Smith for their support and financial guidance.

I also want to express my sincere thanks to Nigel Stoneman, who has guided all the publicity and promotions for my novels for many years. Nigel's constant support, enthusiasm and generous spirit make life on the road a pleasure. Also, thanks to Tory Macdonald who is my personal assistant and a jewel I am fortunate to have beside me.

Chapter 1

It was the first dinner party Lena Fulford had agreed to attend since the separation from her husband. She was eager to show off her new image, although she couldn't help a shiver of trepidation at being on her own. She had chosen to wear a new, and very expensive, figure-hugging Ralph Lauren white cocktail dress. Her thick blonde shoulder-length hair was loose and she'd made sure her make-up was perfect by going to the beauty salon that afternoon. She had decided to take herself to the dinner party, and she felt more in control by doing so. However, she began to doubt her decision as there was not a parking space to be found on Richmond Hill. After having to go past her host's house twice, in frustration she decided to leave her car in the guests' area at the Richmond Hill Hotel. From there she walked to the Berkoffs' house, which was midway up the hill. Nervously she clutched her small white bag and flushed with embarrassment when the hostess opened the front door and shrieked.

'Oh my goodness, JUST look at you!' Maria Berkoff was her usual theatrical self.

She was a large overweight woman, which was accentuated by her tight red evening dress. But her hair was well-coiffed, and she wore chandelier drop earrings along with a multitude of pearl necklaces.

'Lena, you look absolutely stunning, darling, and you seem taller than I remember. I might need a divorce so I can get to slim down and look so good – you must have lost pounds.'

'Marcus and I are not divorced quite yet, and I think the weight loss is down to all the stress.' Lena gave a small smile.

'Oh how awful, but I thought it was all very amicable?'

'It is, but I have been so busy organizing a new children's themed party business, designing toys and–'

'Really,' an uninterested Maria said as she turned away.

'I've called it Kiddy Winks. It's been exhausting having to deal with all the hire of new staff and–'

'Oh Kiddley Winks – what a super name.'

'It's Kiddy–' Lena started to say before Maria interrupted.

'The Middletons have had the most fantastic success running just the same sort of thing, so I'm certain yours will be strong competition. Now come and have a glass of champagne and let me introduce you to everyone. I think you have met most of them before at some time or other.'

Lena followed Maria into a large glass conservatory, where numerous well-heeled guests were gathered. Maria's portly and effusive husband Sasha hurried to hand her a drink.

'How lovely to see you, Lena! We do miss old Marcus, he was always the life and soul of our little events. How is the old chap doing?'

'He was very well the last time I spoke with him,' Lena assured him.

'Good, and what about that daughter of yours – Angie, is it?'

'No, Amy; she's doing very well and enjoying boarding school.'

'Jolly good, now let me introduce you to a very dear friend – he used to play squash with your husband, thrashed him regularly.'

Lena found it all completely excruciating, even more so as everyone was eager to know how Marcus was doing and repeatedly told her how much he was missed. Although she had met most of the Berkoffs' guests before she had always been accompanied by her husband on such occasions. Now she had to endure being the focus of everyone's attention simply because she was single. At dinner Lena found herself seated next to a much younger man and had to put up with Maria, always delighted with an excuse to gossip, giggling that perhaps her glamorous looks were down to her finding a 'toy boy'.

Lena was infuriated and said curtly that she had no interest in forming any new relationship.

'My latest business is my priority right now,' she added.

'Just teasing, darling, you are such a clever lady and very successful,' Maria said as dinner was served.

For Lena it was three courses of substandard tasteless offerings, made worse by having to listen to one guest after another recalling previous evenings when Marcus had held court. He was a great storyteller, often with self-deprecating anecdotes about himself and his failed business ventures. The fact that Lena had invariably financed his thwarted attempts at success was never acknowledged. Being attractive, and somewhat vain, Marcus always relished the attention, and would have enjoyed listening to everyone repeating how much he was missed.

'So will you be staying on in that gorgeous house?' Maria asked.

'I'm not sure, we haven't discussed or finalized anything as yet.'

'So where is that ex of yours living?' Sasha asked, pouring himself some wine, and then proffering the bottle to Lena for a refill.

'He has rented a flat in Mayfair from a friend who is abroad,' she said and placed her hand politely over her wine glass. 'I'm driving so I will just stick to water, thank you, Sasha.'

'Mayfair! Well do pass on our warmest regards, and email us his address. He never answers his mobile or the messages I leave him, and Maria and I would love to see him.'

'I think he has a new number, and I'll remind him to call you,' Lena managed to promise politely.

At the earliest opportunity after coffee and mints, she excused herself, saying that she had a business meeting scheduled for early the next morning.

'What, on a Sunday?' Maria demanded loudly.

Lena flushed and explained that due to the success of Kiddy Winks she needed every spare moment to deal with the ever growing sales and orders for more stock. The by now rather drunk Sasha guided her to the front door, his sweating hand clasping her elbow and moving to her waist as his flushed face came too close.

'Perhaps we could have dinner one evening,' he suggested, leering. 'You know Maria and I have a sort of open thing and I'd like to get to know you on a more personal level.'

She moved away from him, and reached to open the door herself, but he was persistent.

'How are you fixed for next week? There's a new restaurant opened in Chiswick. I think Maria saw Marcus there one night.'

She gave him an icy stare, refusing to even contemplate answering. He opened the front door wider as she edged past him without saying a word. As she walked down the short path and headed back to where she had parked, she was horribly aware that he was standing there watching her. It had been a really hideous evening and one she would not consider repeating. She had been separated from Marcus for two years, yet tonight for some reason it felt as if it had only just happened. She had refused many other invitations to parties and dinners, but badgered by Maria she felt forced to attend this one, even though she knew full well the Berkoffs were really Marcus's friends, as were most of the people seated round the dinner table.

It took a while for her to ease the car out of the parking space, moving backwards and forwards and becoming even more agitated as the hotel car park was by now full for a big function. Why had she agreed to go? She'd known what it was going to be like. By the time she had succeeded in manoeuvring out of the tight space she had answered herself. She had wanted to prove that she could do it. She also wanted to tell everyone about how successful Kiddy Winks was becoming. This latest business venture had played a major part in getting her life back in order, and then deciding that if she could make the business work then she could also do something about herself. The marriage had been very strained for some time before the separation, and she had allowed herself to overeat and had spent days in an old tracksuit. She had not bothered with hair or make-up, her skin had erupted in patches, and the depression that had dominated her life was only relieved by her determination to make a success of Kiddy Winks. But now she'd lost the extra weight and was back to size twelve.

It had been a strange relief when Marcus had suggested they first separate or take 'time out', as was his crass way of putting it. Marcus had moved out; his design company was already in financial trouble, and shortly before his decision to leave he had wondered whether he should continue keeping it afloat. Lena had been impatient; this was not the first business venture that had failed. Over the seventeen years they had been married, she had constantly diverted money from her accounts to his in the hope that he would, as he had always promised, repay her with interest. This last time she had refused, and after taking advice from her accountant she had confronted her husband with worrying discrepancies in their joint bank account. Marcus had withdrawn thirty-five thousand pounds, leaving no money to pay for the mortgage on their substantial house in Richmond, the household staff or the utilities. Lena had to arrange to pay from her private account or they would have been taken to court.

Lena cancelled the joint account and Marcus had given her one of his childish shrugs, saying that she should consider what it meant. She could hardly believe that he was insinuating that it virtually signalled their marriage was over. In reality it was the start of their already strained relationship reaching breaking point, so by the time he had suggested they have a trial separation, his 'time out', she knew the marriage was heading for permanent closure. She had loved him, and they had been an enviable couple to their mutual friends, who were breaking up or divorcing throughout their seventeen years together. What few of even their close friends knew, as had been obvious that evening, was that Lena had always been the main breadwinner. She had never so much as hinted at it, she had cared that much for Marcus. He had tried numerous career moves, and with every new venture she had been supportive and encouraging. The fact they all turned into failures, and lost money – her hard-earned cash – never really bothered her as she had always felt badly for him. He appeared on the surface to take a positive attitude, refusing to feel sorry for himself, and always determined that the next idea he dreamed up would be successful. She knew deep down he was crestfallen and disappointed, and that he refused to show how much it affected him, for her benefit. So she had thought it churlish to complain.

It wasn't hard to pinpoint when exactly the change in her attitude towards him began to take seed. Prior to the separation she had embarked on opening new companies and he had been dismissive, suggesting that surely she had enough to keep her occupied. His attitude had only made her more determined and her animal-print cushions and handcrafted nursery furniture companies became a success and, like her new venture, Kiddy Winks, were all doing very well, taking orders from John Lewis, Harrods and Harvey Nicks. Dealing with the orders and travelling to the various factories and small producers had meant that her schedule was fully packed. Choosing the fabrics and designs alone was time-consuming, and she had by now fifteen women sewing and making the cushions. She was not exactly working twenty-four seven, but close. The past two years had been made easier because their daughter Amy had started at a weekly boarding school in Berkshire. Lena or Marcus would collect her from the school mid-morning on the Saturday, so she would be home for the weekend and returned before seven o'clock on the Sunday evening.

Lena did try not to work on the Sunday, but often Amy had friends to see and parties to attend, so she was not as dependent on being amused, especially now that she was fifteen and increasingly self-sufficient. Lena used the time to check over her accounts and sales orders. She had even stopped making the obligatory Sunday roast – it had always been just the three of them around the kitchen table, but since Marcus had left, and with Amy having alternative arrangements, she would mostly have a BLT and a cup of coffee. There had been a minor emotional upheaval when they had told Amy about the so-called trial separation. She had cried for a few days but calmed down after both assured her that they were still to be friends and she could, if she wished, spend alternate weekends with her father in Mayfair.

When divorce was eventually discussed, Amy had grown used to her parents being apart. She had begun to quite enjoy the freedom of choosing whether or not she spent the weekend with her mother or her father. There had also been numerous times when Amy had actually stayed with a friend so had not been at home with either parent.

The house in Richmond for just herself and Amy was large, and did require a lot of maintenance, but as Lena had paid for the mortgage from the moment they had bought it shortly after they were married, it had never occurred to her that she would be forced to sell. She had also furnished it, and it was very much her style throughout. Marcus had never taken much interest in decorating, or for that matter, what furniture Lena collected, and since they separated she was happy to remain living there; she even redecorated the kitchen and the master bedroom. Amy had kept her bedroom as it was, and she had rarely if ever brought up the fact that her father was absent. He obviously was, but then if Amy were not at his rented flat, but at home with her mother, he would call, so he was a constant and regular part of her life.

Lena had begun to really see the benefits of her new business, and financially she felt more secure than she had been when Marcus departed. It took a while for her to begin to enjoy having extra cash to spend on new clothes for herself and

Amy, but they had done some serious damage on a couple of trips to Chelsea on Saturday shopping extravaganzas. Working hard for so many years she had rarely if ever spent time on herself or her appearance until recently. It was very obviously successful, as the remarks from everyone that evening proved.

A meeting with Marcus had been arranged for Monday morning to discuss their divorce proceedings. Only once had Lena asked her daughter if Marcus was living in the rented flat alone, or if he was with someone, but Amy had been dismissive, saying that she had never met anyone, or seen anyone with her father. She did later mention that she thought someone else had been staying as there had been make-up left in his bathroom, but her father had said that it belonged to a friend of the guy he was renting the flat from.

Lena never for a moment thought Amy was being evasive, and in some ways she was relieved that there was no new figure in either of their lives. She in fact congratulated herself that, unlike many of their friends, they had succeeded in separating without too much emotional trauma. Amy did appear to have totally accepted the arrangements, and showed no outward signs that she was in any way distressed they no longer all lived together. The family home ran smoothly; the gardeners came and tended the garden every Thursday, the housekeeper came in every day at nine and left at five and always had the weekends off. Lena's driver, an ex-manager of a small repair garage, was diligent and polite and kept her Lexus immaculate. He also did a lot of maintenance work around the house, when not required to chauffeur Lena to her places of work. Sometimes he had worked weekends on the school collection when Marcus had called to say it was not convenient for him to pick up Amy, and even when Marcus had excused himself as being too busy to have Amy stay for her weekend, it had not caused any rifts. Lena was so organized, if arrangements were changed, she was able to quickly alter her diary. Basically, her entire life was taken up with work, and rarely if ever did she have any kind of life outside her day-to-day schedule. At weekends she would arrange something to do with Amy if she was available, and they would go to a local restaurant and take in a movie together. So her social life was built around her daughter, and her weekdays were concentrated on business. She had not sought any other social activities until this evening, even though she was feeling healthier and looking better than she had for years. She was aware that she would be subjected to prying questions about her separation and whether or not it was just a phase and she and Marcus would be getting back together. He was now to all intents and purposes a single man in his early forties, a very different dinner guest to his rather reclusive ex, who had never had been over-eager to gossip, and had little to add to their banter.

Lena had been helped to get her life back on track by her therapist and was now on medication, but it had been many months before she was able face the fact that she needed to make some drastic personal changes. As the business ran smoothly she had begun to take more interest in her appearance. It had not been easy – diet and exercise had dominated what little free time she had – but she made sure to style her hair, and had regular massage sessions at a beauty clinic. She had even had numerous Botox treatments around her brow, eyes and lips. Amy being a weekly boarder at school had allowed her to focus on herself.

Amy had been due to spend the weekend with her father but had chosen to have a sleepover in Fulham with one of her best friends, Serena, a young girl that Lena did not particularly like, who had in the past stayed at their house in Richmond. As always there had been emails back and forth to verify that Amy would be collected from school by her friend's parents and returned there on the Sunday evening.

Driving the short distance to her home from the Berkoffs' gave Lena enough time to calm down. She turned in through the big wrought-iron gates, and didn't bother going further down the private lane to the large double garage, but parked outside her front door, sitting for a while resting her hands on the steering wheel. Then she took a few deep breaths and slapped the wheel with the flat of her hands.

'Now just stop this, Lena, you knew what it was going to be like this evening, and you know why you agreed to go, and whether you hated it or not it was proof that you have taken major steps forwards. When Marcus sees you he'll want you back, that's what this is about, now admit it, and stop being silly, you have accomplished every-thing you planned and worked so hard for. When you meet him on Monday he is going to get a big surprise.'

She snatched up her little white evening bag and stepped out of the car, slamming the door shut and locking it with a bleep. Everything was going to be all right, she would have all of Sunday to plan exactly what she would wear from her new wardrobe of elegant clothes. She immediately felt better and did a small sashay dance step to the front door, as the security lights came on like a floodlit stage, and she opened her little bag with a flourish to take out her house keys.

It was strange how quickly her mood changed. Suddenly she realized it was the first time since the separation that she had returned to what felt like a very empty house. Maybe she had previously been too busy to notice she was opening her front door to darkness, or perhaps it was the fact she had so rarely been out so late alone. Lena had forgotten to leave lights on in the hall and landing, so it felt even darker than usual. She dropped her handbag on a chair in the hall, switched on the lamps and made her way up to the first-floor landing and the master bedroom. She undressed, chucking her evening clothes onto a chair by her dressing table; she'd hang them up in the morning. She placed anything she wanted washed into the white laundry bags hanging on a knob of one of the long rows of wardrobe doors. Naked, she walked into her en-suite bathroom, cleaned her teeth and removed her make-up with cleansing cream.

Returning to the huge master bedroom she picked up her nightdress that had been left folded on her king-size four-poster. Getting into bed with just a small bedside light switched on, she drew the duvet around herself and reached for the TV remote. The big plasma screen lit up as she nestled down, flicking from channel to channel, but nothing appealed. She switched to a re-run of *Law & Order* but had already seen it, so she turned off the TV and lay back on her huge pile of frilled white pillows. It was the first time she felt lonely. It was not that she wanted Marcus to be beside her, because she truthfully didn't, it was more an overpowering feeling of being totally alone. She closed her eyes. There were all the staff she knew so well at all of her successful business ventures, and yet none of them had ever become in any way a friend; none had ever even been invited back to the house.

She left the bedside light on, because she didn't feel sleepy – in fact, the opposite. Her mind was still buzzing, replaying the entire course of the dinner party: the many compliments she had received on her new slim self, her dress, her hair, even the many implications that she must have found someone to replace Marcus, although the truth was she had not even contemplated a new relationship. She had not even been looking to find a replacement, toy boy or not.

Knowing sleep was refusing to come, she reached up to her bedside cabinet for one of the various bottles of sleeping pills. She opened the top and inched out half of a tablet. She usually used them only when business deals had made her restless. She sipped from the bottle of water on her bedside table and swallowed the Ambien half, then replaced the small plastic container. She had got them years ago, when they had been in the US on a Disney World holiday, and she had been unable to sleep due to the time zone difference. Marcus had in actual fact got them for her. He was in her mind yet again, and now she thought about the meeting scheduled for ten on the Monday morning. He had suggested she find a divorce lawyer as he had felt it was time they confirmed that there was no possibility of them being re-united. She had agreed and engaged Charles Henshaw, a divorce solicitor, to represent her.

Lena had had only one brief phone call and meeting with Mr Henshaw, who was very pleasant and had a quiet unassuming demeanour. He had asked if the divorce was on a friendly footing, and she had said confidently that it was, and doubted there would be any animosity. Henshaw said that a 'Collaborative Divorce' meeting with Marcus and his solicitor would be the best way forward so they could reach an amicable agreement without going to court. There was no issue of custody as they had made arrangements for Amy to spend time with each of them. Lena did, however, point out that she paid for her daughter's education and had been the main breadwinner throughout their entire marriage. Mr Henshaw had enquired about the house and Lena had made it clear that she had maintained the property, and paid the mortgage throughout their marriage, and could see no problems with continuing to live there. Furthermore, at no time had Marcus even brought up altering the living arrangements as it was obviously their daughter's and her own main home. It was also her main place of work. Henshaw cautioned that it

27

was to be a meeting to discuss how the divorce would proceed, and until they were privy to what Marcus's wishes were, he advised that she should allow him to broach the subject. To date, he had not been given any more details. The only information he had been able to ascertain was that, like herself, Marcus had acquired a divorce lawyer, a Mr Jacob Lyons, who would also attend the meeting.

The only time she had felt a slight unease was when Henshaw remarked that Lyons was rather a formidable gentleman with quite a reputation, and that he had previously represented rather well-known clients. It had surprised her because that suggested Lyons was not cheap – probably more expensive than Mr Henshaw. She had rather naïvely not given much thought to the fact that her husband would also be represented, but she presumed that Marcus must have been earning enough to hire such a prominent figure. It also dawned on her that she had no idea exactly how Marcus was financing himself, unless one of his ventures had at long last been successful.

Waking later than usual she slipped on her thick woolly rather unattractive dressing gown and went down to the kitchen. She brewed a pot of coffee, made two slices of brown bread toast, buttered and spread them with honey, put them onto a tray, collected her newspapers and returned to bed. She skim-read the *Mail on Sunday* and *The Sunday Times,* finished her coffee but hardly touched her toast. It was almost eleven thirty by the time she tried to call Amy on her mobile but it went straight to voicemail. She left a short message to say she hoped she was enjoying her sleepover, sent her hugs and kisses and asked if she would give her a call to say all was well. The rest of the morning she spent having a long leisurely bath and washing her hair. Even though she had not heard back from Amy by early afternoon she was not unduly worried. Heading for her office, she checked her emails, finding none from Amy but a huge number from her business. It took her until almost five to answer them all, sorting out the various collections and deliveries, but finally the paperwork was all in order, the receipts and payments double-checked. Next, she made a list for the grocery shop to be done on Monday by her housekeeper. She made out cheques for the gardeners, and left a memo for them to also clear the guttering as there were a lot of leaves and she was concerned about drainpipes becoming blocked. She was about to close down her computer but hesitated, deciding to Google Jacob Lyons on the internet. Old Mr Henshaw had not specified any of the famous names Lyons had represented, but a quick Google search soon revealed that he was indeed notorious, and an exceptionally tough operator, with millionaire movie stars and rock singers his main clients. He had gained massive maintenance orders and won the unlikeliest of custody battles, and so the press described him as a Rottweiler who never lost a case. She was stunned that Marcus had felt it necessary to hire him, and it was obvious that he was very expensive. It made her feel increasingly uneasy.

Lena opened a bottle of wine; she had still not eaten so she cooked up some eggs and bacon, making another call to Amy as she did so, but her daughter's mobile yet again went to voicemail. The lack of response was starting to be irritating, but then she reckoned Amy was probably having a good time. She was in two minds whether or not to ring Marcus and ask if he had heard from her, but decided against it.

Lena went through her wardrobe, choosing what to wear for the meeting in the morning. She chose a smart new Jaeger suit, a white silk shirt with bow tie at the neck, and took out her black Louboutin high heels and some fine black ten denier tights. By the time she had hung up everything she was to wear and chosen pearl earrings and a necklace, she was ready to go back to bed. Unusually for her, she broke another sleeping tablet in half and by ten she was almost asleep. The wine had helped – almost three-quarters of the bottle of Merlot. She lay there wondering if there was anything else she should have done as she would not be going into work – her appointment was for nine thirty with Henshaw in Mayfair and her driver would collect her at eight thirty to make sure she was on time.

Harry Dunn had arrived earlier than needed as he wanted to valet and wash the Lexus. He remained sitting in the car when it was finished, and at promptly eight thirty Lena walked out of the house. Harry gave her a polite good morning, holding the passenger side door open as she got into the car. She always sat beside him, never in

30

the rear seats unless she was with a business associate.

The offices of Henshaw, Froggat and Co. were in North Audley Street in Mayfair, in a large elegant house on four floors with various other legal companies listed on the brass plate outside. Mr Henshaw was waiting and ushered her into a panelled boardroom. He was immaculately dressed in a pinstriped suit, crisp white shirt and Old Harrovian tie, and appeared the epitome of old-world charm. At just after ten, his secretary tapped on the door to say that Mr Lyons and Mr Marcus Fulford had arrived. Lena was nervous; she had not actually met with Marcus for almost a year, possibly even longer.

Lyons was small, wearing what was probably a very expensive suit, with skinny trousers and five buttons on the jacket, but it looked too tight for him. He had a bright pink shirt, with a matching pink silk tie and heavy gold cufflinks. His hair was slicked back, thinning, and gave his over-large head a gnome-like appearance, and whether or not his suntan was genuine, it had an unattractive orange tinge. This made Lyons' teeth even more unnaturally white, and he had wet lips that were spread in a wide smile. He greeted Henshaw like an old friend, and then turned to introduce him to Marcus.

Marcus was wearing a navy pinstriped Armani suit she had bought him, but instead of a shirt he had on a white T-shirt, and wore two-toned shoes with no socks and dark glasses. His hair was longer than she remembered, still thick, curly and dark, and his face bore signs of a slight stubble. Hand-

31

some as ever, he also gave a wide friendly smile as he was introduced to Henshaw, and then glanced towards Lena.

She wished he had taken the glasses off, as it was obvious that he was taken aback by her new image, and she would have liked to see the expression in his eyes.

'You look well, Lena, better than ever.'

'Thank you.'

She was introduced to Lyons, who gave her a wet handshake, not even looking at her as he chose which chair to sit in, and then gestured for Marcus to sit beside him, both of them across the large mahogany boardroom table. Lyons snapped open a brown leather briefcase, took out some paperwork and a notebook which he laid on the table. He removed a gold pen from his inside jacket pocket, unscrewed it and set it beside his notebook.

'Right, let's get down to business, shall we?'

Marcus turned his chair so he didn't have to look directly at Lena, who now had the opportunity to take a good look at her soon-to-be ex-husband. He seemed if anything to be enjoying the situation, leaning back, crossing his legs, over-relaxed, and why the dark glasses? She thought it was silly, as if he was playing at being a rock star.

What happened next left Lena in a state of distress. First Lyons suggested he start off the meeting and not waste time on pleasantries.

'Now you must be aware, my friend, that my client is in a dire financial situation, and heavily in debt, and as such he will require substantial alimony to be paid, since his wife, as you, my friend, must be more than aware, is a very successful businesswoman.'

Lena could hardly believe how Lyons continued, saying that he had done a discreet valuation on her house, it was worth in the region of four million pounds and Marcus wanted it to be sold and the profit split equally between them. Lyons went on to inform them that Marcus had listed, as best he could recall, the furniture and items from the property, which should also be divided between them, as he would soon need to purchase and furnish a flat.

'My client is currently renting a property but only for a short while longer and will need two-bedroom accommodation for himself and his daughter. He has made it very clear that Mrs Fulford has been the main breadwinner but he has always been encouraging and helpful in her business and he feels it is only fair to have a fifty-per-cent share of all her companies, along with alimony payments to enable him to live in the style he was accustomed to. Again my client wants it made very clear that caring for his daughter is his paramount concern.'

Lena was having palpitations, catching her breath and sipping her water. Henshaw had not as yet uttered one word. She glanced towards him angrily and was about to say something when he gestured for her to remain silent. Lyons flicked over several pages in his notebook and then tapped with his nasty manicured fingers what appeared to be a list and sums written in black felt tip pen. He looked through his paperwork, removing some printed sheets that were stapled together, and rudely slid them across the table to Lena and Mr Henshaw.

'My client has obtained an up-to-date detailed list of Mrs Fulford's business and private bank accounts, as well as her projected earnings for the next financial year, which as you can see, Mr Henshaw, are substantial.'

Lena gripped her fingers tightly, watching as Henshaw flicked through the copies of her bank accounts. It was unbelievable – Marcus had somehow got his hands on all her personal details, not only of her savings, but all her different projects and they were so up-to-date she hardly knew the amounts herself. She wanted to get up and slap her husband's gloating face, sitting across from her smirking as if he expected praise for obtaining her private information.

Henshaw gave a light cough. 'You originally agreed to a Collaborative Divorce meeting between our clients, Mr Lyons, so an amicable settlement could be reached. I am not prepared to discuss your requests at the present time, and I will need to have a consultation with Mrs Fulford before we agree to any of Mr Fulford's demands.'

'By all means, but it is very obvious that the marriage was in difficulties for a considerable time,' Lyons observed loftily. 'Mrs Fulford left her husband with no other alternative than to leave the marital home. Admittedly that was some time ago, but he has had time to reflect and realizes that reconciliation is no longer an option. It is a very emotional decision for his own well-being as Mrs Fulford put her work and ambition before any attempt to show she desired the marriage to continue.'

Lyons flicked his notebook closed and shrugged. He opened his nasty little briefcase and replaced his paperwork and notebook and then gave a cool look towards Lena.

'Kind of a reversal of fortunes, is it not, Mrs Fulford – it's usually the wife who makes claims on her husband's earnings and estate. However in this instance it is quite obvious that you, as a successful businesswoman, will be made an example. No discrimination meant due to you being a woman, but I think my client has asked for only what is fair and his right as your husband of seventeen years.'

Lena simply sat there as Lyons and Marcus did more handshaking before leaving. As the door closed behind them she wanted to scream. How dare he claim that he had always been encouraging and helpful? He had done nothing, everything had always been down to her. She drank the remains of her water and placed the glass down, her hand shaking. He was divorcing Lena claiming that it was due to her unreasonable behaviour, that she had placed too much effort and energy into her work and career and added to that it appeared she had not acted quickly enough because Marcus had put in his divorce petition first.

'What if I refuse to give him a divorce? I don't care if it never goes to court.' She got the words out with difficulty.

'I'm afraid the divorce proceedings are already in motion, and to be honest even without a divorce your husband can still claim to be given financial security,' Henshaw replied. 'You can counter-claim but quite frankly it really does not make any difference because it does appear that the marriage has broken down irretrievably.'

She was tight-lipped with anger. 'You tell me why a fully able-bodied man can have the audacity to want me to pay alimony. Why doesn't he get a job? I refuse to pay him anything, and I am not going to sell the house. He can sue me and if he thinks he is going to get a percentage of my companies, he can go to hell. It just is so unfair, he was the one that walked out for his so-called trial separation, it was not my suggestion but from what I can gather I have to be the guilty one and made to pay out to him.'

Henshaw allowed her to rant on, until she burst into tears. 'He left me, I didn't leave him, and it's disgusting,' she said through her sobs.

Henshaw passed her a box of tissues and she plucked one out and blew her nose. He held up the copy of her accounts Lyons had given him.

'These could have been printed off anywhere from downloaded files and impossible to trace back to a particular printer. Is there someone in your business that would have given him access to all your company accounts?'

She sighed and shook her head. As Marcus had nothing to do with her work, it was unlikely he had ever had more than a fleeting conversation with the staff she employed. The older women that did the sewing were in the country and hardly ever came to London. She couldn't think how he had obtained such recent figures; some of the future earnings she hadn't even calculated herself.

'I don't know how he knew so much about

Kiddy Winks – my God, I've only just got it running smoothly. He was never interested in any of my business ventures when we were together, not one iota, he never helped me in any way at all. I don't know how he has got all those details.'

Henshaw sighed and gave a quick glance at his wristwatch. 'Well somebody has evidently had access. Obviously he had access to your joint bank account, but the copies of your business account statements are as recent as last month.'

'Maybe Marcus or Lyons hired one of those professional hackers,' Lena suggested.

'Possible, but very risky for Lyons as a respected divorce lawyer. I'm sorry to say it would appear somebody close to you is untrustworthy. That said, it would eventually have been necessary to divulge that information to Mr Lyons. You see, you may decline to give him a divorce, but the reality is after a separation of two years your husband can be granted one without you agreeing. He simply files for a divorce on the grounds your marriage has broken down irreparably.'

'Christ, you sound as if you are on his side,' she snapped.

'Absolutely not, Mrs Fulford, and I will endeavour to find the best solution to your predicament as is possible. I will in the interim require you to give me your own estimation of the value of your property and also the value of its contents.'

'He's not getting so much as a stick of furniture. I bought the lot. He never paid for anything.'

'Nevertheless, I am afraid he is entitled to–'

She snatched up her handbag. 'I don't think you heard me, I used the inheritance from my grandparents to put the deposit on that house, and to help start up my business. None of it came from him and I am not giving him a cent, and he can drag me through whatever court he wants because I am not prepared to prop that loser up as I had done for seventeen years.'

Henshaw didn't attempt to stop her as she swept out, banging the door behind her. He had seen it all before, though as Lyons had said it was usually the husband who screamed about being used and refused to pay up. Lena Fulford had a sizeable amount of wealth, albeit hard-earned, and from what he had learned her husband had not been very successful – in fact, to the contrary. However, seventeen years was a long marriage, they had a daughter together and somewhere at some point there had to have been positive times. He sighed and checked his watch. His next appointment was due in half an hour; in the meantime he would look through the copies of Mrs Fulford's earnings left by Lyons in the hope that he might be able to persuade her to make a deal with her husband for a one-off payment, no strings attached. He would leave it for a few days for her to cool down. As he plucked a tissue from the box and picked up her empty glass left on the table, he reflected that people's marriages never ceased to amaze him; she was such an attractive woman, beautifully dressed, very classy, unlike her husband. He had to admit Marcus Fulford was a good-looking man, but there was something seedy about him, and to have worn the dark sunglasses throughout the meeting proved to Henshaw that he was probably afraid to look his wife in the eyes. Maybe that was at the root of their marital problem – he was scared of her, or perhaps he had been in awe to begin with and it had gradually been chipped away by his own failures. At some point he had gained enough strength to walk out.

Henshaw, a wily old man, guessed there would be another woman at the root of it, but neither had brought up a third party as a reason for the divorce. A weak man like Marcus Fulford, he was certain, had someone, and it had to be someone very close to Lena to have passed on such personal details. Gone were the days of extramarital affairs affecting the results of divorce proceedings – they no longer had any bearing on the outcome. It was now immaterial whether one's spouse had been unfaithful; all the court needed was evidence of the breakdown of the marriage. It had been so much easier in those days!

Chapter 2

Agnes Moors had left a message that she was going to collect the dry-cleaning and then do the grocery shopping so would not be back until after lunch. She had made sure the kitchen was spotless and gleaming – in fact the whole house was always polished to within an inch of its life. She had a mild obsessive-compulsive disorder that Lena put up with, simply because she was such a methodical and good housekeeper. Irritating little things, such as her obsession with straight lines, the way she organized the cushions on the sofa, the bed, and even the decorative pillows were an anathema to Lena – everything had to be too neat and precisely lined up. The curtains had to be exactly symmetrical, each drawn across the same distance, no showing of the silk lining that Lena rather liked, so it was a ritual that Agnes would hang the curtains dead straight and Lena would flick them around and tie the coiled loops more loosely.

Agnes was about sixty, square-shouldered, thickset, with an oval-shaped and age-lined face, and small unblinking piercing brown eyes. She wore reading glasses when she worked so that she could see every speck of dust or finger mark. She used over-the-counter hair dye, and it was hard to detect her original colour, as her hair was now reddish brown with darker almost black streaks and a quarter inch of grey growth at her roots, which were very obvious as she had a prominent widow's peak.

Lena, still seething, had uncorked a bottle of wine and sat fuming about the meeting. She opened a bag of Kettle Chips and munched one after the other, unable to think about anything other than the fact she felt as if she was being harassed and for no reason but Marcus's greed. It took a while for her to eventually calm down; she had a shower and dressed in her towelling robe and then returned to the kitchen. She'd forgotten that she had switched off her mobile at the morning's meeting and switching it on now she saw that there were fifteen unanswered calls, and numerous text messages about a new delivery of fabric from India. Simply scrolling through them made her head ache. She realized that she had not heard from Amy, and there was no message or text from her. However, there were two from her school requesting Lena make contact regarding Amy's attendance. She rang Amy but it went straight to voicemail, and checking the time was after three, she decided she'd wait until classes ended at four before calling the school matron. She was not unduly concerned – often, if Amy had been on a sleepover, she returned to school later than usual.

Lena replied to a few text messages that needed to be attended to directly, but then didn't have the energy to return a couple of social calls. Instead she sat scrolling through her contacts, wondering if there was anyone who could have been passing over information to Marcus. She also wondered if one of her women friends might have been having a closer friendship with her husband than she knew about. No names jumped out, and in many instances she had not even been in recent contact with them. It started to really niggle her, as Henshaw had said whoever had passed on her business details would have to have had access to her accounts and it was more than possible it was someone very close to her. She tapped her fingers on the polished glass surface of the kitchen table. Who knew her password? Someone had to have gained entry into her computer, but she doubted anyone would know it; the only possibility was Amy, although she always hated anyone – even her daughter – using her computer.

Agnes arrived with the dry-cleaning and groceries, and began to unload the shopping, crossing backwards and forwards to the cupboards.

'Everything go all right earlier today?' she asked.

'No, and I don't want to talk about it.' Lena picked up her half-filled glass of wine. 'I'll be in my office. See you in the morning.' She paused in the doorway and cocked her head to one side. 'Agnes, have you ever used my computer?'

'Good heavens, no. Is there a problem with it?'

'No, I'm just concerned that somebody has been going through some personal files.'

'You mean you've had some kind of virus?'

'I don't know. Don't leave anything out for dinner – I'm not hungry.'

Agnes continued putting away the remaining groceries, then wiped around the sink, and gave a squirt of glass polish to the kitchen table that didn't really need it. Deciding she'd take the dry-cleaning upstairs the following morning as Lena was clearly not in the best of moods, she turned off the lights, and since it was by now almost five she let herself out and went home.

Lena was in her Spartan immaculate high-tech office. Shelves and filing cabinets were the only furnishings apart from her desk, computer, printer and telephone. It was clear of any knick-knacks. Her filing system was brought up to date every Monday; mail to be checked over was in a drawer in her desk as she hated it piling up on the desktop. She paid bills promptly or by direct debit, and records of these and wages for domestic staff were in separate compartments. She had a small cash box with usually two or three hundred pounds for any emergency, and always kept receipts, which she collected regularly to be switched to her tax drawer. All her bank statements were clipped together in yet another drawer. Everything was neat and orderly with nothing out of place, and it really frustrated her to think that someone had to have had access to be able to give such details to Marcus and his solicitor. Question was, exactly who, and she sat wondering if it was Agnes, but somehow she didn't think it could be, and then depressingly she began to return to the idea that it had to be Amy. Amy would be the only person that could possibly guess her password, and it made her feel so betrayed that she at first wanted to cry, but then became really angry.

Amy's mobile went yet again to voicemail. Frustrated, Lena called the school communal house phone. A bright girlish voice answered and Lena said she wanted to speak to Amy Fulford, as it was quite urgent. The matron came on the line, and said that they had been trying to contact her, as Amy had not turned up for school. Lena was perplexed, but hardly concerned as she suspected that Amy had simply decided to stay, as naughty as it was, with her friend who had arranged the sleepover.

Harriet Newman, the mother of Serena Newman, answered the phone and sounded rather confused. She knew that her daughter had asked Amy to spend the weekend, and they had collected her from the school at eleven forty-five on the Saturday morning. However, Amy had said that she wanted to see her father on the Saturday afternoon, and would return in the early evening. Serena had been very disappointed as they had arranged to go to see a film together, but Amy had never turned up. Mrs Newman presumed that the girl had decided to stay with her father, as she knew that Amy often did so when not at home with Lena.

'Did you try to call her?' Lena asked nervously.

'Obviously, yes we did, and I left you a message on your house phone, but we never heard back from anyone. Serena went to the film with some other friends and we returned her to school Sunday evening.' Mrs Newman sounded more irritated than concerned, as if Lena was blaming her in some way.

Lena realized that with the dinner party, the pending solicitor's meeting and other things on her mind she had not bothered to check any missed calls on her landline since Saturday. 'Thank you, I'm sorry to bother you. I think I will just call her father and sort it out as she has not returned to school.'

'Well, I can understand you must be worried. Serena told me you're going through a divorce so it has to be a difficult time,' Mrs Newman said, more friendly now.

'Yes it is, but Amy is handling it very well as it's amicable. We've made sure she didn't find herself caught in between us. Thank you again.'

Lena replaced the phone, angrier because the least Marcus could have done was to let her know that Amy was staying with him. She had a good few sips of wine before she called him, only to reach his voicemail.

'Hey, it's Marcus, leave a message and I'll get back to you.'

Trying to keep her voice from becoming shrill, she said, 'Can you please ask Amy to call me? She is not at school and I am concerned as she has made no contact with them or with me.' She sat beside the phone, willing it to ring, even while admonishing herself for being stupid and impatient, but she was angry at having to call the last person she wanted to talk to, especially after their meeting that morning. She finally turned her attention to her computer to check the latest emails but there was nothing of any urgency and she didn't feel like looking at any business arrangements for the following day as she would first have a serious talk with her daughter, and insist she drive her to school to apologize personally.

Amy's bedroom was just along the landing from her office, with a sign hanging on the door: 'Privacy Please'. Usually she was very aware of giving Amy exactly that, knocking before entering if she was at home, and rarely if ever going into the bedroom when she wasn't. Agnes changed the sheets, cleaned, and collected any dirty laundry and dry-cleaning. This evening Lena opened the door and stood looking into the room. It was not at all girly or draped in pink, but tasteful, with pale blue fitted carpets, white curtains and wooden slatted blinds. The small double bed had a duvet and frilled pillows, and an old teddy bear that Amy had kept since a toddler. He was worn and moth-eaten with one glass eye missing but was very much loved. She used to always carry 'Teddy' around and sleep clasping him tightly, although at about eleven years old, she had stuffed him into a drawer for some reason. Lena couldn't recall exactly when he had resurfaced but he was now always placed on her pillow. A pair of mule slippers were left on the floor beside the bed, but the rest of the room was exceptionally tidy. Fitted wardrobes took up an entire wall – the sliding doors opened to a bank of drawers and then full-length hanging sections. Winter coats were hung together and all her winter dresses and skirts were colour-coordinated and then there were a few evening dresses and rows of shirts and jackets. Her jeans were folded on the top shelf of the wardrobe alongside hats and scarves. Rows of boots and shoes were lined up along the bottom. Lena didn't touch anything, she just stood there admiring how neat and tidy everything was. It was hard to believe this was a bedroom of a fifteen-year-old; there were no posters of rock stars on the walls, in fact they were devoid of any kind of pictures apart from some family photographs. The bedside cabinets were uncluttered, with only an alarm clock, two matching lamps, bedside house phone and a stand for her mobile. Beneath their tops were rows of paperback books, all stacked together by size and width. Lena looked at the large antique dressing table; this was placed in front of the window and faced the large garden. A hairbrush and comb were in a blue pottery jar next to a hand mirror and a large bottle of 'Daisy' perfume sat beside a tube of moisturizer.

Lena began to look through the neat rows of dresser drawers, starting from the left, and found everything neatly arranged. Lena knew that Agnes was more than likely the person who carefully folded each bra and matching panties, rolled the tights into small balls and tucked them into the plastic dividers: black tights, woollen tights, socks, white tennis and sports socks all rolled up and tidy.

The bottom dressing-table drawers held old school books, sketchpads and envelopes in one, in another some Christmas cards still in their packaging. Only one drawer was locked, a small one on the top right-hand side. Lena had no idea where the key would be, and even had she known she would not have unlocked the drawer to discover what it contained. She reckoned it was probably Amy's diary – as a child she had always kept diaries but once her schoolwork intensified, she was given her own computer and abandoned the ritual. Then before Christmas she had asked for a journal: she was inspired to write short stories and wanted something special to put them in. She asked to have a proper bound one with a lock and key. Marcus had bought her one with her name embossed in gold letters; it had been very expensive, in dark green leather.

Lena stood in the centre of the room looking from one side to the other. She then went to close the wardrobe and she saw the stack of matching suitcases, in three sizes – small, medium and large. Lena knew Amy also had an overnight cabin bag at school, which she used when visiting Serena's or her father's, and it was the only one missing.

By the time Lena went to her bedroom, it was after seven, and she had still not heard from Marcus. She was loath to call back yet forced herself to do so, but it went straight to voicemail yet again and she didn't leave a message. She

47

tried Amy's mobile phone one more time and that too was on voicemail. She next called the school to ask if Amy had turned up or if they had heard either from her or her father.

The matron said they had not, and asked if she would call as soon as she heard when they could expect Amy to arrive. They did not approve of unplanned absences or really allow pupils to return after lights out, but if she was expected to be back that evening there was always someone on duty.

'I hope there's nothing wrong?' the matron asked and Lena, keeping her voice pleasant, replied that she suspected her husband had taken their daughter to the theatre. It felt lame even to her. Replacing the receiver she lay back on her bed, wondering if the school knew about the impending divorce. Because Amy stayed alternate weekends with her father they might very well suspect some kind of marital problem, even though Amy spent her school holidays mostly with Lena and she always allowed her friends to stay. The truth was, it was so much easier if Amy did have a friend to stay as it kept her occupied and Lena didn't have to arrange activities. It was much easier now that she was a teenager, but when she was younger, having to chauffeur her around had usually fallen to Lena. Marcus said he loathed having to remember which mother was which, and hated the obligatory small talk. The reality was, whenever they had both been to a school function, Marcus had appeared to thoroughly enjoy chatting to the mothers, flirting and being as charming as he could be. Lena had always taken a back seat on these occasions, usually because she was tired out having had to work flat out all day. She remembered a couple of times she had not even managed to wash her hair or get changed. Marcus on the other hand was wearing his Armani suit, shaved and immaculate. He had installed a gym in a studio above their garage so he would work out, for hours on end, then shower, and this he did virtually on a daily basis. In some ways she was grateful he was at least not hanging around the house trying to start yet another business venture, or becoming depressed because one had failed.

Lena rolled over, thumped the pillow with her fist. Just thinking about what had happened that morning made her furious all over again. Two years' separation and here she was still annoyed by all the things Marcus did, and had done before he had left. Yet again she was wasting her time on him.

At some point she must have fallen asleep, and with all the bedroom lights on. The phone ringing woke her with such a start that for a few moments she was completely disorientated, but then swung her legs to the ground and grabbed the receiver. It was seven a.m.

'Lena, it's me, I've just noticed your missed calls,' Marcus said abruptly.

'You took your time getting back to me. I have had the school calling me; I have tried ringing her, just what the hell is going on? Where is she?'

'She had a sleepover,' he said, and his voice sounded slurred.

'Yes I know, but she told Serena's mother on

Saturday afternoon she was going to see you, and she never went back there so Mrs Newman presumed she was staying with you.'

'She wasn't with me, I never saw her.'

'What?'

'I just said Amy never came here to me, I haven't heard from her all weekend or yesterday. I thought she was with her friend. I mean, she mentioned some sleepover – I dunno, what's all the panic about?'

Lena wanted to scream.

'Is she at school?' he asked stupidly.

'No she is not, I just told you, they called here, and I have not seen her.'

'What about this girl she was staying with?'

'For heaven's sake, Marcus, don't you listen to what I am saying? I have spoken to them. I talked to Serena's mother and she picked her up on Saturday morning and drove her to Fulham. Amy then told Mrs Newman she was going to see you and would be back in the evening, but she never turned up.'

'Why didn't they call me?'

She gritted her teeth. 'I have no idea, but we have to find her. If she didn't come over to you on Saturday afternoon, it means she's been some-where else since then and she is still not back at school.'

'Well I don't know where she is,' he said lamely, almost as an excuse. Clearly he still hadn't rea-lized that something could have happened to his daughter. Lena swallowed and gripped the phone tighter.

'Marcus, she has not been seen for over two

days now. Don't you understand how serious this is? Now think if there is someone she might have gone to see.'

He said something inaudible, and Lena had to ask him to repeat it. But he cleared his throat.

'Sorry, I was just thinking, you have talked to Serena?'

'No,' she snapped. 'Only her mother.'

'And they had no idea where she is?'

'For God's sake, Marcus, try and concentrate. I am asking you to think if she was friendly with anyone you've met recently?'

'Erm, to be honest I've not met any of her friends. When she's here they, well, they might come over but on the whole she's usually on her own and we go out to see a movie, or just watch TV...'

'Think, Marcus. Is there anyone she might have gone to see?'

'I'm fucking thinking,' he groaned.

Lena closed her eyes and sighed with impatience. 'Were you at home on Saturday afternoon?'

'No, I was at a football match.'

'So she could have gone to see you and you weren't in. Does she have a key?'

'Yes of course she does, but if she was here she never left me a note and I didn't get back until Sunday...'

'You mean you were staying somewhere else?'

'Yes, at a friend's from football.'

She squeezed her eyes more tightly shut, clenching her teeth. 'Okay, what about a boyfriend, do you know if she has a boyfriend?'

'She's not mentioned one. Look, you know you're firing off questions but I could be asking the same ones of you. Do you know if she was seeing a boy? And you'd know more than me who her close friends would be. We should start ringing around.'

'But her friends are at the school, so they would be there and not with their parents. Marcus, I don't know what we should do. I mean, do we wait until a bit later this morning and call around or...' Her voice trailed off.

'Let me just go over it all. She was last seen on Saturday afternoon, and no one has heard from her since and it's now Tuesday morning, so what about her mobile? Have you tried calling her?'

'Of course, it goes straight to voicemail; I've tried numerous times. I think we should go to the police.'

'Hang on, hang on. Obviously we have to think about that, but at the same time, we could be getting into a panic over Amy just being a bit of a truant and taking off with a pal.'

'She has never been a bit of a truant, for God's sake. She has never done anything like this before, and it's totally out of character. She always calls me when she stays over with you, she calls me if she's having a sleepover. I have never known her not to make sure I knew where she was and the more I think of it, the worse I am starting to feel. Something is really not right.'

'Okay, call the hospitals,' sighed Marcus. 'She may have had an accident, and we can both start doing that.'

'You start calling them, Marcus, I am going to

the police. If anything, I should have gone to them earlier. I'll call you, stay by your phone.'

She didn't wait for him to reply but slammed down the receiver. She pulled on a pair of jeans, sneakers, a polo-neck sweater, and a camel-hair coat. She didn't even comb her hair or check her make-up. She was in the Lexus within minutes of hanging up on Marcus, and she drove to the local Richmond police station, so tense her knuckles were white as she clenched the steering wheel, all the while keeping up a mantra to herself of 'Please don't let anything bad have happened to her, please don't let anything have happened to my baby.'

Chapter 3

Marcus had woken early with a terrible hangover and raging thirst. He had drunk a pint of water, taken four paracetamol tablets and a spoonful of Andrews Liver Salts as his stomach churned from the curry he'd eaten the previous evening. There had been the wine before the Indian, then he'd had a lot with his meal and was very drunk by the time he got home and collapsed. He was about to go back to bed when he noticed his answer machine blinking. It was all too tempting not to pick up his calls and, on hearing Lena's terse message, he was at first in two minds whether to bother calling her back. But he could see she had also made a second call with no message so knew something must be up.

The previous evening had not exactly been a celebration but he felt the meeting with the lawyers had been more than productive as Lyons assured him they would be successful and he even insinuated that Marcus might not have to work again but could live well if he invested carefully. They had a good lunch, Marcus paid, and it was expensive, as Lyons had chosen a very posh restaurant in Regent Street, but so far he'd been worth his heavy fees. During the lead-up to the meeting he'd been quite aggressive, constantly reminding Marcus that he would require extensive details of his wife's income and the value of the property and its contents. There was no point in 'pussyfooting' around – he had calculated that after seventeen years of marriage Marcus would easily be awarded alimony for the rest of his life. He was certain that he would be awarded half of the monies from the sale of their 'goods and chattels', and he would try for fifty per cent of his wife's very successful business. Marcus did not exactly like the pugnacious and egotistical lawyer, but he had been advised to secure his services as fast as possible just in case Lena might hire him. Lyons loved the notoriety he had garnered from previous cases and he was not just an A-list divorce lawyer, but the toughest of tough operators.

After a long lunch with Lyons Marcus had gone to meet his present girlfriend, Justine, a twenty-six-year-old, very glamorous and curvaceous blonde. She aspired to a modelling career but was working as a receptionist in a very fashionable hairdressing salon where she was also being trained by the salon's top stylist. Justine had a list of client confirmations and cleaning up to do before she could leave with Marcus. He had been quite happy to sit in one of the comfortable chairs in the waiting area, leafing through the recent glossy magazines, with one sly eye on the other attractive stylists. They had left together just after five, and returned to her small rented flat in Pimlico. Justine shared the place with another girl who was a waitress at a restaurant, so as they arrived she was just leaving for work. They had a few glasses of wine, went to bed, had sex, and then showered together before leaving at around nine to have a curry in her local Indian restaurant. Justine was not too keen on going back to his place as she had an early start with a very important client, one they always opened specially for to give her streaks and a cut before anyone else was in the salon. Marcus dropped her off in a taxi in Pimlico and then it drove him to Mayfair. He had eaten quite a substantial lunch and then the curry, so it was no wonder he felt ill and went straight to bed.

He was still feeling hung over but not as bad as when he had first called Lena. He took a cold shower, and, intent on doing as she had asked, began to seriously try and recall who Amy might have gone to see. There had been no note or signs that she had been at the flat, but he had another look around before he went into her bedroom. It would be quite difficult for him to know if she had been there while he was not at home. Her room was, as always, a shambolic mess. Unlike his wife, he had no housekeeper or cleaner and attempted to manage the place himself. There was a small utility room with a washing machine and dryer, and what clothes he needed washing he chucked in there, but bed linen went to the laundry, along with all his good shirts and dry-cleaning. Amy often didn't bother even straightening her bed, which irritated him, but he didn't make a thing of it. All her clothes were left in untidy heaps, and books and DVDs were stacked beside the bed. Shoes and boots were piled outside the wardrobe, the doors of which were usually open. Posters of her latest craze, the vampire movies, lined the walls, and she had a big thing for a new, very young group, and had forced him to watch them on TV. It was the floppy-haired lead singer who was the big attraction, and Justin Bieber had lost his place as her favourite.

He tried to recall his exact weekend activities. On the Saturday, as he had told Lena, he had been to a football match. It was a last-minute decision as he'd bought a single ticket from a guy in the pub who couldn't go. He'd then gone out with friends for hamburgers, taken in a movie with Justine and stayed the night with her. He had told Lena he was at a male friend's to avoid listening to her making cutting or flippant remarks. On the Sunday, he had nipped home to get changed, and then gone out with Justine and spent most of the day with her. He would have stayed overnight but, because of his meeting with Lena and the lawyers on the Monday, he had returned to get a good night's sleep. At no time had Amy called, or left a message on his mobile, and he was a bit ashamed that he had not even attempted to contact her. Knowing she was spending the weekend with her friend, and would be returning to school on the Sunday evening, it had not occurred to him to double-check the arrangements. It was also obvious that Amy did not get along with Justine, not that he ever discussed it with his daughter. It was just a fact and one he refused to get into any kind of argument about as he felt it was none of her business. But when Amy came for her weekend he would not have Justine stay over. Whether or not Amy had mentioned Justine to Lena was yet another subject he had not discussed, and it was not as if Justine was the first woman he had been seeing – there had been quite a number of others over the past two years, but most of them never even got to meet his daughter.

Amy's dressing table was heaped with cheap jewellery, perfumes and make-up, bottles of shampoos and conditioners, a matted hairbrush and comb. Marcus searched around, opening a couple of drawers, discovering creased underwear and old tights, vest tops and nightdresses. He then thumbed through all the latest magazines from the pile on top in case there was something between the pages, and tossed them aside to look under the bed, only to find old slippers and a few books covered with an accumulated level of dust. He couldn't recall ever vacuuming beneath it and he doubted Amy bothered. The bedside-table drawer was full of broken bits and pieces of necklaces and beads – no letters, no notebooks, or photo albums, nothing of any use. He next checked out the ward-robe, opening a suitcase, a couple of backpacks and a smaller vanity case. All were empty. Left plugged into a wall socket was her mobile charger, but no phone. Standing in the untidy room he could see nothing that gave any indication of where she might have gone, or who she might have been with.

He returned to the kitchen and brewed up a strong black coffee, sitting on a stool by the breakfast counter as he wondered if Lena had any news. He was about to call her when he glanced at the wall calendar pinned up beside a cork notice board. Amy had begun by circling the weekends she would be staying, but had not bothered for almost six months as she simply called him instead. The corkboard was full of receipts, dry-cleaning tickets, phone numbers for his gym and hairdresser, and invitations to dinners and cocktail parties. There was nothing connected to Amy, no old message left for him, but there was a picture cut out of a Sunday supplement of a King Charles Spaniel puppy. Amy had always wanted a dog, but it was just not possible.

Meanwhile, Lena was at Richmond Police Station, sitting in front of Detective Constable Barbara Burrows, a fresh-faced young woman with shoulder-length auburn hair. She worked on the Richmond Missing Persons Unit and was painstakingly and methodically writing down details for the 'misper' report. The slow procedure was beginning to frustrate Lena and she felt that someone of a higher rank should be talking to her. By now she was very concerned, and to be asked so many questions and forced to repeat herself over and

58

over again about her marriage and separation was irritating. DC Burrows was taking care to cover every angle, as she needed to have a very detailed report to put on the Met's missing persons database and also the National Missing Persons computer. Burrows explained to Lena there were three risk categories for missing persons – high, medium and low. Due to Amy's age, and the circumstances, it was possible she had run away and would probably be treated as a medium risk; however, enquiries and searches to try and locate her would still be carefully orchestrated. She told Lena her unit detective inspector was due in shortly and would be checking the report and classifying Amy's risk category. Lena had become very impatient when asked about boyfriends; to her knowledge Amy did not have any, nor had she ever mentioned she was seeing someone. Burrows had asked about whether or not her father would know, and Lena had replied rather sharply that he did not, and she had asked him to stay home and call the local hospitals.

'And he's doing that now, is he?'

'Yes – do you want me to call him?'

'I think so, as hopefully he may have already talked to your daughter.'

Lena took out her mobile, to find a message that as from a short while ago Marcus had no further news about Amy's whereabouts. Now she was growing increasingly anxious watching Burrows making copious notes but not appearing to show any cause for alarm, and it was starting to make her lose her temper.

'My daughter has not been seen by anyone I

know of for the entire weekend or yesterday, she has not even turned up for school, and it is now Tuesday. I need you to tell me exactly what I should – or what the police should – be doing, as I am really very concerned.'

Burrows stood up and closed her notebook. 'Leave this with me for a moment. Would you like a drink of some–' Lena interrupted.

'You want me to wait in here?'

'Yes please, Mrs Fulford. I need to talk to one of my colleagues.'

The small room was stuffy and Lena unbuttoned her coat, drawing it low to her shoulders. Her right foot was twitching with impatience. With nothing else to do she called Marcus, who answered immediately, sounding concerned.

'Did you get my message?' he demanded. 'I've tried everything we thought of but got nowhere. I've been waiting for you to call. Where are you?'

'I'm at the police station. I've been here since I last spoke to you. I've got this young detective woman driving me crazy, asking me the same questions over and over. Did Amy have a boyfriend, Marcus? It feels as if she thinks Amy's simply run away, but I know she wouldn't do that. She's always so good about keeping in touch with me when she's not at home – this is the first time I can remember her not checking in. So, was she seeing some boy?'

'Not that I know of – she never mentioned having anyone to me. You know how she was always texting and using her iPhone so there's no address book, or notebooks here, nothing that would tell me how to reach her friends. I know she was with

Serena, is it? For the sleepover – I knew about that. Christ, you don't think she's gone off with a teacher? There was that case a few years back when the girl went off with her teacher–'

He was talking very fast, his words tripping over each other, and she had to ask him to be quiet so she could think what next to say. 'I have met all her teachers and I don't think that is even a possibility; but I speak from my side – I have no idea what you two did, or if she met someone, maybe a friend of yours.'

'For chrissakes, nobody I know would date my fucking daughter – that's preposterous.'

'Marcus, I am here by myself, and if you had any thought for me left, you would be here with me. This is a nightmare and I am seriously worried that something has happened to Amy, because she would not simply take off without a word to you or me.'

He gave a heavy sigh and, obviously trying to keep himself calm, said he would come to the police station, if she thought it was necessary. Lena told him that he would have to be interviewed if there was still no word from Amy.

'Call the school again, Marcus, see if there's any news, and at the same time ask for contact numbers and email addresses for all Amy's friends.'

'What are the police doing to try and find her?'

'Nothing as yet,' Lena replied dismissively. 'I have been left in a dank little interview room, so I don't know what if anything anybody is doing. The officer took details for a missing person report and said she had to discuss the situation with her detective inspector and he would decide what

61

happens next. It's nearly three days since anyone saw Amy and to be honest I am starting to feel as if they are not taking it seriously enough, and I am at my wits' end.'

'Okay, listen, hang in there, I'll call the school, and get back to you. Stay positive, I'm certain there will be some reason she's not returned to school, and I'll do my best to find out, okay? Lena? Are you all right?'

'Yes, but call me if you hear anything.'

Marcus made the call and had a frustrating conversation with Amy's headmistress. At first, instead of being helpful, she was anything but, explaining that she could not give private email addresses or contact numbers of other pupils without their parents' permission. Eventually she said she was obviously very concerned and would, if he wished to come and see her, seek permission for the details he requested. She also said that according to the pupils' logbook, Amy had signed out for her weekend and they had given Mrs Newman a copy of the letter confirming that Amy was permitted to have a sleepover with their daughter Serena. They had expected Amy to return on the Sunday evening, but Serena had returned on her own, saying that Amy was staying with her father. On Monday morning when she had still not returned, they called Mrs Fulford and left several messages before they heard back from her. Marcus thanked her for the information and asked if under the circumstances she would be willing to give him Mrs Newman's phone number, as he really needed to speak with her. The headmistress agreed.

Immediately the woman hung up, Marcus called Mrs Newman to ask her exactly what she recalled about the Saturday afternoon.

'I am so sorry that you still haven't heard from Amy. It must be very distressing for you both, but I really can't add anything to what I already told your wife.'

'Would you mind going over it again for me, please, from when Amy and Serena got back to your house from school?'

'Well, Serena told me they had originally intended to go shopping and then see the five-thirty showing of a movie at the local cinema. It was shortly after arriving here from school that Amy told Serena she had to go to see you as she wanted to collect something.'

'What did she need to see me about?'

'I don't believe Amy was specific on the matter, Mr Fulford. Anyway Serena decided to stay here, wash her hair and wait for Amy's return. Serena was rather angry because she waited in all afternoon, and even left messages for Amy, but got no reply so she went to the cinema with some other friends.'

'Did no one think to call me or Lena?'

'We don't have a number for you, Mr Fulford, and I did leave a message on your wife's house phone but got no reply. I feel very guilty about not being more worried at the time, but Serena said that Amy often stayed weekends with you and she would no doubt turn up at school on Sunday.'

Marcus had listened patiently, and although annoyed that Mrs Newman didn't do more, kept his calm and asked if she could give him contact numbers of Serena's friends. She took an age away from the phone before returning and giving him details of three girls who were friends of Serena's from her previous school. She thought they did know Amy, but she couldn't be sure.

'Do you know if Amy had a boyfriend?'

'No. It's not something I ever asked her or that Serena mentioned to me. I'm so sorry that I can't be of more assistance, Mr Fulford, but if there is any way that I or my daughter can help you or your wife then please don't hesitate to call.'

Marcus thanked her, and she said he should really call her by her Christian name.

'It's Harriet, and my husband is Bill.'

'Right, Harriet, I appreciate you taking the time to talk to me.'

'Please, under the circumstances you must be frantic. I hope nothing serious has happened and would appreciate it if you keep me updated.'

'I will – thank you, Harriet.'

It was now approaching eleven a.m. Marcus rang Lena, who sounded really tense, to give her a brief rundown of what he'd been doing. He suggested they go to the school to talk with the headmistress, but Lena said that she'd have to call him back as a policewoman had just walked in.

Lena accepted a cup of tea, as the uniformed officer apologized for keeping her waiting but DC Burrows was having a meeting with her superior, DI Reid, and he would be coming in to talk to her in a moment.

'If you think of anything more that might be important, often just the smallest thing can be extremely helpful,' the policewoman said.

Lena closed her eyes and sighed. 'I just can't understand it. She has never done anything like this before, it's totally out of character.'

'Would you like a notebook and pen?'

'What?'

'Just thinking, before DI Reid comes in to talk to you, if there is anything you think might be of use, it's very difficult to be kept waiting, but he has only just come on duty and is going over all the information.'

The tea tasted stewed and Lena was exhausted. She shook her head and then burst into tears. 'I don't understand it. I mean, she's very clever and has no problems with exams and I've wracked my brains thinking what could possibly be the reason she's not contacted us. My husband has been trying to talk to someone that might know, but...' She took a tissue out of her coat pocket and blew her nose.

'Will he be coming here to be with you? Your husband?'

Lena wiped her eyes, and gave a shrug. 'I don't know – we're actually going through a divorce so we don't live together, but she was not staying with either of us but had a sleepover with a school friend. I've told all this to what's-her-name, the other policewoman that interviewed me. I have been here for hours and I am really getting very anxious. How long do I have to wait until somebody does something?'

'I'll go and see what's happening. Would you like another cup of tea?'

'No, I really want to get some guidance as to

65

what I should be doing – better still, what the police should be doing.'

Left alone, Lena blew her nose again, and stuffed the crumpled tissue back into her coat pocket. She drew the notebook closer, picked up the pen and stared at the empty page. She truthfully could think of no reason why Amy would have gone for such a length of time without making contact with either her or Marcus.

In his office on the first floor of the station, DI Victor Reid was still thumbing through the neat meticulous notes made by Burrows. He had been late getting into the station as he had been held up by a gas leak that had made the traffic snarled up around Richmond town centre. Before that he had been stuck behind a long line of traffic over Twickenham Bridge, and the build-up had turned a journey that usually took ten minutes from his flat in St Margarets into almost an hour.

Barbara sat in front of him, watching as he read each page, back and forth, before he stood up to put his jacket back on. DI Reid was quite a snazzy dresser. Today he was wearing a pale blue shirt with a dark blue tie, a well-cut grey suit and suede shoes. He had the kind of thick curly hair that made his chiselled face boyish, but there was a steely quality to his dark eyes. She'd noticed that often he needed to shave twice a day as he had a five o'clock shadow by early evening.

Although in his late thirties, Reid only had ten years' police service, all of which had, up until his promotion to detective inspector, been as a uniform officer. A 'late joiner', he had previously worked for a very reputable estate agent's for many years, gradually moving up to become an area manager and then head of corporate business sales. He was respected, well paid and travelled extensively round the UK, but found the work tedious and never really made friends with other employees in the business. He found them to be mostly pompous ex-public school boys in cheap grey suits and down-at-heel black shoes, whose aggressive attitude infuriated him. An only child from a lower-middle-class family, he was doted on by his parents. They were proud at him gaining a grammar school place and then attending Kingston College; sadly, they both died when he was in his twenties. He owned his small flat outright and, having bought it when he was an estate agent, he got a good deal. He had thought long and hard before finally deciding to join the police service and it was partly due to his long-standing relationship with a lawyer he'd met when showing her round a property. He'd intended to marry her, but she broke off the relationship and started to date a barrister. It had been a painful time made worse when she said she left him because he was boring, but the break-up instigated his decision to finally change careers.

Reid had so far enjoyed his police service and found detective work both challenging and rewarding. He was ambitious and hoped to make detective chief inspector within the next three years and eventually make superintendent. His goal was to be a member of the elite murder team, moving away from mispers to something he felt would be more rewarding.

He was well liked by his small team of six police officers and a civilian administrative assistant. He made them feel they were members of a 'top team', and always listened to and valued their thoughts and opinions. Even though he was very ambitious, his professionalism and unparalleled dedication had won him respect and admiration. It was obvious that he was moving up the promotional ladder at a steady rate.

Barbara fancied him, even though he was at least ten years older than her, but he hardly seemed to notice she existed outside of the station, and when he suddenly looked up, catching her staring at him, she flushed.

'This is very good, and you will need to upload it onto the Met and national misper databases and update things as we go, but you've asked the right questions at this stage. What is she like?'

'The daughter?'

'No, the mother. You mention that she is going through a divorce, but according to her it is an amicable arrangement between herself and her soon-to-be ex-husband, the daughter spending her weekends between them both, right? So, tell me, what she's like?'

'You mean emotionally?'

'Yes – is she very anxious? Does she have any gut feelings about what might have happened?'

Barbara paused. 'I'd say she is very worried, but she is quite controlled. She runs her own business.'

'Okay, and the husband is not with her, so I will need all his contact numbers as he will have to be interviewed today.'

Reid patted down his jacket, picked up his mobile phone, notepad and, running his fingers through his hair, came out from behind his desk.

'Right, let's get started, and I want you taking notes. If I appear to be repeating a number of the questions you've already asked it's to confirm she's being honest. Right now I am treating this as medium risk but, dependent on the next twenty-four hours, I may have to seek permission to upgrade it to high. If that is the case a homicide and serious crime team will take it over, so I want everything ship-shape.'

'Yes, sir.' Burrows opened the door for him and he walked past her into the corridor, asking for her to organize some fresh coffee, as he had not had any breakfast.

Lena half rose out of her seat when Reid entered the interview room and crossed directly towards her with his hand out. 'Mrs Fulford, I am Detective Inspector Victor Reid and I will be overseeing the inquiry.' She registered that he was over six feet with a strong presence and a firm handshake and she was slightly taken aback.

'Please sit down, Mrs Fulford. I've ordered some fresh coffee, and I apologize for keeping you waiting but I needed to assess the situation with DC Burrows before talking to you,' he said as he sat down beside her.

He took in Lena's appearance fast – her face devoid of make-up showed beautiful pale unblemished skin, wide pale blue eyes, and a thick sheet of blonde hair parted in the middle and resting just below her shoulders. She wore a polo-neck sweater, jeans and her expensive camel coat

69

was loose around her shoulders; she was a slim elegant woman, the type he liked. He even noticed she wore no wedding ring – in fact no jewellery at all – and her hands were delicate with short-cut nails.

Reid continued, 'It's imperative we do not waste time, so we will be circulating Amy's description and missing person's form to every police force in the country via the national database and other relevant agencies on the internet for public access. I will also be seeking authority for a press release. Rest assured, Mrs Fulford, we will do everything in our power to find your daughter as quickly as humanly possible.'

Lena felt more at ease and thanked him for his thoughtfulness. It was such a relief for her to be speaking to a senior officer, and at last she felt her fears were being taken seriously.

'I apologize if I repeat anything DC Burrows has already asked,' Reid went on. 'However, to progress the investigation I need to familiarize myself with everything that has occurred concerning Amy over the last three days and her home life in general.'

The more he spoke the more Lena felt confident he was an astute and caring detective who had a real grasp and understanding of the situation and her predicament.

'I may ask some questions that seem intrusive about your personal life and relationship with Amy. I'm not here to judge or pass comment on anyone. I want to find your daughter safe and well, but the more information we can glean about a missing person the more thorough and productive my team's investigation will be.'

Lena nodded, but Reid could sense that she was nervous.

DC Burrows entered with a tray of fresh coffee, two mugs, sugar, milk and a plate of biscuits. He placed one mug in front of her, picked up his own and heaped in three spoons of sugar but no milk.

'DC Burrows will be taking some notes, and as I said I would like to make as much headway straight away before I come to any conclusion. Your husband is helping to try and trace Amy?'

'Yes, he's called the local hospitals and the school. He is staying at his flat in case Amy calls.'

'But he has a mobile so she could contact him that way?'

'Yes, we both have, and Amy also has one; we have called her numerous times but it goes straight to voicemail.'

Reid nodded and said it would be a priority to trace the locations of Amy's iPad and iPhone as they could contain crucial information, and he muttered quietly to Burrows to get on to it straight after the meeting with Mrs Fulford. He wondered to himself if Amy was not answering any calls because she had run away. He then turned back to Lena and drew his notebook closer, reached into his pocket and took out a felt tip pen.

'Right, you do not know if she has a boyfriend or is in any kind of a relationship; have you any possible clue to Amy having a secret friend, male or for that matter female, in her life?'

'What?' Lena asked in complete disbelief.

'Is she dating anyone?' Reid asked, encouraging

Lena to answer.

'No, she has never mentioned it to me. She is quite young for her age, but at the same time socially very accomplished as we have travelled extensively on holidays.'

'How about her schoolwork – is she about to take exams?'

'Yes, her GCSEs. Amy is quiet and studious and always in the top three in her class. She's very bright and to be honest has never had any worries regarding her schoolwork; she's also very athletic.' Lena was visibly less tense as she re-counted her daughter's abilities.

'Is there anything, even the smallest detail, that you can think of that might help us?'

'I forgot to mention that one of her drawers in her dressing table is locked and I know she used to keep a journal, so it could be in there. If it is, should I read it? Perhaps it'll give more inform-ation that I can pass on to you?'

'It would be helpful, and if you do find the journal I'd like to see it myself, not to be intrusive but something that may appear trivial can actually be very productive.'

'What else are you going to be doing? I mean, should we get posters printed?'

'We will deal with posters and flyers, but I will need a recent photograph as soon as possible.'

Lena reached into her handbag and pulled out a silver-framed picture of Amy. 'I brought one in as I thought you might need it,' she said, holding back tears. Reid gently took it from her and looked at the lovely face of her beautiful young daughter.

'Thank you,' Reid said sympathetically; he undid

the rear clips and slowly removed the photo from the frame.

At first, Lena was offended by what she thought was a rather cavalier attitude towards her daughter's picture.

Reid noticed the look on her face. 'I will take a copy of this for the report and national circulation so you can take the original home with you.'

At once Lena felt more at ease and thanked him for his thoughtfulness as he handed the frame back to her.

'From what I have gleaned so far you feel it's out of character for Amy to have run away.'

'Totally, that's why I'm so worried something has happened to her.'

'Do you know if any of her clothing, wash stuff, make-up or anything like that is missing from your house?'

Lena told him that there didn't appear to be on first sight and Amy would have taken some things in a cabin bag to Serena's from school. She also informed him that Marcus had checked Amy's room at his flat and found nothing to suggest she had run away.

Reid picked up on the cabin bag and asked Lena if she had questioned Mrs Newman about it. She hadn't thought to, as she'd become so worried about Amy's disappearance. He used the bag as a subtle means of probing into Amy's state of mind at the time.

'It would be reasonable to assume that Amy took a case to Serena's. If it's not there now, then she must have taken it with her when she told Serena that she needed to go and see her father and if it's not at Mr Fulford's then...'

'I know what you're insinuating, but I simply cannot accept that Amy would run away.'

'When did you last see your daughter, Mrs Fulford?'

After thinking about it, Lena admitted that it was over two weeks since Amy had actually spent a weekend with her as the one before she went missing was spent with Marcus.

'But you alternate weekends with your husband?'

'As best we can, but it's quite an informal arrangement and isn't always strictly adhered to. She rang me from school regularly or I rang her and she seemed perfectly fine.'

'Young people often don't like to share their worries and fears when they are depressed, especially when their parents' marriage has broken down.'

'Marcus and I have lived apart for two years now. At first, yes, she was upset, but we remained on friendly terms and Amy came to accept our separation,' she insisted.

Reid closed his notebook and was about to stand up when he saw Burrows timidly raise her index finger, and nodded for her to go ahead.

'You mentioned that Amy has an iPad and I just wondered if she uses any social or chat sites on the internet like Facebook, Bebo or anything like that?'

Reid was impressed with Barbara's question, as it was something he'd forgotten to ask, having never used or looked at such sites himself. He was also aware that it could be critical to the inquiry and that there was a danger Amy had arranged to meet a stranger through the internet.

The look of worry on Lena's face was obvious as she realized the implications behind DC Burrows' question. The officer had raised something that was crucial to know yet frightening to contemplate.

'I honestly don't know,' Lena said, becoming very distressed.

Reid could hear the fear in her voice and see the redness in her eyes. 'Don't look so worried, Mrs Fulford – millions of people use Facebook every day of their lives and no harm comes to them.'

'I want my daughter back, Inspector Reid ... I just can't cope not knowing what's happened to her ... please find her, please.' She began sobbing and took hold of his hand as if she and Amy's life depended on him.

Remaining calm, he gently eased his hand free, and then gestured to Barbara to assist Lena. Barbara got some tissues out of her pocket and put her arm round Lena.

Reid couldn't help but be moved by the turmoil Mrs Fulford was going through, and realized how inexperienced he was in dealing with this kind of missing persons case. In the few months he had run the unit he'd only dealt with two high-risk cases and they were resolved before the homicide unit became involved. An elderly man had disappeared from a care home, and was found in woodland a few days later, having died from hypothermia. The other was a five-year-old boy who had wandered off when his mother's back was turned and tragically drowned after falling into a neighbour's pond. In both cases there had been some form of resolution for him and closure for the grieving families. But Amy's case was different as there were so many unknowns about her disappearance. He wanted it to be resolved quickly for Lena Fulford's sake, but he knew that he was playing catch-up, with three days having passed since she went missing. He wondered if he should maybe consider her case as high risk and report it to the chief superintendent, but worried that it would look as if he were panicking and jumping the gun. His mind was made up; at present Amy would remain medium risk until there was evidence to suggest that she had come to any harm. Besides, after five days, if she was not found alive and well, protocol dictated he would have to inform the DCS.

Reid waited for Lena Fulford to regain her composure before he suggested it would be best for her to return home and get some rest. He offered to get Barbara Burrows to drive her home but Lena said that she had her car with her and would be fine.

'I will try and visit you at your house later, Mrs Fulford, as I'd like to meet your husband as well. For now I need to fully brief my team and get the ball rolling in the search for Amy. I will instigate house-to-house enquiries where your husband and the Newmans live, as well as in your own area. I can assure you, Mrs Fulford, we will leave no stone unturned – every bit of available CCTV will be recovered and viewed so as to track and trace Amy's movements and successfully find her.'

Burrows was surprised by what DI Reid was

saying. He was rattling off everything the missing persons manual advised, but the feasibility of doing everything he said was nigh-on impossible with such a small team on the Richmond mispers unit. Most of their cases were cut and dried – care home or disadvantaged kids who regularly ran away, and in most cases were located within a few days without calling in the cavalry from the murder squads. Amy Fulford didn't fit the usual profile – she was from a wealthy family, at boarding school, and from her photograph an exceptionally beautiful young girl. Burrows hoped she would be traced quickly.

Chapter 4

Agnes was emptying the dishwasher when she heard the door. 'Hello, Mrs Fulford, you were out early this morning.'

'Agnes, there's a police officer coming round, I've forgotten his name, but he will be here to talk to you about Amy.'

'Oh my God, there hasn't been an accident, has there?'

'No, but she's been missing since Saturday afternoon.'

Agnes shook her head in shock, but Lena had already hurried up the stairs. She threw her coat over the bed and pulled off the polo-neck sweater; she needed a shower as her nerves had made her sweat. Hurrying into her bathroom she turned on the shower as she took off her jeans and kicked her shoes aside. She physically jumped when Agnes tapped on the door.

'Is there anything you'd like me to get you, Mrs Fulford?'

'No, I'm going to get changed quickly and, Agnes, there's a drawer in Amy's dressing table that's locked – have you any idea where the key would be?'

'No, I've never even seen the drawer open,' Agnes said quickly in a defensive tone.

'I'm not accusing you of anything; I'm simply trying to find the key. Do you know where it is?'

'Not a clue. Maybe Amy keeps it with her?'

'Yes. Well, have a look around, I'd like to open the drawer; and Agnes, can you prepare a tray of coffee and sandwiches? Marcus is also coming over and I haven't had lunch.'

Agnes went back to the kitchen, thinking that if her daughter Natalie was missing she wouldn't be ordering coffee and sandwiches, she'd be out searching for her. She never had much to do with Amy, as she was off at the weekends, and always stayed with her daughter in Milton Keynes. By the time she came to work on the Monday, Amy was already back at school. She opened a packet of fresh honey-baked ham and selected some tomatoes and lettuce. Making up the sandwiches, she wondered whether or not Mrs Fulford would prefer the best china, but knowing how particular she was, she decided to wait until she came down.

Lena closed her eyes; the warm shower was relaxing her. She washed her hair at the same time, soaping up the frothing foam and then using the residue to wash her armpits and then gritted her teeth to turn on the cold water to rinse. As the warm water had relaxed her, the icy cold made her body tingle and she then gave herself a really hard rubdown with a snow-white towel. Naked, she went into the bedroom and turned on the hair dryer, not bothering to carefully style her thick hair, but simply running her fingers through it to dry it as quickly as possible. She gave her still damp hair a few brush strokes and chose underwear, a silk blouse and suede trousers with high-heeled leather boots. Staring at her face in the magnifying mirror on her dressing table, she saw she looked paler than ever, but her skin was fresh and glowing from the icy-cold shower. She brushed on a light powder foundation, soft brown eye shadow and then some mascara to darken her eyelashes. She was very adept at making it appear she wore no make-up, but of late the telltale lines had started showing between her eyes and at their corners, and from her nose to mouth. The only sign that Lena, beneath her carefully created image of fresh innocence, was quite a tough woman were her eyes. They often gave off a steely cold expression, and her mouth frequently turned down into not exactly a grimace but a tight thin-lipped line.

The doorbell ringing made her hurry out of the bedroom, but by the time she had reached the bottom stair Agnes had let Marcus in. He still had his own key, but Lena had asked him never to use it and threatened she would change the locks if he did.

Marcus looked dreadful; he needed a shave, his

jeans were crumpled, as was his shirt, and he wore an old leather bomber jacket. She didn't waste time on any pleasantries, but asked him to come with her into Amy's bedroom.

'Have you found something?' he asked.

'I don't know yet; there's a locked drawer in the dressing table and maybe Amy's diaries and journal are inside it,' she said as he followed her up the stairs.

'What happened at the police station?'

'I gave every detail that I could think of to a policewoman, and spoke with an Inspector Reid who was the detective in charge. He's starting house-to-house enquiries and was very positive about finding Amy.'

Marcus gave a cursory look around as he followed Lena up the stairs and onto the first-floor landing. The house looked more or less the same as he had left it. Always the fresh flowers in large bowls, a profusion of plants, and the pictures that they had bought together over the years. The fitted carpet was new, but in the same deep moss-green as it had always been, but there were new brass stair rods, and walking along the landing he also saw there was a new chandelier.

'You've done some redecorating,' he said quietly.

'Yes, mostly to freshen up the place. I have a decorator that comes in over the holidays.'

She opened Amy's bedroom door, and he walked past her. 'Did you tidy it up?'

'No, this is how she left it. The locked drawer is the smaller one, top right.'

As Marcus crossed the bedroom, he stared at himself in the wide mirror. 'Christ, I look a wreck, but I didn't have the time to shave this morning and I had a fair bit to drink yesterday after the divorce meeting.'

She turned towards him, and suggested that the less they discussed the meeting with their lawyers the better it would appear to the police. 'I have said we have an amicable separation, and to be honest I almost believed we had, until you appeared with that despicable toad of a man, but I won't discuss it until we know about Amy.'

'Whatever,' he said as he bent down to try and open the drawer.

'I should have brought a screwdriver up. I mean, under the circumstances we should just break the lock open.'

'Do you want me to go down and fetch one?' he asked impatiently and she sighed, nodding her head. He paused at the door. 'It's strange coming back here – I'd forgotten how big the place is. Do you know how long it's been?'

'Yes, I am aware,' she snapped and he looked at her and then walked out.

The gates to the large house had been left open and DI Reid was able to pass straight through to the wide drive before parking between Lena's Lexus and a convertible Mini. The Lexus was highly polished, but the Mini was mud-splattered and looked as if it had not been cleaned for some time. He peered inside it, noticing old parking tickets, newspapers and a pair of jogging shoes, and jumped in surprise when Harry Dunn, Lena's driver, asked what he was doing. He explained who he was and Harry apologized, and said he was just about to give a quick dust to the Lexus.

Reid went up the three pristine white steps, past two huge pillars, to the blue-painted front door with its magnificent carved brass lion's head on a big looped knocker. Noticing there was also a doorbell, he pressed that. From his former career as an estate agent, he appreciated the value of upmarket property, and this one he reckoned was worth at least four million pounds. It was truly impressive.

Agnes introduced herself as she led Reid into a sitting room. If he had been impressed with the exterior of the property this vast room was stunning. It had huge white sofas with decorative cushions placed in front of a stone fireplace, wooden logs stacked in the grate. The many windows looked out over a spacious manicured garden; on the York stone paved terrace stood carved tables and chairs. He took off his raincoat and folded it over the side of the sofa arm, but did not sit down; instead he walked around, gazing at all the many collectible items – snuffboxes and a profusion of scented candles which were grouped on side tables; over the mantel there were silver-framed photographs. He was about to take a closer look at these when Marcus walked in.

'I'm Marcus Fulford, Amy's father,' he said, and indicated the screwdriver in his hand. 'I was about to try and unlock a drawer in my daughter's dressing table – Lena thinks her diary might be inside.'

DI Reid handed him his card and was introducing himself as Lena walked in.

'I've had some sandwiches made, and there's coffee.'

'Thank you, that's very kind.'

Lena called to Agnes to bring in the tray and gestured for Reid to sit on one of the sofas. 'This is Agnes Moors, my housekeeper.'

Agnes gave a polite nod, putting down the tray, wondering whether or not Lena wanted her to pour the coffee.

'Thank you, Agnes, I'll serve. Marcus, do you want to sit down?'

'Sure, unless – do you want me to try and prise the drawer lock?'

Lena looked to Reid, and he shrugged, but then added that perhaps Mr Fulford could have a chat first as he had already had a lengthy conversation with his wife. Lena poured the coffee and re-called that Reid took it black with sugar; it was all very civilized, yet very tense. Marcus perched on an arm of a sofa and began to tap the screwdriver in the palm of his hand. Reid would have liked to take a sandwich but felt it was perhaps not a good idea as he needed to get started questioning them both, especially Marcus. He had already taken in the man's untidy appearance, and thought that although he was undoubtedly good-looking, he seemed more agitated than his wife and overall as a couple they didn't quite fit to-gether. Reid noticed that she had changed her clothes, and appeared even more attractive than before. She passed her husband a coffee, and then lastly poured herself one. She also took a sandwich and nibbled at it, with a napkin bal-anced precisely on her knee. Marcus refused one, but started to drink his coffee.

'Okay, I need to clarify from you, Mr Fulford, exactly when and where your last interaction with your daughter was?'

'What do you mean?'

'Where and when did you last see her, how did she behave and what did she talk about?'

'It was the weekend before the one just gone; I picked her up on the Saturday morning from school, around eleven thirty. On the way home we stopped for a hamburger at one of the drive-in McDonald's and ate it in the car on the way back to my flat. Amy went to her room and stayed in there on her own until about five p.m. when she got changed and we went to a movie at the local cinema in Fulham. We usually try to go to the one in Mayfair but there was nothing on there that she wanted to see...' He paused, frowning and thinking to himself.

Lena listened, still nibbling at the sandwich. She loathed McDonald's and would not be seen dead in one of its restaurants, never mind ordering a takeaway and eating it in the car.

'I've remembered the film – it was one with vampires, and she had a thing about the actor in it. Anyway, afterwards we went over to Chelsea in my car. The shops were all open and we walked up and down until about nine. Amy went into Zara as she was looking for a dress that one of her friends had bought but they didn't have her size, so then we went to an Italian restaurant in Beauchamp Place – San Lorenzo. We had dinner and went home. She went straight to bed, and then we got up early in the morning and had a walk in

Hyde Park; after that we sort of lounged around – I had some calls to make and she watched TV. She made us a brunch – eggs and bacon – and then I had to pop out to see someone. I got back around six and drove her to school as she has to be there by seven.'

Reid made no interruptions; he jotted down a few notes, and appeared to listen intently until Marcus finished talking. 'So, did she seem in any way different? Worried, even? Did she mention anything to you that would give you an indication she was upset about something?'

'No. Only upset they didn't have her size in the dress she wanted, but she was her usual lovely, easy-going self. I think she said she wanted to work on an essay, which she might have done while I went out on the Sunday afternoon, but she never mentioned that anything was upsetting her, and when we walked together we chatted about how she was doing at school, usual things, but she never brought up anything that would indicate to me she had any worries.'

'What about discussing your present situation – the separation, the divorce proceedings?'

Marcus shrugged. 'No, it's always been a sort of unspoken thing between us: I don't talk about Lena, and the separation is not a recent thing – we've been apart for two years. I don't think when she is with her mother that she discusses me; whether or not she tells her what we did, I don't know.'

'We don't talk about Marcus when she is with me,' Lena interjected and went on to say it was not a rule but it was just their way of dealing with the separation.

'Do you see each other when your daughter is at school?'

'No, we don't,' Lena said, glancing at Marcus before she continued. 'We did meet this Monday with our lawyers and as I said before we have an amicable separation for Amy's wellbeing.'

'So neither of you can think of any reason why your daughter would take off without making contact?'

Lena put her unfinished sandwich back onto the tray. 'I have said this over and over again: this is totally out of character, she is an exceptionally well-behaved and thoughtful girl, and she has never ever taken off without telling us where she's going and leaving us names and addresses. Obviously, we also keep phone contact.'

'On these occasions when you say she's "taken off", where did she go?' Reid asked without looking at either of them.

'Well, she's had sleepovers with school friends, weekend activities with the school, parties that she would be late home from – I meant nothing that would sound alarm bells.'

Reid tapped his pen on his notebook, then said he'd like to see Amy's bedroom and suggested that Marcus or Lena open their daughter's locked drawer to see if there was, as suspected, a diary kept inside. He also said that he would like to talk to Agnes, and also Lena's driver.

Following them up the stairs, he was even more impressed with the immaculate decor and style of the house. Entering their daughter's bedroom was a surprise as it was so devoid of any girlish designs; everything was in its place, neat and tidy. Too tidy, he thought to himself.

Marcus bent down to use the screwdriver on the locked drawer but Lena stopped him. 'Wait, let's try and find the key first. That is a really good piece of furniture, it's an antique...'

Marcus looked up at her in disbelief. 'Lena, we've got to open it, there may be something in there that can help us!'

'Of course, you're right. I'd just hate for Amy to be upset with us when she comes home. It's her privacy.'

'This is an unusual circumstance, Mrs Fulford,' Reid interjected. 'She'll understand, but if it makes you feel any better you can tell her that the police instructed you to open it.' Lena gave him a grateful look and nodded for Marcus to proceed.

Reid stepped towards the wardrobe. 'Any clothes missing?' he asked Lena.

'I don't know every bit of clothing she owned as she liked to buy things herself. Obviously she would have taken some to Serena's in the cabin bag. She would wear her own clothes to go back to school, and then bring them to be washed and ironed by Agnes the weekends she stayed with me. She also has a sort of double-up wardrobe of clothes she keeps at her father's.'

'Would you know if anything is missing, Mr Fulford?'

'She keeps a load of stuff at my place, but I honestly wouldn't know if any were missing.'

Marcus twisted and jerked the lock with the screwdriver but it wouldn't budge. As Lena bent down and asked him to let her try and he refused,

Reid could detect tension between them.

'You want me to have a go? I maybe have more experience,' he offered, smiling, but neither of them looked at him, and then there was a click and the lock sprang back. Lena almost pushed her husband aside as she opened the drawer. Inside were three old diaries from years back and Amy's passport, but nothing else.

'Where's her journal?' Marcus said as Lena took out the three small books. 'The journal I bought her had "Amy" embossed in gold on the front. Those diaries are years old.'

Lena turned to Reid. 'Do you still want to have a look?' she asked. Reid took the diaries from her out of politeness and glanced at them; one had a flap and another a small stud lock, and one was tied with a red ribbon. He opened them, but there was nothing loose between the pages, and as he flicked through he told Lena he would take them with him and examine them thoroughly later.

'If you find this journal you've described, please let me know. It's good that we found Amy's passport as that suggests she hasn't gone abroad. Now, I'd like to have that talk with your housekeeper and driver.'

'Why do you need to talk to them?' Marcus asked.

'Just in case they were privy to anything or aware of something – it's a formality. I will need to talk to all employees, staff, friends and neighbours.'

'Don't you think there has been enough talking?' Lena asked. 'Isn't it obvious that neither Marcus nor I have any idea where Amy is? Shouldn't you be doing a search or whatever is necessary?'

Reid gave a light touch to her arm. 'As I said at the station, Mrs Fulford, we will do everything possible to trace your daughter but I need to be aware of anyone close to you, or friendly with you, who may be able to give us further information.'

Reid walked out of the bedroom and headed down the stairs, leaving Marcus and Lena standing beside the empty and broken dressing-table drawer.

Chapter 5

A very uneasy feeling was beginning to form in the pit of Reid's stomach. There was some agenda here he couldn't quite grasp. The Fulfords' daughter appeared to be a picture-perfect fifteen-year-old, but he knew that was very doubtful in reality. Her room was too tidy, devoid of any personal items, and he would need to see how it compared with her bedroom at her father's. He also wanted to have a private interview with Marcus without the presence of his wife; he was all too aware that, while he liked what he knew of Lena, he found the husband rather shallow.

Reid went into the kitchen as Agnes was placing the crockery into the dishwasher. He closed the door, went to the kitchen table and drew out a chair. The plate of uneaten sandwiches was sitting there, wrapped in clingfilm, making him realize he was starving.

'Mind if I have one of those?'

Agnes had a plate and a fresh mug of coffee in front of him within seconds, telling him to help himself, which he did with relish. Between mouthfuls, he asked if she would sit down, as he needed to have a talk to her. Taking out his notebook, he set it on the table.

Agnes wore two green slides pinning back her thick hair to keep it off her face. She was very articulate, with a slightly haughty voice, and she just didn't seem the type of woman Reid would have expected Lena to employ as a housekeeper. Though he had to admit he hadn't met many housekeepers before.

She explained that she worked Monday to Friday from nine to five each day. On the rare occasion she was needed over the weekend, she would stay in a small bedroom on the third floor of the house. She was then able to serve dinner or help if Mrs Fulford entertained. She said she always did the grocery shopping and served lunch to business associates on quite a regular basis, as Mrs Fulford had numerous small companies. She added that the Kiddy Winks business had taken off and for the past six months or more, Mrs Fulford had not entertained anyone on a social footing. It had all been professional, customers coming to the house to discuss the growing orders for the new venture. Reid was on his third sandwich but giving Agnes his full attention and encouragement, nodding and smiling. He wiped his mouth with the napkin.

'But if Mrs Fulford did entertain in the evenings, you wouldn't know as you said you leave at five.'

'Yes, but I would know because, as I said, I do

the grocery shopping – that includes the wine and champagne. Also, when she does have anyone visiting, there are always things left to be cleaned: cutlery, glasses in the dishwasher, that sort of thing. I usually leave her a covered plate of salad and cold cuts, but sometimes she has been so busy upstairs in her office she doesn't bother to eat. Of course, when she does go out, Harry her driver is on call, but he always gives me his itinerary, in case I needed to contact Mrs Fulford.'

'You run a tight ship,' Reid said, smiling.

'I have to, as Mrs Fulford is very particular, and I value my job.'

'How long have you worked for Mrs Fulford?'

'Almost two and half years; before that I worked for a furnishing company outlet. I was made redundant, so I was very pleased when I got the job. I'd been unemployed for quite a while – when you get to my age it's not easy finding work and I had some health issues. I had a very difficult time because I was divorced and my daughter was going through emotional problems. In many ways I totally understood Mrs Fulford's situation, having been through an unpleasant time myself – my husband is Spanish and an alcoholic, and our daughter had a lot to put up with.'

'How old is your daughter?'

'Natalie is thirty-four. We see each other every weekend unless, as I said, I am needed here.'

Reid tried to calculate the time between when Agnes had been made redundant, got divorced and started work for Mrs Fulford. He felt that she had glossed over just how long she had been unemployed but had no wish to get into her

91

health issues. He suspected Mrs Moors was over-qualified for her job and, judging by the way she was eager to explain herself, was a woman you didn't want to get on the wrong side of.

'Tell me about Amy.'

'She is very self-opinionated – clever, I believe – and very attractive. Even when she is on school holidays, I hardly see her, as she's always going away and they rent a cottage in Devon. I'm often here by myself.'

'Her bedroom is very tidy for a teenager.'

'Yes, like her mother's – they are very similar. When she has a friend stay, which is quite rare, they spend most of the time in the TV room watching DVDs, but as I have said, I leave at five on a Friday and have little to do with her.'

'How do you think she's coping with her parents' separation?'

'Well, I suppose it must have affected her, but we never had a conversation about it. My own daughter took my divorce badly, but then he was a very violent man and we both suffered. Mr Fulford is very easy-going and Amy spends every other weekend with him, but when I first started work here, he was still living with Mrs Fulford and there was some friction. He seemed to spend most days in the gym above the garage.'

'What kind of friction?'

'I hope I am not speaking out of turn by saying this, but I think Mrs Fulford was relieved when he moved out.' Agnes suddenly gave a small laugh and wafted her hands about.

'Did you ever hear Amy mention boyfriends, or do you know if she is seeing anyone?'

'No, and to be honest, even if she did have a boy-friend, I doubt very much if she would mention it to me.' Agnes shrugged. 'You know, I don't want you to think that I am in any way not concerned about the fact she is missing – it must be very worrying – but I feel sure she has simply gone on some adventure, because in my opinion she is almost too quiet, too well behaved, as if she doesn't want to be even noticed.'

'You do her laundry?'

'Yes, she comes home in her uniform, changes and dresses in her ordinary clothes. I wash and press her uniform for her to take back the next weekend. They double up all of their clothes for school, and whatever she has worn of her own, I also wash and press the following week.'

'Any unusual stains?'

Agnes sat back and frowned, and he saw the round eyes become like flints.

'Underwear stains,' he said quietly.

'She has begun her menstruation, but is very modest about herself, careful. I know only one occasion she had period stains, and she told me to get rid of the panties, refusing to wear them even if I washed them clean.' She hesitated, and bit her bottom lip. 'I have a daughter and I am fully aware of what teenagers can get up to – I know because I have monitored Natalie, who did go through a wild period, so if you are referring to semen stains, there have never been any indications of such.'

Reid stood up to signal the interview was over, and Agnes immediately sprang up and reached for his plate and napkin. He thanked her and asked if she would be kind enough to see if Harry Dunn was available, at which point she left him alone in the kitchen and hurried out into the hall.

This gave him time to put in a call to the station, keeping his voice very low as he spoke to DC Burrows.

'Any news on Amy Fulford's iPhone?'

'Cell site analysis shows it was last used to send a text on Saturday to Serena's mobile and the location was from a cell mast near Marble Arch, but it hasn't been used since.'

'If Amy was running away then the text to Serena could have been deliberate to give her more time without creating suspicion,' Reid suggested.

'There's also the possibility she purchased an unregistered pay-as-you-go mobile that no one knew about.'

'Good point, Barbara. I'd like you to put together a list of every call Amy made a week prior to and up to her disappearance, see if we can dig up any unknowns.'

'I have already put in a request for the last two months of historical calls and texts but, due to murder squad cases taking precedence, my request was low down in the pecking order and the results will be a few days yet.'

Reid sighed in frustration. 'Bloody typical. Just keep pressuring the line provider then. Any luck on tracing her iPad?'

'There is a "lost or stolen" application on it, but at present it's dead, so either the battery is flat or it's switched off. If it goes online they will inform us immediately.'

'Thanks, and keep up the good work. Got to go

now as I'm about to speak to Mrs Fulford's driver.'

Harry Dunn wiped his feet on the doormat thoroughly before Agnes ushered him into the kitchen. She closed the door and Harry stood nervously waiting for Reid to indicate he sit himself down at the table. The kitchen was very high-tech with the latest model of Aga, glass-cased wall-to-wall cupboards full of china, and sheets of black marble worktops. The table was made of steel and glass, with matching chairs, and Harry carefully inched a chair back to avoid scratching the polished York stone flagged tiles. He was around five feet nine, a small neat little man in a grey suit, white shirt and an unbuttoned navy overall. He excused himself for not removing it but said he was polishing Mrs Fulford's car.

As he sat opposite Reid, he seemed nervous; his elfin face framed by floppy brown hair was at odds with his worn hands. Reid also noticed he was wearing rather dapper shoes – brown brogues that were old-fashioned and highly polished.

'I suppose you have my background details?' the man asked quietly. Reid looked up, slightly puzzled, as he had not even begun to question him. As he did not reply, Harry explained that he had been on the straight and narrow for more than five years and valued his present job.

'Mr Dunn, this is not about your previous record...'

'Oh, jumped the gun a bit then, did I?'

Now that his suspicions were raised, Reid asked for further details and jotted down a few notes as Harry explained that he did in fact have a long

record for house burglary and had served numerous prison sentences as a youngster. When he
straightened himself out he got a job as a garage
mechanic and became the manager and after that
had become a driver, or chauffeur as he liked to
think of it. Mrs Fulford had employed him two
and a half years ago, around about the same time
as Agnes had begun work.

'Thank you for being open with me, Mr Dunn,
but I am here on a matter concerning Mr and
Mrs Fulford's daughter.'

'Has she done something wrong?' a worried-
looking Harry asked.

'Amy has been missing since Saturday afternoon, and as you were one of the last few people
to see her I need to ask you a few questions.'

'Oh my goodness me.'

Harry was shocked about Amy, but somewhat
relieved that there was no complaint against him,
and that Reid was not concerned with his criminal
record. He was more forthcoming about Marcus
Fulford than Agnes had been and said he was a
lovely bloke and very friendly, but that he had little
to do with him as Mrs Fulford employed him. He
said she was a really special lady and had taken
him on knowing his past record and they had a
good working relationship. He was unable to give
any real insight into Amy Fulford, bar the fact she
was a sweetheart, always polite, and seemed to
him to be a very well-adjusted young woman.

'I drive her sometimes to her dad's, but she never
talks much, and unlike her mother she always sits
in the back of the Lexus – Mrs Fulford always sits
beside me in the passenger seat. She spends a lot

of time texting, and using her iPad during the journeys. When I've taken her back to school on her own she hardly ever says a word to me; I just drive into the school, hand over her case and she waves me off.'

'You ever overhear her talking to anyone on her mobile?'

'Oh yes, she chatters away to friends, always laughing and kidding around, but then when she cuts off the call she sits back all quiet. She's a lovely-looking young girl, but sort of old-fashioned in the way she carries herself, if you understand what I mean. I know her mother's very strict with her, and if they are both in the car together she often talks about her business to Amy, and Amy seems very interested. They make a good team, and she's doing this new business about party planning for young kids and often they throw ideas around – what sort of cakes or cupcakes, what games kids like nowadays.'

'Do you join in their conversations?'

'No. I take good care of Mrs Fulford as she gets tired out, and she never stops – here and there all over London and then into the country, meeting women who do her sewing and stuff. I drive her to the factories and then when they go to Devon I usually drive them there, leave the car and get a train home.'

'How do you think this divorce is going down?'

He shrugged, and now more relaxed, he smiled, saying he had been divorced once when he was young, but had been happily married to an older woman now for many years. He suggested married life was probably easier for someone who didn't have anything worth fighting over.

'Were Mr and Mrs Fulford fighting over it?'

'Not in front of me, and I never saw him with another woman or her with a bloke she was interested in, which considering her looks, you'd think they would be queuing up.'

Harry went on to say he had taken Mrs Fulford to a few events but not frequently as she was working all hours to get her new business off the ground.

'I think she was lonely,' he suddenly said and Reid looked up, wondering whom he was referring to, and then realized he was talking about Amy.

'Why do you say that?'

'She wanted a puppy, but Mr Fulford told her it was not a good idea; this would be a good few months ago – she said she wanted a King Charles spaniel, because King Charles made a decree that that breed of dog could go anywhere because he had a whole load of them, and Amy said to me that if she had a puppy she would take it to school; she was just joking but...'

Reid waited and eventually Harry gave a shrug of his shoulders. 'It was just the way she looked – she has very expressive eyes, like her mother but different. She's a bit young for her age, I think. Course, I said she'd never be allowed to take a puppy, King Charles or not, to school.'

'She ever mention boyfriends, or did you overhear her talking to any boy?'

'No, but then you know she spends a lot of time with her dad, so maybe she has one, but I never heard her mention anything like that – like I said, she's kind of young for her age.'

Reid closed his notebook. Harry half rose out of his seat and then sat back. 'You think something bad has happened to her?'

'I sincerely hope not.'

'Christ, I hope not too; it's something you can't really think about – you know, happening to people that you know; I'm sure she'll be with a friend somewhere, but that said – she's such a lovely little thing and I just hope to God no harm has come to her.'

'So do I, Mr Dunn. Thank you for your time. Oh, just one thing – this last weekend, where exactly were you?'

'I was with my ex-wife's sister, in Somerset; she was getting married again, and Mrs Fulford gave me the weekend off even though she had a dinner party to go to. I was using a hired Mercedes to drive the bride, so I wasn't even in London.'

Reid shook his hand, indicating he could leave. He put his notebook back into his pocket and was screwing the top of his pen back when Agnes knocked and walked in, announcing that Mr and Mrs Fulford were in the sitting room should he need them. As he passed Harry he could feel that there was not a lot of love lost between the two members of staff; Agnes, holding the door open, almost clipped Dunn's polished brogues. Reid paused and opened his wallet, taking out two cards.

'If you think of anything that might assist in tracing Amy, please call; this is my direct line and I may need to talk to you both again.'

Lena and Marcus sat side by side on a sofa. It

was obvious she had been crying as her eyes were red-rimmed and she was clutching a handkerchief. Reid walked into the room and picked up his raincoat, eager to leave.

'Well, thank you both for your cooperation. Mr Fulford, I need to see Amy's room at your place as soon as possible.' He looked at his watch. 'Can I meet you at your flat in, say, forty-five minutes?'

'Of course,' Marcus said, looking at his own watch as he and Lena accompanied Reid to the front door. Marcus followed him out, saying he needed a quick cigarette, and Lena watched from the doorway as the two men walked to their cars. Once Reid drove away, Lena closed the door, leaving Marcus searching his glove compartment for a lighter.

Inside the house, Agnes was standing by the kitchen, but Lena walked past her and up the stairs. 'Is there anything I can do, Mrs Fulford?'

Lena glanced over the banister as she continued along the landing. 'Just tell Mr Dunn to wait around in case I need him, and I'll leave the business answer phone on as I don't want to be interrupted. I'll only answer the private line.'

Agnes heard the bedroom door slam shut, just as Dunn rang the front doorbell. She let him in, and he wiped his feet methodically; he had finished polishing the Lexus.

'What do you think is going down?' he asked, following Agnes into the kitchen. She placed the kettle on the Aga, and fetched a mug to make him a coffee. He watched her, and then drew out a chair to sit at the kitchen table.

'I hope nothing bad has happened to her,' he

said and Agnes pursed her lips.

'I never had any trouble with Natalie.'

Dunn waited for her to hand him his mug of instant coffee, hoping he was not in for a lengthy discourse about her precious Natalie, whom he had never met. Agnes opened a biscuit tin and held up a chocolate Penguin biscuit; he nodded and she threw it to him to catch.

'I've got to say I am surprised she would just take off,' he said. 'Do you think that's what's happened – she's met some kid and run off with him?'

Agnes picked up a damp cloth and began wiping down the already pristine worktops. 'If Natalie had ever met a boy I didn't approve of, I'd know about it, but with Amy staying here one minute and the next at her father's flat, well I doubt either of them knows who Amy is mixing with. I tell you, I'd never have sent Natalie to a boarding school.'

'I'm taking my coffee over to the garage. If she needs me, gimme a bell on the mobile,' Harry said.

She picked up the wrapper from his biscuit and tossed it into the pedal bin just as Marcus knocked to be let back in. Agnes breathed a heavy sigh, and went into the hall to open the front door.

'Mrs Fulford is upstairs,' she said and Marcus nodded, thanking her and heading towards the stairs himself. She could smell smoke on him and it made her instantly crave a cigarette, so she shut the kitchen door, opened a drawer and took out her mobile, a packet of cigarettes and a lighter. Lighting a cigarette, she sank onto a chair and rang her daughter.

'Hello, darling, I hope I'm not bothering you at

work, but we've had quite a time here – Amy is missing and the police are making enquiries.' Natalie asked her to hang on as she was talking to a client.

Agnes dragged on her cigarette, and let smoke drift from her snub nose, taking another drag immediately. Mrs Fulford did not approve of smoking and she rarely if ever lit up at the house, but this was an exception. She'd use the expensive Floris lilac room spray so that 'she who required scented candles from the White Company to permeate the house to avoid any domestic smells' would not detect her nicotine addiction. Natalie came back on the line, and Agnes repeated that Amy was missing, but before she could continue her daughter had another call to take so she hung up. She took a few more drags before running the cigarette butt under the cold-water tap, and then she wrapped it in a tissue and tossed it into the pedal bin. It was now three o'clock and she sighed, realizing she had another two hours before she could leave. Meanwhile the dual phone lines on the kitchen telephone were blinking, but she saw that it was the business line, which seemed to be ringing continuously. It was very unlike Lena not to take business calls but under the circumstances it was quite understandable that, as she had said, she was only answering calls on the private line.

Agnes went up the stairs and along the corridor towards Lena's bedroom; she thought that perhaps she should ask if she was required to stay on later than usual. She hovered outside the bedroom door, listening to Lena and Marcus talking but unable to make out what was being said. She

102

hesitated and gave a light knock. Lena snatched open the door, and Agnes had to step back hurriedly.

'What do you want?'

'Just to say I will be going off at the normal time but if there is anything you need from me I can stay.'

'No, thank you, you can go; sorry if I sounded sharp, I am just at my wits' end with worry.'

'I understand, and I hope you'll get some news. Having a daughter of my own I know how you must be feeling; I don't know what I would do if it was me and Natalie was missing. So if you need anything please let me know.'

'Yes, thank you, Agnes.' Lena closed the door and returned to Marcus, who was sitting on the edge of the bed; she sat beside him, curling up close.

'You really should get some rest,' he said gently, touching her arm.

'I can't, I feel like I must do something, anything that can help. I need her home, Marcus, I can't bear this.'

'I know.'

Lena got up. 'I'm going to check her room again. There's got to be something...' Marcus stood up; even though he wanted to go home to shower before Reid got there, he followed Lena into Amy's bedroom.

Lena began searching through the drawers, and then again inside the wardrobe. She looked under the bed, and inside the bedside tables – nothing. Then in an instant she saw it: the green leather journal tucked in amongst the other books on the shelf. She rushed over and pulled it out. 'Her journal, it's here.'

Marcus reached for it. 'We should call Reid back.'

'Not yet,' Lena said, stepping away and sitting down on the bed. 'I want to look through it first.'

Marcus moved towards her. 'I think we should at least let him know we found it.'

Lena looked at him, considering what he had said. 'Yes, but we don't want to waste his time; if there's anything useful in here we'll call him.'

Marcus agreed, and sat beside her. 'Why don't we look at the last entry first?' Lena started at the back and flipped through the pages.

'Just some recipes,' she said.

'Well, that doesn't help us,' he said with a disappointed sigh as he stood up. 'I don't want to be late for Reid, so I'd better get going. Call me if there's any news, and I'll do the same.' As he hurried out, Lena was still flicking through the journal.

Chapter 6

Harriet Newman lived in an elegant town house off the Fulham Road. She was a very attractive tall woman with curly red hair and was wearing jeans, high-heeled knee-length boots and a cashmere sweater. Her two youngest children, who had just been returned from their junior school by the live-in nanny, were noisily having their tea in the big open-plan kitchen. The two detectives from Reid's team, DS James Lane and DC Timothy Wey, known affectionately by his colleagues as 'Takeaway' because of his Chinese ancestry, were invited into a large living room that had pine wood floors, throw rugs, plush-cushioned cream sofas, and walls lined with bright paintings. The large fireplace had a gas log fire, which was lit, and above it was an enormous plasma screen television. No sooner had the two officers sat down than the two young boys came running into the living room, chasing each other.

'Enough, you two, can't you see we have guests? Now get back in the kitchen and stay there or go up to your rooms as I don't want to be interrupted.'

The boys went instantly quiet and shuffled out of the room as Harriet, who had a somewhat scatty manner about her, offered the detectives tea or coffee.

'No thank you, Mrs Newman. We need to speak to you about Amy Fulford as she is still missing and we wondered if you noticed or sensed anything untoward when you saw her on Saturday,' DS Lane said.

She shook her head. 'How awful for her poor parents. I'm happy to answer your questions but I've racked my brains since I last spoke to Mr Fulford and I can't think of anything unusual about Amy that might help your investigation.'

'Can you go over the course of events concerning Amy on Saturday for us, please?' DC Wey asked.

'She had been given permission to have a sleepover with my daughter Serena, so I collected them both from the school at around eleven forty-five in the morning. We got back here at about one as there had been a lot of heavy traffic and then I prepared a lunch for the girls and my two boys.'

Harriet spoke quite quickly and was about to continue when DC Wey asked her to pause a second as he needed to take notes of what she was saying. He nodded when he was ready for her to continue.

'After lunch I left the girls here and took the boys to the War Museum in Chelsea with my husband. They are only five and six years old and love the playground inside the museum as well as all the uniforms on display.'

'Did the girls, or Amy in particular, say what they were going to do?' Lane asked.

Harriet paused to think. 'As I recall, they were going to go shopping and then see a film later in the afternoon. We were about to leave for the museum when Amy said she wanted to collect something from her father's flat, but Serena did not want to go with her as she wanted to wash her hair. I offered to drop Amy off on the way to the museum but she said she'd make her own way.'

'Did she say what she needed to collect from her father's?' Lane asked.

'No, and regrettably I didn't ask. Bill, that's my husband, and I got back here at about four thirty and Serena was here on her own. She said she had not heard from Amy and had called her on her mobile but it went straight to voicemail so she left a message to meet up at the Fulham Odeon for the five-thirty show. Serena thought that Amy was going to meet her at the Odeon, but she sent a text saying she couldn't make it as something had come up at her dad's. Serena then called some other friends who went to the pictures with her.'

'Is there anything else you can think of that might help us?' Wey asked.

'Not really. I feel really awful about this and wish I could be more helpful. I had bathed the boys as, what with it being Saturday, it was their nanny's night off. I put them to bed, and then called Serena to see if she was coming home for supper. She said they were going to have a hamburger and she'd be back at around ten. I didn't even ask if Amy was with her, I sort of thought that she was, and then I made dinner for my husband and myself, and Serena arrived back at...' She shook her head. 'It was later than we had agreed, it was near eleven, and I was a bit tetchy with her because, you know, she is only fifteen and that was when I asked about Amy.'

Harriet continued to explain that she was not overly concerned, because Amy had said she was going to her father's and later sent the text that she was there, so they had presumed she had just decided to stay with him.

'I didn't think any more about it. Then on the Sunday we had a pre-arranged kids' party that the boys were invited to. I took them there and my husband stayed in to watch something or other on the TV. Serena went shopping to find a pair of shoes, and then came back in time for Bill to collect the boys and drive Serena back to school. I think he did try and contact Amy, but there was no answer and by this time Serena was really a bit miffed about it, and the boys were being very naughty – probably over-tired after their birthday party. They saw the Legoland signs on the motorway and wanted to be taken there and then became boisterous when Bill said they couldn't go – I think he said it was too late, too dark and they weren't open...'

Detective Lane had made copious notes and now asked if Amy had left any kind of overnight bag as she was supposed to be staying the night. Harriet jumped up and apologized.

'Gosh, I never thought about that. Let me go and have a search of Serena's bedroom.'

They could hear her running up the stairs, and then shouting down to the kitchen to her by now rowdy boys, telling them to stay in there as she was still busy. Lane looked to Detective Wey, who had also been taking notes.

'We need to ask Mrs Newman exactly what Amy was wearing on the Saturday and visit Serena's school to go over everything with her,' Wey said. Lane nodded and then glanced around the pleasant room and tapped his notebook.

'This isn't looking good, Takeaway; because nobody realized she was missing from Saturday through to the Monday, when the school reported she hadn't shown up, it's bloody nearly three full days and nights.'

'Yeah, maybe ask about the relationship between her daughter and Amy, and we should also talk to the husband.'

As if on cue the front door opened, and shrieks and yells came from the hallway as the boys realized their father was home. Bill Newman walked in, stopped and looked at the two officers. They rose to their feet and introduced themselves, soon realizing he appeared to not even be aware that Amy Fulford was missing. He held up his hand for them to wait a moment and went into the hall to chastise his sons, who were now running up and down yelling at the tops of their voices. They heard him loudly telling the boys to go into the kitchen and stay in there until he came in to see them; he then shouted instructions to someone called Nicky to put on a DVD and keep them quiet.

Newman returned, closing the door, and offered the detectives a drink, which they refused. This didn't stop him from helping himself to a glass of red wine from an opened bottle before he sat on the arm of the sofa. He was good-looking, and wore a thick woollen suit and a checked shirt with a dark red tie. The detectives took the opportunity to ask about his daughter's relationship with Amy, but he was unable to give details as, he explained, he had only met her maybe once or twice. Serena, as far as he was aware, had a number of friends and as she always came home on weekends he shared the pick-up and collection with his wife. He said she still had a number of friends from her old school in Fulham, and had been at the same boarding school as Amy for just over a year. He said they felt the weekly boarding was a good way to give them breathing space as the boys were a bit of a handful and it helped his wife Harriet have less to do. As if hearing her name, she returned empty-handed.

'I'm sorry to take so long, but I did a really thorough check – wardrobes, under the beds, everywhere – and there is no case or anything that I don't recognize as belonging to Serena.'

Her husband got up and kissed her, placing his arm around her shoulders. 'I feel so bad about all this,' she said, 'it's just dreadful, and I really blame myself for not being more diligent – poor Lena, she must be frantic.'

'Do you know Mrs Fulford well?'

'No, I'm afraid I don't, just from school projects and events when we've met each other – she seems a lovely person.'

'What about her husband?'

Harriet looked to her own husband and he shrugged. 'I don't know him; I think they're separated or getting a divorce, but like my wife, I have only met Lena a few times, and usually she was with her husband. Marcus, I think he's called. I met him about six months ago when he dropped Serena home as we had a sports event for the boys; he seemed very nice but he didn't come in, just waved to us from his car.' Harriet sat close to her husband, resting one hand on his knee as he sipped his wine.

When she was asked if she recalled what Amy was wearing, she screwed up her face.

'Oh gosh, let me think – she was wearing her school uniform when they arrived, then before lunch I think they both changed. Probably Serena would be able to remember, but I think it was jeans and a sort of leather and denim jacket maybe; I'm so sorry but I didn't really take much notice. Oh, shoes, she was wearing the same shoes that Serena wanted to buy – they were flat blue suede ballet-type shoes with a sort of bow in dark leather.'

Detective Wey finished writing and then glanced up. 'So if she changed into clothes while she was here, then she would have brought some kind of overnight bag or suitcase?'

'Yes, right, but as I have said it's not upstairs, and I am trying to remember if she took it with her. I'm so sorry but my mind is just a blank; hang on, let me go and ask Nicky – she was here at lunch.'

Harriet disappeared and Bill again offered the detectives a drink but they declined.

'It's a full-time job over the weekend with the boys, and Serena home, and me!' He grinned – he was a very affable easy-going type, but by now neither detective was feeling relaxed; they had gained little and were concerned about losing precious time.

Nicky Martinez, the Newmans' nanny, was about twenty-two, French, petite, with two long blonde braids and food stains over her T-shirt. She spoke good English and as Bill went to sort out the row emanating from the kitchen she took up his perch on the arm of the sofa.

'Amy was wearing blue suede ballet pumps from LK Bennett. I remember because we had talked about how much they cost at lunch.'

Wey wrote in his notebook as DS Lane asked her to continue.

'She was also wearing a maroon sweater with frilly cuffs and a pair of black leggings. I can't recall what jacket she wore, but she was very eager to see the movie as it starred Robert Pattinson.'

'Did she seem worried or upset about anything?' Wey asked.

'No, not at all, there were no signs and she was okay that Serena would wait at the house and do her hair while she went to see her father and get her watch.'

Lane and Wey looked at each other as this was the first mention of Amy going to get a watch and it tended to suggest that she was not meeting anyone or had any prior arrangement.

'Can I ask how you knew Amy was going to her father's about a watch?' Lane asked.

'I was a bit angry about Amy not contacting us as I had to go with Mr Newman as he was driving Serena back to school. On the way there I asked her why Amy had gone to her dad's in the first place and she said something about getting a watch. I didn't ask anything more as the boys started playing up in the back of the car.'

Nicky was unable to help any further and said that she didn't ask Amy about the watch and neither did Amy say any more about it.

Seeing them out, Harriet offered further guilty apologies and added that she was unaware of Amy mentioning the watch.

By this time the detectives were anxious to travel to the school and interview Serena. They headed into Fulham Road, trying to work out the route that Amy would have taken to get to her father's flat in Green Street, Mayfair. The most likely would have been to catch a number 414 bus towards Marble Arch, get off in Park Lane and walk down to Green Street.

Now armed with at least some description of what their missing girl was wearing, they reported back to the station, and said they would also ring DI Reid.

Reid was at Marcus Fulford's flat when his mobile rang. He glanced at it, excused himself to Marcus and went into the hallway to take the call. He listened without interrupting as DS Lane updated him about the clothing and the watch, and agreed they should visit the school and interview Serena that evening. Returning to the living room, Reid decided that before broaching this new information with Marcus he'd ask him more about his relationship with Amy.

'I adore her. We get on exceptionally well and she is very loving towards me.'

'Was she ever upset or jealous about any of your girlfriends?'

'No, never, and I make sure my relationships never encroach on my and Amy's weekends together.'

'What about Amy, does she have any relationships that you know of?'

'No,' replied, upset with Reid's line of questioning.

'Do you suspect that she may have a boyfriend?'

'It's possible, but I'm pretty sure she would have told me or her mother if there was one.'

'Even if it was a sexual relationship?' Reid persisted.

Marcus fidgeted in his chair.

'Although Amy can sometimes appear older than her fifteen years, she is a very innocent and naïve young girl and I don't believe she is sexually aware. I am certain that she has no boyfriend or any fixation on a teacher or anyone I know of.'

'But you can't be sure?'

'She's my daughter, Inspector Reid, and I am certain I know her better than you. The time we spend together is always very relaxed and she likes to cook for me some evenings and sometimes we go out to dine together. We also both like the cinema and theatre, and sometimes Amy even manages to drag me to the shops and boutiques. Her mother is very generous with her monthly allowance but Amy also likes to ask my opinion about the clothes she buys and wears.'

'I know you may think I'm being intrusive, Mr Fulford, but the more I know and understand about Amy, the better our chances of finding her.'

'You have to understand that this is totally out of character, she has never ever done anything like this before, and it just doesn't make any sense to think she might have run off with someone,' Marcus said and took some deep breaths before continuing.

His eyes were brimming with tears as he touched Reid's arm. 'The phone call a minute ago – it's bad, isn't it? You think something has happened, don't you?'

Reid refused to be put on the spot. 'It was positive news, Mr Fulford, and, we now know what your daughter was wearing when she left the Newmans'. Their nanny heard from Serena that Amy was going to go and see you on Saturday afternoon to get her watch.'

'Her watch?'

'Yes, maybe she left it here sometime before.'

'Well she hasn't been here in over a week and if she left it I'd have thought she'd have rung me at least,' Marcus insisted.

'Nevertheless, I'd like to see Amy's bedroom for myself, please, Mr Fulford. There's also the possibility she came back here and changed, so her overnight bag may be in her room as it was not at the Newmans'.'

Reid was totally thrown by the untidy mess of a bedroom Marcus led him into. Turning to him, he asked if he had caused the state of it, perhaps looking for clues. Marcus shook his head, and explained that this was how it was usually. He excused the disarray and said that as Lena was so anally retentive, he allowed Amy to just do what she wanted, and unlike his wife he could not afford a housekeeper. Reid said nothing; the room was a total tip: dirty underwear, nightdresses, tights, panties, bras were strewn around, or left in small piles, the sheets looked grey and food-stained. The carpet was dirty with crumbs and half-eaten pieces of toast left on mildewed plates; even her pillow had make-up stains.

'Christ, it is a mess,' Marcus said, standing in the middle of it, looking around. He was embarrassed when he saw a used sanitary towel tossed in a waste bin with soiled tissues and torn-out pieces of magazines. The wardrobe doors were open, clothes on and off hangers, some crumpled underneath the dirty shoes. Reid was loath to touch anything because he wanted a forensic team to be brought in as it was not to his mind the normal mess of a well-brought-up teenager.

Unlike her bedroom at her mother's, this room was covered in posters of pop groups and the vampire movies, stacks of cheap magazines littered the floor and were strewn under the bed. Marcus gestured towards them and said he had flicked through them in case there was a letter or anything Amy might have left between the pages. The dressing table was a mess of spilt powder and creams and asking about a wristwatch was laughable as the surface was piled high with junk jewellery and beads all mixed up.

'If she did come home on Saturday afternoon, it would be hard to tell. But is there somebody who might know – a porter maybe?'

'There's a sort of general dogsbody, but no one on duty. Listen, I did shift some stuff around looking for anything that might give us Amy's contacts, anyone she could have gone to meet. I was very hung over and none of the drawers I looked through had an address book. She was always on her iPad, and I didn't find anything like letters...' His voice trailed off as he continued to look around.

Reid used a pen from his pocket to sift through items on the dressing table, and again mentioned that Amy had said she was coming to the flat as she wanted her wristwatch.

'As I said before, I don't know if her wristwatch was left here from her last visit,' Marcus said, rubbing at his hair. 'Yes, she usually wore one but I just can't remember when I last saw it. Lena'll know.'

Reid decided it was time he got back to the station. He asked Marcus not to remove any items or search the bedroom again as he wanted one of his team to check through the clothes. Privately he made a note to get the underwear checked by forensics and if there were any traces of semen get a DNA profile raised.

Driving back to Richmond, he was confused by the totally opposite states of the missing girl's bedrooms. The Amy as described by her mother and her staff was such a meticulous and caring girl, but the bedroom she occupied at her father's showed a very different side. It was filthy. Reid couldn't help wondering if the dirty underwear indicated she wasn't as naïve as everyone would have him believe.

After Marcus had gone, Lena had continued reading the journal, trying to quell her rising fears. The book contained more than just recipes; the first half was filled with personal thoughts about their family and the people in Amy's life. There was nothing that could help them discover her whereabouts but plenty of disturbing and shocking entries about Amy's disdain for everyone. Lena had used small Post-it stickers to indicate what she felt were relevant pages, and she was also using a highlighter pen on some sections. She was still deeply stunned by some of her daughter's copious notes, and confused by the revelations about not only herself but also everyone Amy came into contact with. She had just begun to read a section headed and underlined 'Daddy' when the telephone rang. It made her jump and she quickly answered it to avoid its jarring noise.

'Hey, it's me. DI Reid just finished here and I

thought I'd check in. Any news?' Marcus's voice sounded weary.

'No, I'm still reading the journal. There's more to it than I thought but I haven't found anything that might give us a clue to where she is or who she could be with. It's quite upsetting though... I don't think she loves us, Marcus. Some of the things in here are just cruel. It's like I don't even know her.'

'Don't think that. Of course she loves us; all teenagers write horrible things in their journals – it doesn't mean anything.'

'I pray you're right,' Lena said, the tears welling up again. She hung up the phone and opened the drawer in her bedside cabinet and plucked a tissue from the box inside. Beneath the box were a few birthday cards that she had kept, a Valentine's card and a list Amy had written of what she wanted for Christmas. Puzzled, she took out the list, studying the handwriting, and then she opened the birthday card from Amy to her a couple of years ago: 'To my darling beautiful mother, from her daughter who would hope to be as beautiful when the same age.' It was a cartoon card with a funny monkey inside that stuck out its tongue ... but it was the handwriting that interested Lena, because it was spidery, looped and uneven. When she compared the handwriting from the cards and gift list against the overtly neat, tightly written pages of the journal she saw it was totally different.

Lena placed the list against one of the pages of the journal. It was impossible to believe that the same person had written both. She flicked through page after page of the journal until she came to the entry she had been about to continue reading... 'Daddy'.

Chapter 7

Lena had not moved from her bedroom. The unfinished journal lay discarded beside her as she sank back in a state of utter despair and confusion. She could hardly believe the pages and pages of what she had to accept were Amy's hidden thoughts about how she really felt about virtually everyone she knew. First and foremost was the vicious depiction of herself and Marcus. This had shocked her to such an extent she had felt sick to her stomach. It appeared that, unbeknown to Marcus, Amy had not only made nasty character studies of his women friends, but also described his sexual exploits in disgusting pornographic detail, such detail that Lena began to think that she must have witnessed her father having sex. Could he have allowed this to occur? Another scenario that sickened her was the possibility he had encouraged her to watch him. This made her wonder if Marcus was abusing Amy sexually and if this was correct, she would have to face him with it and also, obviously, report it to DI Reid.

She forced herself to think carefully about what she should do with this information. As angry as she felt towards Marcus, she really could not believe that he would abuse his own daughter.

The references to herself had been cruel, at times vicious in their description of how she behaved, dressed and put her obsession with her business above everything else. Apparently she was a cold, unloving, determined woman who cared for no one but herself, and looked upon her daughter as a clinging appendage that had neither her looks nor personality. Amy had listed how she was forced to behave around this obsessive woman so as not to create any emotional conflict, and it had manifested itself in never showing any personality traits that would contradict her mother's careful image of the perfect offspring.

Lena moved to sit in front of her dressing-table mirror and moisturized her whole body, soothing and rubbing, and then used another facial moisturizer for her neck. She sat staring at her reflection before beginning to carefully apply her usual make-up. Eventually she chose from her massive walk-in wardrobe a cashmere sweater, grey flannel trousers, and grey boots, and from her underwear drawers took out panties and bra. She put on her underwear, pulled on the sweater, dabbed her favourite rose musk perfume to her inner wrists and neck, and yet again stood staring at her reflection. She was the same weight and size she had been at twenty, and she admired herself, even while carefully replacing every tube and bottle she had used in its exact same spot on her glass-topped dressing table. The rage came unexpectedly, consuming her as she swiped with right hand through everything in front of her, but she refused to cry. Gritting her teeth she kicked over the velvet-covered stool that matched the drapes and bedspread. She wanted to exhaust the anguish she felt, and she continued hurling objects around the bedroom until she was panting with the exertion. Only when her breathing had returned to normal did she return to her walk-in wardrobe and choose a grey cashmere fitted coat, dragging it on as she walked out.

Usually if Lena was wearing her grey outfit she would have chosen a grey soft leather clutch bag, but she was in such a tense state of mind, she snatched up the handbag she had carried earlier from the kitchen. Quickly she searched for her set of car keys and headed out towards the garage. Even though she had not deliberately thought about where she was going, as if on automatic pilot she was going to have it out with Marcus.

It was after eight when Reid finished his report at the station, but he was in no hurry to leave as he was waiting for DS Lane and DC Wey to return from enquiries at the school. He would instigate a press release the following morning and ask for more staff to assist in the investigation. They would require CCTV footage from the different routes Amy might have taken from Fulham to her father's Mayfair address. The bus company would also be questioned in case any drivers had seen Amy. As of that evening she had been missing for three full days and nights and Reid was now considering the possibility she had been abducted. He ran a computer search for any recent abductions, rapes or murders in the Fulham and Mayfair areas, but there was nothing unsolved or linked to his case.

DC Wey and DS Lane returned at nine fifteen. They had brought in takeaway hamburgers and French fries, and joined Reid in his office. Wey placed Amy's overnight bag on Reid's desk and told him that Serena had taken it back to the school on Sunday, anticipating that Amy would be there. While Wey continued, and gave a rundown on the visit to the Newmans', Reid put on some protective latex gloves and started checking through the overnight bag. The fact the bag was left at Serena's suggested that Amy had intended returning to stay with her friend. It was also confirmation that discovering what had occurred after Amy left the Newmans' property was now urgent. They could not be sure if she did in actual fact go to her father's flat, but either way the clock was ticking.

The bag contained her school uniform, tights, black slip-on loafers and clean underwear. There was also a nightdress in white cotton, folded neatly, along with a plastic bag containing toothpaste, battery toothbrush and a hairbrush. There was no make-up, perfume or trinkets, but underneath the clothes they found a paperback of Sheridan's play, *The Rivals*. Serena had told the officers she and Amy were intending doing some homework as they were going to audition for one of the roles in the school's production. She said that Amy was her usual self and not upset about anything, and asked her to accompany her to her father's flat, but she had refused because she wanted to wash her hair. They asked if this had upset Amy in any way and Serena had said that it didn't worry her, as Amy would be back in time for them to go to the cinema together.

Flicking through his notebook, Wey said he had asked why Serena had not been concerned when Amy had not turned up at her home or met them at the cinema. She had called her friend on her mobile, but it was left on voicemail; she admitted that she had been irritated when Amy sent her a text 'bailing on her', as she had done it once before. Apparently it had been some time ago, when Amy had gone to stay with her father and promised to meet up with her for a Chinese. That time she had not even called and when they returned to school Amy had said she had been taken to see a movie with her father and suggested that it had not been a firmed-up date but just a casual possibility they would meet up.

James Lane finished his hamburger, and wiped his face with a paper napkin, and then his greasy fingers. 'Serena was a cute little thing, and didn't seem that fazed by the fact her friend is missing, but she said that as far as she knows Amy has no boyfriend, or has never mentioned one, although they are not that close as Amy always has either a weekend with her father or mother and they both arrange activities.'

Wey nodded, and reached for the ketchup, before continuing. They had asked a number of pupils about who was closest to Amy but they had almost all agreed that she was a bit of a loner. She was also academically a very bright pupil and interviewing her teachers had given them no indication that Amy was in any way a troubled teenager. She was studious, and artistic and a good athlete, and not one of them had said a bad word against her. They were obviously concerned and asked if there was anything they could do to assist tracing Amy.

'Any male teachers?' Reid asked, eating a chip, which by now was cold.

Wey opened his notebook again and named a fencing master and a music teacher. One was crippled and elderly and the other had extreme halitosis, and so both detectives doubted that their girl would find either attractive. They had found the art teacher a very sexy lady, a Miss Polka, and she had been helpful, even showing them some of Amy's artwork, which was excellent.

Reid was getting tired; he yawned and stood up to stretch his legs.

'I'm arranging a press conference with the Fulfords for tomorrow morning and will need your help. No doubt the conference will lead to slews of calls and more enquiries.'

'Any luck with Amy's mobile phone or iPad?' DS Lane asked.

'Not as yet, and there's been no activity on either since she went missing. Barbara got a list of all the calls she made over the few days before her disappearance but it has not turned up anything unusual or productive.'

'If we can find her phone or iPad it would be a big step forward,' Wey remarked.

'I know, so Barbara's asked the phone company to monitor them in case they go live,' Reid sighed.

He could see that both detectives were aware of the fact they could be dealing with more than just a missing young girl and the grim possibility she might even have been abducted. Reid started to pace back and forth, trying to get up some adrenalin, and ticked off on his fingers his gut feelings from the day's interviews.

'The mother is neurotic, but obviously concerned, so that may have been a natural reaction; she's successful, very wealthy, from what I could ascertain, but we need a full disclosure of her business, and the possibility is always that someone she employs might be connected. She runs a very tight ship with a housekeeper and driver that hardly have any contact with her daughter, but she is a model teenager by all accounts, her bedroom immaculate, ditto the whole house.'

Wey yawned as he flicked open his notebook, jotting down what he felt was relevant. Reid continued pacing around the office.

'There's gardeners as well, so we need to check them out, and also run a check on her driver as he has a criminal record, and start to question her neighbours.'

'What about the father?' DS Lane asked.

'Okay, he needs looking into; I don't trust him. He rents this flat, the whole place is a bit seedy and the perfect teenager's bedroom is a shit-hole, and I want forensics in to see if there's any blood or other types of DNA – reason is, there's underwear tossed around, sexy and lacy, and it looks stained. Very different to her mum's place, so it could bring a result. He's a good-looking guy, but bit of a loser, so focus on him.'

'Semen stains?' DS Lane asked.

'Possibly, but that's why I'm calling in forensics to go over Amy's room at the flat.'

'You think he's been screwing his own daughter?' Wey asked, not shocked, just interested in Reid's take on him.

'Who knows, but Amy's excuse was something about needing her wristwatch. I couldn't see one there and he couldn't recall when he last saw it. I dunno ... and we need to check his neighbours, see if anyone saw our girl on the Saturday afternoon. Also check on Mrs Fulford's neighbours.'

Lane and Wey looked at each other, both realizing that if Amy returned to her father's, but never left, there was another even more frightening scenario to consider.

Lane spoke first. 'So do you think she's still alive?'

Reid reached for the last congealing chip. 'We have to consider the very real possibility she is not.'

Chapter 8

Lena kept her hand on the door buzzer, but it seemed an age before Marcus answered and when he did, he sounded quite hoarse. As he buzzed her in and she closed the door behind her he came hurtling down the stairs from his flat.

'Is she home? Have they found her?' he asked desperately.

'No, no, she's not come home; I'm here because we need to talk.'

He sighed and then gestured for her to follow him up the wide marble staircase. The stair carpet had been a plush crimson, but was now rather threadbare and some of the brass stair rods were missing. The hallway had at one time been very grand, with marble mosaic flooring, but two flats had been created from the ground-floor rooms. Marcus occupied the second-floor flat and it was quite a way up. The polished wooden doors of the flats were all the same, with brass numberplates and knockers. He walked ahead of her, barefoot, wearing boxer shorts and a cotton dressing gown that looked as if it needed ironing.

'I was asleep,' he muttered as she elbowed his front door closed, trying to avoid the stack of circulars shoved to one side on the moth-eaten fitted carpet. The high ceiling and cornices gave the impression the flat was large, and probably at one time it would all have been one or two bedrooms, but it was now divided into a small kitchen and breakfast diner, utility room, bathroom, sitting room and two bedrooms. It felt shabby and yet there were some good paintings. As Lena followed him into the sitting room she saw it was reasonably well furnished, with leather armchairs and a low carved coffee table. There were more oil paintings on the walls and on an oak carved dresser were numerous photographs of the owner, Simon Boatly, in sporting attire, plus stacks of dirty coffee cups and mugs.

'Do you know what time it is?' Marcus asked, slumping down onto a worn leather armchair.

'I don't know and I don't care – don't you have a vacuum cleaner?'

'It's broken, and don't tell me you've come round to moan about housekeeping.'

She removed her coat and folding it neatly placed it over the arm of the other armchair. Sitting opposite him, she took in the good-quality silk Persian rug between them, observing as she always did the room and contents. Knowing her of old, Marcus shook his head.

'Everything in here belongs to Simon. I am as you know just renting it – before that it was his aunt's place and I doubt anything has been done since she died; I don't know how long he's staying away but it could be a year or so – anything else you need to know?'

'There's a lot I want to know, Marcus,' she said coldly.

'I am sure you do, but you look as if you are going out for a business meeting. I'd have thought considering the situation you would be at home to see if Amy called – has she?'

'I would have contacted you if she had, and I'm on my mobile.'

He gave a wide-handed gesture, puzzled as to why she was at his flat and picking up from the way she clenched her mouth so tightly that she was very tense.

'I have read Amy's journal and I've got to say it threw me sideways,' she said, trying not to sound angry, wanting to be as calm as possible but now unsure how she should elaborate on why she was there.

'What have you found out?'

'She details your sexual antics with various girlfriends or whores, I'm not sure who they are, but she is very derogatory in her descriptions, but more than that–'

He interrupted her, leaning forward. 'What? I don't believe this.'

'You were obviously having sex with women when Amy was in the flat.'

'Well, maybe, but Amy would have been in her bedroom, so I can't see how she would know what I was doing, and it was not as if it was a regular occurrence when she was here – just what are you suggesting?'

'I am not suggesting anything; I am merely telling you what she has written and in such explicit detail it reads like she was in the same room.'

'Are you joking? What the fuck do you take me for?'

'What I take you for is immaterial, what I am telling you is that from her journal it reads as if she were witness to or even worse partaking in your grubby little orgies.'

He stood up, enraged. 'That is bloody disgusting – orgies? For chrissakes, having a few sexual encounters is not anything I am ashamed of, but if you are implying that I would have allowed Amy to be involved then that is sick, and a total lie; I never would have been so crass as to allow that.'

Lena hated to even admit it, but she was enjoying seeing him embarrassed and desperately trying to extricate himself from her accusations.

'But did you have sex while Amy was here at the flat?'

'Yes, maybe I did a couple of times, but it was weekends, for God's sake, and it's not as if she's a little kid, and I don't think she even met any one of them for more than a coffee.'

'But you admit to having women here and having sex with them while you were supposed to be looking after Amy.'

'I just said that I did,' he snapped angrily.

'Well according to her journal she must have been watching you. I am not about to go into the disgusting details of your preferences or these tarts you bring here, but your daughter describes very explicitly their bodies, and yours, plus what sexual positions you used and your use of sex toys.'

Marcus leaned back in the chair and glared at her. 'You are enjoying this, you're fucking gloating about it, but I am telling you that at no time was Amy ever present, and I resent you implying they were tarts; they were all...' He sighed, realizing that whatever he said made it sound worse, and he truthfully was certain that it could only have happened a few times when Amy was staying.

'Did you abuse her?' Lena said quietly.

'What?'

'I asked if you abused Amy sexually because she certainly makes it sound as if she was privy not only to your prowess screwing up the arse but–'

The slap was so hard it knocked her sideways. He stood over her, clenching his fists, afraid he would slap her again. He then backed away from her, ashamed. 'I'm sorry, so sorry. I shouldn't have done that, and Jesus Christ you know I have never laid a hand on you, but I swear on my life I never even touched my daughter. It sickens me just thinking that you even asked me.'

She shook her head and rubbed her cheek as he crossed to a drinks cabinet and poured himself a brandy.

'If the police read her journal, Marcus, they will

get the same impression.'

When he turned he was shaking. 'I want to read it. Let me see it.'

Lena shrugged and stood up. 'I haven't got it with me and while I'm here I want to see her bedroom.'

He downed the brandy in one gulp and gasped. 'That detective who came here said not to touch anything in Amy's room as he wants someone to check through everything.'

'Why?'

'I don't know – probably forensics or something like that.'

'Well, just let me have a look, then I am going home.'

Although Lena had been to the flat before to pick up or drop Amy off, she had always refused and in fact never actually wanted to come inside, and had only entered as far as the hallway with Amy's suitcase. It had also been upsetting and traumatic as it was very early in their separation and she had not really wanted Amy to spend any time with Marcus, let alone an entire weekend. However, she had been persuaded it was good for Amy to be on amicable terms with both of them so she had relented.

Marcus stood waiting for her at the sitting-room door, and then gestured towards the small corridor leading off. Amy's bedroom was next door to his, with windows facing out onto Green Street. His bedroom door was ajar, and passing it Lena could see a king-size unmade bed with a bright orange duvet half across it and half dragging over the floor. It had the same fitted carpet as all the rest of the flat, and when Marcus opened the door to Amy's bedroom she could see it was similarly in need of hoovering. She stepped into the room and gasped, and turning to Marcus asked if it was in the same state as when Amy was last there.

'Yeah, I mean I looked around for anything that might give me a clue as to where she could have taken off – friends, contacts – but it was in this state, it always is, she's very untidy.'

'Untidy,' Lena said, shocked. The room to her mind was a tip of dirty, clothes, unmade scruffy bed and stained pillowslips; everything appeared to have been thrown around.

'They want to get some forensic guys in to test stuff, her clothes,' Marcus said and pointed to a pair of panties left by the bedside. 'I think they want to check if there's any DNA – you know, to see if she is sexually active. Considering what you've just accused me of, I am not going to even let you go further into the room as I don't want that disgusting bullshit aimed at me.'

'Do you think she is?' Lena asked, still looking around the room.

'No, but if she is she never mentioned any boyfriend to me. I know she has a thing about a movie actor and some boy band, but it's just teenage stuff – those posters have been up for about a year.' He gestured to the posters Blu-Tacked to the wall facing Amy's bed.

'What are those drawings?' she said, pointing to ones pinned beside her bed.

'Stuff she does in art class, I dunno – I know she likes her art teacher a lot, a Miss Polka who I

132

met once when I collected Amy from school.'

'It smells in here,' Lena said, wrinkling her nose.

'Well it's been shut up, and she wasn't the cleanest–' He froze and then closed his eyes. He had just spoken of Amy in the past tense and it hit him like a punch. He turned away, heading back down the corridor.

'Washing machine is not all that good and she hates to iron anything and we just take the sheets to the laundry once a month.'

Lena remained in the doorway of her daughter's bedroom, biting back a sarcastic echo of 'once a month' as they clearly hadn't been changed in a long time. The smell that permeated Amy's room was of stale sweat and an over-sweet cheap perfume. She was finding it difficult to move away from the room, it was so hard for her to see Amy staying in it, using it, sleeping in it, as if she was looking at another teenager's bedroom; it didn't bear any resemblance to Amy's beautiful clean stylish room at home.

'I am just going to look into her wardrobe,' she said, but Marcus had disappeared into the sitting room. She stepped over the items on the floor, and eased her way to the open wardrobe doors. She was careful, gently easing hangers apart and looking at the hanging garments, none of which she recognized, and it was the same for the boots and shoes. These were not high-quality designer labels, but cheap garish Top Shop, Zara and Primark items, many with stained armpits. She stepped back from the pungent smell of the clothes and turned towards the door, stopping to look at the posters before she walked out.

Marcus was sitting with another glass of brandy, and as she came to collect her coat he gave her a sad boyish smile. She had always loved it when he smiled at her in that way – he had such a handsome face and such expressive eyes.

'Please tell me you don't believe for a moment I would abuse Amy?'

She picked up her coat. Folding it over her arm, she bent down to collect her handbag.

'For God's sake, Lena, I couldn't stand it if you thought that. I love her, and to have you thinking for a second I would abuse my little girl sickens me.'

Lena took a deep breath. 'I think tomorrow you need to come over to the house and read the journal for yourself. I'm going home now. I need to be there in case she calls.'

'What do you think has happened to her?' he asked plaintively, his voice quivering.

'I don't know; I am scared to really think about it. I want to remain positive because I want her to come home.'

Lena hesitated, and watching him near to tears she felt she should make amends for the accusation she had made, but as always her control barrier was firmly in place.

'Amy is not very nice about me in her journal, she describes me in such horrid detail. She says I am cold and unforgiving, sarcastically referring to me as "Little Madam Perfect" and a lot more that I don't want to repeat right now. Whatever she really feels about me, I want to try and understand or make her understand that I have always had only her best interests at heart. I want to take time out to be with her, forget the business for a while to make up for...' She couldn't finish as in her mind she could see clearly the neat tight handwriting on one of the pages from Amy's journal: 'Bitch is always busy.'

Leaving Marcus already onto his third brandy, Lena said goodnight and left. By the time he heard the main entry door below slam behind her he had shambled into his bedroom. He got back into bed, drained the rest of the brandy and lay back thinking of what Lena had accused him of. He felt deeply ashamed and confused as to why she would have even hinted at there being anything sexual in his relationship with Amy. Had she been jealous of his girlfriends? She had never shown it, in fact to the contrary. He knew his wife was in many ways very naïve, but he couldn't understand why she had implied that the love he had for Amy was anything other than paternal.

Lena's drive back to Richmond at such a late hour meant the journey was free of traffic. Letting herself in and placing the key chain on the door, she headed into the kitchen and after making a cup of camomile tea she went up to her bedroom. The house was silent, not that it had ever throbbed with sounds – neither she nor Amy used the stereo system on a regular basis; only their televisions were used frequently and she could not recall the last time they had sat together in the TV room to watch DVDs. They had sometimes taken a tray and eaten together but after Amy went to boarding school these evenings stopped.

Passing her office, Lena knew she wouldn't be able to go to sleep for a while, if at all, and so she went in and switched on her computer, which she rarely if ever used for anything but work and research. She opened her emails; there were so many she had to prioritize what was important to enable the business to run without her presence before replying. She gave detailed instructions about deliveries and collections that she felt needed to be dealt with, and then spent a considerable amount of time checking new orders and assignments to go to the various outlets before she began listing everyone that worked for her and their contact numbers to give to the police.

It was three a.m. before Lena went to her bedroom, leaving the printer to continue printing. Last in the print queue were the present financial sales for Kiddy Winks. This created a lot of work as she employed a sales assistant to specifically deal with the contacts and requests coming in for the themed party packages. Lena had compiled a very good list of children's entertainers, venues, and birthday cake bakeries for not only individual orders but also to make cupcakes and party bags.

Changed into her nightdress and ready to remove her make-up, she sipped the by now cold camomile tea. She had placed everything she had worn back onto hangers, and her underwear into the white laundry bag. She noticed that all the items she had swiped off the dressing table had been replaced – what she had broken would be listed no doubt by the ever-diligent Agnes. She creamed off her make-up, brushed her hair and, still feeling wide awake, she decided to take a sleeping tablet because she knew she would be unable to sleep without one. Getting into the crisp pure cotton sheets, first neatly folding the silk bedspread, she lay back, leaving just a small bedside lamp lit. Left on the bed was Amy's dark green leather journal. Reaching out with her hand to touch it, she felt such a weight of sadness envelop her she wept. Gradually the sleeping tablet took effect as she debated whether or not she should allow the police to read the journal – maybe she would see what Marcus felt about it, and whether or not he would admit to her if what Amy had written about him was the truth.

Chapter 9

Marcus had a thick head; his mouth felt rancid and the phone ringing had woken him from his drink-fuelled sleep. He was so eager to reach it he slipped sideways off the bed. Hoping it would be Amy, he struggled to sound coherent as DI Reid asked if he would come to the station as he was organizing a press meeting and had arranged for journalists to be present at a ten-fifteen briefing. He also told him that Mrs Fulford had been in-formed and said she would be there. Marcus agreed and replaced the phone, only for it to ring straight away. He snatched it up, with no idea what time it was, and now his head throbbed. Lena didn't sound like herself; her voice was very subdued as she asked if Detective Reid had made contact about the press conference.

'Yes.'

'I think we should go together if that's okay with you?'

'Sure, I'll come over to your house first. What time is it now?'

'Just after eight, and you need to be here no later than nine thirty.'

'No problem. I'll get dressed and be with you in about an hour.'

'They haven't heard anything,' she said quietly.

'I guessed as much, so I'll see you later.'

'Please wear a pair of socks and look presentable. If we have to meet the press we should at least show up looking decent.'

She hung up and he dragged himself into the kitchen, put a pot of coffee on and opened a bottle of aspirin. He didn't give a shit about looking presentable and it was absolutely typical of Lena to tell him what to wear. She had often treated him like a kid, and it irritated him, but he would shave and make an effort.

Lena was dressed and having her coffee when her housekeeper arrived.

'Any news?' Agnes asked, removing her coat.

'No, not yet.'

'I was telling Natalie about it last night; she was so upset – have they any idea what's happened?' Agnes went on.

'No, and I would appreciate it, Agnes, if you did not discuss this situation with anyone outside the family.'

Agnes pursed her lips and nodded as her boss

went upstairs, then she noticed the mess of cooking utensils left in the sink. It wasn't very often that Mrs Fulford cooked for herself, but it really annoyed Agnes that whenever she did she never bothered to put the dirty pans, pots, plates or utensils in the dishwasher.

Lena sat in her study and wondered how upset Natalie would be if she read what Amy had written about her. Agnes was also viciously depicted as a stone-faced harridan with an obsessive-compulsive disorder. Amy had said that Agnes's obsession about placing groceries into plastic bags and plastic boxes in the fridge, all labelled in her thick black marker pen, was ridiculous; Amy reckoned that if she stood still long enough Agnes would put a plastic bag over her head, and put her in the deep freeze, adding that Agnes would probably describe the contents as 'Rich bitch frozen daughter'.

There was a lengthy description of how Mary Shelley, the author of *Frankenstein,* had craved her father's approval as he was always so cold and vicious towards her, and how she had felt that if she remained still and silent there was nothing he could complain about. Mary Shelley had even practised making her breathing so shallow it could not annoy him. Amy had practised being totally silent around Agnes, never replying to her queries, ignoring her presence, so that eventually she was thrilled that Agnes no longer even looked at her. She had written so many pages describing the housekeeper that it was difficult to make sense of her reasoning. She appeared to have a hatred of her and felt that she was evil and twisted and that her mother was foolish enough not to even notice that the pale round-faced woman was infiltrating the house. Amy was just as vitriolic about Agnes's precious daughter and how much she detested having to hear about her. Natalie she described as a cloying dependant, who was so controlled by her mother she was dysfunctional and needy, and to hear Agnes constantly referring to her as gorgeous made her want to vomit.

Lena called Harry Dunn to say she would not require him that morning but for him to come to the house after lunch. As with Agnes, the descriptions of her driver were vicious. Knowing that he had a police record for burglary, Amy had implied that her mother was foolish to even allow him to have access to the house. She described him as 'rat-like', his small hands and dainty feet as repellent, and also noted he smelt of some odious cologne that permeated the Lexus; again she wrote how stupid her mother was to trust him. She had described his clothes in detail, and knew that he purchased them from a second-hand charity shop in Knightsbridge, noting that his tailored suits and two-toned brogues had probably previously been worn by some dapper homosexual who had more than likely died of AIDS. Lena had still not really digested her daughter's character studies of her household staff, or thought why she had compiled such vitriolic assessments; she had been too distressed at reading about herself and Marcus.

Now she looked out of the window and saw Marcus parking on the driveway, so she opened the front door and stood waiting for him.

'We should drive to the station together.'

'Fine, whatever you want, but I need to look at the journal.'

'We don't have time; it's good to see you have at least made an effort.'

Marcus was wearing a Tom Ford navy pin-striped suit with an open-collared shirt and had put on socks, but she reprimanded him about being tie-less.

'For chrissakes, does it matter?'

'I think so, because we're going to meet the press, but it's too late now. I'll get my coat and we can go straight away.'

Marcus was left standing by his Mini, the door wide open, the keys still in the ignition. Agnes appeared at the front door.

'Good morning, Mr Fulford,' she said and he gave her a brief nod.

'I hope you get some good news.'

'So do I, Agnes; it's all very distressing, but we're trying to remain positive.'

Lena walked past Agnes without a word, and joined Marcus; she glanced at his filthy car.

'Don't you ever have a valet service? It's disgusting. We'll go in the Lexus and you can drive.'

'Fine,' he said, slamming the Mini door shut as she passed him her car keys. Agnes remained where she was, watching as the Lexus reversed and drove out. Lena had virtually ignored her but that was nothing new, and without being asked she went into the kitchen and called Harry, suggesting he should come over and wash Mr Fulford's car. He was not too pleased as he had been told he had the morning off, but he nevertheless agreed. Agnes returned to the Mini and opened it, taking the keys Marcus had left in the ignition and deciding she would ask Harry to clean the inside as well – he could drive it round to the garage so he could use the jet spray and vacuum the interior.

Marcus drove in silence as Lena sat beside him for the ten-minute drive. Lena was nervous, and was glad to have him beside her, slipping her hand through his arm as they walked the final few yards from the car, and he looked down and gave her a small glum smile. Together they entered the station where DC Barbara Burrows was waiting. She led them to the witness interview room, where they took their places on straight-backed chairs behind a Formica-topped table. After a few moments DI Reid walked in, carrying a thick folder, and drew up a chair to sit facing them.

'Thank you for agreeing to come in, I really appreciate it. Obviously you would have contacted me if you had received any news of your daughter's whereabouts, so it is imperative we set the wheels in motion to gain as much assistance from the press and public as possible. I need you to agree to what I can divulge to the journalists or let me know if anything feels inappropriate and you would prefer it not to be mentioned. That said, it is imperative we give them as much information as is possible to have a successful appeal that brings forward information to help find Amy.'

Marcus looked to Lena and then back to Reid. 'I don't think there is anything either my wife or I would not agree to being made public. We are obviously desperate to find Amy so we'll give you whatever you need from us.'

Lena leaned forward. 'What about our address

– do you give our personal details, or just the area?'

'We intend to be protective of your privacy, but that said, it could be discovered, and requesting assistance from the public can also encourage unwanted attention. However, if that happens I will endeavour to have uniform officers stand guard at your premises.'

Marcus glanced at Lena and she nodded her head in appreciation. Reid checked his wristwatch and opened the file, taking out a few pages, and clicked open a felt tip pen. He explained that he had brought in a team of officers to begin house-to-house enquiries, and that he would need access to both their homes. He wanted Amy's bedrooms carefully searched and any items removed would of course be recorded for their information. He seemed pressed for time, skim-reading pages and making a few cryptic notes as he quickly covered the exact time Amy was last seen, and gave a brief outline of the statements so far gathered from the Newman family and the staff at Amy's school.

'Has Amy's iPhone been found or traced yet?' Marcus asked.

'Not as yet. It's still work in progress and we are monitoring it with the phone company. The battery may be flat, but if it is recharged and swit-ched on we will be informed right away and will be able to locate its whereabouts,' he said, collecting the pages and replacing them in the folder.

Reid found them both to be calm, and eager to be as helpful as possible, which he thought ad-mirable in light of the emotional turmoil they must both be going through. He gave an encouraging smile.

'Press appeals help us to gain the public's assistance and more often than not allow us to locate missing persons. I am also hoping to get a slot on a new television crime programme, which would broaden the appeal and in turn increase public interest.'

'Thank you, Inspector Reid,' Lena replied.

He checked with Lena the description of the clothes worn by Amy, as described by the Newmans' nanny: the maroon jumper with frilled cuffs, blue ballet pumps and black leggings. Lena did recall buying a cashmere top from Brora that fitted the description, and added she remembered it distinctly because she had purchased one for herself, which she agreed to give to Reid as it would assist the investigation.

Marcus and Lena remained silent as Reid replaced his chair, checked his watch again and then said DC Burrows would join them in about ten minutes and take them to the conference room. Left alone, they sat in silence until Marcus reached out and placed his hand over hers.

'You okay?'

She nodded, and gripped his hand tightly.

'Are you?'

'No, but at least I feel as if things are being done, and maybe this press appeal will bring her home.'

Lena chewed at her lips and could feel the tears welling up. She found it difficult to talk, her tongue felt swollen and she could hardly swallow. He still gripped her hand tightly, and like her he suddenly found the emotional upheaval difficult to deal with, and was trying to keep his composure when DC Burrows tapped and entered.

'Hello again, just wondered if you needed to use the bathroom before I take you into the conference room.'

Lena stood up and nodded. 'Thank you, I do need to go.'

Lena followed DC Burrows out, and Marcus, left alone, clenched and unclenched his hands. He had been concerned, very worried, even angry, but now he was beginning to feel a terrible sense of dread. Close to tears, he sniffed, and then closed his eyes as he prayed that what he had begun to fear could not be true: he would never see Amy again.

Lena was washing her hands in a small cracked washbasin in the ladies' toilets. She drew down a roller towel and carefully dried them, then stood and ran her fingers through her hair. She had forgotten to bring her handbag with her, and she wanted to freshen up her lipstick and powder her face, as it looked patchy from tearstains. She needed a drink as her throat felt so dry, and when Burrows returned to ask if she was ready she asked if she could possibly have a glass of water. Burrows said there would be some on the table and they were now ready for them to join the conference.

Lena gave the policewoman a pitiful pleading look. 'Tell me, these press conferences, do they bring a result? I mean is it usual that they find whoever is missing?'

Burrows had never before been on a missing person's case, and in today's early morning session Reid had indicated a depressing possible outcome.

Amy Fulford had been missing since Saturday afternoon and it was now Wednesday morning. There had been no contact, no sightings, and it seemed she had disappeared leaving no clue of her whereabouts. Added to this was the fact it was apparently totally out of character – she had never gone missing previously and seemingly had no boyfriends, no history of drug or alcohol abuse, and to date they could find no reason for her to run away. Although DI Reid had not expressed his personal views, he had made his team aware that with nothing on CCTV and no witness sightings they had to contemplate the worst-case scenario. Amy Fulford could have been abducted, held against her will, raped and possibly murdered. However, he still hoped that they would find her alive and well and return her safely to her family.

Chapter 10

The raised small platform in the conference room held seats for the Fulfords, the uniformed Chief Superintendent John Douglas and DI Reid. Behind them was a dark blue curtain with a large Metropolitan Police crest and two large blow-up photographs of Amy positioned on either side. Seated in a row of hard-backed chairs were numerous local and national journalists. Cameras were positioned to film the meeting, and photographers sat in the back row, ready to swing into action when permission was granted. Both Lena and

Marcus had agreed to give statements to the press and if they wished to speak at the meeting they would be allowed to do so. To one side was a large screen on which Reid planned to show the route they believed Amy might have taken that Saturday afternoon.

Chief Superintendent Douglas thanked everyone for being present, introduced Lena and Marcus and then handed over the meeting to DI Reid. Reid spoke clearly and concisely, outlining their concerns and the publicity he hoped the meeting would generate. Amy, he said, was only fifteen years old and her parents were deeply distressed and appealed for anyone with information to come forward. They already knew that Amy, who had a bank account and cash card, had not withdrawn any large amounts of money recently. He continued to elaborate on the problems of tracing the exact route Amy might have taken from Fulham to Mayfair. He added there was a football match on that same Saturday afternoon at the Chelsea Stadium, Stamford Bridge. This, he said, could possibly bring forward witnesses but it also meant that the area was quite congested not only with vehicles but with groups of fans heading towards the match.

The screen lit up to show a map of the Fulham Road with the Newmans' street, Harwood Road, flagged up, and this led directly onto the Fulham Road. The most viable means of transport Amy might have used to reach her father's Mayfair flat were bus and Underground, and they were asking for any witness that saw her either on the street, Tube or a bus to come forward. Bus stops were flagged, as well as the route from Fulham Road towards Knightsbridge, Park Lane, Marble Arch and Mayfair.

Lena had calmed down and Marcus kept his hand over hers as they listened intently to the lengthy press conference. Reid said that MISS-ING PERSON – APPEAL FOR ASSISTANCE flyers had been handed out by officers in all the aforementioned areas, but as yet there had been no witness that actually saw Amy after she had left the property in Harwood Road. Reid expressed the importance of the press coverage and des-cribed Amy as a caring, quiet, well-educated girl and said it was doubtful she would have accepted a lift from anyone she did not know. He went on to say they were considering the possibility Amy had been abducted off the street and that if so someone out there must have seen or heard some-thing, but there had been no kidnap threat or ransom demand.

He then turned to the Fulfords and asked if either of them would like to say a few words. Lena gripped Marcus's hand tightly, afraid to say anything.

Marcus cleared his throat. 'I'd like to thank DI Reid and everyone for their dedication in trying to find our daughter Amy.' He released Lena's hand and sipped from a glass of water. He coughed again, almost unable to continue, then spoke in a very emotional voice.

'Amy is our pride and joy and the most beloved and caring young girl, and I beg anyone who saw her, or knows where she may be, to please come forward and tell the police. My wife and I are desperate for our daughter to return home. Thank you.'

It was some considerable time later when the conference eventually broke up. DI Reid had asked for an officer to follow Lena home to retrieve the jumper identical to the one they believed Amy was last seen wearing. Meanwhile, he wanted to have a few private words with Marcus and as he had driven Lena to the station he arranged for a squad car to take her home. Marcus waited in the same small interview room they had previously used.

'You mind if I just ask you a few personal questions, Mr Fulford?' said Reid when he finally joined him.

'No, not at all, anything you need to know, please go ahead.' Marcus kept his voice level but he was nervous, worrying if Lena had mentioned what they had discussed the previous evening.

'Right, we need to have our forensics people check over your flat, specifically your daughter's bedroom, and we will also require the same permission from your wife. I would like you to be present, so if you could be available early this afternoon?'

Marcus nodded, promising to return the Lexus to his wife's house and drive straight home.

'Do you think your wife would like to have a family liaison officer present? It must be a very emotionally draining time,' Reid said.

'I think that is a question you need to ask Lena, but I will be giving her as much care and attention as I can.'

'You are separated and live apart – do you feel

149

this could have had an adverse effect on Amy?'

'No, not at all, it's been two years and it was amicable.'

Reid nodded and, choosing his words carefully, he said that he would need to know Marcus's whereabouts during the time Amy had been missing. This would mean that he needed the names of any girlfriends or partners Marcus was involved with. He pointed out that they had made no reference at the conference to the fact he and his wife were involved in divorce proceedings but it would probably become known if the investigation was to continue.

'What do you mean, continue?' Marcus asked.

'Well, hopefully we will find her. If that occurs then we will not continue the search, but what you have to understand is that is exactly what will be going on – an extensive and at times very invasive search into your backgrounds. Your privacy will feel as if it is being invaded, but we cannot skirt any possible area that might give us some indication of what has happened to your daughter.'

Marcus nodded; he was starting to sweat profusely and he was certain that Reid's probing questions had a hidden agenda.

'I will give you anything you need, if you just tell me what you want from me.'

Getting to his feet, Reid thanked him and said he would discuss it further that afternoon. Marcus was ushered out, while Reid went up into the incident room, which was a hive of activity but so far with no result. Amy Fulford seemed to have disappeared without a single sighting. He'd by now asked for checks on the properties that Lena

Fulford had rented in Devon, and had received the background report on the prison record of Harry Dunn. It was surprising that someone with such obvious business acumen as Lena Fulford would employ as her driver a man with a lengthy record of burglaries. Reid was unsure if he actually approved of Dunn being given a chance to keep on the straight and narrow, but he had worked for her for over two years with no apparent problem. Reid would want to question him again and also the housekeeper, Mrs Agnes Moors, who it turned out also had a rather chequered background of employment with various companies but never as a housekeeper, and had been made redundant rather too many times.

Reid also had a strange feeling about Marcus Fulford, although he couldn't actually pinpoint what it was exactly that worried him. He had asked for both Lena and Marcus's financial situations to be looked into. She was the obvious breadwinner, so perhaps his insistence that their separation was amicable might not be exactly true. By now it was after one and Reid needed something to eat as he had been at the station since before seven that morning, so he took himself up to the canteen. Barbara Burrows was finishing her lunch and gave him a warm smile. She was a little in awe of him and was obviously trying to think what she should say, eventually blurting out, 'No news yet?'

'No,' he said as he fetched a tray and lined up for steak and kidney pie and French fries. He sighed. No news, not so much as a whisper, and he had hoped the press releases would at least

151

bring him something to act on. Taking his tray to a vacant table, he sat with his back to the rest of the room, not wanting to be joined or forced to have a conversation with anyone.

Harry Dunn had almost filled a large plastic rubbish bag with old newspapers, food cartons, cigarette stubs and empty beer cans from the car's interior and now he was giving the Mini a final polish. He was in a quandary as to what exactly he should do about discovering a Cartier watch that must have fallen between the front seats. He guessed it must have been there for some time, as there were mud stains on the carpet and smudges on the watch face. Right now, it was in his pocket. He'd had a job to vacuum up the dirt from the carpets, having to get on his hands and knees and use a stiff brush to lift the dried mud from the driver's and passenger sides. As he buffed the dashboard and stood back admiring his work, he decided he would simply not mention finding the watch and if a good enough length of time elapsed he'd sell it to a friend he'd used on many occasions to fence stolen goods. He got into the car, drove it round to the front of the house and parked up, taking the keys in to Agnes. He was hoping for coffee and a Penguin biscuit, but a police car drew up with Mrs Fulford in it and so he made a quick exit via the garden doors and returned to the garage. He would finish clearing up in there, rewind the hose and wait to find out if he was needed.

Lena hurried up the stairs and into her bedroom. She opened the door to the section of the wardrobe containing all her sweaters and took out the one she believed to be identical to Amy's. It was fine cashmere with a scooped neck and long sleeves, the cuffs frilled with a small band of maroon lace. She returned to the waiting officer and handed him the sweater, which she had wrapped in tissue paper. Assuring her he'd have it photographed, he also asked if she would allow it to appear in any TV re-enactment. Lena agreed. Agnes had been listening and asked Lena if there was any further news, but Lena didn't reply and walked away.

Back upstairs in her bedroom she noticed the heavy thick white curtains that were lined with a pale green satin had been moved. She knew straight away that as always Agnes had, instead of leaving a section of satin showing as she preferred, straightened them to hang down without any lining visible. Irritated, she flipped them open further to reveal the green material. She couldn't help but remember what Amy had written about Agnes, and although Lena was aware of her housekeeper's curtain fixation, she had not, she realized, bothered to draw Agnes's attention to the fact she liked to be able to see the lining.

Agnes had made the bed, stacking the many cushions in a dead straight line along the raised pillows, and Lena had a moment of panic when she realized the journal had been placed on her bedside table. She wondered if Agnes had read any of it, and hoped not, but just in case she placed the journal in her underwear drawer. At the sound of Marcus's voice drifting up from the downstairs hall, she hurried to join him.

'I've got to go back to my flat to meet up with

153

DI Reid. Can you give me the journal to take with me?'

'No, it's better it stays here with me,' she prevaricated. 'Come over this evening and we can discuss it then, because I still don't think the police should have access to it. It's not as if it contains any details of where she might be or who she might be with, and it's full of too many personal details.'

Marcus hesitated but then agreed and went into the kitchen to collect the keys to his car from Agnes. She mentioned that she had asked Harry to clean it, and he thanked her then took out his wallet and passed her a ten-pound note. 'Give this to him from me.'

Agnes took the tenner and said she would see that Harry received it. She walked Marcus to the front door, asking him if he would like a sandwich, as it was way past lunchtime, but he declined and got into his gleaming Mini. It would probably have cost treble that amount if he had taken it to a valet service, but he was short of cash and hoped he had enough petrol to get him back to Mayfair.

Agnes headed round to the garage and Harry physically jumped as she walked in. She handed him the ten-pound note, and he gave a shrug of his shoulders as he pocketed it. The Cartier watch was still in his jacket that was hanging up by the hosepipe.

'Do you know if she will be needing me this afternoon?'

'No I don't; they came and took away something she gave them, but I've no idea what it was.'

Lena went into her office, sitting for a while in front of her computer, but was unable to concentrate, or even contemplate thinking about business. She was completely drained, and opening a drawer took out a family photo album that she used to keep on her desk. So many photographs were of Marcus and Amy and herself on various holidays and now with their pending divorce she couldn't stand to even look at it. Slowly she turned the thick cellophane-covered pages depicting their happy times. The first photograph of Amy with white-blonde hair sitting on a beach with a bucket and spade aged three years shocked Lena at just how beautiful her daughter was then, and page after page delivered the same emotional impact. Amy was stunning, always smiling and playful; photographs of them together brought back a flood of memories. Marcus tanned and athletic, carrying his daughter on his shoulders, Marcus and Amy swimming and diving, Amy riding a little pony she had adored. Lena smiling in a sundress with Amy clinging to her. Page after page showed her daughter getting older, but even minus front teeth she had retained such perfect features – she had been a gorgeous little girl. Lena knew she had spoiled her; every Christmas photograph showed a mountain of gifts stacked under a decorated tree. Towards the end of the album were pictures of Amy at thirteen; she was not smiling as much, but more often staring wide-eyed into the camera. The last photograph was taken more than two years ago; it was Amy in her school uniform, glum-faced and holding in her arms her old worn teddy bear that she now hated ever to be parted from.

Closing the book, Lena wondered where their old home movies were as she began to think she should maybe select something to give to the police. All the while she ignored the flashing light on her business line, refusing to even listen to the messages, ten in all. Now she was intent on trying to recall where the tapes would be, opening one cupboard after another, until she found the old box with them in, all neatly marked by year and occasion. She thought she'd thrown out her old video player but just in case she decided to check and see if it was still in the garage. As she ran down the stairs Agnes appeared, asking if she wanted lunch, but she waved her away, heading out into the garden through the glass conservatory doors. Harry jumped up, startled, as she ran through the rear door of the garage.

'I'm looking for the old video machine,' she told him as she turned round. He shrugged and said that he couldn't recall ever seeing one, but offered to move some boxes that had been left neatly stacked and stored on one side of the garage. She was determined to find it, hurling boxes aside, along with old duvets, cushions and rugs no longer wanted, muttering that they could all go to the charity shop.

'I'll take them away for you,' he said, having no intention of doing so but instead planning to take them home for himself.

Lena was frantic, becoming hysterical as she threw one thing aside after another, until she let out a shriek on seeing the video recorder. Panic-stricken, she asked Harry over and over if he could see the remote for it, but he was doubtful they would find it amongst the mess that was now strewn around. Suddenly she saw it and grabbed it, along with the video player, and wouldn't let Harry carry it back to the house, insisting on taking it herself.

'Will you need me to set it up for you, Mrs Fulford?'

'No I can manage, thank you.'

He watched her stumble across the big garden – some of the stone steps around the fishpond were very uneven where the paths from the shrubbery led up to the house. He shut the door and looked over the mess she had left, before methodically he began to sort through the contents of the boxes, selecting what to keep for himself and what at some point he'd take to the charity shop. He had been busy for about fifteen minutes when Agnes appeared and said that Mrs Fulford did not require him for the rest of the day so he could go home. Curious, she moved further into the garage.

'What are you doing?'

'She wanted the old video machine, said all this junk can be thrown out.'

Agnes immediately started choosing items for herself, remarking that her daughter could do with some cushions and she'd have the duvet. Between them they began to divide up the goods, and Harry was thankful he'd already packed one box for himself. Agnes was grabbing items and putting them aside, saying they would be useful for Natalie as she didn't have much and had recently moved into a new flat. The two of them were like scavengers, checking labels and making their selections, and never at any time did they discuss Amy. Eventually Harry suggested that perhaps Agnes should return to the house in case she was needed. Agnes was sweating with the exertion of repacking the boxes but no way was she going to let Harry have all the goods; she'd even got a nice bathroom and toilet set, plus towels and a bathrobe. He wondered how she was going to take everything home, as he knew she didn't own a car, but by now he reckoned he'd got the best of what was on offer.

Delving into one of the tool cabinets he took out a reel of thick packing tape and began binding his boxes shut. 'I'll give you a few quid to take these to my daughter's, otherwise I'll have to get a taxi,' Agnes offered hopefully.

Harry simply said she should pack up and he'd maybe help her out in the morning, but he was going home. He pressed the button to open the automatic garage doors. The Lexus was parked by the front door of the house so he walked along the back lane, and then drove it back to the garage to stack up his boxes. Agnes was still there on her knees inspecting some pillowcases and stuffing them into the cardboard box by her side. While he opened the boot of the Lexus and carried out his share, Agnes carried on rummaging through the remainder of the boxes, taking out some pans and dishes.

'You'll be needing a removal van,' he said, packing up the Lexus.

By the time he had stacked his items and closed the boot, Agnes was finishing off the packing using the tape; she was red-faced and her hair hung in sweaty rat-tails. He remembered the watch left in his jacket and collected it. Agnes said she would call a local taxi unless he would return and help her but he pretended not to hear.

'See you tomorrow then,' Harry said as he used the automatic key ring to close the garage door. He then drove off; it was not unusual for him to take the Lexus home and return with it the following day – often on occasions Mrs Fulford had called him back, wanting to be taken somewhere or other, but he hoped she wouldn't bother him today as he was intending to unpack his goods and see what he could sell on.

Lena was sitting in the TV room, and having plugged in the video player she was choosing tapes ready to begin watching the footage of Amy. Hunched on the stone-flagged floor, with the remote in her hand, she pressed play: nothing happened. With a sinking feeling she realized the remote needed new batteries. She was close to tears with frustration as she went into the kitchen to ransack drawers, knowing they always kept a selection. Frantically she tossed aside neat stacks of napkins and tea cloths until she found a box of AA batteries and returned to the TV room, shutting the door firmly behind her.

Agnes had by now packed up virtually everything else, leaving only a few items that neither she nor Harry wanted. Returning to the house she saw the TV room door shut, so headed into the kitchen and stood surveying the mess. She began to methodically refold the napkins and tea cloths, restacking them into the drawer as she checked

159

her watch – it was almost four o'clock, just another hour and she would be able to leave. The telephone rang on Mrs Fulford's business line, but she answered it anyway and in a posh voice announced, 'Mrs Fulford's residence.' It was the assistant from KiddyWinks asking to speak to Mrs Fulford and so Agnes informed her she was unavailable but would pass on a message.

'It's Gail, and I really do need to speak to Mrs Fulford about arrangements for delivery – could you ask her to call me?'

'Yes, Gail, I will do that.'

Agnes replaced the phone, and wrote down the time and name for Mrs Fulford to return the call. She hesitated as to whether or not she should go into the TV room but decided against it. She stood in the hallway listening, but hearing nothing she returned to the kitchen and closed the door, then rang Natalie.

'Hello, dear, I've got some lovely things that you will be able to use. Mrs Fulford was going to take them to a charity shop but there's some very nice bed linen and a double duvet.'

She listened as her daughter asked if there was any news about Amy. She gave a sigh and said in a sorrowful voice that as far as she knew there was nothing.

'Oh my goodness, that is just terrible,' Natalie said, mimicking her mother's tone.

'Yes, just awful, and there's a nice bathroom set and some pots and pans.'

'I've got to go, Mum, another caller on the line.'

Agnes replaced the phone. There always seemed to be another call; she was hardly ever able to have

160

a lengthy conversation with her daughter. Still, she reckoned, she'd be with her at the weekend, and they'd have a nice time sorting through the goods. Only now did she really think about Amy, and counted the days in her mind. Missing for almost five days – she didn't think it was a good sign, and for the first time she seriously wondered if something terrible had happened. She knew that if it was Natalie missing she would have been in a terrible state, not shutting herself up in the TV room like Mrs Fulford – she'd have been out searching the streets.

Agnes had no conception that over forty officers were out on the streets attempting to find some clue where Amy Fulford might be. House-to-house enquiries were being conducted and the neighbours around the Fulfords' property were all being contacted and questioned. Agnes did wonder if she would be questioned again, because when making up Mrs Fulford's bed she had picked up the journal. She had flicked through it, not intending to read it, but catching her name on a page she couldn't help herself. Learning exactly what the spoiled little bitch thought of her was appalling and she would have a few things to add to her statement. Fortunately she had not had the time to read more than a couple of pages because she had heard the police car drawing up. She had quickly placed the journal on the bedside table before hurrying down the stairs to open the front door.

Now, knowing that Mrs Fulford was still in the TV room, she crept up the stairs hoping to read more, but looking around the bedroom, she was

161

unable to find the journal. She reckoned there would be another time when she would be able to have a good search around – Agnes when left alone spent considerable time looking over private papers but was always very careful to replace them in the exact same order. Returning to the kitchen, she made herself a cup of tea and sat brooding about how Amy had described her; it would be another subject she and Natalie could discuss. It never even crossed Agnes's mind that Mrs Fulford had read what her daughter thought of her; in her opinion she was an exemplary employee and kept the big house immaculate and she firmly believed that Mrs Fulford could not manage without her.

Chapter 11

Walking up Green Street, Reid stopped and looked at Marcus's polished Mini and peered inside it. He recalled it had been filthy the last time he saw it, and found it strange under the circumstances that Fulford had found the time to have it valet-cleaned inside and out. Up ahead he saw two SOCOs about to enter the house and hurried to join them. He'd had to park a considerable distance away, but didn't want the team to go in without him. They carried their forensic equipment in silver cases and paper suits under their arms.

Marcus buzzed them into the house, whereupon the SOCOs asked to be shown Amy's

162

bedroom, while Reid sat waiting in the sitting room. When Marcus returned he poured himself a Scotch and offered Reid one, but he declined. Marcus sank into the other old leather armchair.

'I've had some news – the press releases will be out in the morning papers and hopefully the *Evening Standard*. We would like to run a *Crime Night* appeal as well; it sounds awful but because we are still treating your daughter as a medium-risk misper and possible runaway, high-risk cases may take precedence. Would you be prepared to take part in an interview, should they agree?'

'Yes of course, but as my wife and I keep saying, we honestly do not believe that Amy would take off – it would be totally out of character. I am really becoming terrified that something appalling has happened.'

Reid leaned forward. 'We are obviously very much dependent on the public coming forward with information, but rest assured we are being very dedicated and thorough in our investigation.'

Marcus nodded, sipping his Scotch, and Reid asked casually why he had cleaned his car. For a moment Marcus looked confused, and then shrugged before explaining that his wife's house-keeper had instructed her driver to wash and valet it – he had not asked for it to be done, but admitted that it really needed it. Reid made a mental note to speak to Harry Dunn.

'You said you would give me the names and contact numbers for your girlfriends. I will need to question them, specifically about the afternoon and evening of the day your daughter went missing.'

Marcus got up and crossed to the drinks cabinet, picked up a notebook and returned to his seat. He tore out two pages and handed them to Reid.

'My current sort-of girlfriend is Justine Hyde, the others are more or less just friends that I occasionally see. Although I am in the process of divorcing Lena, I am not some kind of Jack the Lad – I enjoy female company but there is no serious relationship ongoing, just casual.'

Reid looked at the list of women and asked if he'd had sexual relationships with all of them. Marcus hesitated and Reid could sense the unease emanating from him as he confessed that he had. He explained that when his daughter came to stay he made sure that he was able to give her his undivided attention and rarely if ever introduced Amy to his girlfriends.

'What work do you do, Mr Fulford?'

Marcus helped himself to another Scotch and stood leaning against the cabinet. Yet again he seemed uneasy, describing his various design projects, how he was self-employed and had not had a lot of success recently due to the credit crunch. He eventually admitted that he was presently unemployed and receiving benefits. He explained that the flat belonged to a long-time friend, a Simon Boatly, who was abroad, and he was renting it for a low price. Again, Reid showed no reaction but thought that compared to the large property Marcus's wife resided in, the Mayfair flat seemed rundown, albeit in a very expensive location.

Marcus repeated what he had been doing on the

Saturday Amy went missing, and that after the football he went with Justine to a film and then her place for the night. He agreed that even if Amy had returned to the flat, he would not have been aware of it, but he had asked his neighbours and none of them could recall seeing her. Reid flicked through his notebook and asked about the watch that Amy had told her friend Serena she wanted to collect. Marcus gave an open-handed gesture. 'You asked me about that before. Anyway, Lena said she gave Amy a Cartier watch on her last birthday, and it was inscribed on the back with her name and date of birth.'

'You've not found it here in the flat?' Reid asked.

'No – to be honest I haven't even thought about it, but it's very expensive and she is only fifteen. According to Lena it's what she wanted and my wife has a habit of buying whatever Amy asks for.'

Reid flicked back and forth between pages in his notebook. It irritated Marcus as every time Reid closed it, he would open it again as if he had thought of something else he wanted to ask.

'I will be talking to Justine, Mr Fulford, and just so I've got this right, you spent Saturday night and part of Sunday with her and were not concerned that Amy didn't contact you?'

'Correct, but Amy had already told me she wouldn't be coming as Serena had invited her to a sleepover. I didn't get back here until late Sunday, and I had an appointment with Lena on the Monday morning. Neither of us were concerned about Amy not contacting us. I think Lena turned off her mobile for the meeting.'

Reid nodded and continued his questions as he wrote in his notebook. 'So this meeting on Monday that both you and your wife were present at, even then neither of you knew Amy was missing and had not turned up at school?'

Marcus was now becoming really tetchy and snapped that he had said numerous times that this was the case.

'What was the meeting about on the Monday morning? The school have confirmed they left messages but none were returned.'

Marcus sighed and explained they were at a meeting with their divorce lawyers; he said a Charles Henshaw was Lena's and he was represented by Jacob Lyons. Reid glanced up at Marcus, saying nothing but acutely aware that Lyons was a well-known and very expensive divorce lawyer who was often in the headlines. For a man who claimed to be on benefits it was a strange choice.

'Did Amy have any concerns about the forthcoming divorce proceedings?'

'No, she did not. As I have said repeatedly, we have been apart for about two years and Amy is fully aware we are divorcing. Lena and I had separated and the reason she was sent to boarding school was that it would give her a good strong routine, and as it was only weekly she would be able to spend every other weekend with her mother or myself. If Amy had been finding our weekends difficult to handle she would have told me. Anyway, I am beginning to get really frustrated about this repetition and surely you should be out there looking for my daughter rather than questioning me.'

Reid gave an apologetic nod of his head; Marcus got himself another refill, seething with tension. His hand shook as he poured the Scotch – whether he was trying to control his temper or his nerves were run ragged it was hard to tell. Reid closed his notebook, slipped it into his pocket and stood up.

'I'm sorry if this appears tedious, Mr Fulford, but I am simply doing my job and trying to ascertain what emotional state your daughter might have been in. If she was at all traumatized by the present situation between yourself and your wife it could be a reason that she has run away.'

Marcus banged down the glass. 'She was perfectly happy, she was showing excellent results at school, she had many friends and behaved like any normal teenager!'

Reid couldn't help thinking it rather odd that when angered he spoke of his daughter in the past tense.

It was at this point that one of the SOCOs tapped on the door and gestured for Reid to join him in the corridor. After a short private conversation Reid accompanied him to Amy's bedroom and was met with the sight of loads of evidence bags, mostly filled with underwear and clothes, which were to be removed for forensic examination. However, that was not why he had been asked to join the officers: inside a plastic bag was a selection of hardcore pornographic magazines, which had been discovered under the bed, covered by an old pair of jeans. Numerous X-rated adult VHS videos had also been found in a large shoe box inside the wardrobe. Reid was shocked by the discovery of such explicit material in a fifteen-year-old's bedroom. He inspected a few copies in distaste and was about to walk from the room when his attention was brought to something else. A poster stuck to the plasterboard wall had been pulled back by one of the officers, revealing a small nail-size hole. Reid looked through it and saw that it gave a direct view to the master bedroom and the king-size bed. The SOCO remarked that the poster was clearly a young girl's and was maybe used to hide the peephole, and that the various markings of Blu-Tack could suggest that the right side of the poster had been pulled back and re-placed. Reid realized that there was also a possi-bility that Amy had deliberately put the poster up to stop someone looking in from the master bedroom.

Reid closed the door and returned to the living room, perching on the arm of the chair he had previously been sitting in. He wondered if Marcus, who was now silent and subdued, had drunk more Scotch as his face was flushed.

'I need you to agree to the SOCOs searching your bedroom.'

Marcus sighed, shaking his head, and gave an open-handed gesture. 'Search wherever you want.'

'Thank you, Mr Fulford. I am going to be straight with you because my men have discovered some disturbing items in Amy's bedroom and I need you to be honest with me.'

'What items?'

Reid quietly told him about the selection of

hardcore pornography they had found beneath Amy's bed and in the wardrobe.

'I don't believe this.'

'The tapes are explicit adult porn films. Do you have a VHS video machine?'

Marcus got unsteadily to his feet and ruffled his hair. 'No, and the tapes are not mine and certainly not my daughter's. I do not have an old video player, I use DVDs, and you can bloody check the lot because I have never owned a porn film in my life.'

He suddenly clapped his hands and then looked at Reid. 'I know whose they could be and the tapes have probably been left here for years. As I said, this is not my flat, it's Simon Boatly's and he was into all that stuff. I got the DVD and stereo unit along with Sky Plus set up when I moved in.'

'There's something else. We discovered what appears to be a peephole between Amy's and your bedroom.'

Marcus looked surprised. 'A peephole?'

'Yes. I looked through it and it gives a direct view to your bed and vice versa into Amy's room.'

Marcus took a deep breath before shaking his head and slumping down into the leather arm-chair.

'Listen, I have no idea about any fucking peep-hole or how or why it got there; all I do know is I am damned sure that neither Amy nor I would use it, it's preposterous. You sure it's not just a crack? There's enough of them around this place as it's old and not been decorated for years.'

'It looks as if it's been made deliberately, and you can look at it yourself in a minute.'

169

Marcus leaned forward, resting his elbows on his knees, head bent low. His voice was quieter as he explained how he had moved into the flat and done nothing in the way of decorating in any of the rooms. When it was agreed that Amy could stay weekends she had simply moved into the spare bedroom, and even the bed linen belonged to Simon Boatly. Marcus continued describing Simon, who was in his early forties, single, a photographer who'd been left a considerable amount of money so had never really been forced into legitimate employment. Reid asked where Boatly was now and Marcus, almost inaudible, said he was travelling abroad and he didn't know when he would be returning to the UK.

By now the two SOCOs were at work in the master bedroom and had removed the bed sheets, pillowcases and quilt cover to check for DNA. As Reid walked in, one of the men joked that it was a bit of a hovel – almost as bad as the daughter's bedroom – but the DI was not amused. Eager to leave, he glanced at his watch and asked that they show Mr Fulford the items they were removing and get him to sign an inventory. He then went into Amy's bedroom and as he stood in the doorway staring around he noticed shoved into a corner a small TV set with a built-in video machine.

Marcus needed another drink to calm his nerves. Talking about Simon had set an alarm bell ringing in his brain about the reason Lena had come round the previous night – her suggestion that he had abused their own daughter, telling him about the sexual contents of the journal. If the police were to be shown it they would come to the same conclusion as she had done. Shaking, he knew he had to see Lena as soon as possible because of what Reid had told him. He physically jumped when the officers tapped and entered the room with the plastic evidence bags of the assorted magazines and tapes. He signed an inventory without checking all the items as he felt sick to his stomach.

Reid was coming out of the bedroom as the SOCOs said they were ready to go, and he asked them to list the dates of the magazines and to call or email him later with the details.

Marcus looked shaken as Reid gestured for him to come to Amy's bedroom. Once inside he pulled the poster to one side so Marcus could see the peephole. He moved closer, bent down and could see into his bedroom.

'It's evident from the Blu-Tack marks on the wall that your daughter's poster was pulled back frequently and there is also a TV set with a video recorder in here.'

'What are you implying?' Marcus snapped angrily.

'That the peephole was used on a regular basis by a person, or persons, who had access to this room. As your friend Mr Boatly has not been here for some considerable time and is abroad I–'

Marcus walked out, his fists clenched as he headed into his own room. 'It belonged to Simon and I took it out of my bedroom as I bought a small flat-screen TV.'

Reid followed him. Marcus stood beside his unmade bed, the mattress left exposed, and stared towards the wall. Hardly detectable on the floral wallpaper was the peephole from his daughter's bedroom.

'I swear before God, I did not know that was there,' he said in a voice so low it was hardly audible.

Reid headed for the front door. 'I'll be in touch, Mr Fulford. Thank you for your time, you've been very courteous and I appreciate it. Will you be staying here tonight?'

'No, I will go and comfort my wife this evening, but my mobile will be on if you have any news,' a strained-looking Marcus replied.

Reid hurried down the stairs; although there had been some developments as a result of the search they were still no closer to finding where Amy Fulford could be, but it was looking increasingly like the perfect teenager might not have been as naïve as everyone had suggested.

Chapter 12

Back at the station Reid realized he was starving. Having told everyone to gather in the briefing room in half an hour for an update, he decided to have a quick sandwich in the canteen. Already seated there having their dinner were DS James Lane and DC Timothy Wey; like their superior both had been busy all day conducting in-depth interviews, but sadly they had no direct information regarding the whereabouts of Amy.

Having grabbed himself a toasted cheese sandwich and coffee Reid headed for an empty corner table as he wanted to go over his notes before the meeting, but no sooner had he sat down than a press officer came up to his table.

'We've got good coverage in the *Evening Standard* and we'll get the early issues of the morning papers as well, and they'll all run with the appeal for information about Amy Fulford. I've also had a call from the *Crime Night* TV people and have a meeting set up for tomorrow. If you want a reconstruction I'll need time to get it organized and arrange a lookalike.'

Reid said he would make the decisions after the meeting, hoping they might have more details that would warrant a slot on the show. He took a bite of his sandwich, and asked between mouthfuls if any useful CCTV footage had been recovered. The press officer said that was his responsibility and if his officers found any CCTV of Amy to bring it to him, as the TV people would love it.

Marcus knew he'd had far too much Scotch to drive, but felt the two mugs of strong black coffee had sobered him up somewhat. By now he had a five o'clock shadow and was looking scruffy; he'd not even combed his hair and just pulled on an old fleece jacket to see Lena.

By the time he arrived at the house Agnes was long gone. He rang the doorbell, and then, as he had a key, he waited only a few moments before he let himself in. The house was in darkness so he turned on the hall lights and called out for Lena but there was no reply. He swore impatiently, wondering where she was, when he heard the faint sound of laughter from the TV room. He listened at the door and then heard Amy's voice; it shocked him and for a second he thought she was in the room, but then came the sound of Lena sobbing. He tapped on the door and eased it open. She was sitting curled up on the sofa, and had taken a blanket and wrapped it round herself. She gave him a wretched look and then gestured towards the TV.

'I've been watching all our old home movies. I had to get the video machine out of the garage to play them.'

Although he felt he should go and put his arms around her he hesitated and asked if she would like him to fix a drink. She pointed to an open bottle of wine, and suggested he get himself a glass.

'I've had that detective round at my place all afternoon, along with forensics guys taking Amy's stuff to be examined. I think they will also want to do the same thing in her bedroom here.'

Lena shivered and hugged the blanket closer. 'I gave my identical sweater to an officer, it's apparently what she was wearing when she left the Newmans'.'

Marcus came and settled himself beside her as she spoke.

'I've watched all the videos, some of them from when she was just six or seven years old, right up to the time just before she went to boarding school. I was just replaying one earlier of Amy ice-skating at Hampton Court Palace; you were like a lunatic falling over and she was laughing so much she had tears streaming down her cheeks. Anyway, the reason I played it again was because, I mean I might be wrong but...'

'Wrong about what?' he demanded tensely.

Lena stood up and rewrapped the blanket around her like a cocoon.

'It's the way she looks – no, that's not right, it's something else, an expression in her eyes. In some of the videos I hadn't even watched before I noticed she never smiles, or laughs, and there is a hooded look to her. I can't explain it, but a couple of times when she looks directly into the camera she seems to be angry, and on two occasions she puts her hand up to hide her face, not wanting to be filmed.'

'How old was she then?'

'Thirteen, why?'

'Well she'd have started puberty so was probably just being stroppy – you know, with her hormones...'

'I don't think it was just that, it was as if something else was disturbing her.'

'Can you get to the point, Lena, because I need to talk to you about something serious.'

'I am being serious, for heaven's sake,' she snapped, then stood up and started to pace around the room. 'Looking at the videos, and seeing the change in her manner, it could be something happened to her, something that neither you nor I were even aware of – do you understand what I'm saying?'

He reached out, took her hand and drew her in to sit beside him. 'Please just keep quiet for a few minutes and let me tell you why I'm here.'

'But it's important – don't you understand what I am trying to tell you?'

'Yes I do, but what you're thinking about her change in behaviour may be more recent.'

He still held onto her hand, too tightly, and she tried to ease it from him but he wouldn't let go. Finally she relaxed and waited as he gave a long sigh, then she listened intently as he explained what had taken place at his flat that afternoon and in particular the discovery of the old porn films and magazines that Amy might well have looked through.

Chapter 13

It was seven p.m. and Reid was sitting up on the platform, Chief Superintendent Douglas beside him, and the briefing room was filled with detectives and uniform officers, some seated and others standing lining the walls, all chatting about the long hard thy they'd had.

Douglas spoke in a loud voice. 'Right, ladies and gentlemen, let's have a bit of silence now and get this meeting underway so we can all be brought up to speed on the Amy Fulford investigation.'

The room went instantly silent as Douglas indicated for Reid to stand and address the officers.

'Thank you, sir. Okay, first up, have any of the interviews with neighbours resulted in any useful statements or information we can work on?'

One officer raised his hand and Reid nodded to

him to speak up. 'A neighbour across the road from Mrs Fulford said that there had been considerable activity around the garage and numerous boxes were seen being loaded into the Lexus by Harry Dunn, Mrs Fulford's driver.'

'When exactly was this?' Douglas asked.

'Earlier today, sir, just after Mrs Fulford returned home from the press conference. The neighbour said the double garage doors were open so he could see everything clearly. The housekeeper Agnes Moors was also present, and they had been packing up boxes and bin bags for some considerable time, before the garage was closed and the Lexus driven off by Dunn.'

'It's odd behaviour but well after Amy went missing,' Reid remarked.

Douglas sighed. 'It may be something or nothing, DI Reid, but nevertheless needs to be checked.'

'Yes, sir. Did the neighbour see Mrs Fulford in the garage?' Reid asked the officer.

'Only briefly. I did ask him if he knew Mrs Fulford, but he said he had very little to do with her and though polite she was not very friendly. He knew Marcus Fulford moved out two years ago and he had not seen or had any conversation with him since. However, when he was there he was always pleasant and had often chatted to the neighbour. He was unable to give details of regular visitors, or any vehicle regularly parked in the front of the house.'

'What about Amy? Did the neighbour know her and when did he last see her?' Douglas asked impatiently.

'He knew who she was and would say hello if he saw her, but never engaged her in conversation. He last recalled seeing her about two weeks ago getting out of the Lexus in her school uniform.'

Statements from all the neighbours surrounding Mrs Fulford's property virtually said the same thing. Not one of them was friendly or associated with the family. Basically it was apparent that neither Lena nor Amy made any effort to be neighbourly.

DI Reid listened and like Chief Superintendent Douglas was becoming impatient as nothing appeared to have any important connection to Amy's disappearance. It was hard to believe how lacking in attention or interest Mrs Fulford's neighbours could be.

'Right, what about the team that visited Marcus Fulford's neighbours? Who was in charge of that?' Reid asked.

A detective put up his hand. 'The couple living next to Marcus Fulford knew who Amy was, but were unable to recall ever having a conversation with her. An elderly lady occupying one of the flats below had likewise seen but never spoken to Amy and rarely if ever left the apartment as she was very infirm. She suggested that perhaps the reason for not noticing the comings and goings was that her sitting room was at the back of the property and she always had her TV turned up as she was very deaf.'

The detective's remark caused some laughter in the room, but Douglas was not amused. 'Get to the point, officer. Did any resident see Amy Fulford at or near her father's flat on the Saturday –

or Sunday for that matter?'

'No, sir.'

'So the house-to-house in Mayfair takes us no further forward either,' Douglas remarked.

'Did any of them have anything of interest to say about Marcus Fulford?' Reid asked, hoping that there would be something positive.

'Only the man who occupied the flat above, divorced ex-Guards officer who said he knew Marcus reasonably well as he had been on very good terms with Simon Boatly, the owner of the flat. He described Boatly as from a wealthy aristocratic family and was eager to give some rather lurid details about Mr Boatly and the "lovely girlies" he often had coming and going...'

'What exactly did he mean by "lovely girlies"?' Reid asked.

'He was sort of non-committal at first, but when I pressed him he suggested that Boatly may have paid for their company.'

'You mean prostitutes,' Douglas said in a blunt manner.

'Yes, sir, but from the description maybe more like high-class call girls,' the officer said.

Douglas shook his head in bafflement. 'They're still prostitutes, Detective.'

The detective then generated a few laughs, even from Douglas, when he mimicked the gentleman's posh Army accent: 'Absolutely gorgeous totty, old chap. Dear Simon's a bit of a party animal and I must say I wouldn't have minded a bit of the action on manoeuvres myself, but I never even got a bloody invite!'

'Did he say anything about Amy?' asked

Douglas, bringing the laughter to a stop.

'He recalled meeting Amy on the stairs a few months ago when she was with her father. At first he wondered if Marcus had the same predilection as Boatly for young girls, but Marcus introduced her and he discovered she was his daughter.'

Reid looked around and then they moved on to Detective Wey. He had been assigned to examine Marcus Fulford's finances.

'Marcus Fulford is bankrupt and running up quite extensive debts. He was paying Simon Boatly rent every month by direct debit, but he's currently behind by six months. His previous business ventures appear to have been financed mostly by his wife and have been a litany of failures. He's been surviving on benefits for the last eight months.'

'Other than the location of the Mayfair premises there were no signs of luxurious living in the flat,' Reid added.

DC Wey continued. 'I also spoke with Mr Jacob Lyons, a very expensive and renowned divorce lawyer, who is representing Marcus. He wasn't very helpful, underlining client confidentiality as the reason for not disclosing many details about his fees and how Mr Fulford paid. He did say Marcus would be asking for alimony, plus a share in the sale of the Richmond property which is in both their names, so maybe the fees will come out of that.'

'Usually it's the wife who would attempt to gain a secure financial settlement, but nowadays equality reigns,' Douglas said as if having some personal experience of such matters.

Reid asked Wey what Lena's divorce lawyer had to say and he described Mr Henshaw as a completely different type of man to Lyons.

'He was a gentleman, and although mindful of client confidentiality, intimated that the divorce was not as amicable as had been implied to us by the Fulfords. Marcus Fulford wants a substantial settlement of half the value of the house and a big monthly alimony payment. As yet no settlement has been agreed, but if Marcus gets what he wants he'll never have to work or claim benefits again.'

'Were they both telling the truth about the time and place of the meeting?' Reid asked.

Wey nodded and said that both Henshaw and Lyons confirmed the fact, but Henshaw added the meeting ended acrimoniously shortly before lunch.

'Okay, moving on, what do we know about Mrs Fulford's bank and business accounts?'

DS Lane spoke next. He had been through lengthy Customs House papers, bank statements, and business transactions as well as speaking to an accountant, who was very helpful 'off the record'. His last comment seemed to please Douglas who smiled as he was an 'old school' type of police officer, who was happy to cut corners where necessary.

'On paper she's in a very strong financial position, however, the numerous different companies are at present in reality robbing Peter to pay Paul, but once the dust has settled on Kiddy Winks she stands to make huge profits.'

'How much?' Douglas asked.

'Millions ... which may explain why Marcus

wants a big payoff, but if the new venture fails she could, within six months, be in a critical situation financially as her outgoings are high. To maintain supplies for her cottage industry endeavours requires a number of staff and she owns two small vans and has drivers who make the deliveries and collections, not to mention sales assistants and a receptionist.'

'Does that leave much in her business account?' Reid asked.

'Currently just over quarter of a million, but this fluctuates because of the salaries and rents due, and she has to pay in advance for orders. She pays herself a monthly salary of ten grand from the business into her own private account, which currently has a hundred and twenty thousand in it, and from this she pays the domestic staff's monthly salaries and all the household bills.'

'What about the house in Richmond?' Wey asked.

Lane shrugged his shoulders. 'It appears Marcus has never paid a penny towards it, even though it's in both their names. The accountant remarked that the Fulfords were not exactly *War of the Roses* but might possibly be in rehearsal for it.'

There was some laughter round the room then Reid asked about Amy Fulford's financial situation and DS Lane said that he had checked into it. 'She's in far better shape than her father, with ninety thousand in a trust account and five thousand in a current account.'

There were a few gasps, whistles and remarks around the room that such a young girl should have so much money, but DS Lane explained that the trust find had been left in a will by Mrs Fulford's father and could not be touched until she was twenty-one. Her current bank account was topped up monthly with five hundred pounds on direct debit by her mother. Most significantly, and alarmingly, there had been no movement in Amy's current account since her disappearance, but she had made a couple of substantial payments to her father. One, six months ago, for two thousand, and another more recent for one thousand.

Reid drummed his fingers on the tabletop. 'Any details of wills made by Mr or Mrs Fulford in respect of who the beneficiaries would be for the house and business?'

Lane nodded. 'Mr Henshaw's company drew up a will for Mrs Fulford that stated the contents, house and assets all go to Amy should she die, and nothing was left to Marcus.'

'But if Amy was deceased, also Lena, Daddy could get the lot ... could be a motive?' Reid added, and there were nods of agreement round the room.

Next it was the turn of the officers who had made enquiries along the Fulham Road, at Fulham Broadway Tube station and the bus depot. Due to the football match at Chelsea's Stamford Bridge stadium, extra buses had been laid on. They had questioned drivers around the time it was believed Amy might have caught a bus, but no one was able to identify her from the photographs. CCTV from all the buses and Tube station entrances had been seized and was still being viewed, but as yet there were no sightings of Amy.

They had also seized CCTV from various shops along Amy's possible route, but none of the shop owners could recall her.

Barbara Burrows raised her hand and announced that there was one possible sighting she had discovered from her enquiries. Everyone sat up to listen with interest.

'It's from a security camera from a private house at the end of Harwood Road and taken on the Saturday afternoon Amy went missing. It being close to Fulham Road and the football ground, drunken fans going to or leaving a match sometimes cause damage to cars parked in the residents' bays outside their houses, and some cars have been broken into. They installed the camera facing towards the street and their Mercedes as a security measure and to identify the culprits.'

Reid leaned forward impatiently. 'Good work, but is it ready for us to see, Barbara?' he asked brusquely.

'Yes, sir,' she said and all eyes turned to the screen as Barbara inserted the disc into the DVD player.

Although the picture was colour it was poor-quality and a rather grainy image appeared on the large screen. Numerous groups of men wearing bobble hats and scarves were seen passing by on their way to the match. Eventually a slim young girl came into shot and the room fell silent as Barbara hit pause. It was almost too good to be true as the girl stopped right beside the Mercedes and everyone in the room agreed it was Amy Fulford. Now they could see exactly what she was wearing on top of the maroon jumper. It was a bomber jacket in dark leather with a mock fur collar. She wore a mini-skirt, not leggings as they had first believed, and knee-high boots. It was obvious that she must have changed again before leaving the Newmans' house. Her head was bent down and it looked as if she was texting someone on her mobile. She also had a small shoulder bag and as Barbara pressed play they watched as she put the mobile into her bag and zipped it closed. Suddenly there was a clear shot of her face as she tossed her long blonde hair back, before continuing on her way out of camera shot.

Reid asked Barbara to play the footage again and commented that it was a very important sighting, which they could run on *Crime Night* and which might produce fresh witnesses.

Another group of officers had been assigned to seize and view CCTV from around Marble Arch and Park Lane. Numerous CCTV and top-level security cameras were positioned in this prestigious area, such as by the Dorchester, the Grosvenor and Marriott hotels and the exclusive car sales garages. There was the possibility Amy had caught a bus as far as Park Lane and then walked to Green Street, but as yet they had not discovered any footage or found anyone who recalled seeing her.

It had been a long day for everyone, and most of them had been on foot for nearly all of it. Reid stood up and said he had made some developments that made for uncomfortable hearing but might possibly shed a different light on the inquiry. According to all the statements from family and staff, their missing girl was described as shy, studious, very naïve and a model teenager with no hang-ups or boyfriends. Reid now elaborated on what had come to light in Marcus Fulford's flat, from the pornographic videos and magazines to the unpleasant peephole into her father's bedroom.

The possibility that their missing girl was sexually active, or even being sexually abused, could no longer be ignored.

Chapter 14

Lena had made some toast and heated a bowl of tomato soup for herself and Marcus and carried the tray into the TV room. He looked up briefly from the sofa before skimming over the final section of the journal, which consisted of lists and lists of recipes.

'They can't read this,' he said, depressed and shaken.

She put the tray down but he didn't feel like eating as the contents of the journal had made him sick to his stomach. She sat on the floor and drew her bowl close, dipping the toast into it and sucking at it.

'Jesus Christ, Lena, I can't believe what she has written, it's disgusting, but I can understand why you thought what you did. You have to believe me, I swear before God that I never had any indication of any of this, it's appalling – what on earth was going through her mind to write this stuff?'

186

'She's very unflattering about me, about every-one, and I honestly never suspected, never had a clue what she was really feeling. It's as if she hates me and then there's what she implies went on with you. How could we both be so incapable of not getting so much as a hint about what she's been feeling? She's only fifteen but it's written like a hardened vicious woman.'

'Don't do that,' he snapped.

'Do what?'

'Slurp your fucking soup – you always did it, dipping your toast and sucking it like a kid.'

'If that is all you have to get uptight about you need to get your act together, because that detective found that pornographic filth at your flat and he is going to have just as many suspicions about you as I had if he reads the journal. I mean, you can tell me that you never had any idea what she was doing, but it doesn't read that way, and I believe you, I do, I honestly do, but whether or not DI Reid will–'

'For God's sake!' He jumped up, exasperated.

'Marcus, it reads like you were letting her watch your antics in the bedroom, that you knew she was either in the room or looking through the peephole they've found – she's certainly very graphic, and it was no wonder I thought you'd enjoyed it.'

'Don't do this to me, Lena.' Marcus held him-self completely rigid. 'I swear on my life I had no idea and you implying that I did disgusts me. Please don't make me feel even worse than I do already. You have to trust me, I need you to trust me, because you and I have to try and fathom out what went wrong, why she's written this filth.'

Lena finished her soup, and calmly raised her head to meet his eyes. 'What went wrong is that you left us. That's the root of our daughter's problems.'

'You never had enough time for her – don't just claim it was because I left, you know we had not been getting along for a long time before I moved out. It was your decision to send her to boarding school, not mine – you were so intent on your business you were hardly ever at home.'

Lena glared and snapped that she was forced to travel and spend days away finding all the people for her companies. The fact she was worried about not being at home for Amy and had to make other arrangements had not been just her decision, they had all discussed it, all three of them. Marcus sighed; it was the same old record being played and he couldn't stand much more of it. He got up and strode to the door.

'Where are you going?'

'Lena, I didn't come here to argue with you; you are doing my head in going over old ground. Amy is missing, for God's sake, and making untrue accusations about me isn't helping. We were together for just over seventeen years and most of that time we were okay.'

'You think?'

'What?'

She stood up and placed her soup bowl onto the tray.

'I said, you think it was okay? Well, for your information it was not okay and it wasn't for a very long time, but you know what?'

'I'm sure you'll enlighten me,' he said and sighed.

'I just got too tired to end it before you did. I should have kicked you out ten years ago, but I didn't because I always hoped that maybe, just maybe, you would get your act together. I put up with you and all your failed attempts at making a living, I always felt as if I had two kids, you and Amy. I truly believed as long as I could keep bailing you out from one disaster after another and keep you happy we'd stay together, not for me, but for her sake, because you could do no wrong in her eyes.'

She picked up the tray and carried it to the door. She paused beside him.

'You know, maybe what really happened, Amy began to see you for what you are, the rose-tinted glasses broke, because she had to take in the way you were living, and I think all you have been waiting for was that meeting with your nasty toad of a lawyer. If you think I am going to move out of this house that I have paid for, that I have furnished, that I have covered the mortgage on from day one, you are mistaken. You've never paid one cent, so if you think you are going to screw money out of me in a settlement, make me pay you bloody alimony for the rest of your miserable life, you have another think coming.'

She passed him with the tray, the soup spilling from his untouched bowl, she was shaking with such anger. She went into the kitchen and hurled the tray onto the draining board. She thought he would follow, but when he didn't appear she took down another bottle of wine and uncorked it, getting out clean glasses as she slowly calmed herself down.

Marcus was watching a video, an old one of a holiday they had taken together in Tuscany, and he was sitting with his legs tucked under him on the sofa. She placed the wine and glasses onto the coffee table in front of him. He gave a glum smile as she sat beside him.

'Long forgotten good times,' he said quietly as she poured them both a fresh glass of wine. Together they continued to watch one video after another, neither speaking, simply taking in the past when they had been happy. Lena changed tapes as he drank and asked if they should watch the most recent ones to see if he also picked up how different Amy appeared.

'Do you think something happened to her, something neither of us knew about, because the way she's behaving is so strange, she looks sullen, she was always such fun, but here she seems to be so angry, constantly avoiding the camera.'

Marcus shrugged, turned to Lena and reached for her hand.

'I've been thinking, maybe until we know what is going on I should move back in here.'

'But what if she tries to contact you at the flat?'

'She always calls me on my mobile and I have it with me. I just think that it would be better for us to show a united front. What do you think?'

Lena sipped her wine, unsure about his suggestion, and yet to have him with her was a comfort. When the video ended, she didn't feel like watching any more.

She leaned closer to him. 'I honestly don't know,

Marcus. I mean, I have to admit I feel in a sort of limbo because I can't really comprehend that Amy would have just taken off. The longer it is, the worse I fear about what might have happened to her. What do you think?'

'I feel the same, that's why I'm suggesting I stay here – I mean in the guest room obviously – but at least we can be here for each other.'

He got up, turned the videotape off, ejecting it and stacking it along with the others, then returned to sit close to her on the sofa. 'The worst scenario is she was abducted by someone, but you know Amy wouldn't get into a stranger's car. I mean, we always made sure she knew never to accept a lift from anyone she didn't know.'

'What if it was someone she knew?' she said quietly.

'So taking that on board, she accepted a lift with someone or maybe had even arranged with whoever it was to go with them, then wouldn't she have taken her overnight bag? It was left with the Newmans, their daughter took it back to school with her on the Sunday.'

'So if that isn't what happened, is it possible she arranged to meet someone and there was an accident or something else that meant she was unable to contact us?'

Marcus sighed; all the London hospitals had been contacted and there was no one fitting Amy's description involved in any accident or taken to A&E. He got up and started to pace the room as he threw out another possible scenario: Amy did have a boyfriend, perhaps one she knew neither of them would approve of, and she had like many other teenage runaways simply taken off with him.

Lena was sceptical simply because she was certain that if Amy had met someone she would have known about it. They sat together and went through all the people they both knew, but it was obvious none of them could have been involved. Lena could think of no one, not even one of her employees, who appeared to be in any way connected to Amy. Added to that they were all female apart from the van drivers and delivery boys, but she was certain none had even met Amy. Marcus could think of no one, not even any of his girlfriends, as he was certain they had never had more than a few fleeting words with his daughter.

'I had dinner at the awful Berkoffs' last Saturday. Of course, they asked after you, and Sasha said he had seen you in a new restaurant in Chiswick,' Lena remarked.

'Well he must have been mistaken because I haven't been in any new restaurant in Chiswick, seen him or Maria, and considering you always said you loathed the pair of them, why did you go over to their place for dinner?'

'Because they asked me, but it was the same old putrid food and gossip, and she implied because I looked so good I had to have a toy boy – I mean honestly.'

'Well you do look good, better than ever. You used to drag around in that awful old tracksuit, and you'd put on weight, hardly ever washed your hair or showered and spent all day in your office or–'

She interrupted him, her lips tight. 'Don't start. I know how I looked and all I was doing was earning enough to pay the bills and you never could help out, one business after another went bust and I had to bail you out.'

'All right, all right, don't you start playing the old record.'

'What about Simon Boatly?' Lena asked, changing the subject.

Marcus sighed. 'By the time I moved into his flat he was packed and off on his photographic work abroad. He was also out of the country when Amy went missing. Listen, right now we are just attempting to bring up anyone that could be in any way connected. As far as I am concerned there is no one that I know that I could even contemplate as being over-friendly with Amy. I never saw her with anyone I didn't know, and you say you would have been aware if she had a boyfriend – well then, so would I. This is all just circumstantial because the bottom line is we have no clue to her knowing anyone that we were not aware of.'

Lena nodded; she poured more wine for them both. 'Apart from her school friends.'

Marcus agreed, although he was not aware of any close friend, apart from Serena, and Amy had never mentioned anyone as a specific best friend. He recalled asking her shortly after she had started at boarding school if she had one. Amy had said there was no one special but she had made friends with all her classmates.

'I never liked Serena, something about her – probably jealous,' Lena remarked.

'I should have shown more interest, but her reports were always brilliant and she appeared to be really enjoy boarding. I've never heard her complain about being sent there, and judging from all her reports she adjusted brilliantly from day one,' Marcus said.

Lena picked up the journal and suggested he read it again, and to not just concentrate on the pages relevant to him, but to read about certain pupils and teachers Amy disliked.

'What if she was sort of compiling notes for a novel, something like that?' Marcus asked as he flicked through the entries.

'She never mentioned anything to me about writing one or even thinking of doing so and the people in the journal are real and not given character names.'

Lena remained deep in thought as Marcus continued reading, watching him for a while, as he frowned and shook his head. 'Christ, she doesn't like anyone, does she? I mean some of this stuff is really vicious. And all these odd numbers and references to enemies – I can't read any more.'

Lena put another log on the fire and stood with her back to it. He eventually shut the journal and stretched out on the sofa, closing his eyes.

'According to you she's never shown any signs of being unhappy or having trouble at school,' she said. 'It is the same for me, at no time has she ever discussed how she feels; she does often grow quiet, and she does spend a lot of time in her bedroom, but always says it's to do her homework.'

'Sometimes when she's with me she works on her laptop, and yeah, she is sort of quiet, but there's been nothing that's ever alarmed me. If I do ask her about how she's doing she always says that everything's fine!' He sighed.

Lena felt her back becoming too warm from the fire and she returned to sit beside him on the sofa.

'I think something did happen, and it could be connected to the school.'

He stood up and stretched. 'Well it's possible, but you need to tell DI Reid your concerns. Get some sleep. We are in this together – whatever is going on, or has been going on between us, let's put it to one side. I am sure we'll find her, so you feel positive too.'

She looked up into his handsome face and kissed his rough cheek. 'You have a shave and wear a collar and tie with that nice brown tweed suit.' He put a finger over her lips.

'I'll look smart, Lena. I really need a good night's sleep – I've hardly slept the past few days.'

After Marcus left the house, Lena didn't bother washing the wine glasses or the soup bowls but left everything for Agnes to clear up in the morning. She put the fireguard round the still burning logs and made her way up the stairs, climbing them slowly, wishing she hadn't let Reid take Amy's old diaries. She worried Amy might have written about things that troubled her or nasty, disgusting stuff similar to what she'd poured out in the journal, constantly returning to focus on the horrible references to herself and 'Daddy'.

Forcing herself to go to her home office, Lena checked her phone messages and emails and was irritated by how many were from Gail at Kiddy Winks. She couldn't be bothered to answer any of them and told herself she would sort things out in the morning.

Lena changed into a pair of pure cotton pyjamas, cleaned her make-up off, brushed her hair with a hundred strokes, and moisturized her face, neck and hands. Slowly, as if on automatic pilot, she got ready for bed, and turned down the silk bedspread as usual, flipped back the purest Egyptian cotton sheets and eased her feet out of her cashmere slippers. She left just a low night-light switched on by her bedside as she lay back and let her mind wander over the time she'd spent with Marcus that evening. She was restless but didn't want to take a sleeping tablet as it was becoming too regular an occurrence; at the same time she reasoned that if ever there was an excuse she certainly had one as she was so strung out. She'd forgotten to fetch a bottle of water from the small bedroom fridge so she got out of bed and took one; unscrewing the cap she returned to her bed, growing irritated that Agnes must have moved her pills and placed them inside the bedside cabinet. She tossed out various bottles of vitamins and packets of migraine tablets before she found the prescription bottle of Zopiclone sleeping tablets. She tipped them into the palm of her hand and after counting them was certain she should have had more. She wondered if Agnes had taken some and then it struck her that perhaps it was Amy?

Lena tossed and turned. From feeling almost paranoid about her sleeping tablets she next started to get annoyed with herself. Mr Henshaw had suggested that it had to be someone very close to her who had gained access to her private papers and bank statements. She had not even brought it up with Marcus – truthfully she had not even really thought about it, but now she did. Marcus's solicitor, the obnoxious Jacob Lyons, had been able to assess her present earnings and current bank accounts, both business and personal, along with projections of future income. It had to be someone with access to her office at home or her business office that she used at her Kiddy Winks address. Why had she not asked Marcus while he was with her? She needed to know because she was beginning to think that perhaps it was Amy after all. She wondered if it might be Agnes, but then she doubted that the housekeeper would have been able to access the computer in her business office, as she could not recall Agnes ever being there. Then she reckoned that if anyone were computer-literate it would be easy to get hold of all the information from her computer here at the house. She returned to the idea that it had to have been Amy – would she have done it? Surely she wouldn't have fed all the details to Marcus ready for the divorce meeting, especially not if what she had written about him in her journal was any indication of how she felt about him, but then she had also described Lena in unpleasant terms. It appeared that Amy disliked everyone she came into contact with.

Lena's head started to throb; she began to think that she was about to have one of her migraines. Where was her baby, her little girl, her beautiful daughter? If she was upset, if she were in trouble, she would take care of it, and all she wanted was for Amy to come home. She pushed herself up to a sitting position, leaning over the bedside to reach for her migraine relief capsules, and was then unable to keep her balance. She fell face forwards onto the carpet, and slithered down to be prone on the floor beside her bed. Curling into a foetal position she started to cry, and from a whimper her crying became awful gut-wrenching sobs. Lena had drunk too much white wine, eaten just a bowl of soup, and taking sleeping tablets had now aggravated her emotional turmoil. Pain and confusion assailed her from every quarter but dominating everything was a terrible underlying panic for Amy.

Chapter 15

Agnes could not open the front door as the safety chain was on, so she walked up the lane towards the garage in the hope that Harry Dunn was there. The garage doors were closed; frustrated and concerned, Agnes hurried back to the front of the house and dialled the landline. It rang for what seemed an interminable time before Lena answered.

'Mrs Fulford, it's Agnes, the safety chain is on.'

Lena was still in her pyjamas and looked dreadful.

'What time is it?'

Agnes said it was eight fifteen; she was early because she felt she should be at the house at this time of crisis. She'd brought a carrier bag full of newspapers, and reported that the appeal about Amy had also been on the local morning news. Lena slumped into a chair at the kitchen table. She had woken up lying on the floor by her bed; the telephone ringing had made her heart pump as she hoped it was Amy. Agnes took out the papers and then busied herself putting on the kettle and filling the coffee percolator. She placed the wine glasses into the dishwasher along with the soup plates and rinsed the soup pan out. Lena meanwhile scoured every article, which featured headlines such as TEENAGER AMY FULFORD MISSING, PARENTS' FEARS FOR FIFTEEN-YEAR-OLD SCHOOLGIRL GROW and AMY COME HOME. There were requests for anyone with information to come forward and two papers included a photograph, and yet it had not made the front page in a single paper.

'The local papers will make more of it,' Agnes said comfortingly while fetching a cup and saucer for Lena's coffee.

'I'm going to take a shower and get dressed. I'll take my coffee upstairs,' Lena told her, leaving the papers scattered over the table.

Agnes poured herself a mug as Harry Dunn rang the doorbell. He sat with Agnes and looked through the papers as she gave him a coffee and a Penguin biscuit. Eventually he refolded them and slowly tore off the wrapper of his biscuit.

'What do you think?' he asked morosely.

'I don't know. I mean those articles don't say much, do they? They sort of underline that she's missing but you don't get any details, but if she has just run off then surely she'll read the papers and make contact. If she doesn't then God only knows what has happened to her.'

'Is her passport missing?' he wondered, crumpling the biscuit paper.

'I don't know. Mrs Fulford's in a right state, she's usually up by six and in her office upstairs. Not like her to oversleep, unless she doused herself with sleeping tablets – she'd left them out on her bedside cabinet yesterday morning. I think her husband was here because there's two empty bottles of wine and dirty crockery, unless she had some other visitor. She was holed up in the TV room watching videos when I left last night.'

They finished their coffee and Agnes cleared up the kitchen, with Harry still sitting at the table. They both looked anxiously towards the phone as it rang. Agnes let it carry on, expecting Lena to pick it up as the lights showed it was the business line. It stopped as the answer phone clicked in and then it rang again immediately, this time on the house line, and Agnes answered.

'The Fulford residence?' she said briskly.

Lena stepped out of the shower in her bathroom and, grabbing a towel, she snatched the receiver from the wall, to hear Agnes telling her there was a reporter wishing to speak to her and she didn't know whether or not to put him through. Lena had a brief conversation with a journalist from the local newspaper but declined to give an interview. It was by now eight forty, and the home line rang continuously. Somehow the journalists had gained her ex-directory private number and they were persistent and quite aggressive. Added to the barrage of calls on her home line, the business line was ringing literally every minute. Staff from sales, reception, deliveries and even clients called to enquire about Amy, even though hardly any had ever met her, and they left message after message. Lena's mobile was equally active, it never stopped, as her staff unable to get through on the business line reverted to attempting to speak to her via her mobile.

Lena was at her wits' end; the perpetual ringing felt like a nightmare intrusion. She was afraid that even if Amy had tried to make contact she would not have been able to get through.

A journalist with a photographer approached Reid and Burrows as they drew up in their car and asked if there was news. Reid kept his cool and gave them a brief 'sadly not as yet' as he and Burrows hurried to the front door. An anxious-looking Agnes answered and let them both in as the telephones rang. 'Mrs Fulford's in the sitting room and she's really becoming very distressed by all these phone calls,' she confided.

Reid and Burrows found Lena standing by the sofa, wearing a tracksuit and slippers. Her expression for a moment was so hopeful that Reid quickly had to say there were no developments. He asked if she would allow Barbara Burrows to begin fending the calls and mentioned that a journalist and a photographer were outside the property.

'I obviously keep on hoping it will be Amy, so I can't just let it ring.' Lena's face reverted to its former anxiety. 'My business line has also been inundated with calls. I have the answer phone on but I will have to eventually check who has made contact. Right now I just can't face having conversations with anyone.' She clasped her hands together. 'Sorry, what am I thinking of? Would you like something to drink, tea or...?'

'No, no, it's fine.' Reid looked at her steadily. 'Your housekeeper and driver were seen removing boxes from your garage yesterday afternoon – do you know anything about that?'

She frowned, confused. 'Boxes?'

'Yes, we had a report from a neighbour, and I have been instructed to search these premises and that includes the garage. I will be as diplomatic and unobtrusive as possible, but the focus will be on your daughter's bedroom in the hope we will find some clue to her whereabouts. Do you know what was being removed from your garage?'

'I have no idea – there must be some mistake.'

'Both your driver and housekeeper were seen packing the boxes.'

Lena walked to the sitting-room door and opened it. 'Agnes, can you come in here for a minute, please?'

Agnes came to the door, thinking they were going to ask for coffee to be brought in, but Lena looked at her angrily. 'Did you take anything out of the garage yesterday?'

'Yes, you told Harry that he could clear some old things out and I took what he didn't want. Neither of us would take anything without your knowledge or permission, Mrs Fulford.'

Reid held up his hand, and asked if Lena would mind leaving him with the housekeeper so he could talk to her privately. Lena was furious but at the same time confused because she couldn't really remember giving Harry or Agnes permission. Reid asked if Harry was available, as he would also like to speak to him. Lena agreed to go into the kitchen and call him as he was probably in the garage. Throughout these exchanges the phones could be heard ringing constantly.

Agnes folded her arms. 'She was looking for the old video player because she wanted to watch some tapes of her daughter. Harry said he'd been told to clear out the old boxes she'd been storing in there.'

Reid couldn't help but notice how Agnes's round face glistened with sweat and she kept on clasping and unclasping her hands. He also thought it rather rude that she kept referring to Mrs Fulford as 'she'.

'What was in Mrs Fulford's boxes, Mrs Moors?'

She sighed with agitation. 'Mostly old bed linen – well, to be honest, she probably thinks of it as old but to me it was very stylish. Couple of table-cloths and a few pans and some crockery; that was all I took; whether or not Harry took other stuff I wouldn't know ... because he'd already ear-marked a couple of boxes. To be honest, I mean I could be wrong, but I think she didn't like keeping the sheets and things from when her husband was here.'

She paused, twisting her hair back from her face and hooking it behind her ears. 'I can bring it back if you want me to, or if she wants it back, but that's all I took and Harry said she gave him permission. I paid for a taxi to move it.'

'Were there any of Mrs Fulford's daughter's

belongings in the boxes?'

'The boxes have been stacked up in the garage for quite a while, but I don't recall seeing anything of hers.'

Reid thanked Agnes, and as she opened the door Lena walked in, saying that her driver was coming and that a van with SOCOs had drawn up outside.

'DC Burrows said they were forensics officers – do I let them in? Or do you want to talk to them?'

He smiled and said that the SOCOs were assisting in the search and would need to be shown Amy's bedroom, as he would like them to begin there. Hesitating, Lena apologized for the confusion with the contents of the garage. 'I honestly can't remember giving Harry permission, but I must have done – I was in such a state yesterday. I went over to the garage to find an old video player as I wanted to watch some family films and...' She lifted her arms in a shrug.

'Were there any of Amy's belongings in the garage?'

'No, I don't think so. It was mostly crockery and linen. I meant to give it to the Princess Alice Trust months and months ago, but just never got around to it. I'm sorry...'

Harry Dunn tapped on the open door and anxiously eased his way into the room.

'You did give me permission, Mrs Fulford, you said I could take whatever I wanted as they'd been stacked and left in the garage for so long. You had to move them aside to find the video recorder.'

Barbara Burrows stood behind Harry and signalled that the SOCOs were ready to go into Amy's bedroom.

The house phone began to ring and Lena turned to Reid. 'Is it all right if I show them upstairs and DC Burrows answers the phone?'

Reid nodded and Barbara went to take the phone. Harry remained standing just inside the door, and not until Reid signalled for him to come in and sit down did he nervously do as requested, closing the door.

'Agnes told me there was some problems with the removal of stuff from the garage, but I swear I got permission, I would not have taken anything without knowing it was okay to do so. Mrs Fulford said for me to clear the boxes and that's what I did – I mean I can bring it all back.'

'That won't be necessary, Mr Dunn,' Reid assured him, 'unless there were items that belonged to Amy, or anything that could give an indication as to where she might have gone.'

'No, it was household stuff and Agnes took a lot of it, for her daughter. She got a local taxi firm to move it out.'

Reid rubbed at his chin; the simple explanation Harry and Agnes had given made him doubt there was an ulterior motive behind the removal of the boxes.

Harry edged to the end of his seat. 'I've still got the stuff in the boxes at home.'

'There was nothing unusual in any of these boxes?'

Harry looked puzzled, and Reid watched him closely. 'Bad smells, stains, anything suspicious?'

'No, sir. Also, the boxes had been done up with

parcel tape and none of them had been recently opened. I tore it off to check what was inside – you know, choosing what I was going to take – and then Agnes came into the garage and she picked and mixed if you know what I mean?'

'Thank you, that'll be all, and you'll be on hand, will you, if Mrs Fulford needs you?'

'Yes, sir, I'll be here.'

Harry made small quick steps to the door, and froze when Reid suddenly spoke again. 'One more thing. Who gave you the order to clean Mr Fulford's car?'

'Agnes, she give me the keys and I gave it a wash and interior valet as it was filthy inside and out.'

'You did a good job.'

Harry scuttled out, his heart thudding because for a minute he thought he was going to be asked about the watch he'd found between the front seats. He'd stashed it in a drawer at his flat, and now it worried him deeply and he realized he'd better get rid of it fast.

Lena stood in Amy's bedroom doorway, watching the two forensics officers begin their work. After a few moments she went back down the stairs just as Reid walked into the hallway.

He asked Lena about the video films she had been watching and she told him that she would give the tapes to him if he wanted.

'Some of them are from when she was a child, but there are more recent tapes – well, not for the last couple of years but...' She hesitated enough for him to enquire if she felt they were important.

'Can I show you what made me very agitated?

206

It might mean nothing, but it's something I never noticed before. If you'd like to come with me to the TV room the videotapes are all there.'

He suggested that Lena set up what she wanted him to look at as he needed to have a word with DC Burrows in the kitchen, where his colleague was now fending off the calls, which were coming in thick and fast. Burrows nimbly put off the numerous press requests for interviews and to anyone making a personal enquiry she was very polite, saying there was no news at present. She made careful notes on all the callers and was thankful for a tray of coffee and biscuits Agnes brought her.

Agnes was still hovering and Reid asked her to leave them for a moment. DC Burrows gestured to her notepad and said that the majority of calls were press enquiries but Mrs Fulford's business answer phone was full and suggested that perhaps those messages should be checked out.

'I'll discuss it with Mrs Fulford. I want you to call the dog section and get a cadaver dog brought in to go over the garage.'

Barbara looked aghast and Reid was quick to explain himself.

'We need to do everything by the book and I'm just being cautious.'

As Reid entered the TV room Lena turned from where she was standing by the television with videotapes in her hand.

'I want you to see this one first. She'd be eleven – it was a birthday party in Spain when we were on holiday.'

Reid sat on the sofa and watched as five children

tucked into large bowls of ice cream. The focus was on the birthday girl who suddenly took off her sunhat and swirled it over her head, laughing. She was golden brown, her hair bleached white from the sun, and she was standing up on her chair as a birthday cake was brought to the table by her equally suntanned father. She was an extraordinarily pretty child, very slender, and her excited shrieks and laughter were infectious as she clapped her hands and blew out the candles. Lena switched off the tape.

'She was always laughing.' She patted a stack of videos, all dated with handwritten labels. 'All of these are showing how much fun she was, a real delight to be around, and now I want you to look at this tape; it's from a couple of years ago, so she would be thirteen.'

Lena busied herself ejecting one tape and inserting the other, then came and sat close to him. 'I have to be honest – you know, we used to takes reels and reels of videos, and I don't even recall sitting watching these latest ones, and Amy never asked to watch them. I am not making excuses, but this one was taken when Marcus and I were not getting along, although at no time did we ever make it obvious to Amy.' She pointed the remote at the television and pressed play.

Reid found it slightly uncomfortable to be sitting so close to her, not that she appeared to notice. Leaning forward with her attention on the screen, she fast-forwarded, stopped and gestured towards the TV set. Reid watched the footage of Amy, who was wearing another floppy straw sunhat, big round dark glasses, and a white bikini. She was tall and lithe, bordering on skinny, but somewhat surprisingly for a thirteen-year-old, there was a definite sexual quality to her as she walked towards a sun lounger. She was carrying a bottle of water and a book.

'This was when we were in Antigua; we had a cabana opening onto the private beach,' Lena said quietly. Amy bent to a small side table by the lounger and put down her bottle of water and book. She then picked up a folded yellow beach towel and carefully shook it out to fold over the cushions. She removed her sunglasses, holding them in her left hand and with her right she snatched off her sunhat and threw it angrily towards the camera.

'Turn that fucking thing off!'

It was quite shocking to hear her swearing. Her thick blonde hair fell loose to her shoulders and she was stunningly pretty, but her face was contorted with anger. The camera angle moved to the side and then it shut off. There were a few seconds of close-up on sand as the film started again and Lena could be seen using the sun lounger next to Amy's; she was deeply tanned, her body oiled, and she was wearing the same sunhat. The sea was only ten feet or so away; palm trees swayed gently beside their cabana and now Amy was filmed coming out of the water, her wet hair plastered back from her perfect face as she moved closer towards the sun loungers. She bent to pick up her towel and then realized she was being filmed. This time she twisted the towel and began to flick it towards the camera, shouting for it to be turned off.

'Who's doing the filming?' Reid asked.

'Marcus. That's him laughing.'

Reid sneaked a look at his wristwatch as Lena began to fast-forward the footage. He couldn't understand what point she was trying to make, but didn't want to appear uninterested or upset her by asking. She showed another scene of Amy sitting reading her book, and then Amy curled in a foetal position at the edge of the water as it gently lapped around her. Reid was becoming impatient as he really had more pressing issues to deal with and although he appreciated being shown the footage, he decided that he should get on with his job.

'Thank you, Mrs Fulford,' he said, about to stand.

'Please, I'm not finished. You may not realize it, but she is never smiling, not on any of the footage, and I have been trying to recall exactly when this was filmed, because what you have just seen is not like Amy, and there is one section that has really disturbed me.'

Reid thought to himself that it was just a growing teenager with angst who didn't like being filmed. But being polite he waited as she fast-forwarded through what appeared to be candlelit dinners, beach volleyball games, and then she turned to him.

'This section, and before you ask, I actually filmed this because I remember going into her room; we were going to have dinner on the beach.'

The interior of the cabana was very simple – white muslin drapes, white duvet and sheets, and a mosquito net surrounding the double bed. Numerous flickering candles gave the room a shadowy yellowish glow. The slatted door was open and through it could be seen the soft yellow beach beyond the veranda and the glistening dark sea, like a picture postcard of tropical calm. Amy was naked on the bed, her blonde hair splayed out across the pillow. There was just a few seconds of the film before Amy swiped away the mosquito net and her face distorted with rage as she shouted, 'Get out and leave me alone!'

The camera was switched off, and Lena turned to Reid. 'You want to see it again?'

'I can't really see the point, Mrs Fulford.'

'Then you didn't see what she was doing, and nor did I until I replayed it. She was masturbating and she was only thirteen years old,' Lena said, distressed.

Realizing how upset she was, he didn't think it wise to view the tape again.

'I'm sorry, I missed it, but I don't doubt what you saw, Mrs Fulford. There could be an innocent explanation...'

'Innocent? She was only thirteen – why would she behave like that? I'm worried that she may have been abused.'

Reid himself was more open-minded and wondered if it was just the actions of a young girl who was discovering her body when her mother walked in unannounced. He wanted to try and change the subject and end the matter for now.

'I will seek the opinion of a child protection expert back at the station,' he said quietly, without elaborating on what she perceived to be the shocking content of the home movie.

She started walking back and forth, wringing her

211

hands, reiterating that she should have been more aware and how guilty she felt that she had not seen the video before now. Suddenly she stopped. 'Oh God, it was shortly after we returned from the holiday that Marcus suggested the separation. I remember now.'

Reid wondered if she was trying to cast aspersions on her ex-husband, or was suspicious about Marcus's relationship with Amy, but he didn't want to press her in case he was wrong and she became even more upset than she already was. He decided to approach his predicament from a different angle.

'Has Mr Fulford seen the video you just showed me?'

'No, no not yet, but you see when she came home she showed no signs that anything was wrong but there had to be. I feel wretched about it.'

'Well, maybe you should discuss it with him as well and let me know what he says about it. Amy's behaviour may be related to something that happened in Antigua, so it will help if you make a list of everyone you can recall who came into contact with Amy during that holiday.'

'Yes, yes, I'll do that.'

Reid still didn't know for certain if Amy had been sexually abused, and with Lena in this nervous state he felt that it was not the right time to start questioning her on the possibility.

As he opened the door into the hall, Harry Dunn entered via the garden doors. Lena turned to demand of Harry in a high-pitched voice why he was there, as she had not asked for him. Harry apologized as he had been told to vacate the garage by a dog handler.

'I don't understand,' she cried, becoming even more agitated. 'Inspector, just why are you bringing dogs into my house?'

'It's a cadaver dog, Mrs Fulford,' Harry said, and then wished he'd kept his mouth shut as Lena had to grip hold of the back of a dining chair.

'Why? Why have you got them here – is there something you haven't told me?' she asked accusingly. Reid explained it was just a precaution as there had been a lot of movement seen in and around the garage.

'You think her body was in there?'

Reid, increasingly exasperated, again repeated that it was a precaution, and they had no evidence that anything untoward had happened to her daughter. Lena seemed to calm down, and Reid finally managed to excuse himself and went out to the garden. He crossed the wide lawn and made his way to the rear of the garage, where the dog handler was working with a small spaniel. The dog was wagging its tail as his handler made a fuss of him. 'Good boy, that's a good boy.' The dog handler looked towards Reid. 'Nothing, he's been all over the garage with no reaction. I even moved the boxes left on the side there, but it's all clear.'

In the kitchen Harry hovered at the door, listening as DC Burrows continued fending calls. Agnes joined Harry and jerked her head for him to move further away.

'They brought in a cadaver dog,' she said.

'I know, they're still out there; it's just a little

black and white spaniel.'

'It's because of us packing up the bloody boxes and they obviously think Amy's dead.'

'Oh Christ,' Harry said.

At this point the two forensics officers came down the stairs from Amy's bedroom carrying plastic boxes. They had removed clothing, bed linen, and a few items from which, with luck, they could lift Amy's fingerprints. Both men had been taken aback by the immaculate orderliness of the room, and they had found it difficult to find sets of prints, which was unusual. They had been warned about the broken drawer, but every surface had been wiped clean and in the en-suite bathroom they had found no prints at all, although they had removed a toothbrush. Even the hairbrush had been recently cleaned and no stray hairs were caught between the bristles.

'You find anything interesting?' Reid asked quietly, appearing in the hallway to meet them. He was not terribly surprised to hear that they had never come across such a well-cleaned room, especially as it belonged to a teenager. In a bath-room cabinet they had found bottles of window spray, bathroom tile cleaner, marble polish and sets of surgical gloves similar to the ones they themselves used.

Reid told them they should get back to the lab, and to get a move on with testing not only the items removed that morning but everything from Marcus Fulford's flat. He had also ensured that forensics had been given Amy's overnight cabin bag. He then went to have a word with Agnes, who was dusting along a wooden cabinet that looked as if it was already polished to within an inch of its life.

'Do you clean Amy's bedroom?'

'Well, I give it a hoover and obviously change the sheets, but she is very particular about keeping it spotless herself. I mean, I have a daughter, a lot older than her, but she's never been so obsessive about her bedroom. She sprays the shower in there after every use; she can be in there for hours polishing and dusting, and that includes her perfume bottles and moisturizer and she has a place for everything.'

'That's very unusual in a young girl,' he remarked, encouraging the woman to continue.

'Yes, I know. The reason I know just how obsessive, and I am using the right word, she can be is because once I'd moved something or other and she knew, gave me a right ticking off, saying that I was not to touch her personal things. From then on I've never touched anything because she is a right little madam, she can get this nasty tone to her voice, looking down at me as if I'm beneath her. I mean, I don't want to say anything bad about her, but she is a very arrogant young woman.'

This was a somewhat different picture of Amy to her previous description. It was obvious Agnes didn't like her – in fact he was getting used to realizing that the portrait they'd all painted of her was cracking.

'Will you take care of Mrs Fulford?'

'Yes of course. Will Barbara be staying on? If she is, I'll prepare some lunch.'

'That would be very kind.'

In the kitchen, DC Burrows was still answering the phones, but they had quietened down somewhat. Glancing up as he came in, she asked if he would like to look at the names of the callers, which she had divided into two lists, personal and press.

Reid skimmed the list of private calls, remarking that a Gail Summers had rung frequently.

'What's the connection?'

'She helps run Mrs Fulford's children's party business and seems desperate to talk to her; she appears genuinely very concerned. The other frequent caller is a Marjory Jordan – she said she was Mrs Fulford's therapist and again was obviously very concerned about the missing girl.'

Reid passed the notebook back, asking DC Burrows to make a copy for him and to remain at the house. 'And look, if Marcus Fulford calls or makes an appearance, then let me know. I'm going to have to head back.'

'Of course.' Barbara Burrows smiled as confidently as she could, hoping that this was all making a good impression on her boss.

Back at the incident room, DS James Lane was waiting as they had received a call from the television station to say they could do a three-minute slot on their new crime show, *Crime Night*. They were semi-interested in broadcasting a reconstruction, but it would take a few days to set up and would be used the following week – obviously, only if the girl was still missing.

'How did it go at the house?' Lane enquired and Reid sighed, taking his seat behind his desk.

'As you can imagine, there was a highly charged atmosphere.'

'About the cadaver dog?'

Reid smiled. 'A bit, but the dog didn't react to a thing, not even a bloody yelp out of it. Mrs Fulford's got herself all worked up that Amy was sexually abused because she was masturbating in a video.'

'What?' a startled-looking Lane remarked.

'It may be something or nothing, and if you blinked you'd miss it. Thing is, I think she suspects her husband as the abuser.'

'You think it's the father?' Lane asked and Reid shrugged, reluctant to admit that was what he suspected, as he was also loath to cast aspersions until he knew for sure.

Lane pressed him. 'Did she say as much?'

'No, and part of me was worried, in case I was wrong, that if I asked her she'd bite my head off. There's a good deal of dysfunction in the family and to be honest the quiet innocent teenager everyone has described Amy to be is now appearing to be something of a Lolita.'

Chapter 16

Marcus attempted yet another call to Lena, but the landline had been engaged for hours and Lena's mobile went to voicemail. Frustrated and extremely anxious, he decided he would drive over to the house.

Marcus found Lena holed up in her bedroom. 'What the hell is going on, Lena? I've been trying to contact you all morning.'

'The phones have been ringing here since eight o'clock and I'm at breaking point!' she shouted.

He sat her down on the bed. 'I'm sorry, I didn't realize, and I shouldn't have had a go at you. Tell me everything that's happened, but slowly and calmly, please.'

Lena told him about the search in the house, the cadaver dog and the video she'd discovered of Amy masturbating. Visibly shocked, he protested that she should have shown it to him the previous evening. Again she became angry, insisting that at first she had not really taken in what Amy was doing but had shown it to Detective Reid as she felt it was important he should know. Marcus was totally taken aback and almost in tears.

'How could you do that without first consulting me about it?'

'Consulting you? What the hell is the matter with you? Amy was naked and masturbating!'

'I never filmed that – dear God, that bloody detective is bound to think it was me.'

'I told him it was me filming and it was accidental.'

'What fucking else did you tell him that I don't know about?'

She clenched her fists. 'Maybe if you would just think about it for a second you'd see what I mean. For Amy to behave like that, someone must have been abusing her while we were on holiday.'

'Don't be ridiculous; you're jumping to conclusions, and besides, she's a teenager who wasn't expecting you to walk in with a camera.'

'Stop making excuses, Marcus.'

'Excuses for what – your wild imagination?'

Lena paused and stared at him accusingly. 'Was it you abusing her?'

He had to stop himself from slapping her face and shaking some sense into her. He stood up and moved away, knowing he had already been unable to control himself once before, and he didn't want to hit her again as it was so against his nature.

'Was it you, Marcus?' she asked in a distressed voice.

'No, I have never touched Amy improperly in my life. Even the suggestion makes me feel sick,' he said, sinking into a wing-back chair by the window.

'Reid has asked me to make a list of everyone from the Antigua holiday. Last night we both agreed that her behaviour in the Antigua video was different – she's aggressive, and not like her normal self. I even tried to talk to you about it after the holiday, but when we returned you said you needed to have some bloody space, and moved out.'

'Don't try and put the blame onto me, Lena. You know full well that before we even went to Antigua we were hardly speaking. Maybe that was why Amy was different and looked so miserable – because of us.'

She put her head in her hands and started to cry. He sat there watching her, at a loss not only as to how to comfort her, but how to face the fact that their daughter might have been sexually abused and neither of them had been aware of it owing to their own emotional problems. At last he got up and went to her side, putting his arms around her.

'Come on, sweetheart, let's think this through together. Even if we come up with someone, the reality is Amy's gone missing two years later and it might have nothing to do with Antigua, but we need to really think long and hard about whose names we should give to the police.'

He rocked her gently in his arms as he looked over to her bedside cabinet. 'Are you taking your medication?'

'Yes.'

He reached across to look at the label on the sleeping tablets. 'You shouldn't take these on a regular basis.'

'I need them to get some sleep.'

'Are you still seeing your therapist?'

'Yes.'

He stroked her hair. 'Do you want me to ask her to come over?'

'No, I don't want to see anyone.'

There was a light tap on the door; it was DC Burrows, asking if Marcus would ring the station if he intended leaving.

'Is there some news?' he asked anxiously.

'I'm afraid not, but DI Reid wants to see you. He may be coming back to the house later or perhaps you would call him. Mrs Fulford, I have made a list of all your personal calls in case you want to ring back, and your answer machine for your business line is full, so I think you should perhaps check those messages and delete some, because when they can't get through they call on your private line.'

Lena sat up as Marcus took the list from Burrows and passed it to her. 'Come on, it's best you do something. I'll come into your office with you and we can go through them together.'

Lena slowly swung her legs down from the bed, though her head was throbbing and she felt drained of energy.

'Agnes wanted me to ask if you would like her to prepare lunch?' Burrows added.

Marcus said he wouldn't mind a sandwich, but Lena said she wasn't hungry. Burrows noticed how attentive he was, helping Lena stand up and fussing around her. He fetched her hairbrush and was gently brushing her hair while she stood in front of the dressing table as Burrows closed the door.

'We've also got to talk to our solicitors. Jacob Lyons was on the phone this morning – at least he had the grace to ask about Amy – but basically he wants to know when your bloke Henshaw is going to contact him.'

She turned towards him. 'How can you even think about this right now? You disgust me. Is that why you've come round and why you are acting all loving and caring, when basically you are here because you want a divorce settlement agreed?'

'For pity's sake, Lena, I just told you that Lyons called me. Whatever happens we will have to agree to some settlement; right now I can't even cover the rent at Simon's place.'

'Simon? Simon Boatly? I remember now, he was in Antigua when we were there. Do you remember he was on somebody or other's yacht and came over to the hotel and we all had dinner together?'

Marcus sighed impatiently, dismissing any suspicion of Simon, but Lena pursed her lips and, striding out of the bedroom, said that she was going to include him on the list for DI Reid.

Marcus followed Lena into her office as she began to play the messages on her business answer phone. Call after call was querying deliveries and payments, and then there were the repeated enquiries from her staff about Amy. Lena stood pressing delete, delete, and then listened to Gail Summers asking for the details of three children's parties and for her to confirm addresses and times.

'Christ, you'd think she'd have enough sense to look in the order book – it's all in there.'

'Why don't you just call and tell her,' Marcus suggested, leaning on the doorframe, as Lena continued deleting messages. One of the delivery drivers was off sick, so had not come into work, and Marcus watched as she became angry, swearing at their incompetence, before eventually she went to her computer and began to email instructions. He'd always admired how fast she could use a keyboard and he could see the distraction was beginning to calm her. Even though irritated by the slew of queries, she proceeded to work through them.

Marcus finally left her working and went downstairs into the kitchen, where Agnes had a coffee and toasted cheese sandwiches set out on the kitchen table for him. Burrows was still dealing with the phones but thankfully they had been silent for a while. She hesitated when Marcus invited her to join him, unsure about sitting with him.

'Come on, sit down, Agnes can take over the calls. Please.' He gestured to a chair.

'Would you like tomato ketchup, Barbara?' Agnes asked as she set a place for her.

Marcus squirted out some HP Sauce, noticing how Agnes, within minutes of meeting anyone, always used their Christian name. It used to annoy Lena, but it never really bothered him, although he was the exception – she never called him by his Christian name. She was bustling around the kitchen and obviously listening in to their conversation as he turned on the charm and asked Barbara how long she had worked for the police. Burrows, slightly ill at ease, explained that she had recently finished her two years' uniform probation before going on missing persons and hoped eventually to become a full detective and work on the murder squad.

Marcus asked if she had ever been on a missing person's case before and she admitted that their daughter was the first. The atmosphere grew tense as she attempted to explain how the police structured their enquiries – small children were always a high risk, but very often teenagers were quickly traced and the reason why they had absconded was uncovered.

'What reasons?' Marcus asked.

Burrows sipped her coffee, hardly touching her toasted sandwich and wishing she had not agreed to sit with him. She mentioned that exam results, boyfriends, drugs and abuse were factors.

'What, sexual abuse?' he asked, finishing his sandwich.

'Yes, not just sexual but physical abuse; sometimes there are mental issues; very often though it is connected to schooling, failure, bullying. So we have to take everything into consideration.'

She stood up, wiping her lips with the napkin, and asked where the bathroom was. Marcus out of manners half rose from his chair as Agnes directed 'Barbara' to the downstairs cloakroom. He then drained his coffee cup and crossed to use the phone. 'Have you got the number of the local police station, Agnes?'

Agnes, organized as ever, showed him the station number and DI Reid's mobile.

'I'll make the call in the sitting room,' he said, walking out.

Reid had just arrived at the forensic labs in Lambeth when Marcus rang his mobile, which made any immediate conversation difficult. Marcus agreed to wait at the house until Reid was free, and finishing the call stretched out on the sofa and closed his eyes. He recalled the time they had been in Antigua, specifically when Simon Boatly had appeared. With sun-bleached blond hair, tanned and wearing shorts and a T-shirt and rubber flip-flops, he had surprised them by strolling up the beach towards their cabana. Simon was a well-educated Old Etonian and Oxford graduate with a BA in Philosophy and was at the university at the same time as Lena, who studied Biological Sciences. Marcus had attended the local polytechnic where he had studied Design Graphics and had first met Lena in a pub in Oxford city centre. He met Simon in a squash competition against the university and they instantly became good friends and enjoyed each other's company, but there was always the difference in their backgrounds. Simon had money, having inherited a lot when his parents died, including a villa in Italy, a manor house in Henley and the Mayfair flat on his aunt's death. Although years went by when neither made contact, when they did meet up and renewed their friendship it was as relaxed as if they'd never been apart. Before the separation and Simon's travels abroad, they had seen a considerable amount of each other, both being keen squash players with membership of the Queen's Club. Simon had never married and appeared to have no intention of settling down as he continued his laid-back easy-going life. Although he called himself a photographer, there was no need for him to ever have gainful employment, as his inheritance was invested and he lived off the interest. When Marcus, after a strenuous game of squash, had bemoaned his marital situation, Simon had without hesitation offered him the use of his Mayfair flat.

Mulling the Antigua holiday over in his mind, Marcus couldn't recall Simon ever being alone with Amy. He was certain that Simon would not in any way have, as Lena had insinuated, been abusive towards the girl. That one time when he had appeared like the Sun King strolling along the beach, he had seemed to be as surprised as Marcus to discover they were there.

Marcus swung his legs down from the sofa and rested his elbows on his knees. Amy had visited the yacht with him, but only for a very short time because they'd returned to their hotel for lunch. Simon had been his usual witty self, and after about an hour went off on a speedboat, waving to them as he left. He and his crew were going to a different beach to water-ski, as the hotel did not have any speedboats, nor for that matter did it approve of the disruption of the boats' high-powered noisy engines.

That was the extent of the encounter. Marcus was certain that no way could Simon Boatly have had any interaction with Amy that either he or Lena were not privy to. He was determined that his name would not be tarnished by Lena as he was a very valued friend.

The forensic scientists were still working hard in the lab as Reid walked along the trestle table with the young assistant, surveying the items removed from Marcus Fulford's flat. The table was covered in white sterile paper sheets, on top of which were at least ten pairs of ladies' underwear of different styles and colours. There were also separate bagged sheets and pillowcases from Marcus's and Amy's bedrooms. The assistant carried a clip-board, pointing out and checking off the tagged items they had been working on.

The assistant suddenly laughed out loud. 'The end of that thing reminds me of an ice-cream whip,' he said, pointing to a skin-coloured vibrator in the shape of a very large penis.

Reid did not find it amusing, just distasteful. 'Who's in charge so I can discuss your results so far?'

The assistant moved off to a side room and a man in a white lab coat came out and introduced himself. He was in his mid-thirties, dark-haired, slim and had a warm welcoming smile.

'I'm Pete Jenkins, the lead scientist on this case. Thanks for coming in, DI Reid. I'll deal with the bad news first: unfortunately we haven't been able to raise a DNA profile for Amy from the toothbrushes you recovered.'

'What, none of them?' Reid asked, rather surprised.

'It's not uncommon as it looks like Amy gives her toothbrush a good clean after she uses it.'

'What about blood from the used sanitary towel?'

'Too old, decay and bacteria have destroyed any chance of DNA. However, we are trying to raise a profile from hairs removed from the hairbrush found in the bedroom at her father's flat, but this process takes more time. We need a full profile for Amy to compare against the various female profiles recovered and obtained from vaginal secretions on some of the underwear found in her Mayfair bedroom.'

Reid was intrigued. 'Various female profiles?'

'Yes, we have managed to raise profiles on some of the underwear and they must have been worn by different women.'

'What, like they were sharing them?'

Jenkins laughed. 'No, there were no mixed female profiles on any underwear. The DNA indicates each individual pair has been worn by one woman, but there's so far no match to any known profiles on the criminal DNA database.'

Reid didn't quite know what to make of this, but felt slightly relieved when told there were no semen stains on Amy's bed linen, although there were urine stains and unpleasant patches of faeces, and the blood on the mattress was menstrual.

Pete Jenkins continued. 'Marcus Fulford's bed linen was covered in semen and vaginal stains, as well as pubic hairs which are also yet to be tested for a profile.'

Reid smiled. 'That doesn't surprise me as it appears Mr Fulford is quite a womanizer:

'Well it's reasonable to assume the semen stains are from Mr Fulford, but we urgently need a DNA sample from him for comparison. We also found a number of strands of hair on his bed that didn't match in colour the hairs taken from Amy's hairbrush.'

'They may belong to Fulford's girlfriend Justine.'

Jenkins frowned. 'Or one of the unknown women whose underwear we have. We urgently need a DNA sample from every woman Marcus Fulford recently had sex with.'

Reid felt embarrassed at his lack of forethought. 'It's possible Amy had borrowed underwear from school friends, or they accidently left them behind after a sleepover at her father's flat.'

Jenkins' frown deepened. 'Big question then is why, and how, did they come to be in Amy's room?'

'Only Amy can answer that,' Reid said but wondered to himself if Amy was keeping them as evidence against her father or to show her mother as proof of her father's sexual exploits.

Jenkins continued. 'The DNA from the semen stains on Mr Fulford's bed linen matched semen stains recovered from some of the underwear in Amy's room. The semen on the underwear probably got there as a result of seepage after sex. Assuming the semen on the bed linen is Mr Fulford's then it's reasonable to assume he had sex with the wearers of the ladies' panties.'

Reid was stunned, and although finding it hard to follow the forensic data, he understood the implication. 'So his semen is on Amy's panties?'

'I can't obviously say a hundred per cent yes as I need to raise Amy's DNA profile. If it is her profile and his semen then it's reasonable to assume he was abusing his daughter.'

Reid looked sad. 'To be honest, I already had my suspicions, but I doubted myself. Hearing what you just said puts a whole new perspective on the investigation and one that will cause Mrs Fulford unbelievable distress.'

'I deal with fact and draw conclusions from the forensic evidence for the police and courts. I don't envy your job in having to tell victims my findings.'

'Will you call me as soon as you have anything further?'

'Certainly, but above all I need DNA samples from suspects and witnesses for comparison and to confirm, or refute, my suspicions.'

Pete Jenkins went over to a large cabinet, opened it and removed a bag full of DNA sample kits, which he handed to Reid.

'If you need more ring me or get some from your station supplies,' Jenkins said, paused and then smiled at Reid, who looked despondent. 'With the amount of seminal fluid we found I can say you're looking for a suspect who ejaculates enough to fill a whole sperm bank at an IVF clinic!'

Chapter 17

By four o'clock Reid was back at the Richmond house and found a patrol car with a female officer in it waiting as he drove up. Asking her to stay put as he would be back with Marcus Fulford's DNA in a few minutes, he rang the doorbell, and Agnes led him into the kitchen. Burrows looked tired, still sitting beside the phone, and had compiled an even longer list of names. Agnes reported that Mrs Fulford was in her office upstairs and Mr Fulford in the sitting room.

Reid went straight to the sitting room, where Marcus was lying on the sofa fast asleep. He woke with a start when Reid closed the door and, rather disorientated, sat up, ruffling his hair.

'Sorry, I've had hardly any sleep since Amy's been gone.'

'I need to take a DNA swab from you, Mr Fulford.'

Marcus stood up, shocked. 'Dear God, have you found her?'

'Not as yet, but the forensic scientists need it for elimination purposes.'

'I don't understand – eliminating me from what exactly?'

'As you are aware, we have taken numerous items from your flat in Green Street, and it is necessary to identify samples that have been re-covered, specifically from female underwear and from bed linen.'

Having just woken, Marcus stretched his arms and shoulders, and didn't at first grasp Reid's obvious implication, but it dawned on him after a few seconds.

'Jesus Christ, are you seriously suggesting I was having some kind of sexual relationship with my daughter?'

'A DNA sample is the only way we can eliminate you from DNA found in Amy's bedroom and possibly find who may have been having a sexual relationship with her. She may even have run away with that person.'

Marcus eventually complied and allowed Reid to take a DNA swab from his mouth; Reid then took it out to the waiting officer to take it to the lab.

Marcus had poured himself a brandy, shaken not by the process, which was very simple, but by the implications. As Reid re-entered the room Marcus gestured to the drinks cabinet but the de-tective declined his offer. He kept the conversation relaxed, thanking Marcus for his cooperation, ad-mitting it was never easy or pleasant to have to request DNA but it was necessary to move the investigation forward. Sitting opposite Marcus, he took out his notebook and patted his pocket for his pen while asking after Mrs Fulford. Marcus said she was sorting out all her business calls and compiling a list of names of those she felt should be interviewed. Lena had been very distressed, and he felt it was good for her to be occupied. He leaned forward, adding there was something he thought DI Reid should be made aware of.

'Lena suffers from depression; she has been diagnosed as bipolar and is on medication. Sometimes she becomes very lethargic and incapable of getting out of her bed, other times she is over-active, and hyper. She has been suicidal in the past, but until Amy's disappearance she had been exceptionally well and clearly more than capable of running her businesses. In truth her disorder has in many ways been more of an enabling factor rather than an illness.'

Reid sat back, needing a moment to take all this in. 'Did she react badly to your separation?'

'Obviously, but to be honest I don't know why I'm spilling all this out to you, and I don't mean it to be in any way detrimental to Lena. I am probably trying to make myself appear less of a jerk because I instigated the separation, but neither of us ever allowed our marital problems to affect Amy. Lena is a wonderful mother and she is very protective of her, but eventually I think she saw that it was better for all of us.'

'Were you having extramarital relationships before you separated?'

Marcus nodded, and then draining his glass he held it loosely in his hands. 'I'm not proud of it, far from it, but yes, I was unfaithful; nothing that ever lasted and I was always discreet and I think part of my promiscuity was Lena's fault as much as my own. You've no idea what all this is doing to me, especially the insinuation that there was more than a father-daughter relationship between Amy and me. You think I'm stupid? Wanting my DNA, as you so blithely said for elimination purposes. I have done nothing wrong, and I am as shocked as you are to discover that stuff in her bedroom.'

'But you must understand my position,' Reid said calmly. 'I am merely trying to find out if there is a viable reason why your daughter might have run away.'

Marcus refilled his glass. 'I honestly have been a good father. Every time Amy stayed with me I kept the weekend free, and I swear to you that it would only have been on the odd occasion she met my girlfriends, and as far as I can recall Simon Boatly never even visited his flat while she was there.'

'Why have you brought his name up?'

Marcus gritted his teeth. 'Because Lena has got it into her head that he could have been there and abused Amy, but the only time he was with her, with both Lena and myself, was when we were on holiday in Antigua, more than two years ago, and he and Amy were never alone. He's my best friend, for God's sake. I know him and I don't want any aspersions cast on him – he's not even in the country.'

Reid chose his words carefully, explaining that forensic tests had revealed seminal fluid and different female DNA on the panties taken from Amy's bedroom, and he would therefore require a list of everyone that used Simon Boatly's flat. Although they had spoken to his girlfriend Justine, Reid said that specifically he was interested in any other women Marcus had recent intercourse with as they had found strands of hair that were not a match for his daughter's.

Marcus bowed his head, sighing. 'Justine was one regular visitor, but there was another woman.'

'Who, Mr Fulford? Withholding evidence is a criminal offence, so I need to know right now.'

'I have also been seeing one of the women that works for Lena; her name is Gail Summers. I really don't want my wife told about Gail – she's been very helpful to me regarding the divorce and if Lena did find out she'd fire her.'

Disgusted by Marcus's attitude and behaviour, Reid decided that he'd spent enough time with him, and headed out of the room, suggesting that perhaps he put the stopper on the brandy bottle. He closed the door behind him and was making for the kitchen when Agnes approached him and asked if he felt it was all right for her to leave as it was just after five.

'You'd better speak to Mrs Fulford,' he said abruptly, and continued into the kitchen.

Burrows was still by the phones and was more than happy to go back to the station with him, even if it meant trawling through the list of names she'd accumulated during the day. Agnes returned, reporting that she had been told she could go home and that she was going over to the garage to tell Harry that he would not be required either.

'What does he do over there? Sit in the car all day?'

'Oh no, Mr Fulford had a gym above the garage – well, the equipment is still there but after he left Mrs Fulford made it a sort of sitting room. Harry has a TV and small kitchenette with a microwave. Your officers searched it when they were over there with the dog.'

Reid nodded, though he had not been aware that it existed, but hoped, as Agnes had said, that it had been searched properly. He made a note to check the search reports when he returned to the station. By now he was worn out, and yet he hesitated to leave without speaking to Mrs Fulford; as Burrows put on her coat he said he would just have a few words and trusted that was all it would be.

Lena, still at her computer, turned as Reid gave a light tap on the open door. There was always that moment of hopeful expectancy, which he quickly defused by saying there was no news. She looked very pale, and said she hoped he didn't think badly of her but working took her mind off the constant anxiety.

'Of course not. Whatever helps. Would you like me to arrange a family liaison officer to be here at the house overnight?'

'I don't think I'd like a stranger here right now, but thank you.'

He gave a small nod as she pushed back her chair and held out a neatly printed list of names, phone numbers and addresses. The phone on the desk rang yet again. Reaching for it, she gave him a small smile as she answered the call.

He walked out and then paused as he heard Lena talking on the phone. She sounded quite curt and said something about every box being labelled.

'Gail, it's very simple: if they wanted the table-cloth plus napkins with the child's name printed on them, then it's necessary to have three days' prior notice.'

The call continued as he made his way downstairs, realizing that the woman on the phone was the Gail that her husband had admitted to having an affair with. From what he had gathered, Marcus Fulford couldn't keep his dick in his pants, but there was nothing to suggest that Lena, a very attractive woman, also had extramarital flings. Although he reckoned that Marcus was a handsome man, there was a weakness to him, but if his wife indeed had – as he had made a point of stating – bipolar disorder, then perhaps it had encouraged or exacerbated his womanizing. If Marcus was an open and blatant womanizer since his separation from Lena, Reid wondered if Amy knew about or witnessed his antics and what that might say about their relationship as father and daughter.

Chapter 18

It was after twelve when Reid finally got home and fixed himself a stiff Scotch with ice and water. His small flat was as he had left it early that morning. It was more or less a crash pad, with few personal photographs or memorabilia. The furnishings were simple clean lines and the walls a magnolia cream that gave the box-shaped room a feeling of space. The only items of value were a large plasma TV and expensive stereo system, with his collection of CDs and DVDs stacked in alphabetical order in a glass cabinet. A desk, computer, printer and two filing cabinets with a shredder machine wedged between them dominated the small room.

He had a habit when returning home of emptying his pockets of his wallet, ID card and small change and leaving them on the desk. His briefcase would be placed beside the chair and he would set out his notebook and any files he needed to familiarize himself with. Tonight he was too tired for his usual ritual, dragging his tie loose and chucking his suit jacket onto a chair in his bedroom as he carried through his drink. He intended to take a shower, but lying on his bed sipping his Scotch he eased off one slip-on black leather shoe after the other, kicking them onto the floor. He leaned across and drew one of his pillows on top of the other. Sometimes when he came home this tired he would put on some soothing classical music – he had good-quality speakers throughout the flat, and a remote control on his bedside cabinet. But tonight he didn't even have the energy to move from the bed, and he downed his Scotch, closed his eyes and was in a deep sleep within seconds.

Unlike Reid, neither Marcus nor Lena could sleep. She had made an omelette and they had opened a bottle of wine earlier, although he noticed she hardly touched her food. He asked if she had eaten anything in the day and she shrugged, saying she didn't feel in the slightest bit hungry.

She stood up. 'I think I'll take a bath.'

'I'm going to watch some TV, I'll use the guest bedroom.'

He meant to get out of his chair and put his arms around her, yet instead he remained at the table finishing off the bottle of wine. Eventually he switched off the lights and took himself rather drunkenly upstairs. He felt he should go to her bedroom to check on her, but he couldn't face any further accusations. He was not sleeping but lying fully clothed on the bed in the guest room when she came in. He lifted his arm to indicate for her to come and lie beside him.

'I can't sleep,' she said plaintively.

'Nor can I. Come here.'

Lying beside him with his arm around her and resting her head against his shoulder, Lena realized it was the closest they had been for two years. Neither spoke – it was as if they were bereft of words, as if the ghost between them was Amy.

Reid had forgotten to switch on his alarm, but nevertheless he woke around his usual time, albeit with a thudding headache. By the time he had showered and dressed it was seven thirty. Two cups of strong black coffee made him feel wired, but his headache persisted, and he decided he would go into the station for breakfast.

The canteen was filling up, and having said a few gruff good mornings he sat at his usual table with his back facing the majority of diners. There was a low hubbub of chatter, which annoyed him as he ate his scrambled eggs and sausage and pushed aside his two rounds of toast. He never knew how they managed to make toast so chewy, the butter sitting on it like a puddle. Equally bad, the morning coffee always tasted stewed. Reid by nature was never one to complain, so he downed his coffee and got a refill to take to his office.

There was to be a team meeting at nine, but he had a while to take a couple of aspirin and get his mind into gear. Open on his desk was his diary and he picked up a red marker and wrote in large letters FRIDAY, DAY 6, underlined it and then tossed the marker down. By now his coffee was tepid. Nevertheless, he drank it, then uncapped his felt tip pen and began to write down the day's work schedule. DS James Lane tapped at the door, also carrying a coffee but this one was a Starbucks. Reid indicated for him to come in.

Lane didn't sit, but hovered, sipping his drink. 'The *Crime Night* people are interested in doing something on air but they're not sure exactly how to run it yet.'

Reid shook his head. 'A missing fifteen-year-old girl, who may be dead, and they're being non-committal – what more do the bastards want? We need more information and especially some forensic results. This is now day six, Jimmy, and we have fuck all to go on.'

'Not looking good, is it?' James said, dribbling his coffee down his chin and taking out a handkerchief to dab at his shirt.

'The holiday footage in Antigua worries me now, especially the section where Amy was masturbating.'

James seemed more intent on dabbing the coffee stains on his shirt as he spoke. 'So is Marcus Fulford now your main suspect?'

'He's all I've got at the moment, but even then we are nowhere, and there's this family friend Simon Boatly to check out. I also think we need to go back to Amy's school and see if we can get anything – it's more than possible Amy may have confided in a friend, maybe Serena or someone else in her class.'

'That's a good idea.' James glanced at his watch, nearly spilling what was left of his drink. 'It's nearly nine, so we better get down to the briefing room.'

At that moment Reid's desk phone rang and it was Pete Jenkins at the forensic lab, letting him know that he had started work on Marcus Fulford's sample and hoped to have a full profile for comparison before the weekend. Reid gestured for DS Lane to wait as Jenkins continued.

Reid listened, jotted down notes, and said he would arrange for interviews straight away then replaced the phone and stood up.

'It's unbelievable – they have DNA profiles from different females on a selection of the underwear. The lab needs to know exactly which panties belong to who and keep pressing me for samples from women Fulford recently had sex with. He has only admitted to shagging two women – his present girlfriend Justine and then there's Gail who works for Lena Fulford – but there's bound to be others. I think we need to get them brought into the lab to try and identify which underwear is theirs.'

'You think that's wise, or necessary, for that matter? Why not just get DNA samples off them and send them to the lab?'

'Because it will cost thousands of pounds to analyse, which I haven't got on my small-team budget. I know it's cutting corners, but it will save time and money.'

'Well it's your case and your decision. We better get downstairs – everyone will be waiting.'

Reid nodded and adjusted his tie, and had just begun to gather up his notes and files when someone else tapped at the door and this time it was Chief Superintendent Douglas, the senior officer in charge of Richmond Police Station. In his forties, he had red hair, and his uniform jacket just about contained his stomach as he was overweight. Known to be brash in speech and manner, he demanded an update as he was concerned by the lack of any new developments. Reid sat down again and invited Douglas to take a seat but the chief simply huffed and stood facing him across the desk.

'Well, forensics are working on enough knickers to open a Victoria's Secret department, and some have semen stains from the same unknown male,' Reid said, trying to be slightly humorous, but it was wasted on Douglas.

'So what are you doing to trace this unknown male?'

'The scientist and I both think it may be Marcus Fulford. I've taken a DNA sample from him and should know for certain in a couple of days.'

'The father! Christ, sex games going on in the family?'

'I'd say so. He's certainly shagged enough women and the daughter doesn't appear to be the sweet innocent teenager we first believed.'

'Six days missing. Are we looking for a body, Vic?'

Reid looked up and hesitated: the full version of his Christian name was bad enough but the abbreviation was even worse.

'If he was sexually abusing Amy and she threatened to expose him then it's possible he killed her on Saturday or Sunday. Problem is, I haven't got a sighting of her anywhere near the Mayfair flat.'

'So you want to hold back on arresting him at present?' Douglas asked.

'I'd like to try another round of press reports and *Crime Night* first ... see if it flushes out any new witnesses or fresh information.'

Douglas frowned. 'You need to make a decision one way or the other about Marcus Fulford.'

'We've obviously been misled regarding Amy's character, so it's reasonable to think she was sexually aware and may even have had a male friend that she decided to run off with. Perhaps an older man ... there's a family friend we suspect...'

'Who is he and why haven't you spoken with him yet?'

'Simon Boatly, but we believe he's in the Bahamas at present. He's a wealthy aristocrat photographer, but basically living off the interest from a considerable inheritance. He also owns the Mayfair flat Marcus Fulford lives in.'

'Well stop sitting on the fence, get out there and make some arrests,' Chief Superintendent Douglas said as he picked a small piece of fluff from his immaculate trousers. He held it between finger and thumb, screwed it into a tiny pin-size ball and flicked it onto the worn carpet.

'Although we found Amy's passport she could have acquired another one, and we are checking flights around the time she was missing,' Reid said, trying to avoid Douglas forcing his hand.

'I've got a daughter the same age and I find it difficult to believe that a fifteen-year-old teenager never whispered secrets to her school pals. If our missing girl was sexually aware, and having some kind of a relationship with this Boatly bloke, then I would think she would have told someone about him, even more so as she was at a weekly boarding school and sharing a dormitory. If you insist on holding off on arresting people then I think it might be beneficial for you to have another session at Amy's school.'

'Already in hand, sir.'

'Good. I'm having to go over to Scotland Yard, but contact me if anything comes in. I'll give you until Monday and if you're no further forward I'm calling in a murder squad to take over the investigation.'

'Does that include the weekend, sir?' Reid asked, hoping the answer would be no since as a DI he would not get paid overtime.

'Yes, of course it does and I'm ordering you to work.'

'And what about my team?'

'Overtime budget is tight, so you can only have two officers with you.'

'If a murder squad does take the case I would like to stay on board,' said Reid, spying his chance.

'Let's see how you go first, but make sure you keep me informed of any developments.'

Reid remained sitting at his desk as the DCS

left. He had really not intended to bring up his thoughts on Simon Boatly, but now that he had he would have to question him. He sighed, doubting their budget would run to anyone making a trip to the Bahamas, but along with Marcus Fulford, Boatly was earmarked as a suspect. He checked his watch; it was nine fifteen, and it felt as if he had been at work all morning – instead it was only just beginning. His meagre budget was being stretched to breaking point by forensics and the extra uniformed officers assisting in the house-to-house enquiries. If it became a murder squad inquiry he really hoped he could remain on the case, and work alongside such experienced detectives, as it would be an excellent move for his future career.

Chapter 19

Agnes was taken aback at the mess in the kitchen. Again she was left to clear up the newspapers from the table, then wash the dishes and return the kitchen to its usual immaculate order, finishing by using cleaning spray on the granite work tops so they gleamed. As she went into the hall she saw Marcus heading down the stairs.

'I don't suppose you have any cigarettes, do you?' he asked sheepishly.

'Well as a matter of fact I do – it's a pack that Harry left. I'll get them for you.'

The phone rang and she saw that apprehensive look on his face, so quickly said that she would take it in case it was a journalist.

'The Fulford residence, this is Agnes Moors speaking.'

Marcus waited then Agnes turned to him, holding out the receiver.

'It's for you, a Detective James Lane.'

Marcus took the receiver, and after a moment asked Agnes to transfer it to the drawing room. She passed him a packet of Marlboro Lights, which in fact were her own, but she would never admit that she still smoked. Marcus left the kitchen just as Lena walked in.

'Who was on the phone?' Lena asked.

Agnes said it was a detective and Marcus was taking the call in the drawing room.

'Did he have any news?'

'He never said. Do you want me to make some fresh coffee?'

'No, I have a headache. Are there any paracetamol tablets in here?'

'Yes, there's a pack of Mandanol, the ones you prefer, in the first aid drawer beneath the telephone.'

Lena opened the drawer, fetched a glass and poured herself some water before taking out the blister pack. Agnes watched as she popped out four tablets and, without making eye contact, said quietly that they were 500 mg caplets and perhaps four were too many to take at one time.

Lena ignored her, swallowing the capsules one after the other. She drained the glass and left it on the draining board.

Marcus was sitting on a sofa smoking, but when Lena walked in he got to his feet.

'I have to go to the flat and bring my stuff back,' he said quietly.

'I thought you had given up smoking?'

'I have, but for chrissakes don't give me a lecture – the pack belongs to Harry.'

'What did the police want?'

'No news, but I need to give them a couple of contact numbers which are at the flat.'

'What contact numbers?'

He inhaled, and let the smoke drift from his nose. 'They want to talk to Simon Boatly, and any numbers I have for him are in an old address book.' He made no mention that they had also required further details of the women he had been seeing.

'But you said he was abroad when Amy went missing.'

'I know; nevertheless that is what they asked me for and that is what I intend to do, all right?'

Lena nodded as he stubbed out the cigarette; the haze of tobacco smoke and the acrid smell hung in the air. She folded her arms, still standing in the doorway; it felt to Marcus that she was blocking him leaving.

'I'm going, Lena.'

'Did he say there was any news at all?'

'No, darling, he didn't and if he had I would have told you.'

'Did you know that there were police officers looking around the garden yesterday? They have been over all the place, in and out of the garage.'

'Lena, just bloody back off me and let me go home.'

She stepped away from the door and he gave

her cheek a light kiss, but she averted her face as
he smelt of nicotine. Hearing the front door shut,
she picked up the packet of cigarettes and went
into the kitchen.

'Throw these out, Agnes.'

The phone rang and Agnes saw the same look
of fear cross Lena's face, and she quickly answered, repeating her mantra, 'This is the Fulford
residence, Agnes Moors speaking.'

Just as she'd done with Marcus, she held out
the receiver and said that it was Detective James
Lane; he wanted to speak to her. Lena was
shaking as she took the phone. Agnes, all ears,
listened as Lena said that she would begin to find
a suitable section and would have it waiting for
collection. She replaced the receiver, informing
Agnes that the police wanted some footage of
Amy for *Crime Night,* the new television programme.

'That's good – it means they are really doing
everything possible,' Agnes said, dropping the
cigarette pack into the pedal bin. As soon as Lena
walked out she pressed it open again and replaced
the pack in her pocket. The way things were going,
she reckoned she would need to light up soon, it
was all so tense.

Reid was walking back through the busy main
office to his own when DC Wey got up from his
desk and said he had an interesting development
to tell him about.

'I've been questioning "working girls" known to
frequent the Mayfair area in and around Green
Street. I was showing them a picture of Amy and

discovered something interesting, but also quite worrying.'

Reid sat down and told Wey to tell him, and the rest of the office, the information he had uncovered.

'The girls were all glamorous and many drove smart cars, and the majority were Russian ... long gone are the old whores that used to work that area. The new breed of sex workers are attracted to the very upmarket restaurants in and around the place, like Harry's Bar, George's, Scott's and two new exclusive Italian restaurants which are always busy with wealthy and even famous customers.'

Reid wasn't interested in the history of Mayfair prostitution. He sighed and turned his finger in a circular motion.

'Just get on with it, Takeaway.'

'At first I got a load of abuse as they thought I was there to nick them for soliciting and a few even told me to fuck off. Then I got lucky with an eighteen-year-old Chinese tart called Lily Leo...'

'How much did she charge?' DS Lane asked, causing laughter round the room.

Wey himself chuckled before continuing. 'She was rather blunt but she was frank with me, and there was no charge probably because we both have slant eyes,' he said, making fun of his own looks and causing more laughter from members of the team.

Reid smiled and although he wanted Wey to get to the point the constable had a way of making people laugh and the team's spirits needed lifting, so he let him continue without interruption.

'Lily looked at Amy's photograph and was certain that she had been working the street near to the flat she lived in with her father. She could not confirm if Amy was turning tricks, but she had seen her a few times. She also recalled that once she had been wearing a school uniform, but she had not seen her for some time and reckoned it would have been at least two months ago.'

There was stunned silence round the room as everyone sat up and took in this shocking revelation.

'Lily was certain she recognized Amy Fulford,' Wey went on, 'and said she stood out because she was even younger than herself. The area is apparently divided up virtually by paving slabs and older "professionals" had also warned her off a couple of times.'

Reid was astonished by what Wey had discovered and found it hard to accept. 'What about any of the other girls you spoke to – did any of them corroborate what this Leo woman said?'

'None of them would really talk to me, sir, but I did notice a reaction from one or two when I showed them Amy's picture. It was as if they had seen her on the streets before.'

'Well we can't just dismiss what Leo says; whether it's lies or mistaken identity it has to be followed up.'

'I spoke with Westminster Council who told me the plethora of Bentleys, Ferraris and other high-priced cars parked on the meters in and around the Mayfair area are magnets for the girls. More CCTV cameras were recently put up in the area for security as there are two new flashy night-clubs and Prince Harry had been frequenting the one that used to be the old Annabel's,' Wey went on.

'I want you to get at least two months' CCTV footage from any cameras on the streets the prostitutes worked and go through it with a fine toothcomb,' Reid told him.

Wey sighed at the thought of watching hour after hour of prostitutes plying their trade and Reid picked up on this.

'You can share the footage amongst the office, Takeaway, so as to speed things up.'

Wey looked relieved. 'Thanks, guv. I also spoke to a friend on the vice squad. There had been complaints from the residents about all the tarts and about used condoms thrown out of cars, so vice did video surveillance and clamped down on the area a few months ago. They nicked a few and the others moved on, but vice can't do twenty-four seven surveillance in one area alone due to cost and manpower so like a bad penny they keep coming back.'

Reid stood up and started to head for his office. 'Get all the video the vice squad have as well and let's see if Amy Fulford shows up turning tricks.' He instructed Wey to go back to interviewing the 'whores' and if they didn't like it he was to bring them in for questioning. He was to specifically find out which ones had confronted Amy Fulford and if Lily, or any other 'toms', knew Marcus Fulford.

The new information was depressing, but Reid reasoned at least they might get something from the vice squad. Now seemed like a good moment to get the visit to the school over and done with.

He'd wanted to take Barbara Burrows with him as it was a girls' school and they might be more responsive to her, but he knew she was busy with other enquiries, and there was no one else available who could assist him. He was walking to his car when DS Lane approached, informing him that Lena Fulford was looking for a video that the Crime Night programme could use. Justine and Gail had been contacted, but Justine was in Leeds for some hairdressing event. He said it was going to be difficult to organize cars to take them to the lab at different times, and once they had a list from Marcus there would be other women to get hold of.

Lane smiled. 'Picking out their bloody knickers is going to be a farce, but I think we also need Lena Fulford. She will be able to tell if any belonged to Amy. We've got sexy silk, tacky net, G-strings, navy-blue school issue and–'

'For God's sake, give it a rest,' Reid snapped. 'Just get on with organizing everyone. I really don't care if they meet one another or not. And yes, that will have to include Lena.'

'These are women her husband is shagging,' Lane said defensively.

'They are getting divorced. I would say that Mrs Fulford is more than aware of her husband's inability to keep his dick in his pants.'

Marcus turned his untidy bedroom upside down, opening and closing drawers, trying to recall where his old address book was as he hadn't used it for so long. Any calls he made were from his mobile and he hadn't spoken to Simon for months, although he had received a couple of terse notes from his lawyers about the non-payment of rent.

By the time he had searched the entire flat, and finally found his dog-eared old leather address book, he'd been home for over an hour. To his irritation his doorbell rang and it was Detective Wey asking if he could have a few words with him. Marcus buzzed open the front door and stood on the landing waiting for him to come to the second floor.

Marcus led him into the flat and through to the small untidy sitting room, where Wey perched himself on one of the old leather chairs, flipping open his notebook. He took down the contact numbers and repeated each one to make sure they were correct. He then asked whether or not Marcus had used any of the prostitutes known to frequent his area.

'If I had, what on earth has that got to do with the fact my daughter is missing?'

'It may be important, sir, especially if you have used any of them recently, and if so, did they come here into your flat?'

Marcus rubbed at his head and then opened his arms. 'Yeah, I may have used a couple, but not recently, and, let me tell you, never when my daughter was staying here with me.'

'Do you recall their names?'

Marcus gave a long sigh, and shrugged.

'I know they sometimes use fake names, but even a description would help us. This is important, Mr Fulford, and I am sorry if it seems to be embarrassing.'

'I'm not bloody embarrassed; it's not as if I'm some sexual pervert, just on occasions I have booked a girl after an evening out – you know, had a few drinks too many – and they are fucking available around here.'

Wey's face was an impassive mask as he waited for Marcus to continue.

'Okay, let me try and remember – if not their names then what they looked like.' He smiled as if it was a joke but it fell flat.

Reid was on the M3 motorway heading towards Ascot when he received the call from Wey telling him that Marcus Fulford had admitted to using prostitutes on a frequent basis since he'd moved into the Green Street flat. However, he claimed he had not paid for any girls in the past few months as he was in a relationship with Justine.

'This guy gets his leg over more times than I've had hot dinners,' Wey said.

'Dear God, this man is a scumbag, isn't he?' Reid muttered.

'Good-looking guy, not working, lot of free time on his hands, some would call him the fucking lucky one,' Wey remarked.

'Okay, thanks for letting me know. Keep at it and find the women he slept with. I should be back after lunch if you get any further news.' Reid cut off the speakerphone call and continued driving. The sat nav told him to turn off for Ascot and he went past the racecourse and onto Windsor Great Road before turning into Broadlands Ladies' School. It was previously a large Victorian manor but now there were modern outbuildings that seemed to hold gymnasiums, an indoor swimming pool complex and indoor tennis courts. The vast surrounding grounds were covered in playing fields for hockey, lacrosse, and even cricket. Built onto the square courtyard, which was the main entrance to the school, were various cottages used to accommodate the staff, and behind the old house was a large 1960s building that contained the main boarding dormitories.

Reid parked in a visitors' bay alongside numerous cars he presumed belonged to daytime staff. He stood surveying the old manor, which had a plaque on a side door engraved HEADMIS-TRESS AND PRIVATE STAFF ENTRANCE ONLY. As he bleeped his car locked he could see a hockey game in progress on one of the playing fields.

The girls reminded him of those from St Trinian's, but the school's similarity ended there. The gardens were well tended and the lawns mown, and numerous large stone plinths with vast plants stood to either side of the entrance. Immaculate white steps led to the arched double entrance doors, featuring a bell with brass surrounds. He waited a moment before pressing it and, looking around, noticed the wooden painted signs with arrows pointing to dormitories, dining hall, assembly hall and art studio. Three girls wearing grey blazers, white shirts, dark ties and navy-blue pleated skirts walked past, carrying a tray of fresh oranges and water jugs, as they headed towards the playing fields. The tall leggy girls were, he reckoned, about fourteen or fifteen years old, but they did not even glance in his direction.

A small woman with half-moon glasses opened the door. She was wearing a neat blue suit with a bow at the neck of her white blouse. Introducing herself as the school administrator, she led him along a marble mosaic floor with polished side tables filled with magazines and vases of flowers.

'Miss Harrington is expecting you,' she said primly and gestured for him to walk ahead of her towards a polished heavy, door with HEADMISTRESS on a plaque. He could smell a mixture of polish, scented flowers and cooked mince, which, perhaps with the exception of the mince, could not have been more different from his old school.

The headmistress, Celia Harrington, was sitting behind a vast carved desk; oil paintings adorned the walls and the thick plush green carpet looked like one of the playing fields. She was younger than he had expected and rather attractive in a motherly sort of way, with curly grey hair, a printed blouse and slim-fitting grey skirt.

The glass-fronted cabinets were full of books, and there were two green leather chairs placed in front of her desk. She rose to shake his hand, and then placed both her well-manicured hands on top of a large open diary.

'I spoke to Mrs Fulford earlier to express my sincere sympathy as this must be a dreadful time for her. All of us have been greatly distressed; Amy is such a lovely girl and a great asset to our school. She is truly missed and we say a prayer for her every morning at Chapel. We have so many boarders from around the world, and I don't know if you are aware but we have pupils from aged eleven up to eighteen, and we have over four hundred pupils, only a small per cent of whom are day pupils. The girls that are full-time boarders remain at weekends and we try to make things entertaining for them.'

Reid liked her voice, it was soft and cultured, and she spoke unhurriedly and with eye contact. Eventually she gave a sad smile.

'I presume by your presence you have no news yet?'

'No, sadly I don't.' Reid held her gaze. 'I would like your permission to talk to Amy's classmates as well as her teachers, and I will obviously be as diplomatic as possible. She has now been missing six days and I am hoping that perhaps one of them might have some clue about her disappearance.'

'Quite, however we were interviewed previously by a Detective Sergeant Lane and a Detective Constable Wey and they were extremely kind and thoughtful. We will endeavour to give you every assistance but truthfully no one had anything of relevance to explain her non-appearance here; she is an excellent pupil, very quiet and studious and also very athletic and extremely well liked. She was to be sitting her exams, but as she has already shown a higher than average ability in her half-term assessment we doubted that could be a reason for her not to return here.'

Reid took a sly glance at the large clock on the marble mantel. 'I would especially like to speak with Serena Newman, as she was one of the last persons to see Amy and it would seem they were very close.'

'Certainly. I have of course spoken with Serena myself and she was most concerned for Amy and in floods of tears. School protocol and governing rules dictate that I or another teacher must be present when you interview any of the pupils.'

Rules and regulations was something that had crossed Reid's mind, but he was hoping under the circumstances Miss Harrington would not be so rigid. He really wanted to speak to Serena without any teachers present as it might make her feel more at ease. However, he was in Miss Harrington's domain and had no choice but to abide by her rules.

Almost as if she read his mind she pushed back her leather desk chair and said that Amy's class, 11A, were in one of the new buildings and as it was rather a complex route to get there she would walk him over and introduce him to their form teacher.

Reid followed Miss Harrington along one corridor after another, until they left the old manor and crossed a small courtyard to a new annexe. Pupils passing gave a polite good morning to Miss Harrington and he was very impressed by the overall cleanliness and organized notice boards. Along the walls were photographs of past sports teams and trophies in glass-fronted cabinets. On the first floor they passed windowed doors bearing form numbers and lists of pupils; he could hear the muted voices coming from the classrooms, but like everything else it all appeared to be controlled and the girls attentive to their teachers. Reaching the last classroom in the corridor, Miss Harrington tapped and slowly opened the door, causing the ten pupils to all rise in unison.

'Good morning, Miss Harrington,' came the chorus from the girls.

'Good morning and please be seated.'

They sat down and Miss Harrington turned to a florid-faced woman who wore round glasses that gave her an expression like an owl. She was chunky and rather overweight, but had a lovely smile as Reid shook her hand. Miss Harrington introduced him quietly to Mrs Vicks, the history teacher, and then turned to the class. 'This is Detective Inspector Reid of the Metropolitan Police and he is leading the inquiry into finding Amy Fulford. I want you all to pay close attention to what he asks, and think about your answers before you speak. This is a very serious matter and one where we all need to take every opportunity to help in any way we can.'

Reid would have liked to announce himself; the quiet cordial voice was starting to get on his nerves. He also did not want her to remain in the classroom, or the owl-like woman. It came as an unwelcome surprise when Miss Harrington said Mrs Vicks would remain with him and she would be in her study awaiting his return. As she left the classroom he turned to Mrs Vicks; she blinked quickly, even more reminiscent of an owl, but gave him another warm smile and sat behind her desk.

He took off his jacket, folded it and placed it on Mrs Vicks' desk before casually propping himself up on the edge of it. He looked round the two rows of faces – blondes, brunettes, auburn-haired teenagers, all devoid of make-up, with Alice bands and slides, freckles and glasses and open textbooks in front of them. He knew what he was doing as he glanced from one to the next, all the while his mind picturing Amy Fulford as the girl from the missing desk.

'Which one of you is Serena Newman?'

They were very nervous, glancing sideways without moving their heads. Sitting in the back row, Serena put up her hand. 'Stand up, please.'

Serena stood up, chewing at her lips. He smiled to put her at ease and asked her to come to the front as she was very important, and then to tell the class exactly what happened on the Saturday when she was with Amy. He knew already, but wanted to watch the girls' reactions.

Serena was a very attractive girl, not in the same league as Amy, but she was quite confident as she asked if he wanted her to start from when they were both collected from school that day.

'Please explain in detail everything that you re-member from driving out of the gates here to your home. The smallest detail might be significant. Let me give you an example: was Amy chatty and friendly, knowing she was going to be spending the weekend, a sleepover with you – right? That's what you call it, a sleepover...?'

'Yes, and we had arranged it for quite a while, and when we got home–'

'Hang on, hang on – was she wearing her school uniform, what was she carrying, an overnight bag, a satchel? Come on, Serena, start from the top again. I want you to think like a detective having to recall every single detail.'

'Okay, we both had uniforms on, but not our

hats, and she had an overnight bag, with her nightdress and change of clothes.'

Reid nodded encouragingly as she continued, even describing what CD they asked Mrs Newman to play in the car, and how they had sung along together. The girls were attentive, and he watched as Serena got into her stride, almost as if she was enjoying being the centre of attention. Slowly he began to monitor their reactions. After a while a couple leaned their elbows on their desks, chins held in their hands, and not one appeared bored or even restless. They listened intently as Serena explained about going to the cinema, but Amy had said she wanted to get her watch from her father's flat, and that she would meet her later.

Serena paused and turned to Reid. 'I waited most of the afternoon at home after I washed my hair, but when Amy finally texted me that she wasn't going to come to the cinema I called some of my friends from my old school and they said they could come. Afterwards we had a hamburger and fries and when I got home I called Amy's mobile again but it was on voicemail. I think my mum called her mum, but no one answered at her house. I came back to school on the Sunday and I brought her overnight bag with me as it had her school clothes in it.'

Reid nodded and she was about to return to her desk when he put out a hand. 'Serena was one of the last people we know to have seen Amy since she left her house in Fulham on the Saturday. Since then not one person, not one single person has seen Amy Fulford. It is as if she disappeared into thin air, so now–' A red-haired girl put up her hand.

'Yes, Miss...?'

'Allard, Georgina Allard. I know that Amy's watch was from Cartier and it was engraved with her name and she was given it for her birthday by her mother.'

Reid clapped his hands. 'Terrific, good girl – that is a very valuable piece of information. So how do you know about her watch?'

'She showed it to me; she didn't have a birthday party because she was away abroad with her mother. Amy said it was extra-special because it was a Cartier and very expensive.'

'Anyone else have such an expensive watch?'

There was a murmur as several girls said they hadn't got Cartier watches but a couple admitted they had very nice ones. He asked if anyone felt that Amy was showing off, and there were shrugs and more murmurs and then the same red-haired girl said that her sister had one and it had diamonds. It was taking time, but he was encouraging the girls to be more open about how they felt towards Amy and now they freely looked to each other, whispered and hid behind their hands. They no longer sat prudishly behind their desks, but swung their legs to the side, leaning back and forth to confer with each other. Amy was always top of the class, Amy was always chosen first when picking sports teams and was in the hockey, netball and water polo teams and she had even been given the best roles in their plays at the end of each term. The green-eyed monster of envy reared its head as one after another related an anecdote about the missing girl. It was if they had forgotten the reason he was there as he encouraged them and laughed. By now Serena had returned to her desk and sat on top of it; knees drawn up. She was obviously a class leader and prompted a number of the girls to recall some incident or other that was derogatory about Amy.

Reid was surprised that Mrs Vicks remained silent, though he could see that she was frowning in disapproval. He gestured towards Serena, re-marking that although she'd invited Amy for a sleepover he wondered if Serena didn't really like her. She flushed, which made her look even prettier, and gave a pursed-lipped look to the rest of the girls. 'Nobody particularly likes her and I am speaking the truth. She is a liar and very sec-retive; we are not supposed to have our mobile phones after nine o'clock – we have to put them in the phone box, it's a house rule, but she is always using hers even after lights out.'

'Does she have a boyfriend?'

There was a snigger and the girls covered their mouths as one or two guffawed, but when Mrs Vicks tutted they went quiet. Reid felt he had been patient long enough and now his friendly act dropped.

'Listen to me. Amy Fulford has been missing for six days and nights, we have found no trace of her and her parents are desperate for news. If any of you know of a boyfriend, or someone she was in contact with, now is your chance to tell me. I don't care if you liked or disliked her, I am not interested whether you were envious of her, but if you know anything that can help me find her I need to know now. It will not go against you and

I will endeavour to keep any secrets you've not dared tell anyone.'

They stared back at him, and it was not just frustrating but actually infuriating. Serena got down from her desktop and sat behind it. Reid was shocked as she banged the lid of her desk, and within seconds a couple of the other girls started lifting their desk lids and banging them shut. Mrs Vicks clapped her hands and they quickly returned to sitting quietly like sweet innocent girls. Reid picked up his jacket, and before Mrs Vicks could say anything he gestured for her to come outside the classroom.

In the corridor Reid put on his jacket. 'Mrs Vicks, I think one or other of Amy's classmates knows something that might help me to trace her, but they are either refusing to admit it or afraid to tell me.'

'I sincerely doubt that; they are all very good girls and from very good homes. Perhaps the only thing they may be withholding is that Amy Fulford was a very quiet, difficult girl to get to know; she was exceptionally clever and at times it felt as if she was much older.'

'You are using the past tense, Mrs Vicks.'

Her plump hands flew to her cheeks. 'Oh my God. I didn't mean to do that. I am so sorry.'

'So am I, Mrs Vicks, because if we discover that any of the girls are withholding information and haven't spoken up this morning, there will be serious consequences.'

He turned to walk down the corridor as Mrs Vicks called loudly to a girl that she should return to her class.

'I need to use the bathroom, Mrs Vicks.'

'Very well, straight there and back, Alice. I will be timing you.'

Reid slowed his steps, the classroom door closed, and he heard the soft footfall of the girl behind him. As she approached he recognized her as the small quiet girl who had been sitting behind Serena. As she passed him she threw him a small rolled-up piece of paper and continued along the corridor into the toilets. He unfolded it and saw that written in a hurried scrawl were the words 'Facebook – Slut Shaming'.

He paused a moment in the hope Alice would come out, but she didn't and so he headed down the stairs to the ground floor. He made it to the exit of the complex but was then at a loss as to which way he should continue, until he saw one of the painted arrows to the art studio and recalled Detective Lane mentioning a Miss Polka. He decided he would see if she was available and made his way along a narrow path, following a second arrow pointing towards a glass-sided building with STUDIO in black letters over double French windows.

Peering through, he saw something that astonished him. There was a semi-nude female model on a draped couch and eight girls sitting with big white pads on easels sketching her. He shook his head; if that had been on offer at his grammar school he would have definitely taken up art as a subject. Suddenly a voice behind him asked what he thought he was doing.

He whipped round in embarrassment. 'I am so sorry, I am Detective Inspector Reid and–'

The woman interrupted him. 'They are finishing their class in a few moments and I don't want them disturbed. Miss Harrington said you were here, so let me finish up and if you continue round this path and turn left there is a cottage at the end of it. The door is open so please let yourself in – it's lunch time in a few minutes so we can talk there in private without interruption.'

He thanked her and she gave him a lovely smile. DS Lane had said she was very attractive but he was taken aback by just how gorgeous she was. She had what he would describe as Marilyn Monroe hair, that thick curly platinum-blonde, wide blue eyes and a small straight nose and then a mouth not covered in garish red lipstick but pink and natural. He had not had time to take in what she was wearing as he had been so struck by her face. As he walked to her cottage he laughed to himself as she must have first thought of him as some kind of peeping Tom. Even though it was later than he had anticipated being at the school, he had no intention of leaving until he had talked to Miss Polka.

Arriving at the cottage, he let himself in just as the sound of the dinner bell could be heard from the main building. While he had been unable to see what the rest of Miss Polka looked like as he had been so smitten by her face, he now had every opportunity, as lining the small hallway were numerous photographs of her. A couple were of her posed naked like a Greek statue and she was breathtakingly pretty. Although the photos looked as if they had been taken a few years ago, he couldn't resist examining them more closely, with

265

the result that he was caught out yet again as she walked in and he flushed with embarrassment as she laughed.

'I see you've found me. That was taken a while back, Sonoran Desert, Mexico.'

She ushered him into a small sitting room with more portraits of her, and again she laughed.

'I used to live with the artist – nobody wanted to buy them so I kept them all here. Now let me make us a sandwich and put on some fresh coffee.'

'Thank you, I'd like that.'

She cocked her head to one side, her expression suddenly very serious. 'I need to talk to you about Amy; she is sadly missed. If you're interested, there's some of her work over on the window seat.'

The folder was made of cardboard with a red cord around it, and as he untied it some of the sketches fell onto the floor. They were in charcoal, smudged like shadows, and appeared to be of grotesque skeletons. Two were what he realized must be self-portraits, but both were incomplete, as if Amy had deliberately intended drawing only part of her face and leaving the other side blank. They were very good, but also quite unnerving. He couldn't help but wonder why she had chosen to leave her face incomplete.

Chapter 20

Miss Polka carried in a tray of sandwiches and two mugs of coffee, with milk and sugar on the side. She was wearing a simple pale blue shirt tied at the waist with a patent leather belt and a full circular skirt of some soft material.

'Sorry, did I make you jump?' she said, smiling, and then indicated her black ballet pumps.

'I always wear these as I am on my feet for most of the day. A long time ago I wanted to be a ballet dancer, but as often with teenage dreams I never had the opportunity or probably the inclination to put in the amount of hard work it takes to be an accomplished dancer.'

She moved like one, passing him a plate with a napkin and offering him his mug of coffee, then spooning in the two sugars he asked for. She placed a small round table beside him, so he was able to put down his plate and drink his coffee easily. It was strong, and the tuna mayonnaise and salad sandwich on crusty brown bread was delicious. She sat to one side of him on a small round cushioned stool.

'This is just what I needed, Miss Polka.'

'Please, it's Jo, short for Josephine. Just so you know, I don't often allow any of the pupils to be here, it's sort of frowned on, even more so if Miss Harrington were to see all my nudity on display. It's my private little domain and I don't have any other place during term time, but during breaks I travel as much as possible.

He nodded, remarking that he had always felt teachers had it cushy with so many holidays, unlike himself. She smiled and gave a small nonchalant shrug of her shoulders, saying that if teachers' wages were higher then she would agree with him.

'I find Amy's artwork a bit disturbing,' he confessed, finishing his sandwich.

'Yes, but she is very talented, extremely versatile – some of her fabric designs are excellent and her still lifes even more so.'

She nibbled at her sandwich, and then nodded to the portfolio. 'They were done last term. I have hopes of her working in oils or acrylic, but she seems to avoid colours – even her fabric designs are always in black and white.'

'Why has she left half her face unfinished?'

'I don't know – she certainly was able to sketch her own likeness.'

'Yes, I recognized her straight away.'

'She is a very beautiful girl, very tall and slender, but I think her inability to make the usual schoolgirl attachments saddens her.'

'Attachments?'

She seemed flustered. 'By that I mean making friends – she is very much a loner, and it concerns me because it makes her appear very aloof, as if she is much older than the other girls in her class.'

'You like her?'

Miss Polka nodded and turned away from him. He sipped his coffee, watching her, and got the feeling she wanted to tell him something but was avoiding it. Eventually she spoke quietly.

'What do you think has happened to her?'

'I honestly don't know. As you are probably aware she had a sleepover with Serena Newman, but said she was going to her father's place in Mayfair and no one has seen her since.'

'I found it odd that she would even agree to staying at Serena's – not that I have anything against her, but they were never what I would call close friends.'

'I was just with Amy's class and it became evident Serena is a bit envious of her,' he suggested.

'Well Amy does not cultivate friendships, and when I said she is a talented artist, she is also academically very clever, as well as athletically. In fact, everything she does she accomplishes with ease and never appears to need to work at it; she's also very adult and sophisticated for her age.'

'Do you think she is sexually aware?'

Miss Polka blinked rapidly and wafted her hand. The question seemed to throw her, as she stood up and asked if he would like a top-up of coffee. He declined and she sat down again, hugging her knees and lowering her head so he could not see her face.

'Why did you ask me that?' She still did not look at him.

'There is a possibility that Amy is being or has been abused, but I am unable to give you any details.'

He delved into his pocket and drew out the crumpled paper from his pocket. 'Do you know about something called cyberbullying on Facebook?'

'I know that it goes on, of course. You know what teenagers are like. They live for their social network sites and Facebook pages, and even if they are being bullied, cyberbullied, they can't tear themselves away. Of course you can't actually post anonymously on Facebook, but that doesn't stop the bullies setting up fake accounts, specifically to post nasty comments on girls they are bullying. And then there's this website called ask fin that they can connect to through their Facebook accounts. You can set up a profile and invite comments about yourself, and those comments are anonymous, and they can be really vicious.'

'You're very well informed,' he said quietly.

She was running her fingers through her curly hair, still hunched on the low stool.

'I think Amy was being bullied, cyberbullied, and I'm worried that it might have been the reason she has run away.'

'You never mentioned it to the detectives that came here.'

'No, but there is a reason. You see, the girls are not allowed iPads, just their mobile phones to call home. The rules are there for obvious reasons, and God only knows what they would otherwise be watching on the internet under their duvet covers.'

She began to pluck at her skirt, and was becoming agitated, as if she couldn't keep her hands still.

'Did she say anything about being bullied on Facebook?'

Miss Polka shook her head, sprang up and

picked up the tray of dirty crockery and walked out. It was very frustrating, but just as he was about to follow her, his mobile rang. It was DS Lane. Reid went into the hallway to take the call.

'We've got something off the CCTV footage the vice squad handed over. We have a clear picture of Amy Fulford standing on the pavement in South Audley Street for over five minutes, we've got a fucking punter stopping and she leans over as if talking to him, and then he speeds off; we've got the registration, she is wearing school uniform and the date was three weeks before she went missing.'

Reid sighed. 'Whatever was said between Amy and the driver is critical to the investigation. Get the driver traced asap and get him questioned.'

'Yes, guv. Bit of a sad revelation if she was turning tricks.'

'Find the driver before assuming anything. I'll be back from the school in about an hour.'

'You with the delectable Miss Polka? I wouldn't mind taking an art class with her.'

'Get on with your work,' Reid said, then ended the call and returned to the sitting room.

Yet again she surprised him, her ballet pumps made her so silent. She had in her hand an iPad and held it out for him. 'I took this from her because if it had been discovered she would have been on detention, which always means they have to return earlier than scheduled on a Sunday, and I knew how she treasured her weekends.'

He frowned as he took it from her. 'You should have handed it over before now. Does it have a password?'

'I don't know. I'm sorry, but I put it in a drawer

271

and forgot about it.'

She hung her head in an apologetic childish manner, and then spread her hands. 'I am so sorry but I was concerned about possible repercussions.'

'I don't understand.'

'This is very difficult.' She started running her fingers through her hair again.

'Miss Polka, I have just had a call from one of my officers: your exemplary pupil has been caught on CCTV camera by the vice squad, in her school uniform, turning tricks. It seems she was very likely prostituting herself, so never mind about the cyberbullying and what might be on her iPad, I am now concerned that she was picked up by some bastard and he's killed her. You have withheld what could be a vital clue as to—'

At this onslaught she broke down sobbing, and Reid knew he had gone too far. He knew he shouldn't have lost control, but the phone call had sickened him, and now he was ashamed as she was clearly terribly shocked. He did the un-thinkable and put his arms around her.

'Shush. I'm sorry, I should never have let that out, and we do not have confirmation. We also have a situation with her father which I can't really divulge to you.'

She buried her face in his shoulder, her whole body shaking. He kept his arms around her, but his intuition was telling him that Miss Polka knew something. It was when she had said 'repercussions', and now he wondered if she meant for herself or Amy. Gradually the crying stopped and she slowly moved away from him to make her way with dance-like steps to a box of tissues. She plucked one out, blew her nose and wiped her eyes.

'I could lose my job,' she said quietly.

He was certain she was not referring to keeping the iPad, but he was astute enough not to make a reply. Waving the tissue, she gestured to the paintings and nude photographs of herself, and then crumpled the tissue in her hand.

'You know I said I lived with an artist? She was also my partner and when she left me I was devastated. We actually met at art school and it wasn't until I was thirty-two that I began teaching. I have worked at two schools before being employed here, and although nowadays it is probably acceptable I would say that Miss Harrington might not have offered me this position and the chance to live on the premises had she known about my sexuality.'

Reid was taken aback, but managed not to show it. She gave a long sigh, and then began to twirl a curl through her fingers.

'I might as well come clean with you, and you have to understand it was truthfully never my intention for it to happen, but now I feel wretched about it. As a teacher I am obviously to blame and should never have allowed myself to be drawn in, but I was, and now if it was to come out then I might as well pack my bags.'

'I can't promise you anything, but if you know something, and if it is a possible reason for Amy to disappear, then the sooner you tell me the better and I will endeavour to maintain your privacy.'

'Thank you. Loath as I am to admit it, it happened, but it was never instigated by me.'

273

He waited, suppressing his irritation and allowing her the time to admit what he suspected.

'It started last term; she had returned from her weekend with her mother, and she had been brought back earlier than usual. It was an awful night with rain lashing down. Anyway, her dorm was empty, and she told me she didn't want to go into supper as she had already eaten. Sundays I am not on duty but there are always teachers around, but this night for some reason, whether or not it was the truth, she said she was all by herself and felt lonely. I think she might have been standing out in the rain for some time, maybe getting up the courage to come here – either way she was on my doorstep, soaking wet, in just a pair of jeans and a T-shirt. The girls often come back to school at the weekend in their own clothes and bring their clean uniform with them.'

He wished she'd get on with it, but whether or not she was drawing it all out as an excuse, he didn't want to interrupt. 'I invited her in, and as she was soaking I offered to let her use my bathroom and my hair dryer. I put on some soup and boiled a kettle to make a pot of tea, but then she came into the kitchen ... she was naked apart from a bath towel. She said she had eaten and didn't want anything, and I swear to you I did not encourage it, but she dropped the towel and embraced me. It does not make it in any way an excuse for what happened next, but in all honesty Amy was the instigator and I did try to dissuade her but she was very insistent.'

'Did it become a regular thing between the two of you?'

'I hoped after the term break it would not be repeated but she would turn up on the odd Sunday evening. I tried very hard to dissuade her from continuing it, but I was in a sort of Catch-22 predicament. I told her I could lose my job and she swore she would never tell anyone, and she never showed any sign that we were having an affair when she was in my class. She never threatened me, but I always got the impression that if I didn't allow her to be here with me, she could make it difficult.'

'Do you believe that she was experienced sexually?'

'Yes – as I said, she instigated our love-making. I felt guilty as obviously she was underage, but I was also incapable of ending it. I love her, and since she went missing I have been unable to sleep, worrying if I am to blame.'

'Did she ever profess to love you?'

Miss Polka kept her eyes averted and started to cry, shredding the tissue between her fingers.

'No, she never said anything really. She liked to touch me, kiss my body, but whether or not she had experienced a lesbian relationship before me, she never admitted it. The last time she was here with me was about six weeks before she went missing, and I honestly did try to say that we should not see each other, but whenever I attempted to dissuade her she would ignore it.'

'Did she discuss her parents with you?'

'Not really. It's hard to understand, but she didn't talk very much at all. I met her mother a few times at one or other of the parents' days. She was very glamorous and appeared to be very caring towards Amy, and the same went for her father. I met him a couple of times – it's no wonder that Amy is so beautiful as both her parents are good-looking, and her father was always charming.'

'She never implied that she was unhappy at home?'

'No, never; she said that their divorce was amicable, and that she had a lot of freedom because she could choose who she spent the weekends with. She never at any time with me hinted that there was a problem with her parents.'

Miss Polka seemed more at ease and Reid wondered if it was due to the fact that he had shown no reaction. However, when he asked if she felt that Amy was in a way controlling their 'friendship', and that if it did not continue she would expose Miss Polka's sexuality, he saw the first flicker of how she really felt.

'Yes I did, and as I said before I was in a Catch-22 situation, although it never felt as if she was blackmailing me, because she never asked me for anything.'

Eager to leave, he stood up. 'I can't promise not to reveal your lesbian relationship with Amy as it is now part of my inquiry.'

'Will you be telling Amy's parents and the school?'

He didn't answer.

'Should I resign as a teacher?'

He said nothing, refusing to tell her what to do or give her any confirmation of his intentions.

She ushered him out in her little ballet shoes, through her tiny hallway with all her paintings and pictures of herself. Glancing at them again, he noticed one of a pretty young girl with short blonde hair in her late teens; she was on a beach leaping in the air. It reminded him of Amy but obviously wasn't her.

'Is that you?' he asked, pointing to the picture.

'No, it's my younger sister when we were on our last holiday together.'

'She's very pretty. Do you get to see her often?'

'Not any more – she died six months later. Brain tumour. So sudden, it was heartbreaking.'

'I'm sorry, I didn't realize…'

'It's okay. I miss her dreadfully but have many happy memories.' She made it clear the subject was closed.

'Thank you for your time and for being open and honest with me,' Reid said as she opened the front door of her cottage.

'You know, it's a sort of relief, and if I have to leave here then so be it. I hope that I had nothing to do with her disappearance, because I do still love her.'

Deep in thought, he walked back down the path, around the various outbuildings and towards the staff car park. He bleeped open his car, placed the iPad on the passenger seat and drove out. He was just heading past the racecourse when he pulled over to the edge of the road to fully take in what he had just been told. Try as he might to form some kind of profile of the missing girl, he found it deeply depressing that nothing quite made any sense. Unless she was so abused she was reaching out for some kind of comfort – but then he had to consider the fact that she was emotionally blackmailing Miss Polka. Even if this was the case, Reid knew that as a teacher she was responsible for her actions. It mattered not whether Amy was a willing participant in the affair as she was under sixteen. In the eyes of the law she was still a child and therefore unable to give informed consent. He felt Miss Polka, as a qualified teacher, must know that she had abused a position of trust and committed the criminal offence of sexual abuse. Not only had she risked her career, but arrest and if convicted a minimum of two years' imprisonment. Even though Reid was in a quandary about what to do about Miss Polka's admissions, he felt some admiration of the fact that she had been honest with him. Knowing about the evidence taken from Marcus Fulford's flat, the Antigua video and vice squad CCTV footage, he believed that Miss Polka was telling the truth about Amy Fulford instigating their lesbian relationship and for now he would keep it to himself.

Chapter 21

It was pouring with rain by the time Reid got back to the station and he was in a foul mood. DS Lane made it worse by greeting him with the problems they'd come up against as they attempted to arrange the underwear identification at the forensic lab. Reid listened as Lane told him Marcus Fulford had agreed to be there whenever requested, but Justine Hyde, Gail Summers and two prostitutes were due later that afternoon and he couldn't be certain that things would run to schedule. Reid grunted that he didn't give a damn, he just wanted it sorted. 'When's Lena Fulford getting there?'

'Car was sent to collect her ten minutes ago,' Lane said and then in his usual jokey way asked if Miss Polka was also to be present, as he would like to see her again.

'She bats for the other side,' Jimmy Reid said to shut him up but deliberately avoided mentioning her affair with her pupil. 'You got hold of the punter driving the car yet to see what Amy did or didn't say?'

'DC Wey is going to see him as I've got to help you at the lab. He's an art dealer with a gallery in Brook Street.'

'I told you to get it sorted. I want an answer by tomorrow morning,' he barked and Lane nodded before walking off sheepishly.

As Reid drove into the car park at the lab, he could see Lena Fulford heading into the building with DC Burrows. Remembering there was a small waiting room off the main corridor leading to the examination labs, he guessed that was where they would be and as he passed the glass-fronted door he was able to see he was right. He tapped on the glass for Barbara to join him in the corridor, so he could make the suggestion she keep Mrs Fulford waiting until he had time to check out the lab himself. Barbara said Marcus Fulford had called her to say he was on his way in.

'Keep them both in there until I get back to you.'

Burrows, keen as ever to do as he asked, returned to the waiting room. Reid continued down the long corridor until he reached the double doors of lab two, and was just about to enter, when heading towards him was Lane, with two women. They were none too pleased about being there, and Lane hurriedly explained that he had made a mistake and had taken them into lab three. He introduced a Russian girl called Tanya; her companion was a well-endowed Liverpudlian in a faux fur jacket and high-heeled thigh-length boots.

'Bloody liberty this, and I'm losin' money being here,' she said in a strong Scouse accent.

Reid snapped at her that their priority was trying to trace a missing teenager. He told Lane to wait a few minutes, as he wanted to speak to the forensic scientist in charge.

''Ang on a mo, youse bizzies saying we just 'ang out in the corridor, do we?' she snapped back, hands on her hips while switching her head from side to side.

Reid drew her close by the collar of her faux fur jacket. 'I didn't get your name, sweetheart.'

'Joyce, and I ain't your sweetheart or anyone else's.'

'Just behave yourself. You're lucky not to have been arrested, so the quicker you help us the quicker you'll be out of here and back on the streets to ply your trade, so look at this as a good public relations exercise.'

Fighting to keep his temper, Reid went into the lab, where an equally belligerent scientist was tapping his wristwatch, ready to confront him.

'It's almost six and I've been on duty here since eight thirty, so I hope this is not going to be a long drawn-out game show. I have been ready since after lunch and there have been repeated phone calls back and forth to Richmond interrupting me. This is not the only case I am working on, DI Reid.'

'Sorry, you are...?'

'Andrew Bracken, filling in for Pete Jenkins who's out at a crime scene?'

'Just show me the items and we'll get on with it.'

Bracken led Reid to a trestle table where the stained ladies' underwear had been tagged and laid out. Each pair of panties was pinned to display it in an easily identifiable way.

'Okay, I believe you have two girls waiting outside. Let them come in so we can get this over and done with,' sighed Bracken. 'I will take a DNA mouth swab as well for profiling and comparison.'

'How much will that cost?' Reid asked.

'Your job, if you don't follow correct procedure. What we are doing just now is already highly irregular, but I understand your need for quick answers to assist your investigation into what has happened to Amy Fulford.'

Lane led in Joyce and Tanya.

'Okay, ladies, move along the table and if you recognize any item as belonging to you, please do not touch it but just point and state that it is yours,' Bracken said.

The ringtone of Reid's mobile began to sound and he stepped outside to take the call. It was Burrows in a state of some agitation, informing him that Marcus Fulford had joined his wife in the waiting room, Justine Hyde was due to arrive at any moment and Gail Summers was in reception. Reid attempted to calm her, suggesting that she offer them tea or coffee, and pointing out there was a vending machine near reception. He was about to go back into the lab when DC Wey appeared.

'Not missed anything, have I?'

'Stop wasting time, Takeaway – what did you get from the art dealer?'

Wey flipped open his notebook. 'The dealer, a Philip Salver, aged fifty-eight, denied ever kerb crawling, and when told he was caught on CCTV said he'd only stopped to ask directions. He'd been to a private gallery exhibition and was actually going to pick up his wife, who was dining with friends–'

'Just get to the point, for Christ's sake,' Reid said in a raised voice.

'When I suggested his wife might like to see the CCTV he changed his tune and said it was the first time he'd ever kerb crawled.' Wey rolled his eyes and continued to read from his notes. 'Salver said he drove round the block three times and because the girl never moved he assumed she was a hooker so he pulled over and stopped then–'

'Did Amy say anything?' Reid interrupted impatiently.

'According to Salver she leaned in and said, "What do you want?", and seeing how young she looked and the school uniform, he panicked and drove off.'

'So she wasn't soliciting, and didn't say any-

282

thing that intimated that was the case,' Reid remarked.

Wey shrugged his shoulders. 'That depends on how you interpret the phrase "What do you want?", plus she was standing around for a while. Looking at the video, Salver was parked up beside Amy for at least a minute, so a lot more could have been said that he won't admit to and really we can never prove.'

Before Reid could react, Lane came out of the lab with Joyce and Tanya, who had both given DNA swabs, but weren't happy about it.

Joyce took up her swaggering hands-on-hips stance. 'Bloody cheek, sticking that horrible thing in our mouths.'

'You'd think she'd be used to it in her trade,' Wey whispered to Reid, who was not amused.

'What you say, Bruce Lee?' Joyce asked.

'My name is DC Wey and I was just wondering if you recognized any of the underwear.'

'One pair, yeah, but I never left a bleedin' punter without me kecks unless he was paying for them. All I knows is some blokes offer me extra cash to keep me knickers. They're usually sickos who like to wear or sniff them.'

'Has this man ever bought any?' Reid asked, showing her a photograph of Marcus.

'Looks familiar... What's his name?'

'I'm not at liberty to say.'

'Well that's not much use, is it?'

'What about you, Tanya?' Lane asked.

'Nyet.'

Joyce laughed loudly. 'She doesn't understand or speak much English apart from hand-, blow-

or full job and cash up front.'

'Get them out of here,' Reid snapped and the girls were led off. Wey watched them walking down the corridor and couldn't help laughing at the way Joyce turned to give the finger.

'Cheeky cows,' Wey said with a grin.

'Just go into the lab and wait for me there,' said Reid with gritted teeth. He waited in the corridor as Justine Hyde was brought in from reception by Lane, after he had ordered a taxi for the belligerent tarts. Justine was carrying an overnight bag and a holdall bulging with all her hairdressing equipment. She apologized to Reid for not being available earlier, but she had been at a hairdressing event and had come straight from the station.

'I am training with the salon, you see, and so I sort of double up doin' reception work as well as being trained and it was a really good opportunity – it was all about colouring and highlights and–'

Reid interrupted her, eager to get on. 'Lane, take Miss Hyde into the lab. I'll be in the waiting room when you're finished.' As Reid moved off, he could hear Lane saying that he was sorry for the inconvenience and thanking Justine profusely for her time.

Justine followed the sergeant into the lab and he helpfully took her overnight bag and put it down, along with her holdall of rollers and dryers.

'It's very simple: we have a selection of female underwear and we are trying to identify who it belongs to. Please point but don't touch if you recognize anything belonging to you, and try to recall when it was last in your possession.'

Justine said she couldn't wear nylon, but was able to state that a pair of lace and cotton panties belonged to her, as it matched a brassiere she bought from Marks & Spencer. On being asked if she knew how the panties came to be at the flat, she said that sometimes she stayed the weekend at Marcus's and when she did she took a change of clothing, so probably left them in his room without realizing. When asked how they could have got in Amy's room, she suggested Amy might have washed and used them.

Justine agreed to a mouth swab, which made her even more nervous, but Lane was very reassuring as the forensic scientist Andrew Bracken did his work. As he placed the swab into the test tube Bracken was noticeably less irritable, now almost enjoying himself.

'Is that it?' Justine asked, and Lane smiled, picking up her case and holdall.

'Let me get you a taxi, Miss Hyde.'

She hesitated, and asked if they had found Amy, as she didn't quite understand why she had been brought in and wondered if it was something to do with her relationship with Marcus.

Lane held open the lab door, indicating for her to go ahead. 'Amy is still missing, I'm sorry to say.'

She turned to look at the trestle table.

'But I don't understand. I mean, whose are all the other things – are they Amy's? Is this to do with Marcus?'

Lane escorted her out from the lab and Wey watched the doors swing closed. As he wandered along the table, Wey realized that it wasn't funny any more – in fact it was a seedy display.

'Any more women to do a viewing?' Bracken asked Wey.

'Yes. When I worked on vice a lot of men got a kick out of keeping women's underwear and some even liked wearing it. What I mean is, could Marcus Fulford's semen have got on the underwear because he wore it?'

'Well we're not a hundred per cent sure it's his yet, but from the amount on some of the underwear he certainly spews it out – maybe he's one of those guys that jerks off into them, or withdraws before ejaculation as there was so much on the bed sheets.'

'Jesus Christ,' Wey muttered, checking his watch and wondering who was coming in next.

At that moment DS Lane entered and asked if they were ready for Gail Summers, who was in the waiting room. Suddenly they heard raised voices from the corridor and Wey opened the lab door to look, but there was no one there, though the voices were very loud and a woman was screaming. He headed towards the waiting room, and now the row was at full throttle, and when he looked through the glass panel he saw Lena Fulford attacking her husband and DC Burrows trying to step between them, but to no avail.

'You bastard, you are disgusting, and now it's bloody obvious to me just how you knew so much about my business! How could you? You know I depended on her!'

Reid, returning from the toilet, wondered what on earth was going on. Wey explained that DS Lane had put Gail Summers in the waiting room and for some reason it had all kicked off.

Reid knew why and regretted not thinking to make sure Gail and the Fulfords were kept apart. He stormed into the room and shouted, 'Enough!' at the top of his voice. Gail Summers was sobbing, while Marcus was standing in front of Lena, trying to calm her down, as she was obviously spoiling for a fight. Her fists were clenched and she was trying to move her husband out of the way to get to Gail Summers. Reid shouted again and there was silence.

'This is neither the time nor the place to have this kind of argument. Mr and Mrs Fulford, sit down and be quiet, and Miss Summers, please go with Detective Wey.'

A tearful Gail Summers was led out, as Lena sat perched on the edge of her chair. She glared at her husband.

'You really sicken me. How could you? Well let me tell you, she's lost her job – I will have her out of my office in the morning.'

Marcus just sat there not saying a word, but Lena was not about to let go and turned to Reid as if he needed an explanation.

'His nasty toad of a divorce lawyer knew everything about my business, even down to projected future earnings. I couldn't believe it and I even wondered if it could have been Amy, because it had to have been someone close to me. Now seeing that stupid bitch here it's obvious who he got the information from and she's here to see if she left her underwear at his flat. Can you for one second think how it makes me feel? He was screwing my personal assistant. I'll make you pay for this, Marcus; believe me, you will pay for doing this to me.'

Marcus glanced at Reid and then, looking away, spoke quietly but firmly. 'Well, Detective Reid, you've now had a ringside seat to see for yourself how my wife behaves; not very pleasant, is it?'

She was up and out of her seat fast, and she had Marcus by his hair and punched him. She would have got him down on the floor if Reid had not grabbed her by her shoulders and pulled her off her husband.

'Lena, stop it, STOP RIGHT NOW,' Marcus said and she caved in, putting her head in her hands and weeping. Reid instructed DC Burrows to sit between them and told them both he would not tolerate any more outbursts and they should be thinking about Amy right now and not fighting. Finally Detective Wey ventured into the room to let them know that Andrew Bracken was getting impatient and needed to leave soon.

Lena was by now somewhat calmer but there was an uneasy tone to her voice as she glared towards her husband and demanded, 'What have you done? She was our daughter, for God's sake. What have you done to her? WHERE IS AMY?'

'I'm going to take you through to the lab now, Mrs Fulford,' Reid said, taking hold of her hand to usher her out of the room,

She was pale and shaking and her hand was icy cold as she gripped his tightly. He gave a nod to DC Burrows to remain with Marcus. As they entered the lab Reid asked her to look to see what she recognized as her daughter's, and she stared dumbfounded at the array of underwear.

'Oh my God,' she whispered but moved closer, releasing his hand. She walked along the trestle table and stopped. 'These are part of her school uniform – they are my daughter's and under the tab you will see her initials as all the girls wear the same.' She had stopped shaking as she viewed the numerous panties before she paused again.

'These are mine – the silk and lace are part of a set – I hadn't even noticed they were missing; did you find them in her bedroom at the house?'

'No, these were taken from your husband's flat.'

'You mean Amy took them from my bedroom? I don't understand – why would she have done that?'

Reid made no reply but wondered if Amy had taken them to wear. He asked if Lena would have a mouth swab for her DNA to be tested for elimination purposes and she agreed.

Again he took her hand to lead a by now very subdued Lena back to the waiting room. DC Burrows was standing outside the closed door, ready with Lena's handbag and coat. Reid helped her into her coat and asked Burrows to see her to the car and accompany her home.

Lena gave a weak smile to Reid and asked him to tell her husband not to return to her house. Nodding in agreement, he remained standing in the corridor until Burrows had taken her safely out to the reception area. He then opened the door to the waiting room and gestured for Marcus Fulford to now accompany him. Slowly he got to his feet, seeming worn out as he walked down the corridor to the lab.

The fact was that as Marcus had already given his DNA they would soon know if the semen stains on the underwear were his, but nevertheless it was important for Reid to gauge his reaction to the array of stained underwear.

Marcus was embarrassed. 'You may find it distasteful, or even repugnant, that I am sexually promiscuous, but I like sex and always have, and my private life is nothing whatsoever to do with you, my wife or my daughter,' he insisted defensively. 'I have been separated for two years, I am divorcing Lena and have been under immense strain, so although it may disgust you, it was gratifying for me to prove I was not, as she so often insinuated, a total loser. I admit to sometimes wearing the panties, even masturbating when wearing them, but they were always left in a drawer in my bedroom and none ever belonged to my daughter. I have no idea how they came to be in Amy's bedroom – either Amy took them from my room or someone else put them there. I swear to God they were only like schoolboy trophies to me ... a reminder that women found me attractive and I could screw who I liked.'

Reid gave no indication of how much he disliked Marcus Fulford, nor that he thought the man's excuse for his sexual fetishes repugnant and feeble. He had an ever-growing suspicion that Marcus had abused his daughter, and furthermore he had to consider the possibility, abhorrent as the thought was, that he might also have murdered her.

Detective Wey and Reid drove back to the station.

En route, Reid asked the constable to make it a priority to double-check Marcus Fulford's alibi.

Wey looked surprised. 'It's been pretty thoroughly checked out, guv – football match all afternoon and then spent the evening and night at his girlfriend Justine's; she also verified it.'

'Have we looked at CCTV outside and inside the ground, or asked him where he sat?'

'He told me he thought he sat somewhere in the west stand. The ground holds nearly forty-two thousand spectators so it would be a bit like looking for a needle in a haystack even if we viewed all the CCTV, which could take weeks.'

'I don't care. Get it done asap.'

'Yes, sir. Do you really think he's involved?'

Reid nodded, but by now was too tired to go into details, and arriving back at the station simply said he was going home. Wey watched DI Reid drive out and then went upstairs to write up his notes of the interview with Salver. Finally, having completed them, he was on the point of leaving for home himself when he noticed DC Burrows pull up in a taxi. He waited for her to pay the fare and realized when she came over to him that she seemed ill at ease, asking if Reid was still there. Wey explained he'd taken off and he was about to do the same. She hesitated and then asked Wey if he thought she should write up her concerns about Lena Fulford.

'She was very upset on the way back from the lab; she thinks that all the stuff that was going down was because we – well DI Reid – believe Amy's dead,' she said. 'I kept on telling her that although we have not found Amy she shouldn't think like that. She became really distraught, asking me over and over why it was necessary to bring in her husband's girlfriends if we hadn't found a body. I did try to explain the reasons, but she suddenly went crazy, saying she was sure her husband had something to do with Amy's disappearance. I asked why she thought that but she had a total meltdown and was in floods of tears. I offered to stay with her, but she refused.'

'Well you can always call Reid and tell him, but you know we've all been working twenty-four seven on this and he needs a break to recharge his batteries as well.'

In fact, Reid was doing just that, running a bath and frying up eggs and bacon, having already got into his dressing gown. But before he could enjoy either the bath or the food his mobile rang. He listened to Burrows and asked her to repeat what Lena had said. Reluctantly he turned off the bath taps, put his fry-up onto a plate with a mug of tea and called Lena Fulford. The phone rang four times then went to answer machine; he tried again as he began to eat and at his third attempt Agnes Moors answered with an unusual and abrupt tone.

'Who is this?'

'It's DI Reid, just checking how Mrs Fulford is as DC Burrows said she was very distressed earlier.'

'Yes, she certainly was, but she's gone to her bedroom and I will be staying overnight to keep an eye on her. I'll call her therapist and hopefully she will come and see her in the morning.'

A starving Reid forked in his egg and bacon, and wanting to end the conversation, said he would call in the morning. It was a relief Agnes was there as the last thing he wanted was to get re-dressed, drive over to Lena Fulford's house and have to comfort her.

In her bedroom Lena's mood was spiralling down and down. Agnes had brought in a glass of warm milk and having been told in no uncertain terms to get out had placed it on the bedside table and returned to the kitchen. Harry had stayed on late, telling Agnes that it was just in case Mrs Fulford wanted to be driven anywhere, but the reality was he was interested to know what was going on.

'Do you think the detectives know something and they're not telling Mr and Mrs Fulford?'

Agnes lit a cigarette. 'Like they found a body, but don't know who it is yet?'

'Dear God, don't say that, but it's getting to be nearly a week, so it's no wonder Mrs Fulford's in such a state.'

Lena sat in front of her dressing-table mirror, wearing only her underwear, talking to herself as she robotically removed her make-up and brushed her hair. In front of her were numerous pairs of panties she had cut to shreds. She stared at her reflection as with a sharp pair of scissors she cut through the small satin bow that held the cups of her bra together. Removing it and cutting the strap, she threw the two pieces aside as she got to her feet. Next, she cut through the satin ribbon of her underwear on both sides of her hips, and now totally naked she began to wave the scissors side to

293

side. Some years before she'd used small razor-sharp nail scissors to snip nasty cuts on the inside of her thighs and around her wrists; now she used the larger pair to gouge her forearm. Moaning at the intense pain, she watched in fascination as the blood began to trickle in tiny rivulets like red tentacles, taking with it all the tension in her body and mind. After repeating the cutting action on her other arm, she lay down on her bed, closed her eyes and felt much calmer as she drifted into sleep.

Chapter 22

Reid arrived at the station early Saturday morning to work on the *Crime Night* TV appeal. DS Lane told him that Marcus Fulford had agreed to do the show and be interviewed, but he didn't know if his wife would accompany him after the fracas over Gail Summers. Reid said he would call and ask her as he also needed some video footage of Amy from her. He was checking over his reports from the previous day when his office phone rang.

'It's the front counter officer here, sir. I've got a therapist called Marjory Jordan wanting to speak to you about your investigation.'

'Thank you,' said Reid, trying not to show his surprise. 'Would you get someone to show her up to my office, please?'

Marjory Jordan was in her mid-forties, well dressed, very attractive and curvaceous, with shoulder-length highlighted blonde hair, and her make-up was rather thick, with dark red glossy lipstick. Reid registered that she was quite a forceful presence as she shook his hand, thanked him for seeing her and took a seat opposite his desk. Opening her wallet, she brought out her business card and handed it to him, before telling him that as the therapist treating Lena Fulford she was bound by the rules of client confidentiality. Reid was confused by her statement and asked why she come to see him. Miss Jordan explained that a distressed Agnes Moors had asked her to go to Mrs Fulford's house. Now, having seen and spoken with Lena, she had serious concerns and felt it was necessary to speak to him.

'I am aware of the situation regarding her daughter, so under the circumstances I was there within half an hour of receiving Mrs Moors' call.'

'Is Mrs Fulford all right?'

Miss Jordan sighed. 'Again, I have to consider my client's confidentiality, but it was very fortunate that I was able to see her so quickly.'

Reid wanted her to get to the point. If she had bothered to come and see him he knew that there was something she wanted to tell him, irrespective of client confidentiality. He asked her again if Lena was all right.

Miss Jordan took a deep breath and exhaled before continuing. 'Well, it could have been a lot worse; Lena has self-harmed before, but last night she gouged deep wounds to both her arms. Obviously the distress over her daughter, and the forthcoming divorce proceeding, brought it on as she had been well for months. I discovered Lena hasn't been taking her medication – without it her mood can swing from being very agitated one moment to severely depressed the next.'

'I know she has been diagnosed as bipolar,' he said quietly.

'Yes, but I am here to warn you that I do not think she will be able to handle the interview on the *Crime Night* show which she told me you are arranging.'

'I would obviously like her to be present, but I will be guided by your advice and thankfully her husband has agreed to take part.'

She nodded, and hesitated before asking if there had been any news of Amy's whereabouts.

'Sadly none. Did you know Amy?'

'I met her briefly a couple of times when she waited for her mother. She seemed a very calm, well-adjusted girl, very attractive and polite as well.'

'What about Marcus Fulford?'

Again she hesitated, then said Lena had first been brought to her by him as he had been given her name by another client. To understand Lena's problems it had been necessary for her to speak to Mr Fulford, who said that Lena had unpredictable mood swings that had created a lot of tension in their relationship.

Reid smiled. 'Not easy to live with?'

She shook her head. 'Not at all, and for Mr Fulford, not understanding the causes and symptoms was very distressing. It was a long road, but Lena responded well to therapy, and once we got her medication right she improved rapidly. Just as she was controlling her illness, her husband asked for a separation.'

'From what I have gathered it was purportedly a very amicable split,' Reid remarked.

'Lena may have acted as if it was, but mentally it was deeply depressing for her and I was very nearly back to square one with her treatment. However, she opened up another business, which proved to be successful, and in many ways she channelled the energy of her hyperactivity periods to good use.'

Reid had carefully made no mention that he didn't believe the separation to be amicable, both from what he had witnessed and what he now knew. Instead he asked her to tell him what she knew about Marcus Fulford.

'Well I suppose I can talk about him as he was not my client. I found him to be genuinely worried about his wife's mental state, and for him to bring her to me shows he clearly cared deeply for her. She loves him – I think she still does – and I am certain that he really and truly loved her. Before the separation he had taken a lot of abuse from Lena, and her possessiveness made his life very difficult.'

'Do you think that Lena's illness could have affected their daughter and that maybe Marcus did not work because he wanted to make sure Amy was in no danger?'

Miss Jordan wafted her hand. 'No, no, not at all, there was never any question of that. Lena is a wonderful caring doting mother, perhaps over-protective, and we had numerous sessions where I made her understand and accept that Amy should be allowed to spend quality time with her father.'

As she was talking Reid wondered if Miss Jordan had also found Marcus Fulford attractive, perhaps even having a sexual relationship with him. To give himself some time he began to rearrange the papers on his desk before he asked if he could ask her a personal question. She cocked her head to one side and gave him an open smile, saying he could ask her anything he wished as long as it was not going to cross the confidentiality barriers of her work.

'Did you have a sexual relationship with Marcus Fulford?'

She gasped and leaned forward. 'Absolutely not, though I admit he is very attractive, but there is no way I would jeopardize my position. It would be catastrophic, as my concerns are for his wife, as a patient.'

He wondered if she was being a bit too adamant, but didn't feel he could pressurize her further, as she was quite a formidable woman.

'He told me that he had been faithful, and had not had any extramarital affairs during their marriage, but was finding it very difficult to have a sexual relationship with his wife. He also told me at length about Lena self-mutilating and causing scratches and marks on her body that she covered up and even denied the existence of. He said it was making him think about his mother.'

Reid leaned forward. 'His mother?'

'Yes, and before you jump to any conclusions it was not anything sexual. He told me his mother had suffered from severe psoriasis all her life. It's a skin affliction that is very painful – the skin erupts in itchy patches that can become infected and cause weeping sores. Eventually they dry out and form scabs of dry skin. He said his mother was often covered in sores and scabs and could not bear to be touched – for him it was horrible as she would even have it in her hair and would shed her skin, and he described it as like living with a human snake.'

'So when Lena cut herself...'

'He found it repellent. He said that she used to have the softest most beautiful unblemished skin, but when she was in a manic state she hated to be touched. He also started to find it difficult to live with her, so that was really the main reason he had to leave.'

Reid leaned back, silently speculating that the large number of women Marcus was known to be involved with was more likely to be the real reason for his leaving Lena. He chose his next question carefully and asked Miss Jordan if, considering what she had just told him, there was any sexual or physical abuse of his daughter.

She considered his question and took a long time to reply. 'I cannot give you a direct or professional answer as I only had a few brief meetings with Amy. From my interaction with her father I seriously doubt that anything of a sexual nature would have been instigated or carried out by him.'

'But it's possible?'

'In my profession I have come to learn that anything is possible, Detective Reid, but I stand by my answers about Marcus Fulford.'

She picked up her briefcase and stood up. He shook her hand and walked her out of his office and down to the reception, reassuring her that he would obviously treat everything she said as confidential. When he returned to his office, Chief Superintendent Douglas was waiting to see him and slapping his thigh with a thick file.

'Morning, sir, I thought you'd be off on a Saturday,' Reid said with a smile.

Douglas had no time for pleasantries. 'What the fuck do you think you were doing at the bloody forensic lab? It was a shambles of whores and girlfriends and screaming wives. I want an explanation because I need to know just what the hell you think you are playing at!'

Reid sighed. 'I realize it all went a bit pearshaped, sir, but I was trying to save time and money on expensive forensic work.'

'Don't give me that crap. You went against normal procedure and should have informed me of what you were going to do. Whether it was naïvety and inexperience, or just plain stupidity, is debatable.'

It took Reid a considerable amount of time to calm Douglas down and explain the reasons for his actions and that they were waiting on the DNA results. By the time he had gone through all his reasons it was coming up to twelve. Douglas was still uptight and was convinced that it had been unnecessary to subject the mother of their missing girl to a confrontation with Gail Summers, a woman who had betrayed her trust, not to mention that she had slept with her husband.

'Some of the underwear belonged to her, sir, as well as to two prostitutes. Marcus Fulford also liked to wear it and masturbate.'

'Sick bastard. Was Amy stealing the panties of

these women from her father?'

'Well her father said they were kept in his room, so either Amy stole them or someone else put them in her room.'

'Why would she take women's underwear stained in semen from her father's room?'

'Only Amy knows the answer to that, but it could be connected to him abusing her. Until the profile of his and Amy's DNA comes through I've no strong evidence to really question him on.'

Douglas shook his head, flicking through one report after another. It took another three quarters of an hour as he gradually digested the amount of questionable sexual activity in the case, not only concerning the girl's father, but also the fact that Amy had been caught on CCTV trying to pick up punters. Eventually he stood up.

'You know what this tells me?'

Reid gave a quizzical look as Douglas tucked the file under his arm.

'She's simply run off and is shacked up with some bastard. Jesus Christ, I have a daughter almost the same age, but this girl is a modern-day Lolita. Plus she obviously likes to sell her body for sex.'

'We don't know that for certain, sir.'

'She's got plenty of money, her mother's loaded, so soliciting must be like some sort of hobby to her.'

Reid thought it best not to argue the point as Douglas had formed his opinion and wasn't likely to be budged on the matter.

Douglas clicked his fingers and then pointed towards Reid. 'What about that Simon Boatly character – you tracked him down yet?'

'No, sir.'

Douglas yanked open the door. 'Get on to it; my money is on him. He's close to the family, and loaded, and Amy likes the high life.'

'We believe he's still in the Bahamas, sir...'

'Believing is not the same as proving it. If he's abroad, or in this country, track him down and bring him in.'

'Yes, sir.'

'Get the parents to do the *Crime Night* appeal.'

Reid interrupted him to say that Lena Fulford was probably not going to be fit enough.

'What the hell is the matter with her? Her daughter's been missing for nearly a week, and what, she's lost interest in helping us find her?'

'I'll talk to her, but her therapist said she was very distressed.'

'Therapist, I'll be bloody needing one after this load of shit. Just see if she's capable of shedding a few tears. We need to get a result on this, Reid. At the moment it's like a steam train running out of coal.'

Douglas slammed the door shut after him and Reid slumped down onto his chair. He was loath to think like his boss, or describe the situation as preposterously, but the truth was, the more they uncovered, the more it was starting to look as if Amy Fulford had multiple reasons to disappear.

Chapter 23

The *Crime Night* producers had agreed to do the filming on the Saturday afternoon for release on the Sunday evening. The surprise was that everything went smoothly. Marjory Jordan accompanied Lena, who wore a demure dress and her hair drawn into a chignon, and looked very elegant. Marcus Fulford appeared to be more nervous than his wife as they sat apart in the waiting room. The producer had spent time with them, going over procedures and explaining there would be a short interview with them before the footage of their daughter was shown. They would then interview DI Reid, who would make the request for anyone with information to please come forward or phone the incident room.

At this, Marcus became emotional, but Lena remained downcast and silent. The only time she showed any tension was when she watched, on the screen in the waiting room, the footage she had provided them with from the family tapes. It was not the content but the fact it was so short, literally only one and a half minutes. Everyone involved, from camera crew to sound and lights, could not help but be moved by the stunning young teenager, and the director had chosen a section when Amy was on the beach smiling, and wearing the bikini, but without the sunglasses and large straw sunhat.

At one point the producer took Reid to one side, asking if there was also footage of their missing teenager taken by the vice squad. Reid curtly refused to answer but was unpleasantly taken aback that someone had leaked the fact that it existed.

Sunday evening proved to be exactly as Reid had feared. The office phones were ringing virtually nonstop from directly after the programme had aired, and he had nothing but gratitude for his dedicated team who had volunteered to work for no extra pay but a day off in lieu.

The majority of calls were a waste of time, but everything had to be checked out and logged. The programme had also brought about a new round of press interest and the station was inundated with requests for more photographs, as the journalists began to describe Amy Fulford as a Lolita because of the glamorous footage from *Crime Night.*

Reid was under mounting pressure, as all of this activity had still not brought any further leads, and so he was immensely relieved when DS Lane received a call from Simon Boatly's lawyers. They had been able to contact Boatly and confirmed that he was out of the country when Amy disappeared, but nevertheless he would be willing to speak to the investigating officers. Boatly had agreed to return to England a week ahead of his schedule, and would make himself available as soon as he arrived. They now had a new mobile phone number for him and an address in Henley where he would be staying.

It was early Monday morning when the forensic tests finally came in. There was a DNA match to Marcus Fulford from semen on the underwear belonging to Justine Hyde, Gail Summers and the prostitute Tanya. There was no DNA from Marcus on any of his daughter's panties, clothes or bed sheets. A profile from Amy had been raised from the hairbrush in the overnight bag, and matched menstrual blood and faeces on her school cotton knickers.

Reid felt it was dead end after dead end with Marcus Fulford: now there was nothing from forensics to support the idea that he was abusing Amy. Wey had also double-checked and confirmed his alibi for his movements over the weekend Amy went missing. Reid knew the evidence suggested Marcus couldn't have murdered Amy, but there was still the possibility that she might have run away because she was being sexually abused by him.

As the calls still continued to come, with many apparent time wasters, he was certain that if Amy Fulford were still alive she would have made contact. Even if Amy herself had not wished to come forward, if she were with someone who knew who she was, surely they would have been in touch. An alternative of course was that she had not run away but had been abducted by someone. If that was the case then all the publicity surrounding her disappearance might mean it was too much of a risk for an abductor to keep her alive.

Reid had spoken with Chief Superintendent Douglas who, after much deliberation, had agreed to give him one more day before calling in the murder squad. Reid protested, demanding to know why he couldn't work the case with his team, but Douglas said he wanted the case cleared up once and for all and it would be done a lot quicker by a bigger, more professional and experienced team from the murder squad.

Now Reid sat in a sullen mood, sifting through the mass of data that had been accumulated, returning to day one in his notes. The good news was that Simon Boatly was at last available and Reid decided he would drive out to speak with him later that morning.

But first he drove to the Fulford house, where Agnes had the front door open even before he'd managed to park. Harry was outside with the Lexus, waiting to take Mrs Fulford to her warehouse.

Agnes rang through to Lena's office upstairs and then showed Reid into the drawing room, pursing her lips. 'She is being a bit difficult at the moment,' she confided, 'although it's understandable in the circumstances. It's good that she found Amy's journal, as maybe it will help you find out what's happened to her.'

At that moment Lena walked in and heard what Agnes said, realizing immediately that her housekeeper had seen the journal. She had not intended to tell Reid about it, but knew she had to now. 'Thank you, Agnes, I am quite capable of informing the Inspector about the journal.'

Agnes scuttled out, shutting the door. Lena looked rested, and immaculate as ever, as she gestured for him to sit down. Waving her hand, she

306

said that she was concerned about the contents of the journal, but nevertheless if he gave his word that none of it would be made public he could have it.

'I just need to read it, Mrs Fulford, and I will return it as soon as possible.'

'I don't want any copies made. It is a very personal journal and after reading what some of the press are saying about her, describing Amy as a Lolita, it has made me feel very anxious and obviously distressed.'

He gave her a polite nod. She walked out and after a moment returned.

'Here it is,' she said, handing him a manila envelope, her name and address printed on it in red. He took it and, eager to leave, moved to pass her. She rested a hand on his arm.

'I hope you don't feel that I should not go into work, but I have to deal with finding a replacement for Gail Summers. The stupid girl has left a large consignment for John Lewis in the warehouse and it should have been delivered last week.'

'I think it is probably best to keep busy,' he said, thinking it sounded lame under the circumstances.

Her hand still on his arm, she moved closer, looking up at him, and he could see her pupils were enlarged, the dark black making her irises very blue. 'Has there been anything from the programme? I had hoped you'd call, and all the press – surely someone must know something?'

'We're still hoping, but sadly often these programmes create a lot of wasted time, with

wretched people ringing in with sick false information, but every call has to be checked out.'

'How awful that people use such heartbreak to
concoct lies.'

He felt uneasy with her being so close and her
hand on his arm was awkward. Eventually he
gently patted it. 'Don't give up hope, Mrs Fulford;
maybe we will get a call from someone that has
seen her or knows where she may be.'

'Oh I hope so, the house feels so empty all the
time, and I miss her – I cry myself to sleep because it's been over a week now. Have you ever
had a case where a missing girl has been gone for
so long?'

She finally moved her hand from his arm, and
he lied, telling her that often it had been many
months. She held the door open for him and he
could not bring himself to say that a murder
team would be brought in to review the case, as
hope was fading for her daughter to be found
alive. He didn't want to admit it, even to himself,
but for no one to have seen or talked to Amy
since that Saturday afternoon compounded his
worst fears that she was dead.

As he left the house Reid gave a brief nod to
Harry, who was standing by the Lexus waiting
for Lena. Harry was increasingly nervous about
the watch he had found in Marcus's car, as his
intention to sell it had faltered after the press
release and his unwelcome discovery that it had
Amy's name engraved on it. It was still hidden in
a drawer at his home. A Cartier watch would
have been a nice little earner, but he was starting
to think he should toss it into a skip and get rid

of it.

Reid did not open the envelope containing the journal, but drove straight to Henley-on-Thames, feeding into the sat nav the address he'd been given, which was just outside the quaint Thames-side town. He drove along small country lanes, until he branched off into rather a substantial drive with big open gates. The Old Manor was a very elegant two-storey sprawling property with a vast garden and sweeping lawns down to the river at the rear. He drew up outside the white stone steps, which led to a large studded double door with a magnificent stone urn on either side. As he got out of the car a girl on a horse appeared from round the side of a barn and pulled up on the reins.

'What do you want?' she asked.

He was about to take out his ID when the front door swung open and a huge dog that looked like a cross between a wolfhound and an Akita hurtled out. It almost knocked Reid off his feet as it bounded on towards the horse and rider.

'Wally, just behave ... WALLY!' the girl shrieked.

She wheeled the horse round as the dog barked and bounded alongside them. A suntanned man wearing a padded velvet dressing gown and slippers appeared at the door and Reid instantly recognized him from photographs at the flat in Mayfair.

'Mr Boatly, I am Detective Inspector Victor Reid.'

'Sorry about the dog – totally untrained and an

absolute pest. I've not been able to take him for a walk yet so he's a bit boisterous,' the man said. 'Come on in, sir, and please excuse the apparel as I intended to get dressed, but I didn't think you would get here so soon.'

Simon Boatly was at least six feet two, slender, and his hair was bleached blond, while his suntan gave him a rather heavily lined face, with his teeth made whiter than white. He slithered along the polished wooden floor in Moroccan slippers, his ankles a deep tan, and he was obviously naked beneath the velvet dressing gown. It was old-fashioned, worn in places, with a threadbare satin collar, and the sash was frayed at the ends.

'Right, let's get you settled and I'll put some pants on. Go on into the drawing room, help yourself to a drink and I won't be more than a minute.'

Reid looked round the vast room; massive sofas and easy chairs almost as worn as the velvet dressing gown were dotted around a big stone fireplace. The grate was full of charred logs and cinders, dirty wine glasses were left on an assortment of coffee tables and a grand piano was draped in a Spanish embroidered shawl, the fringe puddling onto the floor. Oil paintings were hung in profusion, cups and plaques arranged on various sideboards, and above the fire mantel was a large gold-framed mirror with invitations stuck to the frame and propped up along the marble shelf.

The scattered Persian rugs were threadbare, with frayed edges, and badly stained. Reid eased himself onto a sofa, but then got up as he felt himself to be too low down. He eventually attempted to sit on a large Carver chair, but most of the wicker seat had fallen out. The arms were embellished with wolf heads and were worn to a paler colour of wood than the rest of the chair. The room had a similar feel to the flat in Green Street – old-fashioned, full of antiques and no sign of anyone taking care of it; even the windows were grimy and the draped curtains a pale washed-out green velvet.

It was rather longer than a minute, more like ten, before Simon Boatly returned, now wearing cord slacks and a pale blue pullover, which enhanced his cornflower-blue eyes. He was a very handsome man but with an air of decadence, and a very easy-going manner as he slouched onto the sofa. He had a silk handkerchief that he wafted about, informing Reid it was dabbed in Olbas Oil as, since he got off the plane, he'd felt as if he had combination of jet lag and the onset of flu.

'I obviously agreed to see you as I am shocked to hear about Amy; first thing I did was call poor old Marcus – he's devastated, and it is really not a good sign for her to have been missing for so many days.' He sniffed with the handkerchief covering his nose. 'Don't suppose there's any news?' He leaned forward. 'Obviously not or I don't suppose you would be interested in meeting me, but I can't for the life of me think if I can give you any kind of insight as to where she might have run off to, or who she might have run off with.'

Reid said nothing, but took out his notebook and flicked it open.

'How well do you know Amy Fulford?'

'I wouldn't even claim to know her. I've met

her of course as me and Marcus are old mates; we go back a long way and he rents my pad in Green Street. This place used to belong to the same aunt – if it smells musty to you it's because it's been locked up while I am away. I've just got this elderly local biddy to clean and dust, not that I think looking around she's very diligent; maybe I've got an allergy to dust and not the flu bug that's apparently going the rounds.'

'Did you entertain local prostitutes in the Green Street property?'

'Wow, that is a bit on the nail, isn't it? I may have done in the past, but I was left that place when I was a youngster. Did you know that one can even get a thing called "Gentleman's Navigator" for a mobile phone? It can be used in major cities around the world to locate escort girls, strip clubs and even brothels, along with pictures, reviews and the going rate for sex ... or any kind of erotic pleasure you may desire,' he said with a smug smile.

'No I didn't,' Reid replied tersely.

'I used to be a bit of a Jack the Lad, but I can't say that I have the same active libido, and doing the work that I do gives me a steady supply of lovely models.'

Reid made no notes but he found Mr Boatly a bit over-eager to depict himself as some modern-day Errol Flynn, and the longer and more closely he watched him and listened to the droll upper-class voice, the less he liked him. He constantly flicked at his blond hair, or sniffed at the Olbas Oil on his handkerchief; he still wore no socks and his slippers hung loosely on his tanned feet.

'How did you get on with Lena Fulford?' he asked quietly.

'Well I honestly felt that old Marcus had got lucky – not only was she a beauty but a very keen businesswoman. I mean, he's hopeless, one job after another. I know he had a sort of goodish job when they married, designer for a wealthy boat yard, or let's say the customers were wealthy. He would design very elegant interiors, but then I think he sort of had his work cut out as Lovely Lena was quite a handful. I know she never liked me, in many ways she was jealous of our friend-ship, but it turned out to be more of a mental thing.' He twisted a finger at his temple.

'You met them in Antigua?' Reid asked.

'Good God, yes I did, two or more years ago, I think. I was on the yacht and visiting friends who were staying at the wonderful Carlisle Hotel. They don't have water-skiing facilities, and my chaps and I were told not to use their bay, so we were going to move further along the coast and ski there. The yacht had a speedboat on board with jet skis, plus staff, chef and crew.'

'Did you know the Fulfords were staying at the hotel?'

'I think I had it lodged somewhere in the brain cells, but it was sort of a coincidence really.'

'You met Amy there?'

'Yes I did; we all had lunch and Lena was a bit tetchy as usual. Thing is, you never know with her – sometimes she's all warmth and smiles, next minute she's quite nasty, and she refused to allow Amy to come on board the speedboat when I offered to take her water-skiing.'

'How did Amy react?'

'Just accepted it, no argument. I think she knew not to start one up with Lena – she's a very intelligent girl, quiet, sort of watchful, as if she's an arbitrator between them; anyway, I rejoined my pals and left. I think that is possibly the last time I saw Amy.'

'She's never been in touch with you?'

'Heavens no, and when Marcus mentioned he needed a place it coincided with me getting the photo gig abroad, so I let him rent my old pad.'

'You were never there when Amy spent the weekend with her father?'

'Not that I recall; I've been skipping all over the place and the rent and stuff is handled by my lawyers. I think he's a bit behind actually, but it doesn't really worry me. I have this place for when I'm back in the country.'

Reid spoke quietly as he explained that he was concerned about the amount of pornography discovered in the Green Street flat. Boatly shrugged.

'Well it could be my old magazines and videos? As I said, I was a bit of a lad. My parents died in a plane crash when I was fifteen and my aunt was my guardian. She was my father's sister and not like some old doddery spinster but at one time had been a great beauty, married a couple of times, and was rather naughty, very theatrical. I doubt she had ever cooked a meal in her life, but she could drink, she had hollow legs as the expression goes. The reality was the flat originally belonged to my grandmother, who left it to Aunt Katherine with the stipulation that it passed to me eventually. Poor Katherine ploughed through her own inheritance and I think she even gambled away any money left by her husbands. I would say that she was not the most reliable person to act as a guardian – in fact some of her conquests were not that much older than myself; she'd never use the expression "toy boys", but she had quite a sexual appetite for virile young men. I was still at boarding school so only came under her unwatchful eyes during the holidays.'

Reid was becoming impatient, and not quite sure why Boatly had gone into such detail regarding his aunt. He was about to ask more questions about the pornography when Boatly swung his legs down from the sofa and laughed.

'I admit I was going through all the teenage sexual fantasies, but what happened was not intentional,' he said and laughed again before continuing. 'I was hammering in a nail to hang up a framed picture of some bimbo or other and it went straight through the plaster wall. It's not obviously something I like to admit but it became my peephole into Aunt Katherine's bedroom. I'd wank myself stupid watching her with legs akimbo being screwed by some waiter or other young man she'd picked up. Sadly her prowess with them didn't last as she became such an alcoholic that the trustees felt her to be unsuitable as my guardian. They wanted to get some other distant relative to monitor me, but I'd just turned eighteen and had access to my inheritance, so I refused to accept anyone else and she was carted off to some hospice where she eventually died.'

'Did Marcus Fulford stay with you at your flat in Green Street on a regular basis?'

'Yes, very often, but that was before he married Lena. The place was only used infrequently as I went to Oxford and then would live here during my vacations.'

'Did Amy stay here?'

Boatly frowned, and said she had on a couple of occasions as she used to ride at the local stables.

'Who was the girl riding the horse when I arrived?'

'Oh, she's my neighbour's daughter; they use one of the outbuildings to stable her horse, and she's quite a little madam. They also look after Wally – well, he's more their pet than mine, but when I'm here he stays with me.'

There was a pause as Reid made a couple of notes before closing his notebook. Boatly, thinking the interview was over, stood up, but Reid asked if he could recall the dates when Amy stayed.

'Christ, I don't know off-hand, but it would have been a good few years ago. Perhaps Marcus could give you a better time frame. She was always very quiet and well behaved and a very accomplished rider – and I think did some equestrian shows.'

Reid detected that Boatly was becoming irritated; his right foot tapped the floor and he stuffed his hands into his trouser pockets.

'Look, Detective Reid, I am obviously intelligent enough to know where your questions are leading. My neighbours' daughter is eleven, and very annoying, I have no interaction with her. Amy was my best friend's daughter, and I have not and never had any interest in pubescent females. As you know, I was abroad when Amy went missing, and I have been open and honest about my relationship with her and her mother, but Marcus was my only reason for knowing them. We have been friends for many years, dating back to our Oxford days, though Marcus was at the polytechnic. He was from a middle-class family without much money, and I had my inheritance, but it never created any friction between us. He eventually married Lena, but I still care for him and enjoy meeting up with him occasionally, on a one-to-one basis. I don't like his wife and she has made it obvious that she does not like me and I think she was always envious of our friendship. I thought his daughter was lovely, but your implication that there was something more between us is abhorrent and distressing to me. I feel great compassion for what Marcus and Lena must be going through and hope their daughter will be found; at the same time I am aware of how long she's been missing and I realize the outcome may be tragic. As a friend I will endeavour to be supportive because I know how much Marcus loves Amy and what a good father he is.'

Driving back to London, Reid mulled over the interview. Although he had no evidence to suggest the handsome and suntanned Simon Boatly was involved in Amy's disappearance, he could not allay his suspicions. He wondered if the nail-causing-the-peephole story was a lie fabricated in collusion with Marcus to cover up something more sinister. However, the look of gratification on Boatly's face as he spoke about it suggested there was some substance behind the admission.

Although he knew Boatly was not even in the country when Amy disappeared, he could have been involved in some previous sexual abuse of Amy, maybe even with Marcus present.

Boatly had returned to bed, certain he was coming down with some flu bug as he kept on sneezing and his head ached. He was dabbing more Olbas Oil onto his handkerchief when the bedside phone rang. It was Marcus, asking if everything went all right with the meeting.

'Yes, everything that needed to be was said, I think; there was no need to even mention it. He might want to know when you came to stay with Amy because I couldn't remember; it was when she was horse-mad, but it sort of makes me pissed off.'

'So you never brought it up?'

'I just said so, didn't I, and I'm sorry if I sound a bit tetchy but I feel horrific, like I'm coming down with flu or something. The fucking woman who's supposed to clean the place seems to have done no dusting at all so I might have some allergy, unless it's the bloody dog hairs.'

'Listen, thanks, I really appreciate it, and I'm sorry about the rent not being paid.'

'Oh for God's sake, forget it, you've enough to worry about.'

'Thank you. Obviously the divorce is sort of on a back burner at the moment, but as soon as that's finalized I'll repay you and you know how grateful I am about you funding Jacob Lyons.'

'Let's meet up for dinner. I'll call you when I'm next in town.'

'Right, look forward to seeing you. Bye for now.'

Boatly hung up and sniffed the handkerchief, lying back on the pillow as Grant walked in with a hot lemon and ginger drink. He was as sun-tanned as Boatly, with long hair tied back in a ponytail, wearing torn jeans and an expensive shirt in heavy linen.

'I heard him leaving, thought it best not to be visible. Do you want me to make you some lunch?'

'No, I feel terrible. Can you get me some aspirin and I'll try and have a sandwich or something later.'

Grant put down the mug and went to a drawer in the dressing table, rooted around and took out a bottle of aspirin. 'Here you go, Simon. I'll be cleaning up downstairs, and then doing a grocery shop, so if there's anything you feel like eating I'll bring it back.'

'Thank you; maybe some pasta – nothing too heavy – or spinach soup, get a load in, as I am sure I'm coming down with something, and we need bread and cheese.'

'Yeah, yeah, I've made out a list. Drink up and take the aspirin and I won't be too long.'

Boatly held out his hand. 'What would I do without you, darling one?'

Grant laughed and picked up Boatly's wallet. 'Can I drive the Porsche?'

'Yes, but for God's sake be careful, you've only just passed your driving test.'

Grant opened the wallet and removed two fifty-pound notes, wafting them towards Boatly who was taking his aspirin and sipping at the hot drink. 'See you in a while. Maybe get some more wine as you had a skinful last night.'

'Whatever,' Boatly said, sighing and closing his eyes.

He thought to himself that he was not going to stay much longer in England and wouldn't mind selling up the house and the flat and never returning. The sound of his Porsche being revved up as if at Goodwood irritated him. He got up and crossed to the window as Grant drove out far too fast. The wretched girl from his neighbours' was riding across the lawn, Wally bounding after her. He tried to open the window to reprimand her – not that the lawn was in pristine condition, it was the fact she had been told to keep off his property. But the window was stuck firm and he slapped the frame with the flat of his hand. He was even more annoyed as he saw Wally taking a crap and scratching at the grass, sending turf flying. 'Fucking dog,' he muttered as the horse jumped over a small row of bushes and the girl whooped and hollered. It was then that he recalled how he had been standing at the same window – how many years ago? Maybe two or three? Amy slapping her thigh with her riding crop and wearing her riding hat, hacking jacket, white shirt and a cravat, jodhpurs and black polished boots.

'Daddy, Daddy, are you coming to watch me jump, Daddy!'

Boatly had turned to Marcus, who was naked and sprawled across his bed. They had both got very drunk the previous evening, and he had to nudge him awake.

'Amy's waiting for you,' he had said.

Marcus roused himself and had an obvious

hangover. 'Bugger! 'What time is it?'

It was eight o'clock, and Marcus had been too drunk to return to his own bedroom the night before. He grabbed a dressing gown and stumbled to the window, but even back then it was stuck firm. He hurried from the room and somehow managed to pull on his trousers and a sweater. Boatly followed him downstairs and laughed as he watched from the doorway as Marcus hopped barefoot over the gravel towards Amy.

He remembered she was very angry, shouting and swiping at him with her riding crop. 'You said you would be at the stables to ride with me and I've been waiting ages. I have to have a practice before the fete this afternoon.'

Marcus had apologized and said he'd overslept. He promised he would join her and ride out to the fields to watch her jumping. He ran back over to the house, shouting as he went.

'Simon, SIMON, can I borrow a pair of your boots?'

Boatly smiled as his mind returned to the present and he went and lay back down on his bed. He remembered thinking that Amy was a right little madam; if she'd swished her riding crop a little closer she'd have slashed her father's face. Marcus had burst into the bedroom, asking again if he could use a pair of Simon's riding boots. Boatly had gestured to his wardrobe and said there was a pair in there or a pair of old ones by the back kitchen door. Marcus had sat on the bed, pulling on the black leather boots; they were too large and he had to tuck his trousers inside them.

'Christ, this could be embarrassing. I hate bloody horses. What's the one I rode out on once with you?'

'It's an old police horse – they use him for children with special needs. He's called Puddle; he might not get up the energy for a trot but he won't throw you off.'

'Fuck off, I am going to look a right arsehole.' Marcus stamped his feet in the boots.

It was strange to remember it all so clearly after such a long time. Whether or not it was due to Detective Reid asking when Amy had stayed, or seeing the annoying girl on her horse, he wasn't sure. He remembered when they both returned from the ride and the outcome had made him laugh until he ached. Marcus, covered in mud, described Puddle's slow ponderous walk and how it had left him far behind Amy.

Suddenly confronted by a thick thistle bush, Puddle was spooked and took off at a gallop. Amy described the way she had first been impressed as her dad sped past her – she didn't think Daddy could gallop so well – but then seeing him hurtling through the air headfirst into the ditch had made her hysterical.

Boatly remembered they were all sitting at the kitchen table, with a bowl of hot water and Dettol; Amy dipping in a wad of cotton wool to clean a nasty scrape on the side of Marcus's face. Her cheeks were flushed, her blonde silky hair falling around her shoulders, and she had loosened the cravat of her shirt. Tall and boyishly slender, she tenderly washed out the graze. Boatly recalled how envious he had felt, her adoration and sweetness touching him, because he knew he would never experience that kind of affection from a child of his own. He also remembered just how beautiful she had become when he had seen her on the beach in Antigua, the tiny bikini showing off her perfect pubescent figure. The way she had lowered her sunglasses to look at him, it had felt provocative; even the way she had sipped her fruit-filled glass with a straw had not been like a young teenager. But similar to the way Lena had behaved towards him when they had first met.

When Lena had refused to allow her daughter to go water-skiing, Amy had given him a knowing glance and a shrug of her shoulders. He left after lunch to join his friends on the waiting speed-boat, and when he turned back, she had been waving and smiling. 'Bye-bye, Simon,' she had called out. That was the last time he had seen her, and now it really saddened him that she was missing, but there was also a niggling unease that perhaps Marcus might have had something to do with it. He hoped that he had not, but at the same time it had registered with him that their affection towards each other was very intimate.

Simon suspected Marcus must have persuaded Amy not to tell Lena about staying at the Old Manor as she did not approve of their friendship and would have refused to allow Amy to stay there. They had slept together in the guest bedroom, and Marcus had come through to his room when Amy was asleep. Boatly now found himself wondering if there was something beyond the doting father image that Marcus portrayed. His mind was made up in an instant:

he would sell the flat and distance himself from Marcus, as he didn't want any possibility of becoming embroiled in the police investigation.

Chapter 24

The station was not exactly a hive of activity when Reid returned to type up his report. There were however two phone calls that had generated possible leads. A man had stated that he was certain that he saw Amy Fulford on the afternoon of her disappearance standing by a car on the corner of Fulham Road. He was unable to give any registration number but thought the car might have been a Jaguar and was a grey or silver colour. The occupant was a middle-aged man but he was unable to give a description and said that Amy had got into the car and it drove off. He only recalled the incident after watching the *Crime Night* programme and seeing the video of Amy. Reid sent DC Wey to interview the caller.

DS Lane had also been checking into a second possible sighting, this time from a woman. She was certain she had seen Amy in the Marble Arch underpass heading towards Park Lane. Again she had remembered the incident because of the TV programme, and that Amy had stopped by a street musician playing a guitar and was talking to him while tossing some coins into the boy's guitar case.

Reid decided he would take off home and spend the evening reading through the journal Lena Fulford had given him. He wanted to preserve it for fingerprints and get it over to the lab the next day, so he put on a pair of protective gloves. Opening the envelope, he found that the leather-bound journal had a second envelope tucked inside. This was some birthday cards, and a note, plus a list of items for Christmas gifts. The card had large looped writing in a blue felt tip pen and from what was written it seemed to be the most recent card Lena received from Amy.

To my darling Mummy, have a wonderful birthday and I hope you like my present. It is obviously not as perfect and as expensive as my gorgeous Cartier watch, but it is by Cartier and it is I think very elegant and writes smoothly and is something you can use signing cheques. Haw, haw! From your adoring daughter Amy.

Reid put the card to one side and opened a small square of pink notepaper with tiny pink flowers at the corners.

Dearest Mummy, I cannot thank you enough for buying me exactly what I wanted. I love my watch, and it is the exact one I showed to you ages and ages ago, and I love you for remembering. Amy.

Reid next read a list written in the same large looped handwriting. It was a list of items including shoes, a Mulberry handbag, and an expensive brand of chocolates. Lena had enclosed on her

business card a handwritten note that was underlined.

Please look at these examples of Amy's handwriting.
They are quite recent, and I kept them to have an idea
of what Christmas gifts I should buy her. LF.

He neatly placed the notes together before he
opened the first page of the journal. Here the
handwriting was small, tight, and very different,
with hardly a break between the words, and each
line cramped up close to the next. He flicked
through numerous pages like a pack of cards but
not as yet reading. The pen had changed; there
was a variety of colours, sometimes in biro, sometimes in fountain-pen ink or felt tip. He noticed
that occasionally the handwriting slanted to the
right and then at times to the left. Other times it
was so closely written and so small that it was
difficult to read, but what surprised him, and it
must also have been confusing for Lena, was that
there was no thick looped script on any page as in
the writing on the birthday card and list.

He took out his notebook, and made a comment
about the note, the card and the gift list. He then
turned to read page one.

Permission granted to insert or rewrite for all selected
subjects.

He surpassed his usual tedious self and as a tormentor
continues to play the bountiful but the strings attached
place him high on the list. It must be determined
whether or not he deserves the ultimate punishment,

and perhaps trials should be conducted before the final decision is made. Access to both establishments is now completed, which enables the substances to be planted. Owing to neither subject being aware where the weekend is spent gives considerable freedom, but this must be carefully orchestrated. Movements are restricted due to the stupid bitch hiring a domestic slave that monitors everything but she is not on duty during weekends.

She has certainly surpassed herself hiring this bitch. A is obviously a woman with severe controlling impulses; she cannot stand to see anything that is not in a straight line. She cannot stand to have anything in its original container or package, but transfers everything into plastic boxes and then writes on them with a thick black felt tip pen in old-fashioned lettering. This will include cornflakes and sugar, flour etc. My abhorrence of this woman is such that I have told her never to enter the bedroom. I place hairs across the drawers so that I am aware when she had been sneaking in and nosing around. Her ugliness, her bad teeth repel me to such an extent I have decided that I might attempt to try out a couple of things on her before anyone else. She has square fingernails, stumpy nasty hands and a wide arse and feet in stinking tennis shoes, but worse than her hideous appearance is her ingratiating manner. She is a character worthy of a Dickens novel and I know she hates me. She is so envious of me, of everything I have, that she can hardly bear to look at me with her watery brown bloodshot eyes. The envy is down to the fact she has never had anything of worth in her flatulent tedious existence and she gave birth to an equally wretched creature that quite obviously loathes her and attempts to keep her at a distance. This creature is squint-eyed and has bitten stumpy fingernails, and gives me the shivers as she is forced to have this dragon visit her every week-end. All she talks about is her tedious boring past, her abusive husband, divorced for fifteen years and she still can't stop talking about him. She wishes he was dead and buried but she will be gone before him. I guarantee that. It is just a question of exactly how to get rid of her without it becoming suspicious.

Reid sighed before turning over to the next page and continuing.

She has now acquired a driver, an ex-con, a small despicable little house-breaker who wears second-hand clothes that smell of mothballs and stale cologne. H thinks himself so dapper but he's insidious and creepy, especially around her, and I would not trust him an inch. His sidelong glances to me, my breasts, my cunt, make me loathe to ever be in the car with him. He probably smells my seat after I've got out, he's that repellent, and yet she puts up with him. A and the midget get along when they think she's out, and if only on occasion she would check her groceries because the pair of them are thieving bagloads of food. M of the 'Good morning, Fulford residence, how can I help you?', when in reality she would like to say, 'This is MY house, it's MY residence.' Her envy is constantly glittering in her oddly shaped button eyes, and she knows that I know and so she will hardly ever look me in the face.

Reid turned over the next four pages, which were all filled with strong dark drawings. There were disturbing grotesque figures and faces, all done in black felt tip pen or black ink. He

328

skimmed over them before continuing.

H needs to be got rid of but that should be easy as once a thief always a thief. I will place something tempting for him to be unable to keep his wretched fingers from stealing. One of her diamonds would be good, but she is so lax about security and insurance and constantly out of it mentally that she might not even notice it missing. If this was to occur I could query where the diamond was, but then H could have time to replace it. I think the same choice of endings would be advisable. They both steal food... Carefully does it, one at a time, as there must be no suspicion.

Reid noticed that the handwriting now took on a totally different style, reverting to printed letters with spaces and dashes. He flicked over a few more pages.

Symptoms can vary, including slight gastrointestinal discomfort, and in some cases they can contain a toxin, which can stimulate the immune system to attack its own red blood cells. Angel wing mushrooms can create acute brain disorder, and attack kidney function.
1. Amanita muscaria – dried and consumed it can be psychoactive...V good.
2. Amanita pantherina (panthercap mushroom) – associated with more fatalities than muscaria.
3. Chlorophyllum molybdites (green-gilled) – intense gastrointestinal upset.

After reading such nasty vitriol Reid wondered why passages of the journal now turned into a biology lesson about mushrooms and their effects. He noticed the entry about the *Amanita muscaria* was repeatedly underlined and assumed the 'psychoactive V. good' meant very good as a drug. He'd heard of 'magic mushrooms' and their hallucinogenic effects, and now wondered if Amy had tried them and the entries about fatal or stomach-upsetting mushrooms were an indication of the ones to avoid collecting in woodland. He read on:

The more unusual toxin is coprine, a compound which is harmless unless ingested within a few days of drinking alcohol, as it inhibits an enzyme required for breaking down alcohol. Once ingested the person will feel as if he suffers from a hangover, flushing, headaches, nausea, palpitations and trouble breathing...

Reid shook his head; there was page after page about mushrooms and their side effects, some passages underlined and some with ticks or stars beside them. Also listed was how long it took for the symptoms to begin to show, and there were initials in minuscule writing beside some timings. The onset of the effects mostly took anywhere between four to eleven hours but in some cases as long as two to twenty days.

He started to flick through the mass of data on mushrooms. It could have been for some kind of biology test, but it nevertheless unsettled him. He got up and fetched a large Scotch and ice before he could face any more of the journal. There were further lengthy pages of hatred referring to 'A', 'M' and 'H' and Reid was pretty sure from the content that 'A' and 'M' were both

Agnes and 'H' obviously Harry. One page was a detailed list of how many times Agnes had been searching the bedroom. This was discovered thanks to the fine strand of hair placed over each drawer revealing it had been opened.

He noted that there was never a direct reference to the author. It was always 'she' this and 'she' that, and from the different styles of handwriting it appeared as if a number of people had been involved in composing the journal. He was however beginning to understand why Lena Fulford had not felt it would assist in discovering where or with whom Amy might have run away. No locations were mentioned. He continued to skim-read until he came to an entry about 'S'. The clue was in the description, which indicated it was about Serena Newman. It was a lengthy vicious attack on her so-called friend, whom she labelled as nothing but an envious acquaintance. The method of using the anonymous website to blacken her name and reputation was described in detail and there was obvious intention to repay 'S' for lying.

What shocked him next were the overtly sexual paragraphs concerning the lesbian activities, but these were written in such a way it could be confusing, unless you were aware of Miss Polka's Christian name, Jo. Paragraph after paragraph in the same minuscule writing described how Jo had become so enamoured and obsessed with silken skin, licking and sucking every inch of perfection in an attempt to gain an arousal, but all it had done was sicken and repulse her. The 'Watcher' was underlined, and yet again there was a lengthy description of how being a 'Watcher' had taught her that there could be satisfaction in observing someone obsessed with touching perfect unblemished skin.

Reid thought about the peephole in Amy's bedroom at the flat in Green Street. Was Amy referring to this, and was she in actual fact the 'Watcher'? He put the journal to one side and got a refill, this time adding water to his Scotch, and some ice. It was almost twelve and he felt tired out, but if he was correct then he needed to persist, despite it becoming emotionally exhausting.

The 'Watcher' began describing anal sex as the preferred position of subject 'F', stripped naked and using dildos, but rarely if ever ejaculating into his partner's vagina, preferring the whore's arse. Reid felt like hurling the journal across the room, but if as he suspected subject 'F' was in actual fact Marcus Fulford then it was clear Amy was the Watcher and using the peephole to look into Marcus's bedroom. He knew he had to continue to read the nasty descriptions of anal sex and copulation to learn more about Amy's state of mind.

Page after page gave intimate details of women's bodies, and how the 'Watcher' had found gratification by masturbation. It became so repetitive that he flicked over page after page until he came to subject 'L' and wondered if it was about Lena Fulford.

Reid saw that yet again there was a noticeable change in the style of handwriting. 'L' was described as frigid, mentally unstable, a self-harming yet brilliant person who was self-obsessed and needed to be loved, but was incapable of loving because of her warped jealous nature. 'L' was unable to give up her lust for material wealth and success; she was narrow and blinkered about everything and everyone around her. The writer described how 'she' had been able to exist by becoming invisible, and even breathing had to be hardy detectable as the monster could be so destructive. The writer now referred to the 'Watcher' as if it were someone she knew and had spoken with. She wrote that the 'Watcher' was now able to release its inhibitions and delight in filth and pornography, enjoying stinking and smelling and wearing the vile garments of the whores.

Reid flicked through the rest of the journal to see how much he had left to read. He noticed to his surprise that the back pages were full of lists of recipes, ingredients and cooking instructions for dishes like spaghetti bolognese, risotto and chilli con carne, and laughed to himself that a journal full of vile language and hatred could also contain some simple home-cooking and methods for packing and freezing home-cooked meals.

He still had about half the journal to finish, but he had read enough, so snapped it closed, put it in an evidence bag and removed the protective gloves he'd been wearing. He drained his glass and went for a shower and then to bed. It was, he felt, no real clue as to where Amy Fulford was, but it did give an insight into someone who he felt was a very disturbed young woman.

Tuesday, day ten, and Reid was in his office early. Tech Support had opened Amy Fulford's iPad

333

and it contained some anonymous and unpleasant Facebook comments and emails that showed Amy was being cyberbullied. Although this could be another reason for her running away, the iPad gave no clue of where she might have gone. All the emails and Facebook comments would be checked to try and trace the sender and/or point of origin, but it would be difficult if not impossible if fake IP addresses had been used.

DS Lane was still trying to trace the street musician, but as yet had no luck. DC Wey had spoken with the man who said he saw Amy getting into a Jaguar on the corner of Fulham Road and having visited the spot was able to establish it was a local resident picking up his daughter. The press were still showing the same photographs but interest was dwindling as there was no new information. Reid had a meeting with Chief Superintendent Douglas, and as suspected was told that thanks to the lack of new developments his time was up and the murder squad would take over.

'I've read Amy Fulford's journal and sadly I can see no clues that divulge her whereabouts, but there are disturbing entries that I'd like an expert to look at,' Reid informed Douglas.

'What sort of expert?'

'A forensic behavioural investigator and/or a forensic psychiatrist to analyse the content in respect of Amy's state of mind.'

Douglas was hesitant. 'I don't really see how it will help and apart from that my experience is that those kinds of experts charge a fortune for their time.'

'Marjory Jordan, Lena Fulford's therapist, might have a look at it as a favour and do it for nothing.'

'I have no problem with that course of action,' Douglas said and left the room.

Reid rang Miss Jordan. She was very pleasant and more than happy to help and give her professional opinion of whether or not it as a valid document to assist in tracing Amy. She was true to her word and arrived at the station within the hour.

Reid handed her a photocopy of the journal.

'I'm having the original examined for fingerprints and I must ask that your examination is kept between the two of us as Lena Fulford is very worried about it being read by others and didn't even want copies made.'

Miss Jordan smiled. 'Of course, I totally understand under the circumstances. In essence you are a client so the principles of confidentiality apply and if I can help find Amy then all the better.'

'I feel rude asking this, but I'm up against the wall with my boss and extra money for my investigation...'

'I'm happy to do this as a favour to you and, although they won't be aware, the Fulfords as well.'

'I really am very grateful and–'

'However, if I find anything that would betray my patient confidentiality with Lena Fulford I will be unable to detail this in an official report. In fact it may be best if my findings are off the record so as to protect both of us.'

'Whatever you feel is best,' Reid said, knowing

he was in a position where he had no choice other than to agree with Marjory Jordan.

Chief Superintendent Douglas met with all the team at two o'clock. He praised them for their diligent work but at the same time it was obvious that without any further clues to the whereabouts of Amy Fulford, and with her now being missing for ten days, the case had to be taken over by the murder squad. He told them to complete all their actions and reports as soon as possible for the handover.

Gloomily DI Reid gathered up all his notes, paperwork and files for the handover. He looked up to see that Douglas had come into his office.

'Why so glum, Victor?'

'To be perfectly frank, sir, I'm really disappointed not to have been asked to remain on the case. I've worked long hard hours, know the investigation inside out and although I understand your reasons it–'

Douglas snorted as he interrupted. 'Cut the self-pity, Reid. I've spoken personally to the commander in charge of Homicide and Serious Crime, who has given clearance for you to remain on the case.'

'Really? I'm honoured that he thinks so highly of me.'

'It's not down to your investigative abilities, but simply because you're close to the Fulfords and know them better than anyone else. The experienced detectives on the murder squad may go about their investigation in a very different manner so watch, listen and learn.'

'Thank you, sir, I won't let you down. Who's taking over the investigation?'

Douglas hesitated, glanced at a piece of paper in his hand and rubbed his chin. 'It's a DCI Barry Jackson. By all accounts very experienced, a tough bastard, but he takes the bull by the horns, so to speak, and he'll leave no stone unturned. Do not rock the boat, do as you're asked, cooperate and assist at all times in every way possible.'

He closed the door, leaving Reid alone as he sat resting his elbows on his desk, his head in his hands. He'd never dealt with such a complicated missing person case before and realized how true it was that you gradually build up the image and personality of the person you're looking for. You get to know them, but only through the voices and words of others, and if he closed his eyes he could see the young Amy's beautiful face. It was something he often thought about. They were always smiling, the victims; the photographs that had been chosen to help try to find them for some sad reason always had lovely wide innocent smiles.

Chapter 25

Reid received a phone call from DCI Jackson telling him that his murder team were based at Belgravia and Reid and his misper colleagues were to report there for a debrief and handover. Jackson thought it convenient as it was three miles from

Fulham, where Amy was last seen, and under two from Marcus Fulford's flat in Mayfair. Reid was not so impressed, as he lived miles away in Surrey and the journey would be horrendous during the rush hour. Jackson also told Reid that DC Barbara Burrows could be attached to the murder team as she had been the family liaison officer for the Fulfords. DS Lane and DC Wey were to complete the actions they had been allocated and then return to the Richmond misper unit.

By the time Reid arrived at Belgravia all the files and data he'd accumulated had been loaded on the murder squad computers. He had not yet had an opportunity to share any details about the journal, and knew it would have to be disclosed, but there had been no chance to do so in their opening encounter. Jackson introduced himself and gave him a few words of what seemed like a warning. 'You've not been a detective very long, so you might not like the way I approach an investigation. I've got twenty-five years' service, so my advice to you would be to watch, listen and learn, and don't get under our feet, especially mine.'

Reid felt like he was being belittled, but wasn't going to show it. 'Pleasure to be on board, DCI Jackson.'

'Yes, well, if we'd been given this case earlier we'd probably have cracked it by now; ten days have elapsed and we're playing bloody catch-up.'

Jackson was a big raw-boned man with a bald head and small piercing eyes. He wore a suit that looked a size too large and a wide tie over a crumpled shirt with the collar sticking up at the corners. He also wore thick crêpe-soled shoes that made him walk in a flat-footed way with his feet splayed out, but for such a big man he moved fast and due to his shoes very silently.

Reid and his misper team had a lengthy meeting with DCI Jackson and his fellow members of the murder squad went over everything to date. Already up on the walls were large LCD TV screens with aerial maps of the high-priority locations: Fulham, Mayfair and Richmond. Marker flags with dates and times signalled each alleged sighting of Amy and possible routes that she might have taken were also highlighted. Reid reflected that it was all very high-tech and impressive as Jackson began to list his team's assignments for the following day. Smirking at Reid, he remarked that he had the assistance of forty uniform officers to redo the house-to-house at the priority locations, just in case they weren't done properly in the first instance. He would personally interview both parents, and the Newman family. Standing with his legs spread apart, he clapped his hands.

'You are all aware that there has been an investigation by the small Richmond misper unit into Amy Fulford's whereabouts, with no strong lines of investigation or suspects emerging. For me it has to be one of these three or a mixture: runaway, abducted or murdered. We find Amy, dead or alive, and we find out what happened and why. Enough time has been wasted already and somebody out there saw or knows something and we are going to find that person.'

Reid remained sitting at the back of the incident room, listening as Jackson spoke with authority and confidence that he would solve the case. He proposed to check out any attempted abductions of ten- to eighteen-year-old females, London-wide to start with, over the last two years. He said to look at solved and unsolved rapes, and indecent assaults, and check on anyone with a record of sexual crimes living on or close to the Fulham Road, Mayfair or near the house in Richmond. It was difficult for Reid, as he knew his inexperienced team had done the best they could, but with the murder squad there was a totally different attitude. They were a much bigger unit and appeared tougher, and first and foremost they were focusing on the possibility of abduction. Reid was upset that Jackson hadn't once praised his officers for their hard work, but what depressed him most was the ever-growing possibility they would never find Amy Fulford, dead or alive.

Jackson called Reid into his office, his small beady eyes boring into him as he came too close for comfort. 'You got a feel for this father as maybe screwing his own daughter?'

'I can't be certain. I think there is considerable dysfunction, but we have been unable to break his alibi for the time Amy went missing.'

Jackson prodded him with a stubby finger. 'Listen, Vic, you haven't even viewed all the Stamford Bridge security CCTV or all the Mayfair ones.'

'I only had a small team and there's hours of the stuff—'

Jackson prodded him again. 'If he slipped out during the game he'd stick out like a sore thumb, same if he got there late. If he's in a seat on CCTV and never seen leaving then so what, he may have popped home before going to the girlfriend Justine's place. He could have found Amy getting her stuff together to run away, and, pop, he gave her a beating that killed her. He could have left her there dead, gone to Justine's to create the alibi and disposed of Amy on the Sunday or early Monday morning.'

Reid nodded. Jackson was right and he was quick-thinking around the possible case scenarios; it was his arrogant attitude that galled Reid. He had even offered to be present when Jackson interviewed Marcus and Lena Fulford, but the DCI declined to have him along as he stressed he needed to make his own impression of the family.

Reid had been home for an hour and it was after ten when his phone rang. It was Marjory Jordan and she apologized for the lateness of her call, but she had taken her time reading Amy's journal. She said it was very dark and contained some disturbing emotions, but she didn't really feel she could assist him. A perplexed Reid asked why not and she explained that she was not qualified to give evidence about the contents in a court of law. Reid asked if she would give him an 'off the record' opinion, but she still declined, stating that she didn't want to upset Lena Fulford, breach her trust or break any rules of confidentiality. Reid could see her issues were valid, though he suspected she was making excuses because she just didn't want to get involved in the whole sordid mess. He asked if there was anyone she could recommend to give a professional opinion on the journal. She thought for a moment and then re-called a forensic psychiatrist she had heard speak at a conference earlier in the year – his name was Professor Elliot Cornwall. He seemed to know his stuff and had been giving psychiatric assessment evidence in court for years. Before she rang off she had managed to find Professor Cornwall's prac-tice address and phone number in Harley Street.

Wednesday, day eleven, and DCI Jackson set off with his DS, a younger man called David Styles. Nothing had quite prepared Jackson for the obvious wealth and luxury of the Fulfords' home, and he had not anticipated that Lena herself would be so glamorous. He had seen her on the TV programme, but in the flesh she was stun-ning, and her skin glowed and her perfume was one he had never come across before. It was like fresh roses, and when she shook his hand it felt feather-light; she had an air of fragility, yet a strong sexuality. As they went to the sitting room she gestured to him to be seated and he chose to sit in the centre of the sofa that faced her. She was wearing a soft cashmere dress in ice blue, a set of pearls and her legs were very shapely. As she crossed them he could see the six-inch high heels in a dark navy.

'Mrs Fulford, there is no easy way for me to explain my presence. I am now heading up a murder team that has been brought in to lead the investigation into your daughter's disappearance.'

She licked her lips and glanced towards his DS, gesturing for him to also take a seat. He hesitated and then sat in a hard-back chair by a window.

'My job is to go over every possible scenario and re-question and check every detail in case there has been anything overlooked by DI Reid and his team. That is not to say I am in any way demeaning his officers, but I will be approaching the investigation in a slightly different manner. Firstly I'd like to ask you about your impending divorce.'

Lena nodded, folded her hands in her lap and said she had no reason to think that her daughter was in any way upset by the forthcoming divorce and that it was a very amicable arrangement.

'That's not true, is it, Mrs Fulford? It appears to be a very fraught separation, your daughter caught between her father and yourself. She may have seemed to be physically coping with the situation, but the reality is very different. Your daughter has been caught on CCTV camera by the vice squad attempting to sell her body, and her bedroom in the Mayfair flat was a hovel of dirty underwear, some of which belonged to prostitutes. There is a peephole giving access into the bedroom used by her father and pornographic videos and magazines hidden beneath her bed.'

He had expected some reaction – denial, even tears, but she remained impassive, staring at him.

'So, Mrs Fulford, I am asking you, and now is the time to tell me the truth, I believe your daughter is a very disturbed young woman who is sexually promiscuous and–'

Lena stood up, interrupting him. 'I have told you the truth; you are describing someone else, not Amy. Please don't treat me as some brainless idiot. You have not for one moment considered what it means to me to be told a murder team are now running the investigation. You think she has been murdered, is that right? THAT IS RIGHT, ISN'T IT?'

'In my job, Mrs Fulford, we deal in facts,' Jackson said confidently. 'It is not what I think, but the facts are your daughter has been missing for almost two weeks. We have had no sighting of her that gives us a clue as to where she could be, so I have to consider that she might have been abducted. If you have any doubts about any person who you think might have been involved then I need names. All I'm asking is that you give it up to me.'

She stood in front of him and her mouth formed into a thin tight line. 'Give it up to you?'

She folded her arms. Jackson in all his years in the force had never come across a woman like her. The fragility had gone; she was like steel and her beautiful face looked ugly and vicious. It was the way her mouth turned down, as if she was gritting her teeth.

'I have given DI Reid everything I possibly can, and I find your attitude unsympathetic and painfully brutal. If your intention is to force me to falsely implicate someone close to me in Amy's disappearance then you are sorely mistaken. This really is most distressing.'

'Time is of the essence, Mrs Fulford. All I am attempting to do is find answers, and I apologize if I upset you by giving you distressing details.'

'You have implied that my daughter is a prostitute – just exactly how do you expect me to react? I do not believe a word of it. She is fifteen years

344

old, for God's sake.'

Jackson gave a shrug of his shoulders. 'No matter how distasteful, I'm telling you the truth. Now let me ask you again: if you have any suspicions regarding close members of your family or associates whom I should question, please tell me. I assure you it will be treated with the utmost discretion and without prejudice.'

'Are you implying my husband?'

'I don't know, you tell me.'

'Have you read Amy's journal?'

Lena mistook Jackson's puzzled look as one of confirmation. 'Detective Reid gave me his word that no one else would read it.'

Jackson was taken aback as he had no record of any journal in the files from DI Reid. 'I don't know what you're talking about, Mrs Fulford.' He glanced towards his DS, who shook his head.

'It's written by Amy, and if you are now taking over the investigation then you have my permission to read it, but I want it returned as soon as possible.'

The fragility returned and she was obviously having difficulty controlling her emotions when, to his astonishment, she began to sway and struggle to breathe, flapping her hands as she took gasps of breath. Quickly he went to her side and his DS rushed to help him guide her to sit down.

'Bag, get me a paper bag,' she spluttered and became even more incapable of catching her breath as he realized she was having a panic attack.

The DS ran to the kitchen and informed Agnes, who hurried in with a brown paper bag and handed it to Lena. She covered her mouth and nose with the open end and breathed in and out deeply.

Gradually the panic attack subsided and she sat back, leaning against the cushions on the sofa. She closed her eyes and Jackson decided it would be best to give Mrs Fulford some space.

Jackson went with his DS to speak with Harry Dunn. Agnes showed them where the garage was and, returning to assist Mrs Fulford, found her walking unsteadily in the hall. She was ashen-faced and shaking but no longer short of breath.

'Let me help you upstairs to your bedroom.' Agnes reached out to put an arm around Lena, but she recoiled and moved away.

'Leave me alone, just leave me alone.'

Agnes watched her climbing slowly up the stairs; she could hear her crying and for the first time she actually felt compassion. She had been unable to hear the conversation as the doors to the sitting room had been closed. She wondered if the reason for Lena's panic attack had been the possibility they had found a body or evidence that suggested Amy had been murdered. She quietly followed Lena upstairs, keeping her distance, as she wanted to make sure she made it safely to her bedroom. At a knock on the front door she turned back and opened it. DCI Jackson told her Harry was not in the garage or outside in the garden. She realized he must be in the kitchen and they found him having a coffee and Penguin biscuit.

Jackson asked Agnes to leave, but on closing the kitchen door she decided to listen. She could hear Harry explaining about the boxes they had taken and him being questioned about cleaning

Mr Fulford's car. She heard him say that Agnes had told him to valet-clean the Mini as it was in such a filthy state. Little bastard's putting me right in it, she thought.

Lena sat on the edge of her bed. She suspected Agnes had been trying to listen at the sitting-room door. She had read in Amy's journal about her hatred of Agnes and had started to monitor her herself, noticing just how intrusive she was around the house. It had never really interested her before, but now it did, and she was becoming irritated by seemingly inconsequential things, like how everything had to be in a straight line and the fridge was full of plastic cartons of meals with handwritten sticky labels on them detailing the date and contents.

The phone rang, and it made Lena physically jump. She was about to answer when the red light came on and she knew Agnes had picked it up. After a moment her phone rang again.

'Mrs Fulford, it's your husband.'

She sat on the edge of the bed, peering at the lights on the phone, wanting to make sure Agnes put the receiver down, worried the woman would attempt to listen in on the call.

'Lena? It's me, Marcus,' he said and still she waited for the phone light to go out.

'Are you there?'

'Give me one good reason why I should talk to you after what you did to me with Gail,' Lena said in a distressed voice.

'Because right now we need each other more than ever. Gail means nothing to me, she never did. She offered to get the bank documents and I stupidly agreed, and for that I am truly sorry.'

'I don't know if I can ever forgive you for being so underhand, Marcus.'

'I accept that, but right now I need your help.'

'Why, what's happened?'

'I've just had Simon's lawyers on to me, he wants to sell Green Street and they have asked me to leave.'

She said nothing and he asked if she was listening, but she still said nothing.

'Sweetheart, I have no place to stay, and I was wondering if I could come to yours; I'll sleep in the guest bedroom. Lena, please?'

There was another pause before she agreed and started to tell him about the visit of DCI Jackson, but Marcus was unable to make much sense of what she was saying as she began to sob uncontrollably. He said he would be at the house as soon as he could get there and cut off the call.

Lena lay back sobbing, still holding the receiver, unable to deal with what Jackson had told her. Amy was her precious baby, her beautiful perfect little girl; the disgusting things Jackson had said were lies, all horrible lies, and she couldn't understand why they had told her such hideous things.

Reid had gone straight to the lab first thing that morning with the journal. Once there he had two more copies made, one for Professor Elliot Cornwall and one for DCI Jackson. He had already phoned Cornwall, explained the circumstances of Amy's disappearance and the existence of the journal. Cornwall said he could see Reid at ten

348

a.m., but could only spare about half an hour as he had patients to attend to.

Reid took the original journal to the fingerprint section where he spoke with John Reardon, who was the forensic scientist in charge. He briefed him about the investigation and importance of the journal.

'It would be better to get a document examiner to look at it first before we start treating it,' Reardon said.

'Why?'

Reardon looked surprised by Reid's remark. 'The different handwriting styles – the Questioned Documents section can look at them and compare them against known samples of Amy Fulford's and tell what is or is not her writing.'

This was something Reid had not considered; in fact he'd never had the need to use a handwriting expert before. He felt somewhat embarrassed about his lack of forensic knowledge.

'There's some cards written by Amy in the envelope in the plastic evidence bag containing the journal.'

Reardon shook his head. 'I can tell you now they'll need a bit more than that.'

'I've got some old diaries of hers back in my office so I'll get them brought up.'

'Leave the journal with me and I'll take it down to the document expert. They need to do their magic first before we can do our light source examination and then some ninhydrin testing.'

'What's ninhydrin?' Reid asked, wanting to improve his forensic knowledge.

'A chemical used to reveal fingerprints on

porous surfaces like books, magazines, banknotes and so on; it makes any fingerprints turn a high-contrast purple.'

'Will the purple wear off?' a concerned Reid asked.

'No, though it may fade a bit, and the chemical is harmful, so once we're finished with the treated document we recommend it's destroyed.'

It wasn't what Reid wanted to hear. 'Maybe best leave the chemical stuff out. I don't want to upset the family as technically the journal is their property.'

Reardon shrugged. 'Well that's up to you, but if you miss a fingerprint that could have helped to solve your case then don't blame me.'

'You're right, finding Amy is the most important thing.'

'Tell you what, let me do some non-destructive tests first and see what we come up with, then we can reassess the use of ninhydrin.'

En route to Cornwall's, Reid decided that he would put off telling Lena Fulford about the ninhydrin testing until after the damage was done, as it might not come to anything anyway. He contacted the murder squad office to speak to DCI Jackson about the journal but was told he'd gone to Lena Fulford's house and didn't want to be disturbed unless it was urgent. Reid said he was going to see a forensic psychiatrist in Harley Street and ended the call.

Professor Elliot Cornwall was waiting impatiently for Reid in the reception area and took Reid straight to his office, which was white and very clinical, with the inevitable couch, large pot plants and minimal furniture. Bookcases were filled with reference journals on psychiatry, psychology, profiling and similar topics; some of them looked very old.

Cornwall sat at his desk and gestured for Reid to take a seat opposite him. He was a short dapper man in his fifties with combed-back black and grey hair and a neatly trimmed beard. He looked immaculate in a blue three-piece pinstriped suit and carried himself with an air of authority. He was well spoken, polite and seemed genuinely interested in examining the journal and giving his professional medical opinion on the contents.

Reid handed the photocopies to Cornwall, who asked how quickly he needed a report. Without wishing to appear pushy, Reid said as soon as possible. Cornwall flicked through the pages, quickly scanning them. He then turned the pages back and forth, back and forth, paying close attention to some; others he virtually ignored.

'I agree with you, Inspector Reid, the handwriting in the journal is varied and remarkably different in some sections.'

'So Amy let someone else write in her personal journal?'

Cornwall smiled. 'You misunderstand me, officer. I believe Amy is suffering from Dissociative Identity Disorder, or DID as we now call it in the profession. It used to be known as Multiple Personality Disorder, a severe condition in which two or more distinct identities are present in a person and they alternate in taking control of the mind and actions. We call the different identities "alters" and certain types of circumstances can cause a particular alter to emerge within the subject.'

'So you're saying the various handwriting styles in the journal are done by different "alters" inside Amy?'

'Yes, and although I've obviously not as yet had an opportunity to study the journal thoroughly, I have identified at least three or four alters so far. When a different personality takes control of an individual's behaviour and thoughts it's called "switching" and this can take from seconds, to minutes, to days. The sudden change in hand-writing midway through a page is indicative of the switching of Amy's alters.'

'Would an aggressive alter ever cause actual physical harm to someone?'

'I have known it to happen, and given evidence in some extremely violent cases.'

'So if Amy is alive she could be a danger to her family and friends?'

'Most certainly, yes. If you find her, my advice would be to have her sectioned immediately under the Mental Health Act and have her assessed in a secure clinic,' Cornwall said and looked at his watch.

Reid realized Cornwall was in a hurry as he had patients to see. There was so much more he wanted to ask, but he knew for now his questions would have to wait until Cornwall had time to do an in-depth study of the journal. He also knew he'd better get back to the station and so tucked his notebook and pen into his jacket.

'I'm so glad I brought the journal to you, Pro-fessor Cornwall, and I can't thank you enough for your help. It puts a whole new perspective on the investigation.'

'You need to understand that often people with DID are depressed or even suicidal, and self-mutilation is common.'

'What?' Reid stopped in his tracks. 'Someone else in Amy's head will make her cut or attempt to kill herself?'

'Yes, and Amy will not even be conscious of why or when it happened.'

'This is really frightening stuff to take in, Professor, but what causes DID?'

'Trauma and stress, but research has shown that predominantly it's physical or sexual abuse in childhood and dissociation then becomes a form of defence mechanism. As time passes they begin to develop more and more different personalities.'

'Do you think Amy may have run away and still be alive?'

'If she has totally adopted the persona of an "alter" then most certainly yes,' Cornwall said with assurance. 'She, or rather one of her personalities, could have orchestrated the disappearance very carefully, even down to changing her appearance, dyeing her hair and living somewhere else as that person.'

'I don't think Amy's had the journal very long and we've found nothing else, not even in her old diaries. These were kept when she was quite young and do not give any indication of what you described as "alters" or abusive writing.'

Cornwall looked at his watch again. 'I'd like to see the original journal when your forensic people have finished with it. I'm really pressed for time, Inspector, but I will get back to you when I've made a more detailed study of what's written in the journal.'

Reid stood up and thanked Cornwall for his time.

'Tell me, Inspector Reid, why did you come to me?'

'I met a therapist called Marjory Jordan after discovering Amy's mother is bipolar and she recommended you.'

'She spoke to you about a patient?'

'No, she was quite cagey actually. I don't think she wants to get involved in giving expert opinion on the journal.'

'If you'd like to leave me Ms Jordan's phone number I will give her a call; it may well assist me.'

'No problem, Professor, and thanks for all your help; it also gives me renewed faith that Amy may actually be alive and well.'

'Physically, yes, Inspector,' said Cornwall grimly, 'but psychologically, I fear not.'

'Once a thief always a thief,' Jackson said to DS Styles as they left Lena Fulford's house. 'Dunn's nervous and I don't trust him. Get a search warrant for wherever he lives. Just look at his record – what on earth is she doing employing him?'

Styles reckoned that if Harry had stolen anything he'd be shrewd enough, as an ex-con, to get rid of it after almost two weeks of the police sniffing around. In fact DCI Jackson was seething, taking it out on Dunn because he was furious about this so-called journal that Reid had not mentioned to, him either verbally or in any report.

Jackson rang the station to enquire if DI Reid was there, only to be told that he had phoned in earlier but had gone to an appointment with a forensic psychiatrist.

'What the fuck's that about, and who authorized it?' he snapped.

'Reid didn't say and I assumed you authorized it, sir.'

Jackson cut off the call, saying that Reid would need a fucking 'shrink' after he was through with him. He then instructed Styles to drive to Green Street as he wanted to interview Marcus Fulford.

Marcus had started to pack two suitcases; he would return to get the rest of his belongings some time later. He had tried to call Simon but his phone was continually on answer phone. He was taken aback at how abruptly the lawyers had asked for him to quit the flat, and at first had presumed it was some mistake. However, when he spoke to them they made it clear that it was Mr Boatly's decision and the flat would be cleared of furniture and put on the market. They also requested that he submit the rent arrears forthwith.

Halfway through packing, Marcus received a disturbing call from his solicitor Jacob Lyons' secretary. She had asked for payment due and said that if he wished for Mr Lyons to continue to represent him then he should submit by cheque or electronic transfer the amount outstanding. She also said that Mr Lyons wished to know when they could put in the diary the next meeting to discuss the settlement, and that this

355

would incur a separate payment.

Marcus had said that Mr Boatly was overseeing payment, but he was told that to the contrary they had now been instructed to request payment directly from him. Marcus was at a loss as to why Simon had changed his mind, as he had no funds whatsoever and it was impossible for him to cover the high costs requested by Lyons.

He had just finishing packing when the doorbell rang. Marcus walked out onto the landing to meet Jackson.

'I am sorry, Detective, but this is really not a very convenient time.'

Jackson flipped open his ID with a flourish. 'It's convenient to me, sir,' he announced bullishly. 'I am with the murder squad and am now handling the investigation into your daughter's disappearance.'

A shaken Marcus took a step back and asked if he was there because they had found her.

'No news as yet,' Jackson said and introduced DS Styles.

'I was just packing, but come in.'

From the look on Jackson's face he felt he had better quickly explain that he was going back to be with his wife. Jackson noticed Marcus appeared very agitated as he looked round the flat, pushing open Amy's bedroom door, and then peering into Marcus's bedroom with the packed cases on top of his bed.

'Going permanently, are you?'

'The owner of the flat wants to put it on the market.'

'Really, and what would a place like this bring

to Mr Boatly?'

Marcus shrugged and said probably in the region of three million plus, due to its location, and gestured for them to go into the sitting room. He then confronted Jackson.

'My wife is very distressed and I feel she needs me to be with her. I presume you were the detectives that were at the house earlier, and upset Lena with some very disturbing allegations about my daughter. I think under the circumstances it would have been more diplomatic to speak me first, because you brought on her panic attack.'

Jackson sat on a wingback chair, his legs apart like a sumo wrestler. He explained his murder team were under pressure to get a result.

'Mr Fulford, you have admitted to paying prostitutes and entertaining them here. Then there's the discovery of a peephole and pornography in your daughter's bedroom, as well as female underwear stained with your semen. We even have CCTV footage clearly showing your daughter attempting to pick up a man virtually on your doorstep. Let's stop the bullshit and get to the truth, shall we?'

'I have nothing to add to the many statements I have already given,' Marcus said, hardly able to contain his anger.

'I agree that you have given statements, but I don't believe what you told DI Reid about your movements from the Saturday when your daughter disappeared to when she was reported missing.'

'What in God's name are you trying to accuse me of?'

'I believe you did meet with your daughter, and that she was here in this flat to look for her watch. There was some kind of altercation between you – possibly she threatened to report you for sexually abusing her – and as a result you killed her. Let's be honest, you had more than enough time to dispose of her body over the weekend.'

Marcus was across the room and dragging Jackson to his feet by the lapels of his raincoat. He was in such a fury his face was puce and his fist was clenched to punch Jackson, but Styles pulled him off before Marcus could swing at him.

'You have quite a temper, Mr Fulford. Is that what happened – she made you angry enough to attack her and–?'

Marcus yet again attempted to get to Jackson and this time Jackson pushed him in the chest so hard he fell backwards, landing on his backside. He was panting with rage and gasping for breath.

'That is a bloody disgusting lie, THAT IS A LIE!'

Jackson spread his arms in disbelief. 'We only have your word for that. Now get up, sit down and behave yourself, or do you want me to get the cuffs out?'

Marcus deflated and sank into an armchair, as defenceless as a child. It was wretched to see a man so distressed and shaking as the tears ran down his cheeks. Unable to control himself, he kept repeating that he would never harm his daughter.

Jackson's mobile rang and he told Marcus to remain seated while he went into the corridor and closed the door so he could take the call. The search of Harry Dunn's flat had brought a result. They had found Amy Fulford's Cartier watch shoved into the back of a drawer. Dunn had claimed that he had found it when he was cleaning the Mini, and was going to hand it to the police but had forgotten to do so. Jackson said to arrest Harry and take him to the station for further questioning.

Once back in the sitting room, Jackson informed Marcus he was arresting him on suspicion of murder and cautioned him. He would be interviewed at the station. He then instructed Styles to handcuff Marcus.

'You can't do this, you can't.'

A uniformed sergeant booked Marcus in at the station and read him his legal rights. He was very subdued and used his phone call not to call a solicitor but Lena. She was shaken but stayed calm as he said that they thought he had something to do with Amy's disappearance, but deliberately didn't mention he'd been arrested on suspicion of murder.

'That bastard that came to the house to see you, he was at the flat and making false accusations; I lost my temper and he arrested me.'

'Are you all right?'

'No, I am in a terrible state. Please, Lena, hire someone to get me out of here. I'd packed suitcases to come to the house and my car is still at Green Street. I had a spare set of keys for the flat and car keys made for emergencies and gave them to Amy. She told me she put them in the back of the kitchen drawer at yours. Get Harry to go over there in a taxi and take the cases to the house in my car.'

Marcus's time was up and he had to end the call. He had no idea if Lena was able to deal with the situation; he just hoped she wouldn't get hysterical again.

Lena searched drawer after drawer in the kitchen, until she found the spare sets of keys to the Green Street flat and Marcus's car. Agnes hovered, knowing exactly where they were, but Lena had snapped at her to mind her own business. It was in fact Agnes who had suggested they have a spare set in case of an emergency, and Marcus had agreed.

'Is everything all right?' Agnes asked as Lena, keys in hand, swept past her.

'No it is not. Tell Harry I want him to drive me to Green Street.'

'He's not here, Mrs Fulford. He was with the detectives earlier and then he went home.'

'Then bloody call him to get here straight away. I'll be in my office.'

Lena decided to contact a lawyer she had used when she had a problem with a company that had refused payment for a massive delivery, claiming it was not satisfactory. He had been a tough operator and costly, but it had been worthwhile. She spoke briefly to him and explained that her husband had been arrested for being abusive to a detective and held at Belgravia Station. He politely declined, as he was more a litigation lawyer, but suggested using one of his partners who was a criminal and legal solicitor with a very good reputation. She steeled herself to enquire how much

360

he would charge for a retainer and asked him to go immediately to the station, as her husband was very anxious to have representation.

Lena had just finished when Agnes tapped on the office door and entered.

'I just spoke to Harry's wife and she told me he's been arrested, something to do with stolen property, but the police didn't say what it was.'

'Stupid idiot. I thought he'd gone straight,' Lena said, wondering if he was up to his old tricks. 'I want you to order me a taxi as I have to go out.'

'Yes, Mrs Fulford. Where do you need to go?'

'That's none of your business, Agnes.'

'Sorry, Mrs Fulford. Would you like me to leave something out for your dinner? There's some nice chicken in white–'

'Not now, please, Agnes, just go and call the cab.'

Tight-lipped, Agnes walked back to the kitchen. It was hard to believe that not long ago Lena had been comatose and exhausted after her panic attack. She was now all business-like and short-tempered.

Lena went into her bedroom, took out her camel coat, and went down to the kitchen to wait for the taxi. Once she was on her way she took out her mobile to call Harry Dunn's wife. The woman tearfully insisted over and over that Harry had done nothing wrong, he had been on the straight and narrow for years and was not into any kind of criminal activity because he was so proud of his job driving for Lena.

'Is it connected in any way to my daughter?'

361

'All they said was he'd stolen something. I am so sorry for this as I know what you must be going through and Harry has been so worried.'

Lena ended the call abruptly – as if they really knew what she was going through, she thought to herself. She sat up straight, refusing to even think about why she had been so shocked by the repellent Detective Jackson's wicked assertions about Amy. She clenched her hands, telling herself to not even think about what they had implied, forcing any emotion down inside her by tightening her stomach muscles. Marcus was in trouble, he'd asked her to sort it out, and becoming in control and being needed helped her deal with the constant pain of fear for Amy.

Chapter 26

Lena had carried the first suitcase down to the Mini and returned to collect the second one when she felt herself drawn to Amy's bedroom. Stepping over discarded clothes and shoes, she peered into the wardrobe. The acrid smell of stale sweat and cheap cloying perfume still lingered and was even more nauseating than the previous time she had been there. Now she wanted to touch the discarded clothes, hold them to her face and try to understand what had made her beautiful daughter turn into a slut in this dirty soiled room.

Lena had read horrible things in the journal

she'd given to Detective Reid, but she didn't believe that they could have anything to do with the disgusting things Jackson had told her.

Sitting on the edge of the bed, she faced the wall and the poster that was now rolled up on the floor beneath the peephole. She got up and stood closer until her face was pressed to the wall and she could see clearly into the bedroom used by Marcus and his whores. She knew full well he was and always had been promiscuous. Although she never told him she knew, she had forgiven his unfaithfulness because of her own frigidity. It was not until she had been diagnosed with bipolar disorder, and gone into extensive therapy with Marjory Jordan, that she realized why she had behaved in the way she had. By that time it was too late and he had asked for the separation.

She shook herself. There was no time for her to think about all of that now. Going to collect the second suitcase and walking into the hall, she didn't know who was more shocked, the young man with the ponytail or herself.

'Hey, sorry if I scared you but I didn't think anyone was here. I'm Grant, friend of Simon's, and he asked me to collect a few things, but if it's not convenient I can come back.'

She introduced herself and he smiled. 'I was just leaving and taking Marcus's suitcase back to the house for him,' she said.

'You want me to carry it down for you?'

'Yes thank you, the first one was quite heavy.'

He picked up the suitcase.

'How is Simon?' she asked pleasantly as they headed out onto the landing and started down the stairs.

'Well he's not that well actually, got some virus, and he's in bed; he's been sick since we returned to England, and he's on antibiotics but they don't seem to be helping, plus we've had trouble with his dog Wally – he's a huge wolfhound cross and he just collapsed and the vet thinks he's not going to last.'

They went out of the front door and she opened the passenger door for him to put the suitcase in the Mini. She noticed he wore a thick denim jacket and jeans and a white polo-neck sweater, and that he was very handsome and sun-tanned. The suitcase loaded, he put his hand out to shake hers.

'Nice to meet you.'

'Do you often come to the flat?' she asked.

He shook his head. 'This is my first time and Simon couldn't make it so I offered. There's some photographs he wants and a couple of paintings.'

'Well, please give him my regards. I suppose you know about my daughter Amy?'

He looked embarrassed. 'Simon sort of mentioned it, and I didn't like to say anything. We both hope she'll be found safe and well; it must be a great worry.' He was obviously self-conscious, and couldn't stop gazing into her eyes.

'It is, but Marcus is moving back in to be with me.'

'I am sorry if it's not a good time for Simon to sell the flat, but he makes up his mind about things and I think he's going to put the Henley property on the market as well.'

'Really? Well it's been nice talking to you,

Graham.' She stepped away from him.

'Grant, my name is Grant.'

'Oh I am sorry, well don't let me detain you any longer.'

He walked back towards the house, and then stopped; turning round to see her getting into the Mini, he hurried towards her once more.

'Sorry, do you mind waiting for one second? I've had to park up the road and it's a ten-minute meter, and I can take this space and bring down stuff easier than having to cart it all the way down the road.'

She wound down the window and passed him the residents' parking ticket, telling him he could scratch off the day and time and no need to feed a meter.

'Oh fantastic, thank you.'

She started the engine, waiting as she saw him in the driving mirror running down the road and eventually stopping by a Porsche. He bleeped it open and got in as she started to reverse and pull out from the bay. He took quite a while going backwards and forwards over and over again, but he eventually stopped behind the Mini, waiting for her to drive away. She headed towards the end of Green Street and could see he was still attempting to park as she turned right towards Grosvenor Square. He appeared very young and was obviously a rather inexperienced driver. She wondered if he was a relative of Simon's but doubted it as he did not have the aristocratic tone. She had no idea that her husband's closest friend was a homosexual; to the contrary Simon Boatly had always appeared overtly heterosexual with a bevy of glamorous model girls hanging around him. She had never liked him or the hold he appeared to have over Marcus. She thought it was a class thing, and due to his wealth Boatly had been a constant threat to her relationship from the beginning. When they had first all met she had tried to be friendly, even had dinners alone with Simon, but she was always suspicious of his intentions. It gave her some satisfaction that his forcing Marcus to leave the flat, when anyone with any sense of friendship would have wanted to help, proved that she was right in disliking the selfish egotistical extrovert.

Lena drove the Mini home, parking it alongside the Lexus in the garage. She let herself out via the garden door and entered the house, catching Agnes smoking in the kitchen and reading the papers.

'I'm so sorry, Mrs Fulford, it's just been such a worrying time. I needed to calm my nerves.'

'Put it out and use the room spray, and please, Agnes, if you must smoke do it in the garden, and bring in Mr Fulford's suitcases from the garage.'

Agnes was in a state as she wafted her hands to get rid of the smoke.

'Shall I put them in the guest bedroom?'

'No, Agnes, the master bedroom. I'll be in my office; you can unpack them and take whatever needs washing into the utility room.'

'Yes, Mrs Fulford, I'll do that straight away.'

'Thank you,' Lena said crisply, pausing at the kitchen door. 'Take out something from the freezer for dinner before you leave.'

'Yes, Mrs Fulford, and will Mr Fulford be join-

366

ing you?'

Lena made no reply and Agnes tipped the cigarette butt from the ashtray into the pedal bin. She rinsed the ashtray under the tap and shoved it into the dishwasher. She was angry at being caught out and the way Lena had spoken to her, muttering to herself, 'Yes, Mrs Fulford, no, Mrs Fulford, three fucking bags full, Mrs Fulford.' She went into the utility area, where the big double-door freezer was housed, to get something for the Fulfords' evening meal. Looking through the freezer shelves, she noticed that a carton didn't have one of her usual labels on it, and suspecting it must have dropped off, rummaged around for it. She couldn't find the label and assumed it must have got stuck to the bottom of something else she had already used. Although it looked like a bolognese sauce Agnes couldn't be sure so she took it to the kitchen with some chicken breasts in white wine sauce and laid them on the draining board to defrost. She wrote a note for Mrs Fulford: 'Not sure what this is or when made. Will check when defrosted.'

It took her two trips to bring the suitcases in from the garage as they were both quite heavy. Taking them upstairs into the master bedroom, she chucked them onto the bed and began to take out all the contents. Some items she threw onto the floor as they needed washing, such as shirts, pyjamas, socks and underpants; for the rest she had to go into the guest bedroom wardrobe to fetch more hangers. She hung a few jackets, folded numerous sweaters, and a couple of these she felt needed to have a cold-water wash. Amongst them was a dark maroon cashmere with frilled cuffs, but she didn't really pay much attention as the pile for the laundry was mounting. With her arms full she went downstairs and back to the utility room and began to select items for the first wash.

The huge sink was used for hand-washing and she poured some detergent for woollens and ran the cold water before putting the sweaters in to soak. She held up the soft cashmere maroon sweater and checked the label to see if it was safe to hand-wash; only then did she think that perhaps it belonged to Lena and put it to one side as Mrs F liked her cashmere to be dry-cleaned. She suspected that she would not be able to leave at her usual time as the washing machines and dryers would still be working, so she stuffed what she had not started into the white plastic laundry container. There was no way she was going to stay any longer than necessary, but at the same time she was curious as to why Marcus was moving back in, and into the main bedroom at that, which must surely mean the divorce was on hold. It was something she had never imagined would happen and she couldn't help wondering if the disappearance of Amy had drawn them back together – with two weeks gone it might mean that they were facing the possibility she might never return alive.

Chapter 27

Marcus had calmed down considerably. He had been given a mug of tea and a spare blanket as he felt cold, but he still could not stop shivering. He was forced to wait for the arrival of his solicitor, Angus McFarland, a man he had never met, who had called the station to verify that he would be present within an hour.

Harry Dunn had requested the duty solicitor, who was young and inexperienced, but listened attentively as he took notes and spent considerable time questioning Harry, going over his reason for having the Cartier watch in his flat. Harry explained the Fulfords had gone to Richmond Police Station and Agnes had told him to valet the Mini, where he found the watch almost hidden, as if it had fallen between the driver's and the passenger seat. It had been dirty, as if it had been dropped in mud; he had put it in his pocket with the intention of cleaning it and handing it to Mr Fulford when he next saw him. He maintained that due to the press and the uproar around the missing girl he had forgotten he had it, and then he had left it in the pocket of his jacket and was very concerned he would be accused of stealing it, so chose to say nothing.

By the time he was interviewed by DCI Jackson, Harry was a nervous wreck. Jackson had listened to Harry's explanation, which was being video-recorded, and then looked to his solicitor and shook his head in disbelief.

'Bullshit, Mr Dunn. You find Amy's Cartier watch, you know it's vital to the investigation, but you hold on to it and say nothing. You think you got lucky, but with the missing girl's name engraved on the back it's hard to sell on to anyone, right? You have knowingly held on to evidence with the intention of what – chucking it out? Admit it, you had a hot potato on your hands, didn't you?'

Dunn gave a long sigh. 'Agnes had asked me to wash and valet Mr Fulford's Mini as it was filthy. I don't deny I found the watch, but at the time I never saw Amy's name on it. I put it in my pocket to give to Mr Fulford, but with all the stuff about her going missing I totally forgot about it.'

'So why didn't you give it to him later?'

'Because with my record I was worried I'd be accused of stealing it, and under the circumstances I was just going to throw it away.'

'Ah, but you didn't, did you! Besides, how could you possibly miss Amy's name on it?' Jackson asked and placed the watch, which was in a plastic evidence bag, on the table. He slowly turned it over, revealing the engraved letters.

On seeing it, Harry began to shake. 'It was dirty and covered with bits of dry mud on it. I wiped it clean at home and saw Amy's name and in a panic I hid it in a drawer.'

'What type of mud was on it?'

Harry frowned and then shrugged, saying he didn't know.

'Was it reddish, clay, garden mud or–'

'It was just dirty.'

Jackson stopped the recording, left the interview room and spoke with Styles in the corridor. 'Dunn's a lying little bastard, but he's not a murderer. He thought he'd make a few grand selling the watch. Hold him until I interview Marcus Fulford. After that, Dunn can be released and bailed to return here in two weeks. If there's no evidence against him regarding Amy's disappearance, charge him with theft of the watch.'

Jackson made his way upstairs to the incident room, asking if DI Reid had returned, and when told he hadn't he snapped that he wanted him contacted and told to get his arse back to the station pronto. He had begun to prepare for his interview with Marcus Fulford when Styles returned to say that Reid's mobile went straight to voicemail so he had left a message for him, word for word as Jackson had instructed.

'Right, what do we know about this brief, Angus McFarland?'

'He's got quite a formidable reputation – he's Scottish.'

'Yeah, I fathomed that out by his fucking name. I doubt Fulford will put his hands up if he was abusing or killed his daughter, but we have to put it to him as he's been arrested. If she's dead we need to find her body to have any real chance of nailing him.'

In the interview room Marcus Fulford was going over his arrest with Angus McFarland, who was a neat sandy-haired man in his late forties but who looked much younger, with a pinkish complexion

371

and wet lips. He wore a grey suit with a pink shirt and a striped matching silk tie. He had a large briefcase for his files and notebook. He placed his notebook down on the small table and took out a Parker pen, then cleared his throat and checked his wristwatch.

'They like to keep you waiting, all par for the course. Just stay calm, don't let them rattle you, and if I touch your arm, you let me do the talking.'

Marcus nodded; he felt unbelievably tired, his body seemed heavy and his head throbbed. He held his hands tightly together, his palms wet as he was sweating with nerves, and he wanted to cry he was so numb from the shock of being arrested. He physically jumped when Jackson barged into the room. He introduced himself to McFarland and then gestured towards his DS.

'This is Detective Sergeant David Styles, known to everyone as DS because of his initials and his rank obviously.' If it was an attempt at a joke it fell flat. Drawing out a chair, he sat down, opening a thick file.

Jackson told Marcus the interview would be video-recorded and cautioned him. He was just about to begin when there was a knock at the door; he pushed his chair back and without even an excuse me left the room and saw DI Reid in the corridor.

'Where the hell have you been, Reid?'

'I have been with a Professor Elliot Cornwall and he has agreed to assist the investigation. There's been a development and I–'

Jackson jabbed him in the chest with his stubby finger.

'Whoever he is, you better have a bloody good reason for not informing me where you were going.'

'Maybe, sir, you should speak to Professor Cornwall straight away or at least let me tell you what he said.'

'I have Marcus Fulford in there with his solicitor; when I'm finished he will either be charged with murder or out of here, pending further enquiries. If it's the latter you're to blame for a piss-poor initial investigation.'

'I did inform Chief Superintendent Douglas about taking the journal to an expert and–'

'He may be senior to me but he's not running this investigation, I AM! You are hanging on to your career by a thread because of insubordination; you have the journal of Amy Fulford, right? RIGHT?'

'I did, sir, it's at the lab for examination, but I have a photocopy for you.'

'You should have told me earlier about the journal. Now get out of my sight and I'll see you tomorrow.'

Banging the door closed behind him, Jackson strode back into the interview room.

Two hours later, Marcus was released without charge and returned to Lena's. He had fixed himself a tumbler of Scotch and settled himself at the dining table, which was still set for dinner. By now he was totally drained and had not even turned the lights on, preferring to sit in the semi-darkness, the dining room lit only by the hall lights. He had been sitting there for some time before

Lena came down from her bedroom, wearing a nightdress and matching robe.

'I didn't hear you come home.'

'Sorry, I didn't want to disturb you.'

'Agnes got some chicken in white wine sauce out for dinner – are you hungry?'

'No, I couldn't eat anything.'

'Me neither. I expected you hours ago – you could at least have called me.'

She drew a chair closer to sit beside him.

'Have they found something? Is that why you have been so long?'

'No, they only interviewed me, and thank God for McFarland,' Marcus said, meeting her eyes. 'I really appreciate you arranging for him to be with me; he calmed me down and guided me through the interview – well, if you can call it that; it was more like a bloody Gestapo interrogation by DCI Jackson. I was finding it really hard to control myself.'

'I've been so worried, but I don't really understand why they took you in.'

He sighed and sipped his Scotch. He told her that Harry Dunn had found Amy's watch in his Mini, and hidden it, and he had been arrested and questioned about it. He hesitated.

'I maybe should have told you, because I think Amy might have left it in the car when we went over to Henley one weekend,' he went on quietly. 'You know how she liked to ride there. It was raining hard so she never actually rode out, but I had spare keys for Simon's place so we had a look round – well, Amy more than myself, while I made us a black coffee to warm up.'

'Did they think because of the watch you had something to do with her disappearance?'

'Jackson seemed convinced Harry and I were involved, but he admitted to finding the watch between the seats in the Mini and taking it.'

'Well he's out of a job, the nasty little thief. When I think what I have done for him,' she spat.

'I never asked him to clean the Mini – that was bloody Agnes. Jackson thought I'd asked Harry to valet the car and innocently get rid of any evidence. If I'd known Amy's watch was there I'd have told the police right away.'

'She loves that watch.'

'I know, also that it's a Cartier and you got it for her birthday; anyway, they then went on to question me about...' He paused, not sure how he should tell her.

'Go on, question you about what?'

Marcus explained that there was video footage from the vice squad, and that Amy had been caught on CCTV footage and appeared to be soliciting a passing motorist for sex.

'She was wearing her school uniform, Lena.' He was close to tears.

'Well I don't believe it, it's preposterous. This Detective Jackson is a disgusting loathsome man; he came here and I refused to even continue talking to him. I think they are trying in some ways to implicate the both of us in her disappearance. I am going to make an official complaint against him; it's outrageous that they are treating us like this, scrabbling around in a pitiful attempt to blame us because they are incompetent. As from now I will only talk to Detective Reid.'

He reached out and held her hand.

'It's not looking good, Lena. I mean it's obvious they think that she's met with some nightmare – do you understand what I am saying?'

Lena held his hand tighter. 'They think she's been murdered, don't they?'

He nodded, hardly able to accept it, and yet by Lena being so calm it somehow made it a reality.

'They've a murder team handling the case now. But they still have no evidence of an abduction and...' He couldn't say it, but Lena knew what he meant, that they had found no trace of a body. She released her hand from his and leaned towards him, putting her arms around him.

'We just have to deal with it, don't we?'

'How do you deal with it, Lena? It's as if I have a gaping hole in my chest all the time and I can't face it, because if God forbid it's true, how do we go on?'

She cradled him and kissed him, closer now than they had been for years.

'Listen, darling, I will make you a hot drink and you take a couple of my sleeping tablets; you'll feel more able to cope in the morning. You go up and get into bed and I'll bring in a tray.'

She got up and went to the kitchen, taking a pan and heating up some milk to make him a hot chocolate. She noticed the two cartons of food and the note from Agnes on the draining board. It made her laugh that the ever-efficient Agnes had forgotten to label something. Lena wrote on the note that both cartons were in the fridge and then buttered two slices of bread without the crusts and cut them into soldiers.

Lena carried the tray into her bedroom, but Marcus wasn't there. She left the tray on the dressing table and looked in her en-suite bathroom but he wasn't there either. She went into the guest bedroom and could see by the light from the bathroom that he was taking a shower.

'Marcus, I've made you a hot chocolate. It's in my bedroom.'

He came out wrapped in a big white bath towel, his hair dripping.

'Can you bring it in here? I'm just going to see where Agnes has put my clothes.'

'They're in my room, so you can have it in there.'

'No, Lena, let me just have a really good night's sleep in here. Let's not use what's going on as anything we will regret later. I'm sorry if you got confused about my being here, but I had nowhere else to go.'

She walked out and returned a short moment later with the tray, the bottle of sleeping tablets and his pyjamas, bade him a curt goodnight and left him to it, closing the door. He sighed; at least she had appeared to take it calmly, but he really did not feel like sharing her bed, not this night or any other. Marcus intended to go through with the divorce and was concerned that Lena obviously thought otherwise. He took three sleeping tablets and drank the hot chocolate, but found the bread and butter soldiers unappetizing, as if she was treating him like a child. He threw back the bed cover and changed into his pyjamas before drawing the curtains, already feeling the effect of the tablets. He locked the bedroom door and snuggled down beneath the fresh pure cotton sheets and the featherweight duvet, with hardly time to even think about the events of the evening before falling into a deep much-needed sleep.

Lena was wide awake, and even though she had taken the same amount of tablets as Marcus, didn't feel drowsy. She had hoped to lie in his arms, to be comforted by him, but instead she was restless and angry with herself. She wanted to go next door and slap him, because after all she had done for him she believed that they could be reunited. He obviously had no intention of them getting back together, and she felt not only foolish but infuriated that she had misunderstood his return. She now had to face the fact that he was only in the house because he had nowhere else to go, and her anger built. Throwing the bedclothes aside, she got up and started to pace around the room, resisting the urge to go into the bedroom next door and confront him. She began hurling his clothes from the wardrobe onto the carpet, kicking out at them, losing her control as she attempted to rip them apart. She got a pair of scissors and cut the sleeves off his freshly laundered shirts, and then she attacked the collars, working herself up into a frenzy until she rocked back on her heels, exhausted.

'Stop it, stop it, stop it,' she muttered to herself as she slowly crawled back to her bed and curled up like a child. As the pills at last began to take effect she was already reprimanding herself for her behaviour. If she wanted to get Marcus back this would not encourage him to stay, it would do the exact opposite. What she had to do was stay calm, be in control, and without any obvious persuasion make him want to be with her. This was the first night she had not been haunted by Amy, and in her own confused way she was actually coming to terms with the awful prospect that her daughter was never coming home. Life without Amy would be heart-wrenching, but without Marcus it would not be worth living. Tomorrow she would tidy up the cut clothes, and she would buy him a new wardrobe of designer shirts. With these thoughts she eventually fell into a deep exhausted sleep.

Chapter 28

Reid was already at the incident room by seven. He'd written up his own very lengthy report on his meeting with Professor Cornwall and the research he had done about DID, spending virtually the entire night on it. The team were not due in until nine for a meeting, so it gave him the opportunity to catch up on everything. Details of the arrest, interview and release of Harry Dunn, plus the transcripts from the interview with Marcus Fulford. He guessed that Jackson must have been working at the station until late and noticed the copy of the journal he had left on the DCI's desk was not there. From the interview transcripts, he realized the importance of the missing Cartier watch had been resolved and was now effectively a dead end as Amy might have dropped it in the Mini or it had unknowingly slipped off her wrist. If she told Serena she was going to her dad's to collect it, then it seemed she must have lost or misplaced it.

Promptly at nine o'clock, with the entire team assembled, Jackson made his appearance, a thick file and the copy of the journal under his arm. He bellowed for everyone's attention, and there was a scramble to get seated.

'Right, I have read most of this copy of the journal belonging to Amy Fulford and to say the least it's full of some pretty vitriolic and nasty stuff. I'm no expert in psychology, but DI Reid took himself off yesterday to consult a forensic psychiatrist, so I'll let him tell you exactly what the shrink had to say.'

Reid was not expecting to be put in the spotlight like this in front of the experienced officers on the murder squad, and had wrongly thought Jackson would speak to him one to one first. Not wanting to step down, he decided to seize the moment, picking up a marker pen as he went over to the large whiteboard. Before writing anything, he explained he had read the journal and felt that the assistance of an expert might reveal lines of enquiry and things about Amy and her family they had not so far considered or discovered.

Reid said he would refer to the notes he made of his conversation with Professor Elliot Cornwall and his own research. Using the black marker he wrote 'Dissociative Identity Disorder' on the board and DID in brackets beside it.

'Dissociative Identity Disorder was previously known as Multiple Personality Disorder. Your sense of reality and who you are depends on your feelings, thoughts, sensations, perceptions and memories. If these become disconnected from each other, or don't register in your conscious mind, your sense of identity, your memories, and the way you see yourself and the world around you will change. This is what happens when you dissociate,' Reid said and, looking round the room, could see many confused faces.

He then wrote 'Mild dissociation' on the board. 'Everyone in this room has probably experienced mild dissociation at some time or other...'

'Speak for yourself,' Styles said, which caused a ripple of laughter and some smirks round the room.

Reid wrote 'Daydreaming' on the board. 'In simple terms, just for you, DS Styles, mild dissociation is daydreaming or getting lost in the moment while working or doing something.'

'That's definitely DS Styles,' a detective said, causing more laughter.

Jackson slapped the palm of his hand on the desk. 'Enough of the jokes, now shut up, you lot, and listen to what DI Reid is saying and you might actually learn something.'

Reid nodded his thanks to Jackson and continued. 'Can anyone give me an example of what mild dissociation is?' There were still puzzled looks on many of the detectives' faces.

'Come on, surely one of you can think of an example,' he said encouragingly.

There was a pause while they all glanced at each other and thought about the question, then a young detective spoke up. 'Sort of like driving to work and not remembering the journey or what you were thinking about along the way.'

Reid noticed there were some looks of doubt from some of the team, while others nodded in agreement.

'Good examples,' Reid said and wrote the word 'Coping' on the board. 'Now I'm sure many of you in the room have been to some of the most horrendous and unimaginable crime scenes, and they can leave a lasting impression on your mind, especially if the victims are children. But how do you deal with it ... how do you cope?'

'We deal with it because we are murder squad detectives. It's our job to cope and get on with the investigation, so we don't have or show any emotion,' Styles said in a matter-of-fact way.

Reid said, nothing but he could sense from the shaking of heads and expressions of disdain that many in the room disagreed with this macho cop attitude.

Reid wrote on the board 'Trauma and stress'. 'The reality is, trauma and stress are often very difficult for us to handle or talk about. We may like to think of ourselves as tough police officers, but sometimes we dissociate ourselves from a traumatic or stressful experience that's difficult for us to deal with. Anyone know why we do that?'

'As a form of defence or coping mechanism,' Jackson said.

Reid knew Jackson had undoubtedly seen and dealt with many horrific cases in his long career on the murder squad, and probably more than anyone in the room could relate to what he was saying about trauma and stress.

'DCI Jackson is quite right. We suffer from

natural human reactions and emotions just like everyone else and dissociation is how we, even as police officers, deal with a violent, traumatic or painful incident.' Reid could see that everyone in the room was interested in what he had to say. He knew he'd hit a raw nerve with many of them, and now they would be able to better grasp and understand Amy Fulford's state of mind.

Reid wrote 'Host and alters' on the board. 'DID is a very complex diagnosis to fully understand, even for the professionals, but basically it's where someone splits from their own normal "host" personality and develops other personalities known as "alters" in their subconscious. The alters can cause internal chaos in the mind and behaviour of the sufferer. Imagine looking in the mirror and seeing a totally different face.'

'What causes DID itself though?' another detective asked.

'Sad to say, it's predominantly caused by sexual, physical or emotional abuse in childhood that is severe and repeated over and over again for long periods of time. When a particularly abusive experience becomes unbearable, the child simply exercises a sort of self-hypnosis to go to sleep, which allows an alter to emerge who can handle the situation.'

'So the child steps outside of themselves and perceives the trauma as if it's happening to a different person?' Styles asked.

'Yes, and they may use this coping mechanism in response to stressful situations throughout their lives.'

There were murmurs and whispers around the

room, but the importance of this information was not lost on anyone in the room, even DCI Jackson. Reid had their close attention now as no one had ever been involved in or dealt with a case like it before.

'Professor Cornwall has looked at the journal and he believes that Amy Fulford had at least three or four different personalities and maybe many more. These different alters will have distinctive patterns of thinking and relating to the world, and can be in control of her behaviour and thoughts at different times. Some alters have stronger person-alities than the others and are able to take control of the host whenever they want or think they should.'

The room was now totally silent as everyone took in the severity of Amy Fulford's DID. They listened attentively as Reid spoke about the diff-erent alters 'switching' from one to another within seconds and how it was possible Amy might have been taken over by the most dominant personality, who now totally controlled her mind and actions.

Reid wrote 'Aggressive alters' on the board and spoke of the contents of the journal and how there was hatred directed at her parents, Agnes, Harry and Serena, to name but a few, and there were also veiled threats of harm towards some of them. Jackson asked him to elaborate and so Reid explained that in the journal Amy had written, 'H needs to be got rid of', and he suspected this was about Harry. Another entry, which he suspected was about Agnes, stated, 'It's just a question of exactly how to get rid of her without it becoming suspicious.'

Jackson held up his hand to interrupt Reid. 'All very interesting, and I have read some of the journal myself, but the two entries you just mentioned could mean nothing more than Amy wanted to get them both sacked by setting them up.'

'I don't believe that to be the case and–'

'Let me finish, DI Reid. In the journal Amy writes about fitting Harry up with a bit of jewellery to steal and she clearly dislikes Agnes and wants her out the house. You are letting your imagination run away with you.'

'Professor Cornwall said aggressive alters can and have caried out violent physical harm to those they hate.'

'Did he refer to or mention the specific bits of the journal that you have quoted?'

'No, sir, I asked him if an aggressive alter could be violent.'

'That does not mean Amy Fulford is about to become a serial killer. Granted, she's clearly got mental issues and could still be a runaway, so I intend to call a press conference; we will release our concerns that she may be suffering from a mental illness and be a danger to herself. Also we will get one of our computer graphics guys to use Amy's photograph and show what she might look like with different hair colouring. However, we also have to be open-minded and accept that she may be dead by her father's or a stranger's hand.'

It was at this point that Jackson called the meeting to an abrupt halt and strode into his office, telling Reid he wanted to speak with him. He didn't feel so bad after a few of the murder squad

385

detectives approached him and said his talk about DID was really interesting and they agreed with him that Amy could be a danger to people.

At that moment Reid's phone rang and he stepped out to the corridor to take the call. It was DS Lane and he'd been given a tip-off that *Crime Night* had somehow got their hands on the vice squad's CCTV footage and they wanted to run it on the next show.

'How the hell did they get that?' Reid asked furiously.

'I dunno, all I do know is they want to run it, and repeat some of the material that was used in the last show.'

'Okay, thanks for letting me know.'

Reid knocked on Jackson's door and related the call he had just received from DS Lane.

Jackson shrugged. 'Well that's typical of an underhand investigative journalist. I hope you're not accusing someone on my team, as your lot had a copy before us.'

Reid had a feeling that Jackson was aware of it, and suspected that he might even have leaked it himself. While he didn't want to get into a confrontation with the DCI, he felt it was unethical to show the footage and would be very disturbing for the Fulfords. As he turned away, Jackson gestured for him to come closer.

'Listen, you got a good relationship with the parents, right? I think they maybe should be made aware of how we are proceeding. The mother was very antagonistic towards me, so I want you to go and give them the update on the journal and what that bloke Cornwall said.'

Reid agreed, though he thought Jackson was just using him to do the dirty work. His suspicions were confirmed when Jackson then told him that he should really put them through the wringer to find out what might have traumatized their daughter.

'You know they put out she was Miss Perfect, right? Well we now know differently, and we need to get some answers.'

Reid found the DCI too close, as if he was invading his space, and he took a step back.

'Do you have a problem with seeing them?'

'No, no I don't, but I wondered if we should tell the people mentioned in the journal to at least be on their guard as Amy may turn up looking totally different and assault them.'

'Listen, I am doing as much as I can to digest this bloody journal,' growled Jackson, 'but for me it's just the ramblings of a sick little girl. If DID is caused by sexual abuse at a young age then the suspect is staring you in the face. Now get out there and find me some evidence against Marcus Fulford.'

Agnes had tidied the kitchen and dining room. She was unsure if she should check on Lena, but aware that Marcus was staying, decided not to go upstairs. She gathered up some of the sweaters that she had put to one side to be dry-cleaned and noticed the note Lena had left the previous evening that the two cartons of food were in the fridge. Agnes had a look for them, opened the unmarked container and could see it was indeed a bolognese sauce. She then left a note for Lena saying she'd be back shortly and would she like the chicken or bolognese for her dinner tonight.

Lena had slept longer than she had in weeks, and woke feeling very heavy-headed. She had a cold shower, dressed, dried her hair, and made up her face. Now that she was feeling more refreshed she collected all the cut garments, placing them into a waste bag, and then carried them downstairs to throw into the bins outside the kitchen door. She returned to the guest bedroom and gently tried to open the door, but realizing it was locked decided not to knock and wake Marcus. Then she went into her office, wrote a letter and placed it an envelope addressed to Harry Dunn, before returning to the kitchen and noticing the note Agnes had left about the dry-cleaning and asking what she wanted for dinner. Lena wrote a note back to say she had gone shopping, and might go out to dinner, so Agnes could help herself to the unused cartons of food. She then went to the garage to get the car, leaving the envelope for Harry in a prominent position. She decided to do the shopping in Richmond town centre, feeling very positive, and eager to choose some designer shirts and socks for Marcus.

Agnes returned from the dry-cleaner's and carefully pinned up the tickets on her notice board. Lena's note caught her eye, so she went to the fridge and took out the plastic containers of food as Harry entered the kitchen.

He was tight-lipped, folding the letter Lena had left him and stuffing it into his pocket. 'The bitch has just fired me without the decency to tell me to my face. She better bloody well pay me a month's notice.'

'Good heavens, that's awful, I'm so sorry – did she give you a reason?'

He shrugged, not wanting to get into it, but Agnes continued reminding him how good a job he had done always keeping the car immaculate.

'Yeah, well part of it's your fault.'

'My fault? What have I done?'

'You told me to clean his ruddy Mini, which I did and it was disgusting, full of garbage and fag ends; anyway, I found something, and I swear before God I intended handing it in, I just forgot.'

'What on earth did you find?'

'Amy's watch, but with my record they put two and two together and come up with Christ knows what. I get arrested and spend bloody hours down the station with this prick questioning me over and over. Now she leaves this letter for me and never even gives me the opportunity to explain. I'm out on my ear.'

'Oh I am sorry, it's just dreadful!'

Harry noticed the plastic cartons of food she was holding. 'You making some lunch? I wouldn't mind something to eat before I bugger off.'

'Mrs Fulford didn't want them so I was going to have the chicken. You can have the bolognese if you want?'

'Thanks. After two years that's about all I'll be getting ... fucking spaghetti bolognese.'

Reid drove into the school's horseshoe drive, parked up and walked to Miss Polka's cottage. The front door was open, and so he knocked and then stepped further inside. The small hallway was stacked with all the paintings and framed photographs. He continued into the little sitting room to see even more artwork stacked and two large cardboard boxes filled with books. He turned back towards the entrance, and then stopped as he could hear someone crying. Cautiously he moved to the room next to the kitchen and tapped on the door.

'Who is it?'

'It's DI Reid.'

She was sitting on the edge of a double bed, cases and clothes piled high around her.

'I'm sorry to intrude, but your front door was open.'

'You're lucky I'm still here – a removal firm is coming to put my stuff into storage.'

'You're leaving?'

'Not by choice; I've been given my marching orders by Miss Harrington, and told that if I leave quietly, if I don't cause any further embarrassment, I will be paid up until the end of this term and she'll give me a reference.'

She had obviously been crying for some time; her eyes were puffy and red-rimmed.

'I'm sorry,' he said quietly.

'Not as much as I am; I have no alternative but to accept and hand in my resignation. They have a new art teacher moving in tomorrow, and I am not even allowed to say goodbye to my pupils. I think Miss Harrington has put a stopwatch on me, and will be monitoring my departure through her office window.'

'You're a good art teacher and with the reference I'm sure you will get a job somewhere else.'

'I don't know what I'll do right now, but more importantly, is there any news about Amy?'

'So far we have not traced her, but I believe it is possible she is alive.'

'Really?' she asked, wide-eyed.

'Really – so how about a cup of coffee?'

She ran her fingers through her lovely curly hair and gave a wan smile.

'Okay, let's go into the kitchen.'

He followed her out of the bedroom and into the kitchen next door to it.

He had to stand in the doorway as the kitchen was small and he watched her brew up fresh coffee for them both. He liked the way she moved in her ballet pumps, very light on her feet.

She passed him a full mug. 'Let's go and sit down.'

He sat in the same chair he had previously as she sank onto the low stool, which was surrounded by framed photographs of herself.

'We have been given a journal that belonged to Amy and which she wrote in. It portrays a very tortured soul and we believe through expert opinion she was suffering from a multiple personality disorder.'

Miss Polka, cupping both hands around her coffee, frowned and tilted her head to one side. 'I don't understand?'

'It's a complicated psychiatric disorder and hard to explain, but in short her mind and actions could have been taken over by a person in her head. She could be alive and living under an assumed identity and the real Amy is repressed by another personality.'

She sighed sadly and her expression grew quizzical. 'Oh that poor child. It sounds utterly awful and makes me feel wretched. Is it my fault?'

He had such a strange feeling, wanting to put his arms around her; instead he carefully placed his coffee mug down on the floor beside his chair.

'I don't know whose fault any of it is, but I am trying to find out. The identity controlling Amy may be dangerous and want to harm people they've written about in the journal.'

She was so shocked she spilt some of her coffee, got up and hurried from the room. She weaved around the stacks of paintings and he heard her retching and being violently sick in the bathroom. Concerned, he went to see if she was all right. She was shaking and wiping her mouth with some toilet paper, having flushed the toilet.

'I'm sorry, but there is no need for you to be with me; it's always the way I react to anything upsetting me. If there is nothing else you need to talk to me about I really should get my packing finished.'

'Listen, I want you to know that I never brought up our previous conversation – it didn't come from me, rightly or wrongly.'

'Thank you.'

'Did Amy ever confide in you about anything concerning her mental state or to do with her family?'

'No, never. I swear if she had I'd tell you. I hope you find her, I really do – it's just heartbreaking.'

'Who do you think tipped off the headmistress?'

'Tipped off! I really don't know, but she implied it was anonymous, and asked me directly about whether or not I was a lesbian. Ridiculous but, to be honest, whether or not it was foolish of me, I said it was my own business and would leave directly, so here I am packing and doing just that.'

'Well, I'm sorry. Do you know where you are going?'

'No, but as soon as I do, I have your card and will let you have my address. Obviously I want to know whatever the outcome is for poor Amy.'

'We all do, so, good luck.'

She shook his hand, eager to finish her packing, and looked close to tears again, so he left and heard her crying.

Chapter 29

Lena had returned from her shopping loaded down with shirts, trousers and socks for Marcus. She was about to take all her boutique and designer bags upstairs when Agnes came out from the kitchen.

'Is Marcus up yet?' Lena asked her.

'Not yet, but I think I heard him moving around earlier. Shall I make him some brunch?'

'I'll ask him to come down.' She continued onto the landing and found the guest bedroom door ajar.

'Marcus, Agnes wants to know if you are hungry.' She paused at the door.

'Yeah, I'll just dry my hair. I can't find my

clothes – do you know where she's put them?'

Lena called out that he should come into her room as they were in her wardrobe. She was like a child with presents as she unwrapped and laid out all the new shirts, covering the bed, and then she piled up the new socks and folded the three pairs of cord trousers. She was bending over the bed when he walked in wearing just a towelling dressing gown and put his arms around her.

'Hey, I slept like a log, and you were right, I feel a lot more human now.' He hugged her and kissed her neck and she turned in his arms, smiling.

'Listen, I have tossed out all those awful old clothes and you can have a fashion display. I think I have got all the right sizes.'

He walked around the bed. 'Are you crazy – when did you buy all this gear?'

'This morning, so you take what you want to wear for today and then go and have something to eat.'

He sighed and shook his head. 'You shouldn't have done this, Lena.'

'Oh, and I suppose you want me to take it all back, do you?'

'No, of course not, but you make me feel like a schoolkid whose mummy's gone and got his clothes.'

'You don't like the styles?'

'Of course I do: you always have impeccable taste – not necessarily my own, but this stuff is really nice, thank you.'

She wrapped her arms around him, smiling, and he kissed her cheek. She picked up some dark green cords and then a dark green polo shirt,

holding them out to him, along with new underwear and socks by Calvin Klein.

'Here you go, try these on.'

'At least let me pick what I want to wear.' He
sounded tetchy.

'Oh for goodness' sake, don't be so prissy, and
you need to have a shave.'

He clutched the clothes and gave a rueful
smile. 'Can Agnes make me pancakes?'

'Of course she can. Do you want maple syrup
or bacon with them?'

'Both,' he called over his shoulder as he walked
out. When he got to his room he kicked the door
shut behind him and threw the clothes onto his
unmade bed. It had always really annoyed him the
way she would pick and choose his clothes; it
made him feel not only like a kept boy but a ten-
year-old one. She wanted him to dress like a country gent – tweeds and cords – whereas he preferred
his old shirts and jeans and fully intended retriev-
ing them from wherever she had thrown them out.

By the time he had shaved and dressed in the
cords, with the hideous polo shirt, even pulling on
his new socks, which were cashmere, he felt less
angry and berated himself for being so ungrateful.

Agnes had made a pile of pancakes with crisp
bacon and a pot of honey was open on the table.

'No maple syrup, Agnes?'

'Well there is but Mrs Fulford thought you'd
prefer honey.'

'Well I don't, I want the syrup and black coffee.'

'Yes, sir, that colour suits you – brings out the

green in your eyes.'

He laughed; she flushed and put down his pancakes with the syrup. She asked if she could just say something that he might feel was not her business.

'By all means, Agnes, fire away.'

'It's just that Mrs Fulford's office phone rings constantly and she has spent so little time in there and you know how methodical and tidy she is.'

She poured his coffee as he tucked into the pancakes with relish.

'I happened to be passing the office and there are papers and files on the floor and over her desk; it just seems so unlike her.'

'Well maybe, Agnes, considering the emotional strain we are under at the present time it's no wonder she's not been concentrating on work.'

'I just thought I'd mention it to you, Mr Fulford.'

He put down his fork and turned towards her, becoming irritated by the way she hovered around him.

'And?' he asked.

'Well I took out the garbage as usual and there's bags full of clothes in the bin; some of them have been cut up – all your shirts and trousers.'

He sighed and promised that he would talk to Lena, and if Agnes didn't mind he would appreciate it if she left him to have his breakfast in peace. She obviously did mind as she pursed her thin lips and walked out, closing the kitchen door sharply. He no longer felt hungry and pushed the plate aside, but he drank his coffee as he contemplated having to have a serious talk with Lena.

Not only must she have cut up his old clothes, but he thought he had also better ask her about her work and lastly tell her that if he did remain at the house it would be in the guest bedroom. He decided that he would call Simon Boatly and see if he would reconsider helping him out financially.

Reid had tried to speak to the headmistress again but could spend only a short time with Miss Harrington as she had parents' meetings coming up, and was brusque and impatient. She told him that Serena Newman had been very distressed at the disappearance of Amy and had caught a very bad cold so her parents were keeping her at home until she was recovered. Reid found her to be very dismissive and decided he was not going to go into any details about the journal, but he did ask to speak with Mrs Vicks.

Mrs Vicks was alone in a classroom, marking a stack of exercise books; she replaced the cap on her pen and pushed the books aside as he entered. Thanking her for sparing him some time, he sat himself on top of one of the girls' desks in front of her raised teacher's desk.

'Still no news?' she asked sadly.

He pondered whether or not he should go into the complicated details of the reason he was there, but instead cut to asking if she had been aware of any signs that Amy was distressed about anything before she had disappeared. Mrs Vicks said she hadn't been.

'Would it be possible to look at some of Amy's exercise books? And have you ever noticed any difference in her handwriting?'

'Well I can give you access, but as I said before she is very accompiished in all her subjects.'

Mrs Vicks went to a large cupboard and opened it to reveal neat stacks of different coloured exercise books. She spent some time sifting through them before selecting several with Amy Fulford's name on a white label on the cover. As she was checking them he asked about Serena Newman.

'Yes, the poor girl has come down with a very nasty virus; it will be a few days now that she has not been back to class.'

She placed the books in front of him, and opened the top one.

'This is Amy's history book; we were doing the Roman Empire, and as you can see her essays are very well researched, and I encourage the pupils to add unusual items that will create interest and be informative beyond the dates and historical references.'

Reid saw that the writing was neat and methodical and without a single spelling error, as Mrs Vicks flicked through the pages pointing out her high marks. He asked if she would turn back a page. She leaned over him, pointing with her finger to the essay heading 'The Murder of Caesar'.

'This is very interesting: Claudius Caesar of the infamous *I, Claudius* died of suspected food poisoning and here you see Amy's supposition that he did in fact die from ingesting deadly mushrooms; she proposes that although there was never any proof of this poisoning it was possibly the deadly toxins that attacked the tissues of his body, which could have been the reason behind the descriptions of his convulsions and irregular breathing.

Although death is recorded as a heart attack, his organs failed after eating a mushroom described as "Death Cap", which breaks down the red blood cells.'

He was taken aback, as he recalled reading the mention of mushrooms in Amy's journal, and asked if any of the other pupils had also written about the poisonous mushrooms.

'No – as you can see she was awarded top marks for interest and I believe they were studying different types of mushrooms in biology, which is...' She set down one book after another before finding the biology exercise book. He loathed the way she leaned in so close; she had unpleasant breath, and he eventually asked if it would be possible for him to take the books with him as he would like to study the various subjects because he had noticed a change in Amy's handwriting.

Mrs Vicks dithered, saying that was probably due to the different pens used, from biro to fountain pen to felt tip, and insisted she call Miss Harrington before allowing him to remove them. He also asked her to see if he would be able to speak to the school matron while she was at it. She left him in the classroom so he was able to glance through the biology book. He paused to look at a drawing of a mushroom named 'Ink Cap' and beneath it was an underlined sentence: 'If this is ingested and combined with alcohol, even hours later, it can cause death as the toxins will attack the liver and kidneys and the victim becomes dehydrated from severe vomiting and diarrhoea. The body eventually becomes unable to remove the dangerous toxins that are absorbed into the bloodstream.'

Mrs Vicks returned and said she had been unable to speak with Miss Harrington but that the deputy head had agreed to allow him to take the exercise books, as long as they would be returned. The matron, Mrs Hall, would see him in the surgery, which was outside the new building and inside the second older building on his right as he left the classrooms.

Reid found the so-called 'surgery', which was a small office next to a room with a bed and various medical supplies. Mrs Hall was like the classic version of a matron in a cartoon: she was overweight with enormous breasts that looked like two large balloons, and she wore a loose-fitting blue tunic with a pocket containing a row of pens that had leaked ink in dots beneath it.

She stood up as he introduced himself and was almost the same size sitting as standing, but she had a round pleasant motherly face, devoid of any make-up, and her hairstyle was *circa* 1940, the permed curls like tight sausage rolls.

'I really appreciate you agreeing to talk to me,' he said.

She sat back in her comfortable padded armchair and Reid drew up a hard-backed one from against the wall.

'I have been so saddened by the disappearance of Amy, she is such a sweet gentle creature, not that I knew her well as she was never sick, but occasionally she would come in to see me. I just wish I had more indication that anything was wrong.'

'What do you mean by "more"?'

'Oh well, you know teenagers, they have menstrual problems and she is fifteen, and very attractive but never flaunted it, but I always make sure the girls know that I am here if they want to talk through anything.'

'So Amy came to talk to you?'

'Yes, it was a while ago, but to be honest I wasn't sure what was bothering her.'

'Can you take me through why she came to see you?'

'She said she was having trouble sleeping, and I am not allowed obviously to administer sleeping tablets. I said to her that when she felt restless she should write down in a sort of journal what was bothering her to help get to the root of it. I'm no therapist but I read somewhere that it was a productive way of helping a troubled mind.'

'Did she explain what was making her restless?' Reid wondered.

'No, but you know these newfangled iPhones, Twitter and Facebook things they all use nowadays can also be used in very hurtful ways, and I think she said that someone was writing unpleasant things about her.'

'Did she mention anyone in particular?'

'No, she was quite evasive, and when I asked her if I could do anything to help she said that she could handle it, and now of course I worry that it might have been the reason she ran away.'

She kept on patting her hands together, and he was certain that she had more to tell him.

'When you say she was evasive, what gave you that impression?'

'Detective Reid, what the girls talk to me about

in here is kept very private. I have in a few cases advised contraceptives and asked a few of the girls to consider going on the Pill. This is a very delicate subject, because I make them aware that being in any way sexually active could have severe repercussions, including unwanted pregnancies.'

'Can you recommend using birth control?'

She quickly interrupted him. 'Let me just say I have in the past suggested it, but parental permission is always advisable. I am very loath to even admit that very infrequently I have sent girls to see the school doctor, because although they are teenagers I am aware they are sexually active.'

'Did you advise Amy – I mean by that, did she admit to being sexually active?'

'When I said that she was evasive I perhaps used the wrong word. You see, I did try to understand why she was here with me. I tentatively suggested the reason might be because she was worried about getting pregnant.'

'And was that why she had come to see you?'

The fat hands stopped patting each other. 'No, in fact she was very dismissive, and she was really quite sarcastic. I had recommended some Pepto-Bismol as she had irregular bowel movements and suffered from loose stools – quite regularly in fact as I made a few notes about it – so it was not connected to pregnancy concerns. She said that she was fully aware of taking precautions, and she flounced to the door. It was so unlike her, because she was sort of smirking at me.'

Her round fat face was shiny with perspiration, and she eased herself up to cross to a box of tissues. Plucking one out she dabbed at her top lip.

'She called me a fat menopausal incompetent, who didn't deserve to have the position of matron, and said if I made a complaint she would report that I had been instrumental in a number of girls being prescribed the birth control pill without their parents' knowledge.'

She was quite distressed, still patting at her perspiring face. 'That was the last time I saw her, and quite obviously I did not report her rudeness.'

He stood up to leave. 'How do you feel about it now?'

She gave a long sigh, her enormous breasts rising up and down. 'That she was possibly a very troubled young woman, but you know I am not a psychiatrist, just a nurse, and I try to the best of my ability to look after the girls.'

'Thank you for your time, Mrs Hall. Just one more thing – Serena Newman apparently came to see you recently?'

'Yes that is correct, she had a bit of a temperature and stomach pains; she said that she had been sick at her home, but on arriving back at school felt worse. Due to the various viruses going around I kept her in the sick bay next door, and when she was still feeling poorly I called her parents and they came to collect her and take her home. Apparently she is still not feeling very well as she has not returned.'

She turned her back on him, blowing her nose with yet another tissue; he probably should have said something to comfort her, but he didn't. Time was now catching up with him and he had to call in on the Fulfords.

At the station, the meeting room was packed with journalists plus a TV camera crew from the evening news on standby. DCI Jackson had finished giving them the latest information and the room erupted as every journalist wanted to get their questions answered; it was very obvious that this latest development would give them front-page headlines and this was exactly what Jackson wanted. He had pulled strings and called in favours to get the room jam-packed and it had worked. Press packs were handed out containing details and photographs and he had asked the journalists not to harass the parents, adding that all enquiries were to be handled by their press office. While some journalists jostled for attention, some legged it out fast in an attempt to gain early coverage.

Jackson agreed to give TV interviews outside the station so they were setting up their cameras. This was exactly what he had wanted but even he was taken aback by the overwhelming response. He just hoped it would also bring results. As he was preparing to be interviewed he was told that they had traced not only the Chinese prostitute Lily Leo, who was even now being driven to Belgravia, but that the street musician had been tracked down in a Kingston shopping centre. The officers were bringing him in even though he had argued and become belligerent as he was earning good money from the shoppers.

Lily Leo was taken into an interview room and given a cup of tea, and had to wait some while before Jackson eventually came in to see her with a female detective. The very petite prostitute looked more like a college graduate. Her thick silky black hair was braided and she wore a woollen beret, a neat navy coat and small leather boots with fur trim. She wore no make-up apart from thick dark kohl around her eyes. As she was very nervous, the DCI made it clear that she was not under arrest, simply there to answer questions and assist in their investigation. She was shown the photograph from the CCTV footage of Amy in her school uniform, but she insisted in her slight Cockney accent that she had told Detective Wey everything she knew and could add nothing else.

They then showed her the entire set of Photo-Fit pictures of how Amy might look with various wigs.

'Look, I only ever saw her that once talking to a punter.'

'So how do you know for certain she was trying to sell her body for sex?'

'Some of the other girls seen her hanging around and warned her off because they all had patches they covered. She was an obvious amateur, but nevertheless a threat as she was so young, and the school uniform really got their tempers flaring.'

'Do you know anything about her father Marcus?'

'Don't know the name, but I heard a couple of girls been questioned about their underwear, and admitted to having sessions with her father. They had a nickname for him, "Backdoor Man", and I don't suppose you need me to explain what it means.'

Jackson recalled the 'Watcher' in the journal

describing anal sex and the thought that it was young Amy watching through the peephole sickened and angered him.

'Anything else about him, Lily?'

'I heard a rumour he also used a couple of rent boys, but you know they come and go round there, especially if they pick up a rich bloke who will take care of them, and most are quite young, but I dunno if that's true, just what I heard.'

'Rent boys?' Jackson sighed as no one had ever reported Marcus Fulford with rent boys; to the contrary he appeared to have had numerous women, judging from the array of underwear found in the flat. He decided not to question Lily any further on the subject. Instead he showed her the photograph from the vice squad, pointing to the car as he pushed the photo towards her.

'What about the john in the Bentley – you ever seen him picking up the girls?'

'Listen, there's more Bentleys around that area than red buses in Park Lane, so I couldn't tell you if I had seen him before or not, and on the photo you can't even see his face.'

Jackson let her go; she had given nothing new and he was now impatient to interview the street musician Eddie Morris. He was about to head down the corridor when one of his team suggested he leave it a while longer as Eddie needed to sleep off whatever he'd been ingesting, snorting or shooting up in the Kingston Plaza.

Jackson took himself off to the canteen, saying they should give the bloody pest some strong black coffee.

Marcus had been trying to contact Simon Boatly for over an hour. But yet again the phone went to answer phone and he felt disinclined to leave a message even after the fourth attempt. He went to the back door to look in the bins for his cut-up clothes and, having found them, he decided to confront Lena, but thought he would just give Simon one more try first. This time the phone was picked up, and with relief he asked to speak to Simon.

'He's not here, he was taken into hospital this morning. Who shall I say is calling?'

'It's Marcus Fulford. Who am I speaking to?'

'I'm Grant, I'm taking care of the house. We've had to get the vet out as his dog died this morning, and then poor Simon felt so bad I took him into A&E. That's where I've been all day, as they're keeping him in to do some tests.'

'What's the matter with him?'

'I dunno, some stomach bug he's come down with – vomiting, terrible diarrhoea and he was dehydrated so he's been put on a glucose drip. Doc said it was a gastrointestinal disorder, probably something he's eaten. I just thank God I'm a vegan, but he hasn't actually been able to keep anything down.'

Marcus felt that it was all too much information, and Grant seemed to need to tell him all the details even though they had never met, so he was eager to cut off the call.

'Just pass on my best wishes. I'll maybe try to come out to Henley to see him.'

'We won't be here for long as we're going to Barbados, but I'll tell him you rang, and I know

407

you were staying at the flat in Green Street. It's unbelievable, he's already got a property developer after it – they'll gut it, I suppose, and I think he's also selling up this old pile. All right for some, isn't it? I was never left so much as a toothbrush, and–'

Marcus interrupted, certain this Grant would get into a lengthy diatribe about his family and he knew better than anyone just how wealthy Simon was. Perhaps he would consider lending him a lump sum if he was even more flush than usual.

'Nice to talk to you, Grant. Maybe we'll meet up soon.'

'Yeah, okay. Bye now.'

Marcus slowly replaced the receiver. In the past he had almost hated Simon for his wealth, not that he hadn't been generous, often to a fault, but there had always been on his part a certain amount of envy. Their relationship had really never been the same after he had married Lena. At the time Simon had sarcastically said he would give it a year and Marcus would come back to him. Marcus had felt that originally Lena had really liked Simon, but now she was not interested in having any further contact with him. He had obviously continued to meet with Simon secretly, but after Amy was born their close friendship lessened and they just met infrequently for the odd game of squash, or the occasional lunch. Marcus's inability to gain employment had left him with a lot of free time, so while Lena successfully built up her business he had felt inadequate.

Marcus hated to admit it, but being asked to

leave the flat had hurt him and now after the call he felt a twinge of jealousy about Grant, whoever he was, as like himself he would doubtless be benefiting from Simon's wealth and generosity. The reality was hard for him to even admit, but Simon Boatly was and always had been a very strong fixture in his life. He decided that he would drive to Henley the following day and see him, and he would now sit Lena down and have a serious talk.

Marcus was midway up the stairs when the doorbell rang. He paused as Agnes came out of the drawing room. Waiting to see who it was, he looked over the banister as Agnes opened the front door.

'It's Detective Reid,' she said, looking up at Marcus.

'Yes I can see that, Agnes.' As always there was that gut wrench in his stomach, wondering if there was any news.

'I would like to talk to you and your wife, Mr Fulford.'

Marcus almost ran down the stairs in expectation but Reid said quickly that he was there to discuss Amy's journal.

'Oh. I see. Agnes, please ask Lena to come down and we'll go into the sitting room.'

Reid took off his coat, folded it over the arm of the sofa and then sat down, opening his briefcase. Marcus took a seat opposite him on the matching sofa.

'I have quite a lot to discuss with you, but I feel it is necessary that you both together hear what I have to say as it is quite disturbing.'

Lena hurried into the room.

'Is it bad news, is that why you're here?' she demanded, coming to sit on the edge of the sofa next to Marcus.

Reid cleared his throat, as he explained that he had taken some expert advice with regard to their daughter's journal and felt that it was imperative they should be told of the initial findings.

'What do you mean by advice?' Marcus asked.

'I have spoken with a very reputable psychiatrist about Amy's journal, and he is of the opinion that Amy is unwell.'

'I gave you the journal with the promise you would not allow anyone to read it.'

'Shut up and listen, Lena, please,' Marcus interjected impatiently.

'As you noticed yourself, Mrs Fulford, the writing alters numerous times, and I don't know if you actually read the entire journal because much of it is rather illegible.'

'I read enough to be concerned,' Lena said, tight-lipped.

Marcus nodded and said that he had not actually read every page but had scanned some of it.

They were visibly becoming increasingly anxious, leaning towards him expectantly, making what he had to say even more difficult.

'Okay, the psychiatrist had diagnosed that Amy is suffering from something called DID, which is more commonly known as Multiple Personality Disorder.'

They both leaned back against the sofa cushions in unison. Reid now had their undivided attention as he began to repeat all the information from Professor Cornwall as clearly and simply as possible.

DCI Jackson was led along the corridor to the interview room where waiting inside was Eddie Morris. He had sobered up after drinking three cups of black coffee, and he was now able to answer questions coherently, especially after they'd reassured him that he was not under arrest, but there to assist enquiries relating to Amy Fulford. Jackson looked through the window in the interview-room door, watching the musician adamantly claim he did not know and had never met anyone called Amy Fulford. He was truculent and still argumentative because he insisted they were keeping him from earning his living. Jackson made a good entrance carrying the file with the PhotoFit pictures of Amy. He slammed it down onto the bare table and then drew out a chair to sit facing the greasy-haired Eddie. The musician had spiked black-dyed hair and his face was pallid and unshaven, but he had dark luminous eyes and high cheekbones and his lips were unusually pink.

'Okay, Eddie, this is what I need from you. We have a witness that saw this girl talking to you.'

He set down the photograph of Amy and tapped it. He continued with the date and time and the location at Hyde Park.

'See what she's wearing, a maroon sweater and–'

Eddie interrupted, pushing the photo away. 'Nope, never saw her, and to be honest if I had I would remember as she's a looker.'

'You sure?'

'Yeah, I'm sure.'

411

'It's very important, Eddie, because after the sighting of her in Fulham Road we've only had this witness to say she was sure she'd seen her talking to you in the Marble Arch underpass. So have another look, son, because if she was in that area then she might have returned to Mayfair and–'

'No, I'm telling you the truth, for fuck's sake, and I gave up that patch because of the Romanians hanging around – they bedded down there and it was not a safe place 'cos me money is in me guitar case and twice I got some nicked. They kicked the case over and then pretended to help pick up me money, pocketed most of it, so that's why I'm doing the Plaza in Kingston, and by you keepin' me here I'm losin' out.'

'Tell me about these Romanians.'

'I just did – they erected their tents on the island in Park Lane, they got Tesco trollies loaded with bags and their gear, illegal immigrants. Instead of wasting my time you should check those bastards out.'

Jackson gathered up the photographs and files, stacking them like a pack of cards, and then he looked to the uniformed officer at the door.

'Okay, he can go.'

Jackson tucked the files under his arm. It had been yet another waste of time, but he reckoned before the day was out all hell would break loose when the information from the press conference was made public.

Chapter 30

Reid watched the Fulfords' reaction carefully as he explained the interim diagnosis of Professor Cornwall. It was excruciatingly painful as they digested the possibility that their daughter was alive, but that an aggressive personality might have taken control of her mind and she might actively seek to harm people mentioned in the journal.

'Are we to take this professor's diagnosis at face value, because I find it hard to believe that Amy has taken on another identity. I mean, if this is the truth, does she not know who she is?' Marcus asked nervously.

'If, as Cornwall believes, she is suffering from DID, then if a dominant alter takes over her whole being then the real Amy is not aware of it or what she is doing.'

'Oh my God.' Lena started shaking.

Reid knew he had to continue. 'Dissociative Identity Disorder can be linked back to childhood, if there has been a very powerful trauma. It is possible that your decision to divorce may have been the catalyst that forced her into taking on multiple identities.'

'I don't understand,' Marcus said.

'Each identity will have a separate set of memories. Your separation and the fact that she was placed in boarding school were traumatic for Amy as well.'

Marcus turned to Lena, saying that boarding school had never been his choice. She glared at him.

'Don't start trying to put any of this onto me, you can't blame me. What we should be doing is trying to think back, trying to answer Detective Reid's question.'

'What question, for God's sake? I am at a loss to understand any of this and we don't even know if she is dead or alive.' Marcus was nearly losing it. He jumped up from the sofa. 'If she is suffering from this DID thing I never saw any sign of it. The last time I saw her she was happy-go-lucky and the same as she always was. Now I am supposed to believe she is all these different people and may be living somewhere with a new identity. She is fifteen years old, for God's sake.' He was running his hands through his hair, and what interested Reid was that he appeared not to grasp the situation.

Lena yet again was proving to be far more intelligent than her husband and pointed out to him that at no time had she ever demanded Amy's room be so tidy. 'Isn't it more likely that this multiple personality was actually forming with her father?'

Reid did not want to get into a bickering match with regard to who had done what, or who was to blame.

'It's important for you both to really try and recall any incident, perhaps going as far back as three or four years old, when Amy had some traumatic experience.'

'I don't recall ever being aware of any kind of

414

trauma,' Marcus said emphatically.

'Because she hid it, Marcus; for heaven's sake, sit down and stop pacing around the room.'

'I am pacing round the room because I don't recall or remember anything, and don't start to lecture me–'

'Don't be so childish. Sit down and think about it because I sincerely doubt that Detective Reid is asking us about some trivial childish accident. It's sexual, isn't it, Inspector?'

She looked directly at Reid; her incredible eyes were over-bright. Marcus slowly sat beside her with an incredulous expression on his face.

'Yes it may well be,' Reid said.

'I can't believe you're dredging up that abuse crap again.'

Reid kept his voice low, trying to calm Marcus down, and explained that Dissociative Identity Disorder was frequently a result of sexual abuse as a child.

'Dear God.' Marcus leaned back, closing his eyes, and then turned to his wife. 'How come you know all about this?'

Yet again Lena appeared to be more controlled than her husband.

'Because I know – just don't let's get into what or how I am aware, but believe me, I understand, and we have to acknowledge that something could have happened to Amy.'

Just as Reid thought they were going in the right direction, Marcus went to fix himself a drink. He poured a stiff Scotch and walked back to the coffee table.

'Go back to what you said about an aggressive

alter thing harming people. I mean, if that identity is controlling Amy do we take it seriously?' Marcus asked.

Lena stood up. 'No, no, that can't be right, it's preposterous, and I think we should concentrate on trying to recall–'

'Shut up,' he snapped at his wife, and sat on the arm of the sofa furthest away from her.

Reid felt he was losing control and attempted to placate them by gesturing with his hands for them to be calm.

'I understand that Professor Cornwall's observations and my concerns must be distressing for you, but I believe we need to take the possible threats seriously. All the people referred to in the journal as "enemies" or to whom hatred is directed will be warned to be vigilant. We should also go over the journal together and see if anyone named could have had a connection to the trauma that brought about your daughter's illness.'

Marcus drained his Scotch and his face took on a moody sullen look; to Reid's mind he was being childishly belligerent.

'I will ask you some questions that might trigger a response or a memory. So firstly, has Amy ever attempted suicide?'

They both said 'No!' in unison.

'Have you at any time been aware that she was self-harming?'

Marcus glanced at his wife, and she shook her head. 'No, never to my knowledge.'

'Did she ever have a pet, maybe a puppy or a kitten – something she was very attached to?'

Lena said that Amy had wanted a dog, a King

Charles spaniel, but the time had never been right, and with her going to boarding school it was not an option.

'Why are you asking about her having a pet?' Marcus asked.

Reid explained that it was usual in many cases of DID for the victim to self-harm, or kill an animal they cared about.

'She never had a pet. I need to make a phone call.' Marcus stomped out of the room, taking out his mobile, and slammed the door shut.

Lena gave a sigh. 'I'm sorry, but he's never grown up and I think he is finding this very difficult to deal with, as am I, but I honestly cannot think of any event that might have caused—'

'Do you accept Professor Cornwall's diagnosis?'

'I don't know; what in many ways is sort of helping me is the idea that she is alive, because I was beginning to believe she couldn't be, but if what you have told us is the truth, then it will be imperative we find some answers to your questions.'

Reid could not help but be impressed by her, as she spoke quietly and positively and he admired her for remaining calm, unlike her husband, who came back and stood in the doorway, tears in his eyes.

'Simon Boatly died two hours ago. I just spoke to his partner, a guy called Grant.'

Lena immediately went and put her arms around him, but he pushed her away.

'Leave me alone, leave me alone!' he shouted and, sobbing uncontrollably, left the room.

Lena suggested Reid return in the morning as she felt they could not continue.

'I'm sorry, it must have been a very difficult interview with us, but I am sure you understand that Marcus will need me, he and Simon were very close.' She hurried after her husband before Reid was able to agree to her suggestion.

Reid headed back to the station with a heavy heart, but he knew he had to give a report of the day's interviews. Meanwhile he confirmed Simon Boatly's death with the hospital, asking them to keep the body in the morgue as he would be seeking permission for a forensic post mortem. As he drove towards the station he recalled his meeting with the elegant suntanned man, who had complained of flu-like symptoms. He remembered all the dirty wine glasses left in the untidy sitting room. Reid's mind flashed back to the earlier meeting with Mrs Vicks and Amy's exercise books. He pulled over sharply, the brakes screeching the car to a halt, and reached over to the back seat to grab the plastic bag containing Amy's school exercise books, pulling them out and stacking them on his lap. He flicked open the history book and found the section on the Roman Empire and the essay on the murder of Claudius Caesar. There it was, right in front of his eyes, 'Death Cap' mushroom and organ failure. He threw the book on the passenger seat and again rummaged through the pile on his lap until he came to Amy's biology book. He flicked through the pages until he found the drawing of the 'Ink Cap' mushroom and the words underlined beneath it: 'If this is ingested

418

and combined with alcohol, even hours later, it can cause death...'

A totally stunned Reid sat back in his car seat and the schoolbooks slid like a cascade of cards, one by one, from his lap into the driver's well. He banged the palms of his hands on the steering wheel as it dawned on him that one of Amy's alters intended not merely to physically assault those who had aggrieved it, but to murder them by the use of poisonous mushrooms. He grabbed his phone and dialled the Fulford house.

Chapter 31

Lena took the call from Reid in the kitchen.

'Mrs Fulford, I know this may sound strange but I think one of Amy's alters is trying to kill its perceived enemies by using poisonous mushrooms.'

He heard her gasp, and then she said, 'That is totally ridiculous. How on earth can you even suggest something so outrageous?'

'I know it may sound ludicrous, but her journal has entries in it about poisonous mushrooms and so do her schoolbooks, which one of her teachers gave to me.'

'I really haven't got time for this, Insp–'

'Please hear me out, Mrs Fulford,' Reid pleaded and then went into greater detail about the journal, the schoolbooks and poisonous mushrooms.

Having finished what he was saying, he waited

for a reply, but none came. 'Mrs Fulford, are you all right?'

'I don't know... I can't... I mean why, why would she want to poison people?' Lena said, sounding distinctly shocked by what she had been told.

'You have to understand it's not the Amy you love and know who is doing this, but another personality altogether.'

Again there was a pause and he could hear her crying. 'I don't want to unduly alarm you, but to be on the safe side, please check your fridge and freezer for anything untoward and put it to one side for me to collect.'

She thanked him for his advice and Reid promised he would contact her later.

Marcus was lying face down across the bed. Lena told him it was about time he got himself together.

'Go away. I want some privacy.'

'No I won't, you need to listen to me because DI Reid has just called with some very disturbing news.'

Marcus sat up and listened intently as Lena recounted the conversation word for word. He would have thought it a load of rubbish, but for the fact that Lena was so calm and serious about the matter.

'You took Amy to Henley, and it would be in the time frame when this DID was manifesting itself. Maybe I have been right all along and Simon–'

'Jesus Christ, Lena, Simon would never have abused Amy.'

'What if he was poisoned as some sort of

revenge. How often did she go into his house?'

Marcus let it slowly sink in as he remembered something, and he was visibly shaken.

'What is it, Marcus? I can tell you're hiding something.'

'Amy did go into Simon's house a couple of weeks back when we went riding. She had a plastic carrier bag, but when she came out from the house she didn't have it with her. I asked her if she had forgotten it and she said it was just some dog biscuits for Wally and she'd left them in the kitchen.'

'We'll have to tell Detective Reid,' Lena said as she walked out, leaving Marcus in a state of wretched confusion.

She went into the utility room and opened the large double-fronted freezer. She checked through all the various compartments, rummaging through packets of chicken, beef, fish, bags of frozen chips and vegetables, and began to search for any cooked dishes that might contain mushrooms. Agnes would buy in bulk and prepare the dishes, placing them into plastic cartons neatly labelled with the date. These were used at weekends when the housekeeper was not at the house and Lena was alone. Many of the cartons were enough for two people, and she would defrost them and if Amy was at home for the weekend they ate them together.

Lena took out every single plastic carton or zipped bag containing leftovers or home-cooked meals. Throwing them all into a bin bag, she closed the freezer doors, went outside and dumped the bag in the bin.

Returning to the house, she could hear the phone ringing. Marcus must have picked it up from the bedroom, so she went to the foot of the stairs and called up, asking if it was for her. He appeared on the landing above and told her it was Marjory Jordan. Lena frowned, certain she did not have an appointment.

'What does she want?'

'To see if you're all right. Do you want to speak to her?'

'No, tell her I'm fine and will call tomorrow, and can you come down and look through the photograph albums with me, please?'

Marcus went back into the bedroom as Lena went round the house collecting all the family photo albums. She took them through to the dining room and divided them up for them both to go over to try and pinpoint when Amy's facial expressions noticeably changed to something sinister. Marcus came down after a while and said that Marjory was just checking in, and there was no missed appointment.

He sat beside her and looked at her as she took out a notebook and pen and opened an album.

'You know, you consistently amaze me. I would have thought you would maybe need to talk with your therapist after what we've been told, but instead of you being the one cracking up, I am – I can't even think straight, I'm so emotional.'

She smiled and patted his hand. 'You always have been, darling, and you know, sometimes having such awful things to deal with sort of straightens out my thoughts, prevents my darkness from invading me. That's what it feels like, you know, and it is difficult to control, because sometimes it starts without warning, a terrible feeling of despair envelops me, makes me feel totally inadequate, incapable of thinking straight and unable to cope.'

He couldn't help but give a small smile; the way she was talking about her depression, it was as if he wasn't aware of when these episodes occurred. He had borne the brunt of this darkness for so many years, and here she was talking about it as if he were a stranger to her condition.

They remained silent, looking through the various albums, and yet again it was Marcus that felt a welter of emotion that he couldn't deal with. His eyes brimmed with tears as he turned over the plastic-covered pages of photographs.

'Have you found something?' she asked.

'No, it's just seeing all the good times. Amy building sandcastles, always laughing, and with that golden blonde hair – I don't think I can do this.'

He left her looking at the albums and quietly slipped up the stairs, went into her bedroom and opened her bedside cabinet. Here he found numerous containers of Prozac, and other prescribed antidepressants, citalopram and paroxetine, which were known to lift a person's mood. Reading the pamphlets from the containers, he wondered just how much medication Lena was taking. He carefully refolded everything, returning the containers to the cabinet, then checked the sleeping tablets and took a couple out for himself before he went back down to the dining room.

She was still sitting with the albums and he

rested his hand on her shoulder as he sat down beside her. 'Can I ask you something, and I don't want you flying off the handle, but this bipolar thing you have, it can be hereditary, right?'

She leaned back in her chair as he held her hand. 'I am just wondering if what this professor has diagnosed for Amy isn't this multiple personality shit, and that she isn't being controlled by some monster and planning to poison Christ knows how many people. I mean, could she simply have inherited the bipolar thing from you?'

She released her hand and her whole body tensed up. She wouldn't look at him but picked up her pen and began twisting it in her fingers. He continued persuasively, keeping his voice quiet and calm.

'I know that you are and always have been very capable of hiding your true feelings, but all I am suggesting is that perhaps Amy, like you, is bipolar.'

'Do you really want to get into this now?' she asked and began to tap the table with the pen.

'I think we should. I mean, when did it start with you, because when we were first together you didn't show any signs.'

She sighed, saying that she had never been diagnosed until after Amy's birth and at first she wanted to believe that it was postnatal depression.

'I knew it wasn't – the truth is, Marcus, I've been depressed most of my life; it felt like I had some sort of infection,' she admitted. 'As a child I was always a bit sad, but things sort of came to a head when Amy was a toddler. I so wanted her to be happy and for me to be able to play with her, and I realized that I had never played much in my own childhood – I became paranoid because it felt as if I didn't know how. Can you imagine what that felt like, to be unable to play with her?'

'I never realized that, I never noticed it, and you have always been a good mother to her.'

'Yes I know, because I tried so hard, and when I was finally diagnosed and given medication, it eased a lot of my sadness, but then my way of coping was to make myself feel as if I was totally in control of every element of my life,' she explained. 'That was when I decided to start my business, and I was constantly trying to prove to myself that by being in control I was better. I kept making these schedules, working out how much time I could give to her, and to you – everything depended on how much work I could get done. It was as if I was constantly against a ticking clock, but I was really trying, and when you said you wanted to leave me, or as you put it, create some space between us, I felt as if I was losing it all again.'

'Why did you never discuss this with me?'

'Because I never wanted to lose you, and you were adamant that you wanted to leave. And then you moved into Simon's flat. I just worked harder and harder and kept up this crazy schedule, proving to myself that I was brilliant at business.'

'It was your decision to put her into that boarding school.'

She bit her lip, her face becoming tense, and she turned to face him. 'You see, you blame me – admit it, you blame me, first by saying she inherited my depression, which I know is possible, but Amy did not have my background and I never even considered that she could in any way feel the way I did. She never showed any symptoms – don't you think I would have noticed?'

'Well, you just said you were very capable of hiding how you were feeling, so perhaps that was what she did.'

She sighed with irritation, asking him what the point was of his questioning her.

'I am just trying to understand everything, that's all,' he said, putting his hands on his head and running them through his hair.

She stood up and looked at him. 'Don't you think it's a bit late for that? What we should be doing is as DI Reid said and trying to find out what might have triggered this DID, gain some insight into the fact that she might be somewhere, not knowing who she is, and if anyone else in her journal dies it could prove that she is alive.'

'Terrific – prove premeditated murder. Personally, the more I think about this, the less I believe it.'

'So you think she's dead?' she asked in a raised voice.

'I don't know, Lena, I DON'T KNOW!'

'Don't shout at me, Marcus. I don't care what she might have done, or what she is doing; if she is sick I want to find her and I will never give up hope of bringing her home. If you can't help me then I will do it on my own, because I won't stop, I want to take care of her, and I'll do anything I have to do.'

He hit his flat hand on the arm of the chair. 'All

426

right ... I'll look through the albums.'

He banged one open in front of him and began thumbing through the photographs; everything she had said about trying to be a good mother was evident there, one photograph after another showed them together, always smiling, many of him with Amy, from riding ponies to playing tennis and skiing. He was yet again about to say it was a pointless exercise when she pushed back her chair and gave a strange half-moan.

'What, what is it?'

She pointed to the open pages of the album in front of her; they were not photographs of Amy. In gathering up the albums, she had mistakenly brought one of her own from when she was a child.

'What, what's the matter?'

She got up from the table and walked towards the glass-panelled doors that led into the garden. She stood still and then pressed her head against the cold glass.

'Are you all right?' he asked, concerned.

Still facing away from him, she said in a small quiet voice that she had never wanted to ever open that album. She had kept it in the drawer, hidden away, because it was too painful.

Marcus somehow knew to encourage her to continue, and he got up and put his arms around her, drawing her away from the glass. She leaned against him, and instead of returning to the table he walked with her into the TV room and then sat beside her on the big wide-cushioned sofa. He was trying to think of what he should say, hoping that she might have found some detail that would help them to understand their daughter.

His silence and the comfort of his arms made her want to talk about something she had never told him before, something she had only touched on with her therapist. It was coming out, unstoppable, and she had to take deep breaths as she described what it had been like to be told her mother was dying, the cancer affecting and consuming her fragile body as she slowly lost her mind to the disease. The terrible screams that permeated her mother's semi-consciousness as the morphine eased the pain. She had felt helpless and repelled by the odours at her mother's bedside, but still she helped wash her and clean the bed linen.

Marcus felt Lena's body shudder and he held her tighter, as she described lying awake night after night waiting for the end, and then waiting for her father to come and comfort her. She was eight years old when the comfort became physically abusive and the grief-stricken man professed his love, and then the secret that she must never tell to anyone went on and on even after the funeral.

'I never told a soul, and his drinking spiralled out of control so he would often be so drunk he'd just lie beside me. I was too frightened to move away from him in case he would force me to pleasure him.'

Marcus rocked her in his arms, unable to find a word of comfort, and appalled that she had never trusted him enough to tell him this until now. He was also trying to think about the possibility of her father, Amy's grandfather, ever being left alone with the little girl. He had met him when they married, and he had stayed with them for short periods, but he was a wretched alcoholic and as far as he could recall he died when Amy was two or three years old.

'Are you disgusted with me?' she asked softly.

'What, how can you even ask me that? Dear God, I am disgusted with myself, ashamed that you never had enough faith in me to tell me any of this.'

'Shame is what I have felt nearly all my life, but he made me promise not to tell, and constantly told me it was because he loved me, and if I was to ever tell anyone he would be arrested and taken to prison.'

'So you kept his filthy secret – was there no one you could have turned to?'

'No, when I reached sixteen I had a lock fitted to my bedroom door and he stopped. He was so pitiful I used to feel sorry for him.'

'My God, if only I had known, I'd have beaten the shit out of him, and you let him stay with us, he gave you away at our wedding.'

She was curled up beside him, her head resting against his body. He gently stroked her hair and she pressed her face into his chest.

'It wasn't him, was it? I mean, you don't think he would have touched Amy?'

She gave a long sigh and eased away from him. 'No, I never left him alone with her ever; by the time she was three he was dying, and I was very protective of her. I said to him once that if I saw him so much as touching her, even holding her hand, I would kill him. He was sort of afraid of me, because he knew I meant it.'

Marcus was stunned that she had kept all this from him, and he had never felt so protective of her before. He looked down into her beautiful perfect face, and he kissed her.

'I won't leave you, Lena, we'll go through whatever we have to together. I've been pretty useless of late, but I promise I am going to change.'

'I love you,' she whispered and he lifted her up in his arms, carrying her up the stairs and into her bedroom. He was gentle and caring, and she responded with such adoration, he would have made love to her, but she seemed only to want him to hold her and eventually she fell asleep. He got up and drew the duvet around her and slipped out of the bedroom.

Marcus rarely if ever went into Lena's office, but now he did and stood staring around the usually neat room. Stacks of unopened mail were left on her desk and some had been tossed onto the floor. Every surface was covered with documents and papers and over the carpet were littered torn-up letters and envelopes. The answer machine on her desk was blinking to indicate the memory was full; the house answer phone was also blinking with unanswered calls.

He sighed and glanced over the mound of receipts, some with 'Urgent' stamped across them, payments due for deliveries and orders. He would have liked to open her computer but had no idea what the password could be, and so instead he sat in her desk chair and began to sift through some of the unopened mail, growing increasingly concerned when he found a recent mortgage company letter claiming payments had been late for six months. He couldn't understand why, as he knew she had the finances, particularly after their meeting with the divorce lawyers. Checking more recent demands for payment, he realized that Lena had been ignoring all the household bills since before Amy had been missing. He wondered if she had become so consumed by her Kiddy Winks business that she had neglected her everyday bills or whether she was ploughing the house money into the new venture. He gave a deep sigh, knowing they would have to discuss the situation.

Marcus returned to the bedroom to check on Lena, who was still sleeping, and so he decided to go and find something to cook for them both. As he was going downstairs the doorbell rang then rang again, and when he opened the door there were two journalists asking to talk to him and Mrs Fulford. Marcus curtly told them they were on private property and they should leave. The big wrought-iron gates at the foot of the drive were rarely closed and were not electronically operated. Marcus went out to the garage to fetch a padlock and chain and, returning to the front of the house, again demanded that the journalists leave. As he drew the gates closed, two more journalists drew up, beginning to make him feel threatened, as their cars were parked outside in the road by the entrance. He hurriedly secured the gates with the chain and locked the big heavy padlock.

The journalists called out his name and there was a flash of a camera. Marcus's first reaction after anger was that they must have information about Amy and he dreaded that maybe her body had been discovered. He was just wondering whether he needed to contact the police when suddenly his mobile phone rang.

'Hey there, is this Marcus?'

'Who is this?'

She sounded so friendly that he almost regretted snapping so rudely but she said she would be willing to meet with him and discuss having an exclusive and she would be prepared to pay him a considerable amount. He cut the call, stupefied as to how the press had got his mobile number. When the same caller rang back he said he'd recorded the calls and would be reporting it to the police, who were also monitoring his mobile, and this time the caller cut off. He fought hard to contain the rising feeling of panic.

Lena came downstairs, an expression of dread on her face, and said she'd been watching out of the bedroom window. She had an awful foreboding feeling. 'Have they found her?' she said pleadingly.

'I don't know, sweetheart, I'm just trying to find out what's going on. Let me talk to Detective Reid. Why don't you go back upstairs and stay in the bedroom?'

Lena drew the bedroom curtains and then sat waiting, certain that it was bad news. Eventually Marcus came back up.

'They've not found her. Reid just called. Apparently there was a press conference, in the hope of getting an update – by that I mean they are hoping it will help trace Amy.'

'Let's hope so.'

'I'm not letting the bastards in though. Don't

answer the phone, we don't talk to anyone, do you understand?'

'NO, I don't,' she said shrilly.

'Detective Reid said he would get officers back over here.'

Marcus went round the house, drawing the curtains, and could see that by now there were even more journalists outside the gates. He thanked God he had padlocked them so they couldn't get in, but it meant they couldn't get out.

En route to the station Reid received a call from the handwriting expert who had been examining the journal.

'Due to the many different styles I can't say for definite who exactly wrote the entries in the journal. There is much variation in the handwriting so it's possible more than one person wrote in the journal.'

'Amy has DID, it's a multiple personality disorder, so that may be the reason for the different writing.'

'That would explain it. I've never seen it myself; but I have read an expert forensic article where the subject's different personalities made the entries in different handwriting styles. I would say though that some bits of the journal were similar to Amy's handwriting on the diaries and cards.'

'Well thanks for looking at the journal...'

'Actually there is something about the entries at the back of the journal that is quite worrying.'

'As I recall it was just a bunch of recipes and the handwriting looked the same,' a bemused Reid said.

'It is the same, but not Amy's, and every recipe was for some form of meal containing either poisonous, deadly or hallucinogenic mushrooms and some appeared to be for specific people who had upset the writer.'

Back at the station Reid gave Jackson a rundown on the entries in the journal and schoolbooks which mentioned the poisonous mushrooms. At first Jackson laughed dismissively until Reid told him about his conversation with the handwriting expert and Simon Boatly's sudden death. Immediately Jackson's attitude changed as he demanded a full forensic post mortem on Boatly's body and that everyone in the journal must be told to check every bit of food in their house. Anything suspicious was to be collected by forensics officers and examined for traces of poison.

Reid was almost enjoying seeing Jackson squirm and actually take notice of what he had to say for once, but the moment was short-lived.

Jackson flicked through all the pages of his photocopy of the journal. 'There's no mushroom recipes in the copy you gave me, DI Reid?'

'I hadn't realized the importance of them at the time, sir. I thought it was just maybe something to do with Amy Fulford's cookery classes.'

Jackson smirked. 'Like you thought the mention of mushrooms in the journal were to do with her biology classes?'

'Yes, sir,' Reid replied nervously.

'If you'd bothered to read the bloody thing properly in the first place you'd have seen all the poisonous recipes at the back, wouldn't you?'

Reid nodded. 'Yes, sir.'

'You failed to inform me of the existence of the journal when I took over this investigation. You also failed to give me a full copy of the journal, and had I had one I would have spotted what you so clearly missed.'

Reid doubted Jackson's assertion, but had no choice other than to eat humble pie. 'I'm sure you would have, sir, and I'm sorry if I've let you and the team down.'

'You've let yourself and the police service down, but much more serious is that you may have let a dead man down!' Jackson said forcefully.

'Sorry, sir, I don't see what you mean.'

'It's now Thursday and you've had the journal in your possession since Monday when you met with Simon Boatly and he was still alive. He dies four days later and if it turns out to be from mushroom-poisoning you may have committed a most heinous error of judgement. Do you see what I mean now?'

Reid felt as if his legs were going to give way. He knew he'd made a big mistake, but to be so harshly accused of neglect and inadvertently causing the death of Simon Boatly was shattering. There was nothing he could say as he knew he was in the wrong. He expected to be suspended from duty there and then.

'I'll keep this between us for now,' Jackson said menacingly, 'but let's hope to God no one else in the journal has unwittingly eaten anything with poisonous mushrooms in it. Your career is on the line at the moment, DI Reid, and it hangs on how this Boatly died. Now get out there with a roll of bin bags, visit every person in that fucking journal. Warn them to be vigilant and clear out their fridges and freezers.'

Reid felt totally humiliated and couldn't believe he'd made such a monumental fuck-up. However, Jackson seemed to be giving him another chance, though he wondered if as the lead investigator the DCI could be in trouble as well. Reid knew he had one last chance to redeem himself and didn't dare mention the fact Serena Newman was sick, but decided her family would be his first port of call before revisiting the Fulfords.

Standing outside the Newmans' house, Reid's anxiety continued to mount and his hand was shaking as he rang the doorbell. He was praying that Serena had recovered and was dreading the possibility she'd been taken to hospital in a serious condition, or worse still was dead.

So he couldn't help but let out a gasp of relief when Serena, who looked far from sickly, opened the door. 'You don't know how absolutely fantastic it is to see you looking so well, Serena. Are you fully recovered from your tummy bug?' he asked with enthusiasm.

Serena looked at him as if he was nuts as she invited him in, shouting for her mother, who came down the stairs. Serena explained who he was.

'Good evening. I'm sorry to disturb you and your family, Mrs Newman, but I wonder if I could just have a quick chat with you, your husband and Serena,' he said, as always being very diplomatic.

'My husband's still at work. Have you found Amy?'

'No, but I do need to talk to you about something that is of urgent concern.'

Harriet Newman gave a nod of her head and gestured for him to go ahead of her into the drawing room. Mother and daughter sat side by side on the sofa as Reid asked that the conversation they were about to have remained confidential for the sake of the investigation. Mrs Newman agreed, as did Serena, but Reid had no doubt she'd be on the phone to her school friends as soon as he was out of the door. Without going into detail, he explained that Amy was psychologically a very ill girl and in many ways not responsible for her actions. Mrs Newman got the gist of what he was saying, but Serena sat with her mouth wide open, not having a clue what Reid was implying. He then got straight to the point and expressed his concerns that they might unknowingly have food poisoned by Amy on the premises.

Harriet was up like a shot. She ran through to the kitchen and started rummaging through her enormous, state-of-the-art fridge freezer. Reid followed her and pulled a black bin bag from his pocket as Serena joined them.

'If there is anything suspicious I need to take it for forensics,' he said, opening the bin bag.

'Amy never did any cooking while she was here. I never precook meals or keep leftovers as I don't believe in reheating cold food,' Mrs Newman said, going through the fridge and checking every item.

Reid asked if anyone else in the house had been ill and Mrs Newman replied that they were all well and their GP had confirmed Serena had had a virus. Examining the items in the freezer one by one, she said that there was nothing that she couldn't account for or that would have been there since the Saturday Amy disappeared. All at once there was a loud scream and yells from upstairs. Hurriedly setting down the frozen meals on the counter top, Mrs Newman explained the nanny had a night off and she would have to go and settle down her two boys, who were having a bath. As she left the kitchen, wiping her hands, he thanked her for her time and said he'd be on his way. As he moved towards the door Serena suddenly spoke in a low voice.

'She was over-friendly with Miss Polka, you know, and I think they had a thing going on.'

Reid, knowing the truth, acted surprised. 'Really? What makes you say that?'

'Amy used to visit her on Sundays when she came back to school, and it created quite a lot of jealousy because we all liked Miss Polka.'

'But are you saying that Amy was in some kind of relationship with her?'

'One time she became really nasty because we'd suspected that there was something going on and they were lesbians but she denied it.'

'Did she threaten you when you asked her about it?'

Serena nodded and leaned closer to him again. 'She said she would cause trouble for anyone who gossiped about it.'

'You don't like her, do you?' he asked quietly, and was surprised by her vehement reaction.

'Nobody did, and I am really very sorry for what

has happened, but she was very difficult to get to know, best at everything, first in everything, and what was so annoying was she never even seemed to have to swot up. She was little Miss Perfect, but I think the truth will come out.'

'What do you think the truth is, Serena?'

'That she wasn't perfect at all. That she was a liar and a showoff. If you ever said anything against her it was treated as jealousy, just because...'

He finished the sentence for her. 'Amy was exceptionally beautiful.'

Yet again Serena's reaction surprised him. Her eyes welled with tears and she nodded. 'Yes, maybe that was the problem for all of us, because she was, and I can't sleep for thinking about what might have happened to her.'

'Did you say the nasty things about Amy on Facebook?'

'Yes and a couple of the other girls in my year did as well. I really regret it now, but like I said I wasn't the only one.'

As Mrs Newman returned, Serena hurried from the kitchen, saying she was going to her bedroom.

'Poor thing, she's really been very upset,' Harriet said.

'It's affected a lot of people,' Reid observed as Mrs Newman walked him to the front door.

'We do take this food thing very seriously, and thank you for coming to see us about it, I really appreciate it. It's hard to live with the fact we were the last people to ever see Amy and she was such a lovely girl.'

He disliked the fact she used the past tense, and he would have liked to tell her that Serena might indirectly have had something to do with Amy's disappearance by writing some of the vicious diatribe on her so-called friend's Facebook page.

Harriet was about to open the front door for Reid when a key turned in the outside lock and her husband Bill walked in. There was a look of displeasure on his face as he wondered who on earth Reid was.

'Don't worry, that's Bill's possessive look, Detective Inspector Reid,' she said somewhat sarcastically and her husband frowned.

'Is it about Amy Fulford again?' he asked.

'Yes, sir, your wife's been very helpful.'

'Shame about her mental problems.'

Reid was taken aback. 'Can I ask what you mean by that remark, Mr Newman?'

He pulled the *Evening Standard* out of his pocket, unfolded it and held up the front-page headline for Reid to see: MISSING TEEN-AGER SUSPECTED OF MULTIPLE PER-SONALITY DISORDER.

Chapter 32

On the way back to the station Reid used the hands-free phone and ordered that two uniform officers be assigned to the Fulfords' house to keep the journalists back from the property. He then rang the Fulfords and was as conciliatory as possible on the phone to Marcus, explaining why DCI Jackson had told the press about Amy's personality disorder. He had to lie, claiming it was as a result of having no further development in tracing their daughter. The truth was, he felt appalled by the way DCI Jackson had called the press conference without forewarning and protecting the Fulfords.

The aftermath was explosive, not just from the intrusiveness of the press but also the television coverage that now became a daily matter of interest. Interviews with Professor Cornwall were on most channels as he explained the diagnosis; this then spiralled into further interviews with people who suffered from DID. Breakfast television, the morning shows and news bulletins all repeatedly showed photographs of Amy, and then there was the day when the CCTV footage of her in her school uniform purportedly approaching a man for sex created further excitement. It was relentless and the police were inundated with possible sightings. Every call had to be traced and verified and checked out; Jackson had brought in more clerical staff to deal with the barrage of calls.

Lena and Marcus felt marooned in the house. The gates were kept locked and there were so many reporters and photographers positioned outside from morning to night that they couldn't go outside without facing a battery of questions. Both had refused to give interviews and the pressure on them was appalling. They had resorted to ordering food deliveries to the house and a uniformed officer would accept them at the gates. Reid had arranged for a civilian worker from the independent Victim Support charity to be with them as a quiet and calming presence in the house. The uniformed officers were on duty twenty-four seven, switching over shifts every eight hours.

Agnes had her own key to the padlock and she arrived promptly every morning at nine, and although she was harassed and questioned by the journalists, she always refused to answer any of their questions. Even so she was taken aback when they gained access to her mobile phone number, yet again requesting an exclusive interview, only now they offered money.

Agnes's daughter Natalie was ringing her mother regularly, eager to know what was going on. Agnes whispered that a journalist had offered five, then ten thousand pounds for an interview, but she had refused because she had signed a confidentiality contract with Lena when she was first employed. Natalie could sense the confidentiality clause irritated her mother and told her that she should hold out for as much as possible, and that the contract was meaningless.

'Listen, Mum, you know more about that girl and her family than anyone else; if they want to pay you then do an interview.'

Agnes was very unsure, but the truth was, she had started to rather enjoy the notoriety.

'What are they doing in the house?' Natalie asked.

Agnes knew that Lena was hardly touching any food, and cried a lot, while Marcus was very protective of her, but was finding it all very difficult to deal with.

'Are they back together?'

'I think so; they don't always sleep together

442

though, and I heard him say something terrible the other morning.'

Natalie was eager to continue the conversation but Agnes said she had to go as someone was coming into the kitchen.

'Wait, what did he say, for heaven's sake?'

Agnes lowered her voice. 'That it would have been better if they had found her dead.'

'Oh my God, that's dreadful. Fancy saying something like that.'

'Got to go.' Agnes shut off her mobile as Marcus appeared at the kitchen door.

'Who are you talking to, Agnes?' he asked.

'My daughter, she's very concerned with all this stuff in the papers.'

'Aren't we all? I am at my wits' end, and being cloistered up here is driving me nuts.'

'Would you like some pancakes?'

He shook his head and walked off. Agnes went into the TV room; Lena was with the Victim Support worker, Deirdre Standing, a pleasant woman who had agreed to stay a couple of nights and had moved into a smaller bedroom.

'Morning, Deirdre, I'm just putting coffee on, would you like something to eat?'

'Just coffee, thank you, Agnes. Lena, would you like something to eat?'

Lena was playing patience and didn't look up from the cards. 'I'm not hungry.'

The next day a very nervous and sweating DI Reid was given Simon Boatly's post mortem results by DCI Jackson. He had been suffering from AIDS-related bronchial pneumonia and had died as a result of it. Initial tests had not as yet found any poison from mushrooms, but further toxicology work was still in progress. The report said that it was possible the poison might have aggravated his condition, but passed through his system before he died. Reid had never felt so relieved in his life over the death of another human being.

Reid was at the Fulford house by twelve, where Marcus was waiting with Lena in the sitting room. Keen to put their minds at rest, he came straight to the reason he was there.

'Your friend Simon Boatly died of an AIDS-related infection.'

'AIDS,' Lena said and gave an odd soft laugh.

Reid continued. 'To date no one we had been concerned about has shown any signs of illness linked to mushroom-poisoning nor have we found anything untoward in their food supplies.'

Lena said that although Amy was still missing this came as a huge relief. Marcus however seemed to take the news differently – he asked Reid to repeat it, saying that he was certain it could not have been AIDS, and then asked if he knew whether Grant was also infected.

'I think, Mr Fulford, that a forensic pathologist knows an AIDS-related death when he examines a body. As for Grant, well I've never met or spoken with him.'

Marcus abruptly left the room, and Lena stared after him.

'He is finding this very difficult to deal with,' she said quietly.

'Well, Mr Boatly was a close friend.'

'I don't mean about that, it's the press camped

outside virtually twenty-four seven. It's a total invasion of our privacy and we can't move out of the house. The press and *Crime Night* appeals failed to bring any new or useful information to light, yet they continue to pressure us.'

'They don't give up easily. It's possible if you agreed to do a TV interview, say in the house here, that you would not then be subjected to such media pressure. I can also help you vet the questions before the show.'

She nodded, and sat down again. 'The ironic thing is, my husband has really looked after me, and we have been closer since this all happened than we have in years, so, some good has come of it.'

'No divorce then?'

She smiled again and without replying to his question said she would ask Agnes to bring him a coffee while she talked to Marcus about the TV interview.

Marcus was changing his clothes when she walked into the guest room and repeated her conversation with DI Reid.

'Oh really, they want to tout us out like B-list celebrities, do they? We've already been interviewed; this is like watching us crumble and there is nothing more I can add to what I've already said. That professor has made a big name for himself out of it, spouting bullshit, and all this multiple personality stuff is a load of crap.'

She plucked at the bedspread and watched as he shrugged into the new jacket she had bought him. He then got a pair of new suede shoes from the wardrobe and sat on the bed to put them on.

'What are you doing?'

'What does it look like?'

'Are you going out?'

'I am going to see Grant at Simon's place. I need to know if he's arranging a funeral and what he might need from me.'

'Why would he need anything from you?'

'Because I know he is on his own and doesn't know many people.'

Lena folded her arms, trying to keep her patience.

'You mean you want to find out if there is anything in the will for you?'

'I never even thought about that.'

She went and stood in front of him. 'He kicked you out of his flat, Marcus, and put it on the market. Some friend, and now we know he died of AIDS.'

'Don't pretend like you didn't know, he never hid it, and you trying to insinuate that he might have screwed Amy sickened me.'

That infuriated her still further. 'Sickened you? He sickened me! The big rich friend with all his model girlfriends, yachts and sports cars. It was all an act, he was a queer, a homosexual who always hated me.'

'He didn't hate you, Lena, it was all in your mind. You were just jealous of our friendship.'

'Really? And just how far did that friendship go?'

The slap almost knocked her off her feet; she toppled sideways and then regained her balance to punch him in his chest. He gripped her by her wrists, pushing her away from him, so angry that

446

he would have slapped her again if she hadn't ducked to kick him.

'Well maybe you should have yourself tested,' she hissed.

He just shook his head; this was the side of Lena that he'd always hated.

'You should hope Simon has left me financially well off, considering the shambolic state of your business affairs.'

He knew from the expression on her face and her clenched fists that she was gearing up for an almighty row, but he no longer had the appetite for a fight. Instead he walked calmly out of the bedroom.

'I am sorry but I refuse to be further subjected to any more media interviews,' Marcus said as he joined DI Reid in the sitting room. 'Right now, I am leaving to go to Henley to discuss my friend's funeral.'

'Well that is your prerogative, Mr Fulford; it was just a suggestion.'

'We have gone along with all the police advice and requests so far, Detective, and the result, as you can see outside, is a media circus, and I refuse to have any further part in it.'

Marcus, wearing dark glasses, drove his Mini to the gates and the uniform officer let him out, whereupon the press photographers clamoured to get pictures of him as he drove off.

Reid watched all this through the hallway window as Deirdre from Victim Support, who had been sitting waiting in the TV room, came to stand beside him. She was a sturdy, pleasant-faced woman in her mid- to late-thirties and had a very professional demeanour.

'How are things here?' he asked her.

'Very tense. I am having more to do with her than the husband, he just wanders around smoking and drinking, but she is trying her best to remain calm and positive. Any idea how long you'll need me to be here?' she asked.

'Well it's entirely up to you. I can't force you to stay, but their daughter is still missing, they're being harassed by the media, and our investigation is stalling.'

'Yes, I appreciate that, but I don't usually move in to a family home and I have my own two daughters to look after. I also have other victims of crime that I need to visit,' she informed him in a serious but pleasant manner.

'Can somebody else look after them for you?'

'Not really, but I can liaise with them by phone for a day or two, I suppose. Being the parent of a missing child has many parallels with the experiences of families bereaved by homicide. The emotional trauma, stress and the unknown is like living in limbo for the parents.'

'How long have you been with Victim Support?' he wondered, impressed by what she had to say.

'Seven years now.'

'It must be very hard for you as all you ever deal with is grief and misery. What made you want to do this line of work?'

Deirdre looked at him levelly. 'I volunteered after they helped me overcome being the victim of a violent attack. I got followed off a bus one night by a stranger who dragged me down an alleyway and violently assaulted me. I woke up in hospital the

448

next morning, and no one could have prepared me for the impact it would initially have on my life.'

'I'm sorry, I didn't mean to pry, it was rude of me,' Reid apologized, suspecting that Deirdre had probably been raped as well as beaten.

She gave him a reassuring smile. 'Not at all, talking about it is still a form of release. When it happened I not only had physical injuries but also emotional ones and they were the hardest to deal with,' she said frankly. 'I went through the full range of revulsion, fear, and anger, not to mention a sense of helplessness. I was also terrified about reporting what had happened to the police.'

'But you did report it?' Reid said, concerned that her attacker might still be roaming the streets unpunished.

'Yes, and the young lady detective who dealt with me was excellent and got Victim Support to visit me. It was a great sense of relief to be able to talk about my feelings with someone that was not a police officer, a family member or a friend. Jane from Victim Support was someone who would just listen to me and reassure me that what I was feeling was normal.'

Reid nodded understandingly and with respect for her. 'And that experience encouraged you to join them?'

'Yes, I wanted to give something back and now I'm the person that listens and allows people to talk through their feelings and emotions.'

'I have to say, Deirdre, that is a very moving and powerful story. I chose to change my career because I was bored, but your inner strength and what you have achieved is remarkable. I take my hat off to you.'

'Thank you, DI Reid, that's very kind of you.'

Reid checked his watch. 'Sorry, I'll have to get going. You've been really helpful and I do appreciate what you've done.' As he started to walk away he stopped, turned and spoke softly.

'Did they get, well I mean, did they arrest...?'

'Yes they did. It was three years later on DNA, but working for Victim Support and my colleagues helped me through having to relive the ordeal in court.'

'He pleaded not guilty?' Reid asked with amazement.

'Yes, tried to say I was a prostitute and went down the alley willingly and slipped, causing my injuries.'

Walking to his car, Reid couldn't get over how open Deirdre had been with him, and found himself deeply moved by her story. As he drove out, ignoring the journalists shouting their inevitable requests for information, he reflected that in some ways his fears and concerns about his handling of the investigation paled into insignificance compared to what had happened to her.

Deirdre went upstairs and tapped on Lena's office door, but got a sharp reply of 'Leave me alone, please.' She continued along the landing towards the bedrooms. The guest suite was a mess of Marcus's discarded clothes, his dirty sneakers left beside the bed and tissue paper from a shoe box strewn on the floor; no doubt the vigilant Agnes had not as yet done her speed-clean in there.

Deirdre moved on down the carpeted landing to the closed door at the end, feeling a little guilty about sneaking around as she eased it open. Amy's bedroom was not as large as either the guest suite or her mother's room, but it was nevertheless a fair size with a small double bed. The bedspread covering the duvet was in a pretty white cotton with small daisies and matching frilled pillows. The wooden slatted blinds were partially closed but the room remained very light and airy, with high ceilings and carved cornices, and Deirdre thought how her daughters would love to have a room like it. The row of fitted wardrobes ran the entire length of the room, and gently pushing one sliding door open, she was astonished at the array of beautiful designer clothes. They appeared to be colour coordinated, and beneath them were racks of pristine shoes and boots, all with shoe horns and boot presses. There was also an open-shelved unit with cashmere sweaters in various colours.

Deirdre eased the wardrobe doors closed, and then turned to look at the dressing table. A blue pottery jar, a hand mirror and a bottle of perfume were placed neatly on its surface.

She noticed by the further bedside cabinet a small well-filled bookcase. It contained textbooks and exercise books, rows of sharpened pencils and pens. She bent down to look along the spines. They were all leather-bound classics – Shakespeare, Dickens, Ibsen, Strindberg and poetry volumes by Byron and Shelley. Nothing gave any real indication that this was the room of a fifteen-year-old girl. She sat on the bed and took four school exercise books out to look through them.

451

She was struck by the neat handwriting, and further fascinated by the very advanced level of the content across all subjects. One book contained essays on various historical leaders and notes describing their political context. There were also some long essays about the slave traders, and these had excellent drawings, and down the margins were small red ticks and notes for further research.

She replaced the books, and stood looking around the room; to her mind there was not a single sign that Amy Fulford was suffering from any form of mental illness. Bending down, she peered inside one of the bedside cabinets and found yet more neatly arranged items from aspirin to sweeteners, and two diet books, a stack of vitamin tablets, boxes of tissues and various moisturizers. She moved to the opposite bedside cabinet and in the small drawer she found a Bible and a volume of Sylvia Plath poems. She was careful to straighten the bedcover and ensure she left the room as she had found it. She looked around once more and noticed the room was devoid of any posters, pristine and tidy. Lastly she entered the en-suite bathroom and found the glass-fronted cabinet contained an array of very expensive shampoos and conditioners. There were banks of white towels and face cloths, and hanging on the back of the door was a white towelling dressing gown. She even felt inside the pockets to see if there was anything tucked inside, but they were empty.

As Deirdre was about to leave the room she decided to take a few of Amy's school exercise books to examine more closely. She stepped onto the landing and saw Agnes leaving the guest bedroom with a white bin bag.

'Oh, I don't think you should have been in Amy's room!' the housekeeper said tersely.

'I just wanted to see it for myself, Agnes, that's all.'

Agnes moved closer, glancing round to make sure she was not overheard.

'I was just outside the sitting room when the detective was here and I overheard him saying that Mr Fulford's friend died of AIDS; next minute he rushed out of the room and went upstairs, and she followed him. I was about to ask if they wanted a cup of coffee and I was outside the room when I heard them having a right argument, and what I gathered, right or wrong I'm not sure, was she accused him of being one.'

'One what?' Deirdre said, stepping slightly back as Agnes was so close.

'A homosexual – I wouldn't be surprised because she treats him like a child, buying all these clothes for him. I've seen the prices left in the boutique bags – money no object.'

Deirdre found Agnes objectionable and the thought of her creeping around eavesdropping on private conversations disgusted her. Nevertheless she had been snooping herself, even if to her mind she had good reason as she was there to help the Fulfords. She felt a little guilty even so.

'I wouldn't repeat that to anyone, Agnes, and if you'll excuse me I'll be in the TV room.'

Yet again Agnes followed close on her heels, carrying the rubbish bag and at the same time using the ever-present duster to give a quick polish

453

to the banisters.

Deirdre closed the door to the TV room and sat perched between the plumped-up cushions to leaf through Amy's schoolbooks, growing even more impressed by her intellect and her neat meticulous handwriting. She selected the most recent, noting the date would be a week or so before she disappeared. It was a complicated and very detailed essay on Mary Shelley's life and works and how Shelley's own experiences and fears were reflected in her novel *Frankenstein*. The account of her friendship with Byron was threaded through with descriptions of their villa and the tragic death of Shelley. She had even drawn the removal of his heart. In the margin she had written in neat print her desire to go to Italy and visit these places. Also written in red ink were the school term dates and the suggestion of making a research trip. There were details of flights and costs plus possible hotel expenses. Underlined was the name Miss Polka and the hope was expressed that she would accompany her. She had gone so far as to note her bank balance, and the fact that she had more than enough funds to pay for both of them. In fact if the amount was true she had more in her bank account than Deirdre had ever had saved in her entire life.

Deirdre did not know of Miss Polka or her relationship with Amy, but what she did find of interest was that there appeared no sign that this was written by a girl purportedly suffering from DID. Furthermore, as the entries had been made so close to the time of Amy's disappearance, could the police have missed a vital possibility that, far from anything untoward happening to her, she had simply arranged to fly to Italy? Deirdre physically jumped when the door opened and Agnes announced she was leaving for the evening. She was already wearing her coat and carrying a shopping bag.

'Yes of course.'

'I've left out a selection of salads and cold cuts and, if you want a jacket potato, I'd use the Aga as it always crisps up the skins.'

'Thank you, I'll maybe just have the salad.'

'Well she likes jacket potatoes. I went up and knocked but she won't come out, told me in her usual rude manner to go away, so that is exactly what I am doing.' Agnes sniffed. 'But you know she's been off her food and hardly eaten anything and I've not heard if he's coming back or not.'

'I'll talk to her. Goodnight, Agnes.'

Agnes hesitated, and then closed the door. Judging by the bulging shopping bag, she probably had her own dinner sorted. Deirdre waited for a while before she went into the gleaming immaculate kitchen, noticing a note about the salads had been stuck to the fridge. Lined up inside were plastic containers of ham and chicken. In a dish beside the Aga were two large potatoes.

Deirdre checked the time and saw it was exactly five thirty; Agnes would no doubt return in the morning at her usual prompt nine o'clock. Sighing, she realized she was not hungry and had no need to interrupt Lena until suppertime, but first she needed to have an urgent conversation with DI Reid.

Chapter 33

Agnes stood alone at the bus stop waiting to get her bus to New Malden. She had relocked the gates after leaving, observing as she did so that only one vehicle remained out of the crowd of journalists and photographers who'd been attempting to get an interview. She did not even notice that the woman who approached her had actually got out of the parked car.

'Mrs Moors?' asked the pleasant-faced woman in a camel-hair coat. Agnes had nodded and then looked to see if her bus was coming.

'I have spoken to you on the telephone a couple of times and I was just wondering if you would agree to be interviewed for an exclusive as I know you are the Fulfords' housekeeper.'

Agnes was taken aback but took the proffered card and inspected it.

'We would be willing to pay you a considerable amount, Mrs Moors, and we can conduct the interview at a hotel or wherever would be most suitable for you, but you must have known Amy Fulford well and all we would need is some background on what you thought of her as you'll be very aware there has been considerable press surrounding her disappearance.'

Agnes hesitated and opened her handbag to place the card inside. There was still no sign of her bus, and at first she declined the offer, saying that she really was unable to divulge any personal details as she had signed a confidentiality contract, and would hate to get into any legal situation.

'There would be nothing to worry about, Mrs Moors. You just have to look at it as if you are simply helping enquiries, not invading anyone's privacy, and as I said we are very willing to pay you for your time.'

'How much are we talking about?' Agnes asked.

'Why don't we discuss it together? There's a nice hotel close by, so we could go and sit down and talk, or if you would prefer we can go to your home.'

'Well I don't have much time,' Agnes said, but then agreed to go with the journalist to the very plush Petersham Hotel.

Gripping his phone tightly, Reid listened attentively to Deirdre as she described what she'd just read in Amy's exercise books. He was completely taken aback by the thought that their missing girl could have simply taken off to Italy. However, he knew that her passport had been recovered, and even so they had also made extensive enquiries into the possibility of Amy leaving England and had no result. He also paid close attention to Deirdre when she went on to say that having read through the schoolbooks she had found no sign that Amy was suffering from any kind of debilitating mental disorder.

'We have been acting on a very experienced professional's word, Deirdre, and for you to come up with an alternative scenario is unacceptable,' he insisted. 'Whether or not you have two teenage daughters and feel you know more than either myself or the murder team from reading Amy's essays–'

'I am not as you suggest coming up with any scenario based on my girls,' she replied angrily. 'What I am repeating to you is that judging from what I have read and from her most recent work she had planned to go to Italy and with someone called Miss Polka.'

Reid's grip on the phone grew tighter than ever. 'There's been a very big time-consuming investigation, Deirdre, and you are not obviously privy to all the facts, but I have also read many of those exercise books and there was a very thorough search of Amy's bedroom for any evidence. However, I will call in tonight and read the essays for myself.'

Deirdre bristled and finished the conversation by informing him that Marcus Fulford had not returned from Henley, and she had not had much time with Mrs Fulford, as she was working in her office at the house. She was reluctant to repeat her conversation with Agnes in which the housekeeper had suggested Marcus Fulford was homosexual, but she did, and was taken by surprise when Reid told her that Marcus was bisexual, but that there was no indication that it was connected to Amy Fulford's disappearance.

Just as Reid replaced the phone DCI Jackson strode into the office to inform him that they had just received information that Harry Dunn, Mrs Fulford's driver, had been rushed to hospital suffering from severe abdominal pains. Reid had to swallow hard as he felt sick to his stomach.

Jackson continued. 'I called the hospital and told them it may be mushroom-poisoning and sent them a list of every mushroom mentioned in the journal. They said they'd do what they could, but his condition is critical and they're doubtful he will survive the night.'

Reid's face turned ashen; his mouth was instantly so dry he could barely speak. 'It can't be connected, it can't. I don't think Amy even knew where Harry lived. Both Lena Fulford and Agnes checked everything at the house and threw a load of food out. No one else who works or lives in the Fulford house has been ill at all, and anyway Lena sacked him over the watch. It's impossible, simply impossible for Dunn to have been poisoned.'

'Well you had better bloody check it out.' Jackson slammed out of the office as Reid tried to calm himself down, battling against the sensation of everything closing in on him. Not only was he exhausted but now he was concerned that he had never mentioned the sexual relationship between Amy and Miss Polka. If Deirdre's information led to the discovery of the pair going to Italy, he would have to admit failing to report it. He hoped to God that Harry Dunn was not a victim because if he was, it would be his career finished.

Agnes had a double gin and tonic. She had started by answering questions very diplomatically, but when offered ten thousand pounds, and a second double gin and tonic, her tongue loosened. She was certain that she could easily remove some family photographs from the Fulfords' albums, but asked if she could call her daughter just to make sure she was doing the right thing.

Natalie immediately suggested that her mother ask for another five thousand, and to check that the journalist would ensure that there would be no repercussions over the confidentiality agreement she signed when starting work for Mrs Fulford. Agnes turned off the phone and pursed her lips. She then requested the payment be increased to fifteen thousand. The deal was agreed and Agnes was assured that she would see the article before it was printed, so that any changes could be made.

When DI Reid arrived at Kingston Hospital to enquire about Harry Dunn he found that DS Lane was already there. Harry had died just a short while earlier without Lane having an opportunity to talk to him. He told a shattered Reid that Harry's wife said he came home from work with a container of bolognese from Mrs Fulford's, and that was all he'd eaten with some spaghetti before falling ill. Harry hadn't even had a chance to tell her that he had been sacked over the watch. Reid sank onto one of the hard waiting-room seats and put his head in his hands, wretched with guilt and wondering if he could have done more to prevent Harry's death.

It was some time before Harry's attending doctor was available to speak to Reid and Lane. Harry had been admitted with suspected gastro-enteritis, his symptoms consisting of dehydration, high fever and severe bouts of vomiting. After DCI Jackson had called them they had administered various antidotes for mushroom-poisoning, but to no avail and Mr Dunn had eventually succumbed to a bronchial infection that had resulted in his lungs collapsing, culminating in a heart attack and death.

Harry Dunn's body was being transferred to the mortuary and a post mortem was to be carried out the following day. Reid was shocked and asked if mushroom-poisoning could have brought on the lung collapse and heart attack. The doctor was non-committal until a forensic post mortem was done, and toxicology tests completed.

Reid, grasping at straws, asked if it was possible Harry's lungs collapsed through bronchitis alone. The doctor said he doubted it as his wife said he was perfectly healthy and full of life before suddenly being taken ill. The doctor told Reid that he could speak to Mrs Dunn and pointed to the waiting room opposite them. Reid could see an elderly woman in floods of tears being comforted by a nurse. As much as he knew he should speak to her about her husband, his guilt was so great he just couldn't bring himself to do so. DS Lane could see how upset Reid was and patted him on the shoulder, assuring him he would speak to her and take a statement. Reid thanked him and asked that he take her home and seize the empty bolognese container for forensics.

Reid went to the toilets to wash his face with cold water. To his relief there was no one else about as he stood staring at his reflection in the mirror, observing how his expression failed to hide his anger at his own stupid mistakes, and he banged his fist repeatedly into the metal towel holder, leaving two big dents. Returning to his car,

461

he couldn't get Mrs Dunn's wretchedly sad face out of his mind; by the time he was in the driver's seat the overwhelming emotions became too much for him, and he broke down in floods of tears.

Eventually composing himself, Reid rang Deirdre and said he would not be coming over, making the excuse that he'd been held up, and to tell Mrs Fulford that he would like to talk to her in the morning. A frustrated Deirdre replied she was finding it all rather a waste of time as Mrs Fulford had not come out of her office for hours and still refused to eat anything. She felt like she was wet-nursing her rather than performing her role as a counsellor.

'I could do with some counselling myself,' he said quietly.

'Pardon?'

'Nothing, I'll be in touch.'

No sooner had Deirdre come off the phone than Lena walked into the TV room.

'Would you like me to make a tea or coffee, Lena?'

'I'll make you one,' Lena said, beaming. 'I have been so hard at work all day, and I think I have rectified all the problems. As from tomorrow I will reorder and start getting the business back in shape. Everyone has been very understanding, and I have got the orders coming back and deliveries can be deferred until we are ready.'

'Oh that's good, and a tea's fine for me, thanks.'

Lena clapped her hands. 'Yes, isn't it, and I have also made a decision – whether Marcus likes it or not is not my problem. I want to do a television interview, so I want you to contact Detective Reid and tell him to set the wheels in motion. I will need to have my hair done, and will organize someone to do my make-up, and maybe you can help me choose what I should wear.'

Deirdre was nonplussed. Lena now appeared energized and confident, almost like a different person, and in no way concerned that Marcus had not returned. She could hear her banging around the kitchen. The TV was on very loud in there, and to Deirdre's astonishment Lena reappeared with a glass of chilled white wine for her.

'Here you go, and the fry-up I'm making for us both won't take long. There's an old movie with Doris Day on Channel 5 we can watch while we eat.'

Deirdre accepted the wine, even though she would have preferred a cup of tea.

Marcus was also cooking dinner for himself; he had bought steaks, only to discover that Grant was a very dedicated vegan. He tossed a salad and fried up his steak as Grant opened a second bottle of very good wine. They had already gone over details for the funeral, compiling lists of guests and attempting to contact relatives, but it was not very fruitful as only two of the names they had recovered from Simon's address book were still living. There was an elderly aunt who was in a retirement home and an uncle who was somewhere in Canada. Grant had been in touch with Simon's lawyers to ascertain whether or not his will was up to date, and was told that Simon had very recently made some alterations. Grant had been eager to discover who the beneficiaries were, but had been informed that the legal team were still checking all the bequests.

'Do you reckon he looked after you?' Marcus asked, when he really wanted to know if he himself had been left anything. He had elaborated on how long he and Simon had been friends and tried his best not to sound over-eager, turning the conversation to how long Grant had been Simon's partner.

Grant had been slightly evasive, as he had only been associated with Simon for six months. He explained that he had been hired as a crew member for Simon's yacht and their relationship had become serious only recently. Yet again Marcus prodded for information, knowing Simon had died from an AIDS-related illness. Grant claimed that they rarely had unprotected sex – although Simon had never admitted to him that he was infected, there had been suspicion on his part and he said he wanted to have himself tested.

'What about you?'

Marcus made no reply as he cut up his steak.

'You and he had an ongoing thing, so have you been tested?' Grant persisted.

'No, and we were not active for years, but I'll have myself tested as it can be dormant for Christ knows how long.'

'Yeah, I know, but I also know if he was fully aware then he should have bloody well come clean with me. If there is no cash coming my way I'll fucking sue his legal team that are being so protective about who's getting what.'

'How much is this place worth?' Marcus asked as he finished his steak.

'I dunno, but there's his yacht, the Bahamas villa, his car, the sale of this place and the Mayfair flat, so he must have been rolling in cash. This has got to be four to six million what with how much land it's on, and with the waterfront.'

'Yeah, I guess so – old Simon was never short, and he was always very generous to me, but right now I don't have a pot to piss in. He suddenly withdrew finances for my divorce lawyer and kicked me out of the Green Street flat virtually overnight.'

'Yeah, he could get these whims, one minute chucking cash around, the next querying a grocery bill, but he was generous and I got a wardrobe of great gear from him,' Grant replied. 'What I was thinking was maybe going through his cupboards and packing up stuff that I'd like. I don't know how long they'll allow me to stay on here, unless he has made arrangements for me – do you think he would have done?'

Marcus shrugged, thinking that if he personally had been left money he would go through with the divorce and then go abroad.

'What about your daughter?' Grant suddenly asked.

It threw Marcus; somehow he had shut out the emotional turmoil of her disappearance, as not allowing himself to think about her made it easier to cope with what had just happened to Simon.

'I mean, what do you think happened to her?' Grant persisted.

Suddenly the impact of Amy vanishing hit

Marcus all over again and he gasped for breath, as if his chest would burst.

'I don't know, I don't know, but I have started to believe she will never be found. I can't sleep at night thinking about where she could be, or what could have happened to her. My worst fear, that I may eventually have to live with, is that she could be dead.'

'What about your wife?'

Marcus rubbed his eyes, and then picked up the napkin and wiped his face. 'We broke up two years before Amy disappeared. I had to get away from Lena – I mean, Amy knew how I felt because she would feel the same pressure from her. She's like a ticking time bomb, and you never know when she will explode or fly off the handle. In reality I should have had the guts to leave her a long time ago, but I stayed for the sake of Amy.'

'But you must have loved her once.'

'Yes of course I did, she was the most beautiful woman I'd ever met, and I had no indication that she had problems.'

'What problems?'

Marcus sighed. 'I don't really want to get into this. Just leave it, because if I have to think about it I get to feel guilty. She just has major problems, and I am probably one of them because she won't let me go, she's obsessive, but I believed we could work it out – we couldn't, we can't and now all I want is to walk away from her.'

'Does she know you and Simon were at it?' Grant asked regardless.

'At it? For Christ's sake, don't make it sound so crass, and any sexual activity I had with Simon was a long time ago.' He got up from the table to take his dirty plate to the sink and almost tripped over a large tin dog bowl. He looked down and picked it up as Grant joined him with his dinner plate.

'I should chuck that out as it was Wally's – I meant to do it days ago.'

Marcus ran the water into the sink and went back to the table to pick up his wine glass; he refilled it as Grant put the dog bowl into a bin.

'What did he die of?'

'Wally? It was hideous, what with him being such a huge dog vomiting all over the place; the vet came out a few times but we reckoned it was rat poison from the barns out back – they have horses and with the hay and stuff it's always got mice and rats.'

'Rat poison, is that what the vet said?'

'Yeah, Wally would eat anything but he was almost catatonic by the time he died.'

'Did you feed him?'

'Simon was off his food, hardly kept anything down, and I would fill up a bowl outside with anything he'd not finished for Wally.'

Marcus thought about it as he washed the dishes and continued sipping at the wine.

'You ever take food out of the freezer?'

Grant was pouring himself another glass and heading out of the kitchen.

'Yeah, but like I said, Simon wasn't eating much.' He paused in the doorway.

Marcus drained his wine, and ran the glass under the tap. He didn't want to even attempt to explain to Grant the reason he'd asked, but he felt unsettled and changed the subject.

'You know Simon had some very nice gold cuff-links, a couple with emeralds in the centre.'

Grant grinned. 'Yeah, I know. I'll maybe go up and have a check over the bedroom.'

Marcus waited until the kitchen was clear before he went into the back kitchen and opened the deep freeze. There were shelves of meats and frozen vegetables, French fries, but no containers of ready-made meals. He made his way back to the main kitchen and banged into the doorframe – he was quite drunk. Could it have been possible that Simon had eaten something containing poison, and then if Grant had fed the leftovers to Wally maybe that was what the dog had died from, and not rat poison?

He was still unable to stop thinking about it as he went upstairs and found Grant in Simon's bedroom. He had opened lots of the drawers and small leather boxes had been tossed onto the bed. He continued his rummaging as Marcus started to open one box after another, uncovering mono-grammed cufflinks and gold studs along with gold chains, medallions and heavy gold bracelets.

'He liked the bling, did old Simon,' Grant remarked as he searched through a drawer of silk ties and cravats.

'Yeah he certainly did. Any money stashed around?'

Grant shook his head, but Marcus was sure he would have already searched and pocketed much of what he wanted. He crossed to the massive old Victorian wardrobe, opening both carved doors to reveal rows and rows of suits and jackets, all expensive and tailored for Simon. Cashmere sweaters lay in stacks on the open-shelved unit above racks of trousers.

'Like a men's fashion store in here,' Marcus said, taking out some of the items to check their labels, as he caught the distinct cologne worn by Simon, a musky lime perfume.

'You staying over?' Grant asked nonchalantly.

'Well I've had too much to drink to drive back to London.'

Grant came to stand beside him and put his hand on the small of his neck.

'Maybe not sleep in here – let's take this stuff down and open up the rest of the boxes with a nice glass of wine.'

Marcus cringed slightly and then smiled. 'Yeah, why not?'

Grant returned to collect the boxes from the bed and tossed one to Marcus but as he tried to catch it, he stumbled and dropped it. The large leather case sprang open to reveal a diamond necklace.

'Christ almighty, look at this – are they real diamonds?'

Grant bent down and scooped it up, grinning. 'I'd say they're the real thing, and worth a packet.'

Marcus watched as Grant stuffed the necklace into his pocket.

'Hey, I thought we'd share stuff...'

'Don't worry, I'm just putting it in my pocket to take downstairs. You never know, it might be part of a really valuable set that we can share out,' Grant said and, with his hands full of the smaller items, he walked out.

Lena had shouted to Deirdre that everything was ready. Eggs, bacon, sausages, baked beans and mushrooms were all piled high on a plate, plus she had made fried bread, and was looking in the fridge for the tomato ketchup when Deirdre walked in.

'Wow, this is a feast,' she said.

'Pour yourself another glass of wine, and do you want HP or tomato ketchup?'

'HP for me, thank you.'

Lena plonked down both sauces and then drew out a chair to sit opposite Deirdre. The television set was turned down low, and Lena gestured towards it, saying that Doris Day was singing *'Que Sera Sera'*, and it was about her son being kidnapped, but she couldn't really remember much of the plot. She picked up the remote and turned the TV off.

'Agnes watches all the daytime soaps and the usual crap. Sometimes I come in here and cringe as it's either somebody cooking, or somebody selling or buying a house, so I hate to sit down and eat when she's around. She drives me to distraction, forever washing her hands, and I swear if you stood still long enough she'd put a plastic bag over your head and stick a label on you.'

Deirdre smiled and started eating as Lena banged the sauce bottle against the table, and then ate at an amazing rate, dipping the bread into the egg yolk.

'I often think that this is the best dinner ever, and I love BLTs with loads of mayonnaise, and crispy fresh lettuce with thin-sliced tomatoes.'

'My favourite too,' Deirdre said and between

mouthfuls asked Lena what her business was as she had never been told.

'Oh I recently started a company called Kiddy Winks, it does themed parties for children, so I have people making up the costumes, toys and designs for the cake, tablecloths, balloons with their names printed on – all sorts of things like that.'

She pushed her half-eaten dinner aside. 'I had hired a girl called Gail Summers to help me run it, and I really made her welcome, and I was so helpful explaining everything to her and do you know how she repaid me?'

Lena got up from the table and went over to the sink. There were numerous pans left on the draining board, as if she had used a separate one for each of the ingredients. She almost threw her dinner plate into the sink as she turned to face Deirdre.

'Two-faced bitch gave Marcus details of my earnings, not just present ones but projected ones – he knew every single account. When I met with his divorce lawyer I was totally and utterly stunned he knew so much about my business.'

'I'm sorry – that must have been dreadful to find out.'

Deirdre got up, intending to put her plate in the dishwasher.

'Leave it, just leave it, Agnes can clear it all up in the morning.'

'I don't mind tidying up,' Deirdre said.

'I just told you to leave it!' Lena snatched the dish and threw it into the sink. As she turned back to face Deirdre, her face was twisted with anger. She was so tense and angry her fists were clenched and Deirdre was starting to feel very alarmed by the way she was behaving – from being very friendly she had become abusive and threatening.

'I have faced the truth about my husband: he's a loser, a bisexual leech dependent on his rich friend to pay his legal fees. He was only here because he had nowhere else to go and it was not for Amy, not for me, but for himself.'

'I am sure your husband wanted to be here for you at this very trying time.'

'Trying, TRYING? Have you any idea what it's like to spend day after day waiting for news, hoping and praying she will come home?' she cried, and swept out of the kitchen, leaving the counsellor not exactly cowering, but nevertheless very unnerved. Deirdre followed the sound of banging doors coming from the master bedroom. She tapped and entered but Lena appeared not to even hear her as she was dragging clothes from the wardrobe and hurling them onto the bed.

'Lena, I think we need to sit down and talk things through calmly,' Deirdre suggested.

'I have to select what I am to wear for the television broadcast. I want everyone to know what a disgusting deviant piece of shit Marcus is; he is going to pay for walking out on me today.'

'I don't think that will be a very good or productive attitude to take, Lena. This will be your opportunity to ask the public to assist in any way possible in tracing Amy. If you are antagonistic or belligerent about your husband, it might not do your image any good, and I am certain it will not help find Amy.'

Lena made no reply; she was unzipping her trousers and kicking them away, and then pulled her sweater over her head, throwing it to one side.

Deirdre could see clearly the many thin red circular scars on both arms. Down the inner thighs of both legs were strange butterfly-shaped red scars, from her knees up to her crotch. It was obvious that Lena was self-harming.

She took a dressing gown from the hook behind the bedroom door and held it out to Lena.

'Slip this on, Lena, and we can talk through what clothes you will feel confident to wear, but as we don't have a time schedule as yet, we can maybe choose a few and put them to one side.'

Lena nodded and allowed Deirdre to hold up the dressing gown as she slipped her arms inside the sleeves. To the counsellor's relief she quickly calmed down, and then she began to refold the clothes she had flung across the bed. Suddenly she gave a soft low sob and turned to Deirdre, holding in her arms the maroon cashmere sweater that they had used for the reconstruction of Amy's last sighting.

'Amy and I both bought one – look, it's got these pretty frilled edges on the sleeves, with the matching maroon ribbon threaded through. I let them take this for the girl who acted as Amy when she was last seen on the Fulham Road; she was wearing hers but I have not been able to even really look at it.'

She gently stroked the soft wool and then held it to her face.

'Please don't let her be hurt, I ache all the time

as I miss her and want her to come home.'

Deirdre gently put her arms around Lena and really felt for her as she cried with such heart-breaking muffled sobs, repeating over and over that if Amy were never coming home she would not want to live.

As a Victim Support counsellor Deirdre had dealt with numerous tragedies, giving parents and loved ones a means of knowing they were not alone in their grief. She knew from her training to never get too personally involved, but to be a consistent calm presence. Deirdre could relate to the anguish of Lena's situation. She also felt exceptionally angry towards Marcus Fulford, who was not helping his wife – to the contrary – and she thought his behaviour deplorable.

'I'm here for you, Lena, I'm not going anywhere, and I won't leave you.'

'Will you pray with me?' The woman's voice was like a child's and hardly audible.

They knelt together side by side; Lena had her hands clasped together in prayer and her eyes tightly closed.

'Please, God, bring my Amy home safe and sound, Amen.'

Chapter 34

The next morning DI Reid was anxiously awaiting the toxicology reports on both Simon Boatly and Harry Dunn.

The incident room were all aware of the possibility they might have been poisoned, but DCI Jackson, much to Reid's relief, had not let the error over the poison mushroom recipes in the journal be known to the team. Reid had contacted the vet who had dealt with Boatly's dog Wally and was somewhat relieved when the vet said blood tests had confirmed the dog had eaten rat poison.

There was still no sighting of Amy, and even the crude time-wasting calls had diminished to a few 'sickos'. The mass of publicity had drawn a blank, and DCI Jackson was forced to reassess the next stage of the inquiry. The death of Boatly and Dunn was an obvious concern, but without the toxicology evidence to prove they had died from poison it was a waiting game, or, as Jackson described it, 'a fucking unexploded time bomb'.

Jackson was in a quandary, but at least he was now taking Professor Cornwall's diagnosis seriously, and was aware that Amy Fulford might be alive, albeit under another identity. He also had to consider that she had planted the poisons before disappearing, and had since been abducted or killed. Everyone agreed on one disheartening fact: they were probably looking for a murderer, dead or alive.

The exclusive interview Agnes had agreed to do was not as yet published and she was at work at nine as usual. She found the kitchen untidy and wine glasses in the TV room, so she set about rushing around to get everything in its habitual perfect order.

She collected the dry-cleaning shortly after eleven and returned to the house. She left the items in their plastic covers and took the jackets and trousers that belonged to Marcus, and the maroon sweater that was Lena's, upstairs and hung the sweater in Lena's bedroom wardrobe. She put Marcus's things in the space where Lena had already hung his new clothes.

Agnes had just returned to the kitchen when Marcus called to say he would not be returning home for a while but was remaining at Boatly's house in Henley. He asked about Lena and she was able to tell him that she was well and working in her office. No sooner had she replaced the phone than DI Reid rang and she put him through to Lena's office. Agnes decided to listen in to the call in case there was something useful she could sell to the press.

'Hello, Mrs Fulford. I've spoken to the television producer and they want to pre-record the interview rather than go live, and if you are agreeable will do it tomorrow morning.'

'I look forward to it, Inspector Reid.'

'Good. I'll have a police car pick you up at nine a.m.'

Lena asked Deirdre to come and give her more

advice on which outfit to wear. The counsellor obligingly sat herself down on the bed as Lena went to the wardrobe to pick out some clothes.

'I have always taken care of my clothes – my mother taught me to always replace them onto hangers after wearing them, and always dry-clean cashmere; she loved cashmere, so soft against your skin, and I love that sometimes I can smell my perfume lingering; she always had a sweet lilac essence and...'

She noticed the dry-cleaned maroon sweater in its plastic cover and took it out, frowning.

'Where did this come from?'

'Your wardrobe,' Deirdre said, fearing Lena was losing it.

Lena passed it to Deirdre, then took out the identical one and held it up. 'I showed you this before, the police used it in the reconstruction, so where did the dry-cleaned one come from?'

Deirdre had a sinking feeling in her stomach as Lena was fingering the sweater and visibly becoming more and more agitated. She snatched the dry-cleaned one from Deirdre and hurried down the stairs, shouting for Agnes.

'Where did you get it from?' Lena's voice was high-pitched as she held up the dry-cleaned sweater in front of her housekeeper.

'From Mr Fulford's dirty clothes he brought over from the flat. I didn't really even look at it, I just bundled everything together that needed to be cleaned and took it to the dry-cleaner's.'

'Don't you understand the importance of this, Agnes? If Amy was last seen wearing it then how did it get to be with Marcus's clothes? It means she was not wearing it when she disappeared or...' Her voice trailed off and she looked fearfully towards Deirdre.

'She must have gone to his flat.'

'Something has just come up,' Reid said, barely stopping to knock on Jackson's office door. 'It appears the sweater we believed was worn by Amy the last time she was seen has surfaced. The Victim Support counsellor just rang to say it was in a suitcase amongst clothes Marcus Fulford took to his wife's house. He's staying in Henley at Boatly's and if the sweater is Amy's then–'

Jackson interrupted. 'She went to the Mayfair flat, exactly as she told Serena Newman she was going to do! I want him rearrested and questioned – he has been bloody lying from day one.'

'I agree, but let me first get the full story before we maybe jump the gun. I'm going over there now.'

'Shit, I don't like this – go on, move it, and get back to me ASAP.'

That same morning, Marcus and Grant had been requested to attend Boatly's lawyer's in Kensington regarding the contents of the will. They were both excited about the meeting, wondering exactly what they'd been left. By the time they arrived it was almost twelve and they were led into the prestigious offices by a dour-faced secretary who informed them that Mr Boatly's lawyer would be with them shortly. The office had a vast polished round table, with leather carved chairs, and the walls were panelled with oil paintings of various stern-faced men who all appeared to have the surname Sutherland on polished plaques beneath their portraits. After fifteen minutes a fleshy pink-faced man in an immaculate pinstriped suit entered, carrying a large leather-bound file. He introduced himself as Alistair Sutherland and greeted them with a fleshy soft handshake, gesturing for them to be seated. He spent a considerable time sifting through the mound of documents before he laid flat the final will and testament of Simon Boatly. In his pompous aristocratic voice he explained that his firm had taken care of the Boatly family for many years. He had endeavoured to contact all the beneficiaries, which had taken a great deal of time as many were deceased or living abroad.

'Right, gentlemen, let me proceed.'

Marcus was almost beside himself waiting to hear whether or not he was a beneficiary but he managed to remain calm and respectful. Grant kept on glancing nervously towards him; he was wondering if the bits of jewellery they had both pocketed might be included and if there would be any repercussions.

It seemed like an interminable time as Sutherland listed the beneficiaries' names, deceased as well as living, from second and third cousins to aunts and uncles, and charities. Eventually he said that the entire estate was valued at twenty-five million. Certain specific items were to remain in the Boatly family, but the rest was to be sold to provide the lump sums allocated to the listed beneficiaries.

'To my dearest and closest friend Marcus Fulford I leave three million pounds on the condition he divorces his wife and looks towards a career he wished to pursue during his days as my lover, but never accomplished whilst married.'

Marcus almost fainted; his heart was beating so rapidly, he had to clench the sides of the carved oak chair to stay upright. To Grant he had left twenty-five thousand, thanking him for the affection and care he had been given in their short time together. They could both barely hear let alone take in the lengthy explanation from Sutherland as to how and when the monies would be paid to them. They couldn't wait to get out of the stuffy office and shout out loud in the street, Marcus more so than Grant as three million was like being given a new lease on life.

Reid listened as Agnes repeated exactly how she had removed the clothes, including the 'smelly' maroon sweater, from Marcus's suitcase and taken various items to the dry-cleaner's.

Lena was very subdued, her head bowed, her hands clasped together. She obviously knew what the discovery meant, and yet showed no visible sign that Marcus could have been involved in any way, or that there could be a more sinister meaning. Deirdre however was very aware how high the stakes were, and knew by the way Reid acted that this was a very big development.

Shortly afterwards, a team was sent to Henley to arrest Marcus and bring him back to the station. It was almost six when the police arrived at the Old Manor to find both Marcus and Grant exceedingly drunk and celebrating. The confused and inebriated Marcus was led out in handcuffs and he passed out in the back of the patrol car; they had to support him into the police station. It was decided that until he was sober they could not question him and he was left to sleep it off in the cell.

Early the next morning Deirdre heard a scream and found Lena in the kitchen with the newspaper open, tears streaming down her face as the headline screamed out, FATHER ARRESTED FOR MURDER, and then there were numerous photographs of Amy, and the exclusive interview with the housekeeper Agnes Moors.

'Look what that two-faced bitch has done, she has stolen private photographs and given them to the press as well as saying things about me and Amy. How dare she do this to me? My lawyers will sue her and the paper. She will live to regret this, I'll make her sorry, she is going to pay for this!'

Lena was so enraged her whole face changed, her mouth a thin tight line, and she was virtually spitting as she swore and threatened to take a knife and cut Agnes Moors' throat. Deirdre was quite frightened as she watched Lena pace up and down the kitchen, smashing plates and cups and anything she could lay her hands on. It was a horrible scene that went on and on, and Deirdre was worried that when Agnes made her nine o'clock arrival Lena might assault her.

Eventually, more from exhaustion than anything else, Lena quietened and began cutting out the articles with a pair of scissors and folding them up. This done, she announced she was going to her office to talk to her lawyers, but as soon as Agnes arrived she wanted to know.

Deirdre took the opportunity to call Agnes's mobile and warn her not to come into work. The woman was in floods of tears, and claimed the journalist had twisted what she had said.

'You have done a lot of damage, Agnes,' Deirdre pointed out, 'and please stay away until we have some calm here. Mrs Fulford is talking to her lawyers.'

Agnes sobbed, and again claimed that she had not said all the things in the article, but admitted she had taken the photographs from Lena's private album.

'Listen to me, Agnes, I don't know what the outcome will be, I am just giving you some advice, and I think you should take it and stay away until the heat has died down here.'

'Will I lose my job?' came the pleading response.

'That's not up to me, but stay away from the house for now.'

Deirdre next thought she had better call DI Reid to explain the situation. He had only just arrived at the station, but it was buzzing, not only because of the leak of Marcus's arrest, but also the exclusive interview with Agnes Moors. Marcus had still not been interviewed and was waiting in the cells for his solicitor Angus McFarland. It appeared he was very hung over, feeling unwell and had been sick during the morning.

Deirdre cleared up the broken china and then went to see how Lena was doing. She had locked the office door and after repeatedly knocking Deirdre eventually got a response: Lena said that she wished to be left alone.

'Listen to me, Lena, I have spoken to DI Reid and he is going to try to come over to be here for you, and he needs to know if you still want to do the television interview.'

'I said I would do it, and if they want me to do it, I will do it, now please leave me alone.'

Deirdre returned to the kitchen and put the scissors away, then picked up the scraps of newspaper, rolling them into a ball and tossing them into the pedal bin. The kitchen was quickly back in order, although the phone rang constantly and her head started throbbing as she wondered if perhaps she should answer the calls, but decided against it. She knew if DI Reid wanted to make contact he would call her mobile. Hoping to take her mind off the situation, she decided to read one of the many books in the floor-to-ceiling bookcase in the drawing room.

Entering the vast elegantly furnished room, with its rows of silver-framed photographs on top of the piano and on all the small side tables, she went over to the bookcase. Her eye was caught by the rows of leather-bound photograph albums, and she rested her hand against one, letting her fingers trail across the bindings until she hooked her index finger into the curved leather of one that appeared older. Opening it, she realized it was Lena's album from when she was young and single. She flicked over the plastic covers, noting the various photographs, some in black and white, and was impressed by the neatness and the small handwritten cards denoting the place and year. She turned numerous pages until she reached the last section and was surprised to see a smiling, stunningly pretty Lena in a black university gown, wearing a mortarboard and holding a degree scroll. The note beneath it was written in black felt tip print, very small and underlined: 'Oxford University Graduation – First-Class Honours Degree in Biological Sciences'. Deirdre had had no notion that Lena was so well educated. Turning a few more pages there were pictures of her wearing a white lab coat and with that beautiful lazy smile on her face; written in felt tip at the bottom was: 'MSc Course, Harvard, USA'. The last page showed a serious-faced Lena standing beside a tall elderly man with a shock of white hair; he wore a crumpled tweed suit and a cravat, and beneath the picture was a caption in a different larger print: 'Home with Daddy'.

Intrigued by uncovering Lena's past, Deirdre reached for another album, carefully replacing the one she had looked through. She wondered if this was where Agnes had stolen the photographs for the press, and thought how disgusting it was that the woman had been so invasive and sly. Another album held many photographs of Lena and Marcus's wedding day, and again Lena looked stunningly beautiful, dressed in a couture white wedding gown. As Deirdre turned another plastic-covered page, loose photographs tumbled out and she had to get down on her hands and knees to pick them up. Many featured the same white-haired man but now his face was scribbled over, or blacked out with felt tip pen. She laid the album down flat on the floor and reinserted the loose photographs; one she thought had to be of Lena's mother and it was obvious where she got her good looks. She turned it over and in looped ink writing on the back was the note 'Mama before Cancer'. A second picture showed the virtually skeletal frame of the same woman, and on the back, written in the same childish writing, was 'Mama dying'.

Deirdre closed the albums, and had started to get up when she noticed lined up on the last shelf of the bookcase a row of larger volumes. Some were atlases and one was dotted with small coloured stickers, but not until she eased it out did she realize it was a detailed *Encyclopaedia of Mushrooms.*

Deirdre carried the heavy book to the sofa and set it down on the coffee table. She turned to a page marked by a small coloured tab. There were large coloured photographs of a mushroom called 'The Deadly Amanita', another was of a strange small domed mushroom called 'The Destroying Angel' and one with a flat head was described as 'The Death Cap'.

Deirdre jumped when her mobile rang, and she patted her pockets to retrieve it. It was a very agitated DI Reid, apologizing that he doubted if he could get to her as they had a really worrying situation.

Angus McFarland, Marcus's solicitor, had been taken to the interview room, where he demanded to know why his client had been rearrested. Jackson told him about the maroon sweater, and curtly said Marcus could quite possibly have murdered Amy in the flat, left her body there while he created an alibi by visiting Justine, and then disposed of the body on the Sunday. It had been a heated discussion and when Marcus was then brought up from the cells, he looked flushed, complained of stomach pains, and said he'd been vomiting. McFarland suggested that the police doctor be called to administer some medication for his client.

Jackson thought Marcus was trying to pull a fast one, and, eager to get started, said he'd call a doctor after the interview. He was certain he could break Fulford into confessing to murder and was going to be hard on him. Reid started the DVD recorder and cautioned Marcus. Before Jackson could ask his first question McFarland interjected.

'My client stands by his original alibi; he is innocent and has never lied about where he was on the day his daughter went missing. As for the maroon sweater, Mr Fulford accepts beyond doubt it is his daughter's, and that she clearly went to the flat he rented on the Saturday afternoon, but he was not there. When he packed his bags to move he gathered up the contents of the laundry bag, and without looking through it, simply dumped it in his case. Now unless you can provide any hard evidence to the contrary, or can disprove his alibi, I suggest you release my client immediately.'

Jackson frowned. 'I'll release him when I'm good and ready and I want to hear the answers from Fulford's mouth, not yours, Mr McFarland.'

Marcus had started sweating profusely, which to Jackson was a sign he had lied to McFarland. The next minute Marcus leaned forward, clutching his stomach, and retched uncontrollably, before he suddenly collapsed, hitting his head against the interview-room table. He started convulsing and then seemed to hallucinate, shouting and screaming for his daughter to come home. They tried to give him first aid, called an ambulance immediately and told the crew he might be suffering from mushroom poisoning.

Deirdre hurried to Lena's bedroom as soon as she got off the phone from an increasingly frantic Reid. The en-suite bathroom door was closed and the shower turned on. She called out for Lena, who shouted back that she was washing her hair and to please give her some privacy.

'Lena, your husband has been taken to Kingston Hospital.'

Slowly the shower door opened and Lena, with shampoo frothed across her hair, leaned out. 'What?'

Deirdre repeated what she'd said, and although Lena seemed to register what she had been told, there was little reaction and she simply closed the shower door and continued washing her hair.

'Do you want me to call the hospital to see how he is?' Deirdre asked in frustration.

'I'll dry my hair, get dressed and see you downstairs.'

Deirdre couldn't believe her attitude and decided that she would call Kingston Hospital herself. She explained to the nurse in intensive care who she was.

'He is in a very serious condition and unconscious,' the nurse said. 'The doctors are still treating him, so until I speak to them there is not much more I can tell you.'

Deirdre asked to be called as soon as there was more news as she was taking care of Mrs Fulford.

Reid pulled up outside the Henley property and parked beside a patrol car. Two uniformed officers were already there and they explained that there was no answer to repeated knocks on the door, and that the back door was locked. Reid, fearing for Grant's safety, was about to break open the back door when he saw and heard a Porsche roar up the driveway. A young man got out with a panicked expression on his face, asking nervously what was happening and holding up a bag full of shopping, saying he'd been to the supermarket. Establishing that this was Mr Grant Delany, Reid suggested they went inside and Grant led them into the sitting room.

'Marcus Fulford is seriously ill and in intensive care. We don't know for certain yet, but it's possible he has some kind of serious food poisoning,' Reid explained, not wanting to unduly alarm Grant, who looked worried.

'You're joking; we did get a bit plastered last night, but we were celebrating because he's been left three million quid by Simon.' Globules of spittle formed at the sides of his mouth and he was talking very fast.

'Can you just listen carefully, please? Have you had any stomach pains, headaches, maybe feel as if you have flu-like symptoms?'

'No, I'm fine, but you are starting to freak me out. I am a vegan so whatever I eat I prepare for myself.'

'Can you recall exactly what Mr Fulford ate?'

'He had a steak the night before last, but you lot turned up and arrested him before we ate properly yesterday. Earlier on we drove to London, met with Simon's solicitors to discuss his will and Marcus had a beef burger and I had a veggie one on the way back here.'

'And he wasn't ill at all after the beef burger?'

'No, and we started drinking when we got back. I mean he was ecstatic – three million quid. I got twenty-five grand, but then I'd only known Simon for a matter of months.'

Grant seemed unable to stop talking and Reid in irritation stood up, walking around the room, picking up one bottle after another.

'What did you both drink?'

'Dom Pérignon champagne and red wine I got from the cellar. Well I sort of drank most of the bubbly as I don't really like red wine, but Marcus opened a couple of bottles before he went on to the brandy,' Grant said and pointed to the dusty bottle.

Reid saw that it was a vintage Napoleon in an elegant carved bottle, with just a small residue left in the bottom.

'That's a very expensive brandy – hundreds of quid – I brought it back from Simon's place in Green Street.'

'Was it open?'

'Yeah, and about a quarter full. Simon loved his brandy, not that he told me to bring it back from his flat, I just did because I know he favoured the aged stuff and we didn't have any in the cellar.'

'Did Simon consume any of this?'

489

'Not really – he wasn't well so wasn't drinking.'

'What do you mean, not really?'

'Well, I put a little splash in when I made him a hot toddy.'

Reid suspected that Amy must have put the poison in the brandy hoping her father would drink it at the flat, but as fate would have it the bottle ended up back at Boatly's and both he and Marcus unwittingly drank from it.

'Did you have any of the brandy?'

'No way, can't stand the stuff.'

'Do you know how much of it Marcus had?'

Grant thought for a moment and said that as far as he recalled he maybe had one or two large ones before he got arrested. Reid asked to see the room Marcus was using and followed Grant up the wide staircase and into the master bedroom. There were piles of clothing in different sizes on the floor and bed.

'You both sleep in here?'

His face flushed. 'Er, yeah, but only the one night.'

On the floor was a jumble of discarded old-fashioned leather jewellery boxes embossed with a monogrammed faded gold crown. Grant saw the way Reid looked at the cases and started to pick them up.

'Simon's lawyers mentioned the jewellery they would be collecting, but most of these were empty. That big one must have one time had a tiara or something inside – you can see the indentation on the old velvet.'

'Where's the jewellery from the boxes that weren't empty then?'

'Oh, uh, I've got it hidden away for the solicitors. I didn't want a break-in and for it to be stolen.'

'Very thoughtful of you,' Reid said sarcastically. 'This box you think a tiara was in...'

'Well I'm not sure – it's just the indentations made me think that.'

'If it had been removed ages ago I'd have thought the indentations would be less pronounced.'

'I swear I haven't got it and Marcus was with me when we opened the boxes.'

'Well let's hope he comes round and can confirm that's correct.'

Reid was certain Grant was lying and, along with Marcus, had probably helped himself to the contents of the empty boxes, but he had more pressing things to deal with. He instructed Grant to check the freezer for any opened bags or plastic cartons of food, not to eat from them and to put them to one side. Reid also told him to put aside any other bottles of opened drink he found and he would arrange for their collection later. Lastly he said he was taking the bottle of Napoleon brandy for forensics. Grant picked up on what Reid had just said.

'Wait a minute, you think he was deliberately poisoned and it was in the brandy bottle. Oh my God, I gave it to Simon in the toddy and it must have killed him ... oh my God.'

'You didn't know, and it wasn't enough to kill him, Grant. The pathologist said he died of AIDS-related pneumonia.'

But Grant was in tears and could barely take in

491

what Reid was saying when the detective asked him for a set of keys to the flat so he could search it for any other contaminated fluids.

Deirdre was in the kitchen when she received a call from Miss Jordan, who agreed that after her last appointment in the afternoon she would come to see Lena. Suddenly she heard Lena's voice from behind. Deirdre was taken aback to see that the woman's hair was brushed to perfection and gleaming, she was perfectly made up and wearing the clothes she had chosen for the interview. As Lena crossed the kitchen her perfect legs, slim ankles and stiletto shoes made her look as if she was modelling on a catwalk.

'Have you heard from the producer or whoever is arranging the interview?' she demanded.

'No, but I did call the hospital and Mr Fulford is not well and on the intensive care ward, so maybe you should go and see him.'

'He walked out on me when I really needed him to be here. I think it would be more beneficial if I do this television interview. I have prepared what I am going to say, because my priority is and always has been trying to find Amy. How do I look, by the way?'

'Very elegant.'

Again she gave that smile, and then sighed as she drew out a kitchen chair for herself and sat down.

'My mother was always perfectly dressed; she was adored by my father, but he found her lack of interest in anything other than her designer clothes and beauty treatments irritating,' she said

confidingly. 'He was such a brilliant and intelligent man, but when she became ill his patience
with her evaporated and he could hardly face her.
She had breast cancer, and it spread to her lungs
and eventually her brain. Her last months were
pain-racked until the morphine injections, but
then she didn't eat, and just lay in bed slowly
fading away. I was taught at home by Daddy as
he needed me to look after her; he was a well-
educated university man and the most vibrant
and inspiring tutor, also well-travelled and he
spoke numerous languages.' She flicked back her
glossy hair.

'Did you go to university?' Deirdre asked rather
lamely.

'Oh yes, Oxford just like Daddy, and I got a
scholarship to study for a Master's Degree in
America, but I never felt very happy there.'

'Why was that?'

'I missed Marcus so much, and we were very
much in love. He was very understanding about
me going to Harvard and said we'd get married
when I finished there. Daddy was very disappointed when I insisted we come back to England.'

'Oh, so your father was in America with you?'

She laughed and said that he was never far away
from her, and made another expansive gesture
with her hand. 'I had a few issues, health-wise, you
know, the normal teenager and young women
things, like depression and deep sadness.' She suddenly laughed before continuing. 'I think Daddy
knew from the beginning Marcus was bisexual,
but I didn't even consider it, even though his so-

called close friend Simon Boatly obviously was, as they were always together.'

Deirdre was trying to ascertain exactly where it was all leading. It was her job to help bereaved or anxious families, but this situation was totally unexpected because Lena appeared to be enjoying her disclosures, talking about her husband with obvious affection, even accepting his sexual inadequacies.

Lena pushed her chair back and stood up. 'Why was that sweater in his stinking flat? I have had the humiliation of being told he had whores there; he hardly ever had sex with me, but he had whores and my daughter was forced to watch him screwing them. That disgusting animal Simon has always been like a predatory leech, dangling his body and wealth, enticing Marcus away from me. I wanted to show him just how pitiful Simon was and that he even came on to me in that hideous flat of his.'

She was becoming very agitated, curling a strand of hair around her finger, then pulling at it as if wanting to drag it out by the roots. She suddenly started to gasp for breath, her chest heaving.

'LENA, stop this now, just take deep breaths, try and slow down...'

Deirdre began opening drawers, searching for a bag for Lena to breathe into, but she couldn't find one. Lena's face was now shining with sweat and then she slumped onto the floor.

'Oh my God, oh my God.' Deirdre knelt down beside her, reaching round to support her head. Eventually the awful gasping sounds quietened and slowly her breathing returned to normal.

'I am so sorry, so sorry,' she whispered.

Reid took the brandy bottle straight to the forensic lab, and whilst he was there he was given the toxicology reports on Harry Dunn and Simon Boatly. Much to Reid's relief, Boatly's primary cause of death was HIV/AIDS, though he did have traces of mushroom poison in his body, not enough to kill him outright, but enough to exacerbate his respiratory problems, and effectively speed up his death. The toxicologist had found ingested traces of a mushroom called 'Ink Cap', which if eaten in isolation would have no ill effects, but if alcohol was consumed with it, or even many hours after, a reaction would set in.

Reid was stunned, and he now felt certain that Marcus Fulford was suffering from the same poison. He knew it was imperative that all the 'enemies' in Amy's journal were contacted again and warned of the dangers so they could check not only for food but open bottles of wine or other alcohol that could possibly have been contaminated.

Marcus remained unconscious as his condition continued to deteriorate, while DCI Jackson waited at the hospital in the hope he would regain consciousness and be able to answer questions. Doctors had begun to frantically run tests. Specialists were called in and were discussing what if anything could be administered to halt further organ failure. The seriousness of his condition was causing increasing alarm as his liver was now damaged, and it was suggested they begin a revolutionary medical technique involving an artificial liver machine, which could potentially remove the toxins by filtering his blood through charcoal granules. However, by now his heart was affected and his lungs were collapsing. The medical staff was informed that the usual standard procedure would have been to pump his stomach to remove the toxins, but Marcus had vomited almost as soon as he had been admitted and was again retching and sick the following morning. The most unnerving fact was that with all the new modern science there was no antidote as yet discovered.

Chapter 35

'Truffles!' exclaimed a concerned Harriet Newman. 'I'm pretty sure Amy brought a box of them to the house and they were home-made.'

The Newman family were high on the priority list and were scared, having listened to DS Lane explain that the mushroom poison might also be contained in alcoholic or normal liquids as well as many types of food.

Bill Newman interjected. 'We were worried for Serena and our two small boys when DI Reid told us about the possibility of poisoning. Harriet and I decided to throw out everything in the fridge and deep freeze.'

Harriet nodded. 'And luckily there were no opened bottles of wine and the alcohol is kept in a locked cabinet away from the children.'

'Can you tell me more about when Amy brought the truffles round?' Lane asked Mrs Newman.

She thought about the question before answering. 'It wasn't on her last visit but a previous one a few weekends before. They were a thank-you for having her to stay. The small box was rather elegant, but the sweets themselves had marzipan in them, which no one in our family likes.'

'What did you do with them?' Lane asked.

'I can't recall exactly, but I think I threw the box out,' Harriet said.

'And none of you have had any tummy upsets or suddenly felt violently ill?'

They all looked at each other and shook their heads before Bill Newman spoke.

'Well Serena had a fever and was sick...'

'Let's not exaggerate, darling, it was more like the flu than anything else. She wasn't eating while she felt ill anyway and I made sure she had plenty of water to keep hydrated.'

DS Lane noticed a look of dread on Serena's face. 'Do you know anything about the truffles?'

Serena said nothing at first, but when pressed by her mother to tell the truth she started to cry.

'I took them to my room and hid them in my wardrobe and forgot about them, but the day after Amy disappeared I found them and tried one. I took one bite but it had marzipan in it and I hate marzipan so I spat it out and threw the box in the bin.'

Mrs Newman was beside herself, shouting at and chastising her daughter for failing to remember this before, and her husband had to calm her down.

'The boys could have eaten one of them, for God's sake.'

'Yeah, all right, darling, but we'll not know now if they were dangerous, and we should just thank God that Serena – in fact all of us – hates marzipan.'

'But why did you try to eat it? You don't like marzipan,' Mrs Newman asked, almost shaking with agitation.

All the fight had gone out of Serena. 'I just wanted to see what a truffle tasted like, I'm sorry.'

'Well if the truffle did contain any poison then your mother giving you plenty of water was a good thing, and more than likely flushed out any dangerous toxins. You were very fortunate, young lady,' DS Lane said firmly as Serena started to cry.

Only an hour later, Marcus Fulford's became the third poison-related death. Jackson and his murder team were in a state of agitation over who might be next and whether Amy Fulford was still alive and administering the poison. They were still waiting on the forensic report on the bottle of vintage brandy that Marcus had drunk from, but were reasonably certain that the contents were contaminated.

Deirdre had just got Lena to rest in her bedroom after the panic attack when DI Reid called and gave her the news that Marcus Fulford had died of organ failure. He said he had spoken with Marjory Jordan and she was on her way over to help Deirdre break the news and comfort Lena.

It wasn't long after the call that Miss Jordan

arrived at the house and told Deirdre that the journalists outside already knew about Marcus's death as they had asked her about it.

'How did he actually die?' Miss Jordan asked.

'I was told organ failure, but how the press have got hold of it is beyond me – they must have a contact at the hospital.'

'How has she been?'

'Under the circumstances extraordinarily calm,' Deirdre said cautiously. 'I suggested she visit her husband in hospital, while he was still alive, but she didn't want to. She seemed to think she would be going to the studio for another *Crime Night* television interview, and got dressed and made up ready for it.'

'Well probably for the best that she wasn't subjected to it; the pressure she has been under must be taking a toll – she's really very fragile.'

Deirdre remarked that Lena had told her at length about her past, and that she had been surprised at her degrees and university background. She also mentioned that Lena had told her about her mother's cancer, and that she seemed very enthralled by her father's intellect.

Miss Jordan gave a long sigh.

'I have no intention of breaking patient confidentiality, but in reality I believe that her father married a great beauty with no brains and his daughter inherited both. I doubt she was enthralled by his intellect as he was very dominant and controlled her life for many years. The pressure proved to be too much, because while at Harvard she had a nervous breakdown, and they returned to London, so she never really put her academic prowess to any use.'

'What caused the breakdown?'

'Being apart from Marcus, with whom she was deeply in love, didn't help and some old issues with her father raised their head again,' Miss Jordan replied primly.

'Funnily enough, I wondered why he would have been in America when she was studying. Were they very wealthy?'

Miss Jordan hesitated; again she was very guarded about discussing her patient, and repeated that she was not really allowed to give too many details.

'They were extremely well off, but Lena's father still lived in his old family semi-detached, and to all intents and purposes was very Scrooge-like. Lena was really her mother's sole carer as he refused to hire any nursing staff, but I think the mother came from a wealthy family – big property developers. When they died Lena inherited a considerable amount of money, but her father monitored any access to her inheritance and it was not until his death that she realized she was exceptionally wealthy.'

Deirdre nodded; for someone refusing to divulge any patient details, Miss Jordan seemed unable to stop herself, as she went on to say that as far as she was aware Marcus Fulford was a very kind-natured man, who had never been her patient, but she was aware he had personal problems and his bisexuality troubled him.

Miss Jordan gave a long sigh. 'Lena has bipolar disorder – at times her depression was very debilitating and to be diagnosed really helped her adjust, and with medication she has been able to cope. She's a very good mother, but suffers from a guilt complex that she was not able to be more understanding of Amy, who inherited her brilliance and looks. Lena told me that at times she had overpowering feelings of jealousy towards her daughter. The awful emotional impact of Amy disappearing, I felt, would be very difficult for her to deal with, but she cancelled numerous appointments, and now with Marcus's death she will really need my help more than ever before.'

Deirdre nodded in agreement and started to cry.

'What's wrong?' Marjory Jordan asked.

'Nothing, I'm just tired, that's all.'

'Come on, tell me, Deirdre. I'm a good listener.'

She took a deep breath. 'The stresses and strains of the last few days have become rather overwhelming and I've let them get to me. In my job that's not good and now I'm dreading telling Lena that her husband is dead. I really feel DI Reid should have come over personally to break the news.' She blew her nose on a tissue.

Miss Jordan sat her down and spoke quietly.

'In many ways we are similar, Deirdre. You counsel the victims of serious crimes and families of murder victims, and so do I in cases where it causes psychological stress or damage. I am sure you understand patient confidentiality but I feel I can trust you ... Lena was sexually abused by her father from an early age; it continued until she was sixteen years old and–'

They were interrupted as Lena shouted for Deirdre from the top landing. Miss Jordan picked up her case, saying she would go upstairs and tell her that Marcus was dead. Deirdre was so relieved, the tears that had begun a few moments before now came like a flood and she wept, out of total exhaustion, both emotional and physical.

Chapter 36

By seven o'clock Jackson was ordering the team to get together to decide how to handle the situation. Marcus Fulford's death had become a big issue for the press office and it was fortunate for the team that he had become ill while his solicitor was present, and not found dead in the cell.

The team had cobbled together a timeline of when each victim could have eaten or drunk contaminated food, and they had confirmation that the residue in the brandy bottle contained the remnants of a lethal concoction from a variety of mushrooms, which were still being analysed to identify the exact fungi. The examination had verified traces of the Ink Cap mushroom, which would slowly take effect if alcohol were consumed after ingestion.

Jackson and Reid were finding it impossible to be certain when the poison had been administered, owing to the different times each victim had died and not knowing exactly when the food or drink was laced. However, the dates did match with the period of time Amy Fulford was missing, and now they had the added evidence of the box of marzipan truffles given to the Newmans. They also had a statement from Agnes that she had defrosted a spaghetti bolognese and was going to serve it to Mr and Mrs Fulford, but when they had not eaten it, she had passed it to Harry Dunn who took it home.

They had yet again contacted all the surviving 'enemies' in the journal to warn them to be vigilant; however, Agnes Moors was not at home or answering her mobile. Her daughter Natalie said that she too was unable to contact her mother, and that Agnes was so upset she had gone to visit a friend, but did not say who or when she'd be back. Jackson wanted her tracked down, as the last thing he needed was another murder to deal with.

Jackson was unsure whether Amy was still alive, on the run, or had been murdered by her father, but reckoned that if she was alive it might be worth trying to lure her out into the open. He decided to issue a press release worded to imply that Marcus Fulford had murdered his daughter, and that they were no longer looking for a suspect in her disappearance. Admittedly they had no body but it would not be the first murder inquiry to never recover its victim.

Reid had the distinct impression Jackson was also trying to bring the case to a close, and that if Amy didn't surface, or her body wasn't found after a month or so, he would shut the investigation down. While he didn't want to question Jackson's judgement, Reid worried that if the information about the poison was to surface it could be alleged that the police had deliberately misled the public. He left the station feeling depressed, and in some way appalled that without any real confirmed evidence Marcus Fulford would be named as the man who had killed his own daughter.

Once home he opened a bottle of Scotch, mulling over the entire investigation, and tormented by the guilt of not contacting Deirdre. Finally he rang her mobile. She told him that Miss Jordan had informed Lena of Marcus's death and she had been inconsolable, screaming, sobbing and suffering another panic attack. It had taken considerable time to calm her, but after a sedative they had left her alone in her bedroom to sleep. However, ten minutes later she appeared in the drawing room, started swearing and shouting and insisted on playing the piano.

Deirdre was shocked at such bizarre behaviour, but Miss Jordan maintained if it was her way of releasing the pain they should let her get on with it. Eventually the sedative kicked in and Lena was helped to her bed by Miss Jordan.

By this time Deirdre really felt her nerves could not take much more. She told Reid she was no longer willing to stay at the house and pointed out that as a Victim Support worker she was not obliged to do so in the first place, and had only offered to help him out of the kindness of her heart. Reid tried to persuade her to stay another night, but she refused and said she was leaving and that was that. Reid spoke with Marjory Jordan, who said she could not stay overnight and that it was his responsibility to find someone to be with Lena.

Reid phoned Barbara Burrows. She was at home and had just had a hot relaxing bath, and was about to have some dinner.

'Hello, sir, how are you?'

'Fine, thanks. I really need your help with Mrs Fulford, Barbara.'

'What can I do for you?'

'She's taken the death of her husband very badly and the Victim Support lady has had to leave and Marjory Jordan is busy so I...'

'Need someone to sit with her?'

'You're a star, Barbara. I knew I could rely on you,' he said, assuming her question was a positive answer.

She wasn't actually that keen on going over to Lena Fulford's as she'd hoped to have a relaxing evening, but she did have a soft spot for Reid.

'I'm happy to be of assistance, sir, and chuffed that you asked me to help out.'

'It should only be for a couple of days as Jackson seems intent on bringing closure to the inquiry.'

'But surely he can't shut the case down – won't they still at least search for Amy's body?'

'Yes, that will obviously be continued. There have been many murder investigations where the victim's remains have not been discovered for months, even years.'

'If it's Jackson's decision, he should speak to Mrs Fulford and not lumber it on you.'

He sighed, knowing that would never happen, as he put down the phone. The discovery of the maroon sweater last worn by Amy was basically the linchpin of the investigation, proving that the girl must have returned to the flat her father was renting. No matter what angle he looked at it from, it was difficult to see who else would have placed it there if not Amy herself. He had the statement from Justine Hyde, Marcus's girlfriend, that he had been with her from about five thirty after the football match. If Fulford had killed Amy before the football match, Reid wondered, would he have even bothered to go to the game and then straight to Justine's flat? Reid knew that Boatly had a key to the Mayfair flat. But it had been confirmed that he was still abroad on the day Amy went missing. He wondered, had Amy's watch simply fallen from her wrist one weekend when she was in the car rather than from her dead body?

The unanswered questions went round and round in his head, until in frustration he began to jot down each one and underline it. Another scenario he mulled over was that if Marcus had found out that his daughter was making a hit list of people she wanted to poison, was that a possible reason for a violent argument that resulted in her death?

Even in his exhaustion he forced himself to think back through all the interviews, the mass of statements taken, his trips back and forth to the house in Henley and his original meeting with Simon Boatly. He next moved on to the times he had been to Amy's school, the meetings with Miss Polka and the headmistress, as well as his interview with the school matron. As far as he was able to ascertain, there was never any single mention of Amy showing signs of abuse by Marcus. Miss Polka had owned up to a sexual relationship with

Amy, but Amy herself had never said anything about being abused by her own father – the only abuse uncovered so far was the unpleasant bullying on Amy's Facebook page. Yet the findings at Marcus's rented flat were construed by Jackson as confirmation that Amy was sexually abused, but there was no forensic evidence of his DNA on Amy's underwear or bed sheets.

It was almost four in the morning, and his head was throbbing from concentrating for so many hours, along with the half bottle of Scotch he'd consumed, but he refused to call it quits. When did Amy prepare the poison? When did she pre-plan the infusion of it in the brandy, the truffles and the bolognese that was originally in the deep freeze? Did it take months of preparation, and where did she learn how to break down the mushroom spores to turn the poison into liquid for the brandy? Although her biology and history essays made references to poisonous mushrooms, the question was, when and where did she collect the mushrooms and how did she know the exact measurements? His list of queries got longer and longer, and now, unable to question Marcus Fulford, he began to accept the conclusion, rightly or wrongly, that Amy's murder happened on the Saturday she disappeared, and the subsequent poisoning and death of her victims was a tragic outcome of a plan that had already been set in motion.

There were only two journalists sitting in a car by the gates sipping coffee when DCI Jackson and Chief Superintendent Douglas drew up at Lena

Fulford's house the next morning. Barbara Burrows opened the front door and reported that Mrs Fulford had slept through the night without any incident, and was still dressing but should be down shortly.

They had to wait fifteen minutes before Lena came into the drawing room. She looked pale and drawn but had dressed smartly, wore make-up and her hair was swept up into a pleat. They both expressed their sympathy for the loss of her husband and said that they also now felt he was responsible for Amy's death.

'Did he admit it?' she asked, barely audible.

'We did not have the opportunity to question him in depth as he fell ill during the interrogation, but he could give no explanation as to why your daughter's sweater was found in the flat he rented from Mr Boatly,' Jackson told her.

She at last looked up, her incredibly blue eyes wide and unblinking. 'Do you believe that he was sexually abusing Amy?'

The normally blustering DCI was sweating as he said, as diplomatically as he could, that there was no direct or forensic evidence of the abuse, but the telltale signs, like the peephole they had uncovered in the flat, led them to believe that it was a strong possibility.

There was an awful silence as she slowly looked up again, her eyes brimming with tears.

'I'm deeply sorry, Mrs Fulford, but my experienced and professional opinion is that Amy won't be coming home,' Douglas said, feeling it wouldn't be right under the circumstances to use the term 'murdered'.

Jackson found it hard to meet her eyes. 'We won't give up looking for Amy, but you need to understand we may never find her body.'

Douglas glared at Jackson, annoyed with his choice of phrase at such a delicate time. Lena straightened her back, sitting fully upright.

'Thank you for your kind words of sympathy, but I would like to be left alone, so I can come to terms with the fact my beloved daughter will never be coming home, as I had hoped and prayed. I feel totally and utterly numb, and at the same time I have a terrible sense of guilt that I ever trusted Marcus and loved him to such an extent I did not protect my daughter.'

Driving back to the station, Chief Superintendent Douglas asked Jackson if he felt Mrs Fulford was drugged, as he had never in his entire career come across a woman who had been able to deal with such wretched and heartbreaking facts with hardly any trace of emotion.

'Maybe she's simply no emotion left after the events of the last few weeks. Also Burrows took me to one side and told me she had taken quite a few sedatives,' Jackson replied, somewhat relieved that his ordeal was over.

'Right, well let's hope she doesn't forget everything we told her because I don't fancy going through that again. Her being so quiet, so calm, it made me feel worse than I have ever felt before... I just think God help her when the reality takes over because she's still in denial...'

After the press release the interest in the Fulford

case palled. For the journalists it was case closed, and they no longer rang or waited outside the Fulford house. Marcus Fulford's body was released for burial, the death certificate giving the cause as organ failure, and Lena arranged the funeral at Putney crematorium with only a handful of mourners present. Lena herself did not attend the service, claiming she was too distressed, and wished to be left alone to grieve for her daughter.

DC Burrows had offered to stay with Lena for a few days but she said she'd prefer to be on her own. Barbara had even suggested that she call by or ring her every few days, just to see how she was or if there was anything she needed. Miss Jordan had monitored Lena and although she had not requested any further appointments, she had promised to take her medication on a regular basis. Lena also told Miss Jordan that she was going to concentrate all her energies on her businesses as she had neglected them. There had been a lot of confusion and poor decisions and her finances were in disarray but she wanted to regain all her customers and take on new staff to work in the main office.

Agnes Moors never heard a word from Lena, but did worry about inadvertently bumping into her. She had applied for various housekeeper positions, but without a recommendation from her last employer, she found it difficult to get an interview. The fifteen thousand she had been paid for the newspaper article was disappearing fast. She had written numerous letters to Lena, asking her to understand that she meant no harm and regretted what she had done, and was just asking for a reference so she could get a job. They were all to no avail, and she never got a reply. She was now seriously considering taking Lena to a tribunal and sent her a letter to this effect.

On receiving the letter, Lena felt sick with anger and tore it to pieces. She would have to think very carefully about what she should do about it, as it was an obvious blackmail threat. The last thing she wanted was for the wretched woman to contact the press as she had done previously. She herself obviously had more than enough money to pay her former housekeeper off, but to write a glowing CV would be too much like twisting the knife.

Sitting at her desk, Lena began to compose a letter to Agnes, but she kept tearing it up and starting again. Eventually she decided that she would have a face-to-face meeting with her, but would need to make arrangements first because she would have to be very careful.

She physically jumped when the landline rang and she hesitated before answering. It was a relief that it was DI Reid calling to see how she was, and if Simon Boatly's lawyers had been in contact with her.

'No they haven't. Why do you ask?'

'It appears that Simon Boatly has left your husband three million pounds.'

She was totally shocked and said nothing.

'Are you there, Mrs Fulford?'

'Yes. Are you sure about this money?'

'It may be best that you contact Mr Sutherland, Mr Boatly's solicitor, yourself. I haven't got his details to hand but the office is in Kensington and the address and phone number is on the internet.'

As soon as Reid finished the call she was straight on the computer to get Sutherland's office number. She spoke firstly with the office clerk, who was not fully aware of the inheritance as the office dealt with so many wills. Lena explained that her husband Marcus had been left a large sum of money in the will of a Simon Boatly, who was one of their clients, and that Marcus had died shortly after Simon, but that his will was made some time ago, and everything was to be left to her should he die. The clerk asked if they had any children as they might also be beneficiaries. Lena didn't want to go into chapter and verse about Marcus murdering Amy, and how she had poisoned him, so simply said that they had a daughter Amy, but she had died recently.

'Well everything sounds in order, but of course we would need to see Mr Fulford's will.'

'Certainly, the original is still with my solicitors and I know he had a copy,' Lena said, thinking it highly unlikely Marcus would have made another will since they separated.

'Let me just get the file out so I can have a quick look at the exact clauses.'

A few seconds later the clerk came back on the phone and said he'd found the file.

'So with Marcus being deceased, and his will leaving everything to me, then I should be the natural beneficiary of Marcus's bequest from Mr Boatly?' Lena said.

'Unfortunately that doesn't appear to be the

case as–'

'What do you mean, unfortunately–?'

'Please let me finish, Mrs Fulford. Mr Boatly stipulated a clause that Marcus had to be divorced to receive the money, therefore his bequest in the will is null and void. I am very sorry and please accept my sincere condolences at the loss of your husband and daughter.'

She slammed the receiver down and muttered angrily, 'Fuck you, FUCK YOU!'

Lena took stock for a few moments but then began to wonder if she could contest the will on the grounds that she and Marcus had been about to be divorced. She went to the guest-room wardrobe and took out Marcus's holdall, unzipping it to find it was full of papers and letters, old files and tax returns. She tipped everything onto the floor and began to search for the copy of his will, but instead of being able to concentrate on the job at hand she began to feel a terrible all-consuming weight of sadness. It was truly a pitiful array of his belongings. There were bundles of letters tied with elastic bands, some so old they were worn and torn, and she sat on the floor opening one after another. Love letters from her to Marcus when they had first met, and letters from Amy to him, along with postcards and birthday cards, and numerous florid letters of adoration for Marcus from Simon Boatly. She knew more than ever now that Simon Boatly had always been trying to persuade Marcus to leave her. The letters to Marcus from Amy in her familiar looped childish handwriting made her break down in tears. Sweet, loving letters explaining how much she missed him, and some proudly describing her exam results.

Lena carried all the letters in a small plastic container into the garden, crossing the small path that led to the garage across the flagged paving stones towards the rear of the walled garden. She hopped from one paving stone to another as if playing a child's game of hopscotch. The fir trees and the dense bushes hid the section of the garden that had once been a Victorian vegetable patch, where the old greenhouses, once used to cultivate lettuce and tender vegetables, still stood, although most of the glass panes were broken, and the interiors overrun with weeds and ferns. One part of the ground was blackened from the gardeners burning rubbish and the dark damp ground beside it nurtured the growing bed of mushrooms.

Chapter 37

DI Reid was in the canteen having breakfast when DC Timothy Wey joined him.

'I've just taken details for a new misper case, guy. Young lass in care that's run away again. Work's a bit slow now we are all off the Amy Fulford investigation.'

'We were only ever temporary staff,' Reid said. He loathed discussing the investigation, so said nothing to encourage Wey, who continued regardless between mouthfuls of toast and marmalade.

'I know Marcus Fulford was a bit of a Jack the

Lad with the hookers and girlfriends, but he seemed like a genuine bloke and was really cut up about his daughter going missing. If he was guilty, okay, he was a bloody deviant, but also one hell of an actor, because I would never have put him in the frame.'

'It's over and done with, Takeaway, so let it rest,' Reid said, draining his coffee and eager to leave it there.

'Well it won't be until they find her body. If he did kill her then her whereabouts have gone to the grave with him.'

Reid made his excuses to get back to his desk, but the mention of the Fulford investigation made him unsettled all morning. At lunchtime, not wanting to get into any further discussions on the case, he decided to go out for a breath of fresh air. He bought a Starbucks Americano and a chicken wrap before heading down past Twickenham Bridge and took a leisurely stroll along the towpath. He was sitting on a bench watching some rowers go by and the youngsters feeding ducks with their parents when he saw Deirdre Standing walking along the towpath. She looked well and was wearing a pink cardigan and pretty floral summer dress.

'Hey there, how are you?' she asked, having spotted him too.

'Fine and you?' He thought she looked more relaxed than when they had last seen each other.

'I have taken a sabbatical from Victim Support. After the pressures of the Fulford case I'm not sure it's the right work for me, and besides I wanted to spend more time with my girls.'

'I think it affected all of us in one way or another,' he said as he sipped at his coffee.

She asked if he had heard how Lena Fulford was, and he said that he had only spoken to her once and she seemed to want to get on with her life in her own way.

'What about Miss Jordan?'

'Not spoken to her.'

'I didn't like her very much.'

Reid smiled. 'She was the one who suggested I take Amy's journal to Professor Cornwall. She's quite formidable, always goes on about patient confidentiality, yet still says things she shouldn't.'

'Yes, she did with me as well,' Deirdre agreed, smiling ruefully, 'and I thought it unprofessional when she told me things about Mrs Fulford. Once she started she couldn't stop talking – patient confidentiality went right out the window – but I have to admit it helped me to understand some of Lena's behaviour.'

Reid was paying more attention to the children who were now backing off from a hissing swan. While he didn't want to appear rude, he definitely didn't want to get drawn into going over old ground. 'Well you did a good job under difficult circumstances and I for one appreciated your help. Anyway, I'd best be getting on.' Easing himself to his feet he placed his empty coffee cup in the bin next to the bench.

'Life must have been much more difficult for Lena, having been abused for all those years,' Deirdre observed.

'Well Marcus Fulford was not a very pleasant man.'

'No, I'm talking about her father. His face was scribbled over or blacked out with a felt tip pen in her old family photo albums.'

This was new and surprising to Reid. 'Where were those albums? I never saw them.'

'In the drawing room in one of the bookcases; they were near or next to a big book with lots of little tabs and notes in it.' She paused for a second, thinking. 'The book was called *Encyclopaedia of Mushrooms.*'

At once he sat back down on the bench, blinking rapidly while absorbing the information and its importance to the investigation. 'Did it belong to Mrs Fulford or to Amy?'

'Oh, it was Lena's, as it had a sticker in the front with her name and that of some kind of research project.'

A knot was tightening in his stomach, as he said it was good to see her and thanked her again for her work on the investigation.

'Are you working on anything interesting at the moment?' she asked.

'No, I'm back running the mispers office now and the usual run-of-the-mill cases.'

'It was very nice to see you, DI Reid.'

'Nice to see you too.'

Reid returned to the station, buzzing with a sense of urgency. Back in his office he went over everything that Deirdre had told him, before driving over to the murder incident room, where he asked for the files on the Fulford case. It was shortly after three o'clock when he returned to his flat and began re-reading the copy of the journal.

At first he skimmed through it, often turning back one page or another. He jotted down notes, all the while becoming more and more aware that throughout the journal there was no reference to it being written by Amy. The word 'enemies' was frequently used, and the repeated listing of everyone intended to be 'got rid of' and their so-called crimes, but there was never an 'I' or 'me'. It was always initials, and the constant changes of handwriting added to the confusion, where a different alter took over.

Reid thought back to the first time he'd learnt about the journal. Lena had clutched it to her chest and said that she was very reluctant to release it because the contents were very private, and she had even explained that some of the pages referred to herself and her husband and did not show either of them in a good light.

Clearly included in it were details of Marcus Fulford's behaviour, his promiscuity and sexual perversions, his prostitutes and girlfriends. The murder team had also discovered his bisexuality and intimate friendship with Simon Boatly.

What was slowly beginning to surface in Reid's mind was his suspicion that the journal was not written by Amy at all, but her mother. He recalled Lena showing him the birthday card and the wish list of gifts, the neat looped handwriting in the schoolbooks and diaries, but as far as he could see little of the handwriting in the journal matched the known samples of Amy's. He wondered how much Lena had helped Amy learn to write when she was younger and whether this had in some way created a slight similarity, but he was also aware that different alters would write in different styles.

He knew it was going to be difficult to prove, and without being given any official clearance to investigate further he needed to uncover more evidence on his own. He had now established that Lena Fulford, through her university studies, would have knowledge of deadly mushrooms, but he needed more than the possession of the *Encyclopaedia* to implicate her and prove his theory that it was she herself who had written the journal – and been the one who had poisoned the victims.

All his previous unanswered questions that he had put aside now began to haunt him again, and above all he knew he needed to prove that Amy was of perfectly sound mind and therefore not the real author of the journal. He started to work out a list of people he needed to re-interview and one name he ringed as being of prime interest was Miss Josephine Polka.

By now it was after eleven and pointless to try and arrange anything, so he went to bed, determined that the following day he would, with or without permission, begin his own investigation. His present case could easily be handled by DS Lane or DC Wey.

He knew with dreadful certainty that if he was correct, then the enemies still alive – Agnes Moors, her daughter Natalie, Serena Newman and Miss Polka – would be in the most terrible danger.

Chapter 38

It was ten p.m. when her mobile rang and she was unable to tell the caller's identity as it was withheld. When she answered she did not at first recognize the voice, but then immediately became fully alert.

'I think we really need to have a private meeting as I have something I want to discuss with you.'

'Who is this?'

'It's Mrs Fulford, Agnes.'

'I am so pleased you have called, Mrs Fulford, as I have been bereft since I left and feeling really ashamed about what happened,' Agnes gushed. 'Mr Fulford's death must have been heartbreaking for you to have to deal with.'

'Yes, but I'm keeping myself busy,' Lena said briskly. 'I will be in Esher tomorrow at a big antiques fair at Sandown Park; there is a coffee stall not far from the entrance so we can meet there at three. I was wrong in the way I treated you and I want to make it up to you financially.'

Agnes agreed to the meeting and after shutting off the call, shed a few tears of relief. She was certain that she could get her old position back and a large sum of cash – it would be more than she could have hoped for, and she was determined she would make up for her betrayal.

Reid was at his desk by eight, and started the day

by calling the school to enquire if they had a forwarding address or contact number for Miss Polka. The headmistress Miss Harrington gave him a mobile number but did not know where Miss Polka had moved to, though she had said she might go travelling abroad. The mobile phone number was no longer active. He contacted his friend Agent Morgan from the National Crime Agency to see if he could give him a heads-up on the whereabouts of a Josephine Polka. Morgan said he needed some more information but Reid told him that all he had was her date of birth, her description and that she might have left the UK any time since the date she finished teaching at the school.

Reid knew that if his theory was correct he would need a search warrant for Lena Fulford's house. To get one, along with enough officers to carry out the search, he would have to confront DCI Jackson and explain his reasons. This all meant he desperately needed evidence, as everything was still without foundation and his suspicions alone were not enough.

He had arranged to meet Gail Summers at her two-bedroom Putney flat. She was still unemployed and deeply upset by the revelations about and accusations against Marcus Fulford.

'As far as I'm concerned, Marcus was a marvellous and caring father. He adored Amy and would never have abused her either sexually or violently.'

'Do you not feel he used you to get what he wanted...?'

'No, and I don't deny I was underhand in providing him with the details of Lena's financial situation, but at the time he was living on benefits and was certain that Lena would attempt to hide her wealth.'

'Did he say much about his wife to you?'

'No. It was the other way round. At work Lena was always vitriolic and horrible about him, and would say he was a bad father and role model for Amy. I knew a totally different Marcus and when Lena found out about me it was hideous,' she informed him. 'She was very frightening and I was relieved to quit working for her.'

'When you say she was frightening, describe how she behaved,' Reid said, conscious that he had up to now excused this side of Lena.

'Well, phoning me and being threatening and abusive. She said I would never find work and she would make sure I had no recommendation from her when I applied for a job.'

When Reid went to see Justine Hyde at her flat she was equally shocked by the accusations levelled at Marcus and was still coming to terms with the fact he had died. She was adamant that he had never abused his daughter. She had never met Lena, socially or otherwise, but obviously was very aware of her existence as she said that often when she and Marcus were together Lena would make persistent calls to his mobile about Amy and how he let her do what she wanted. He was also certain that Lena was often outside the flat in Green Street, as if she was stalking him. She had met Amy, and like Gail Summers claimed that she had only ever seen a loving and doting father who she believed put his daughter first. Justine also said she was aware that Marcus had a very strong friendship with Simon Boatly, but just how deep the relationship had gone in the past had not been discussed.

'He was very confident about the divorce, and that he would benefit from it financially, and he wanted Amy to stay with him permanently and not just every other weekend. I was certain Amy wanted to live with him – she never said anything to me about her mother.'

Even though he was beginning to discover more and more about Lena Fulford's behaviour, Reid was only too aware he as yet had no evidence that she was the author of the journal, or that she had administered poison to the victims. He had no choice but to continue his round of interviews.

He returned to the Harley Street clinic used by Professor Elliot Cornwall. This time he was met at the reception desk by a smiling young woman wearing a short white medical coat and rimless glasses. She stood up to shake his hand.

'You must be Detective Reid. I am Professor Cornwall's new assistant and I have to make his apology to you. He has inadvertently been called away on an urgent matter, and asked if you would be able to rearrange the appointment for next week as he is only here three days a week.'

Disappointed, Reid asked if she could contact him and explain that it was very important he see him as soon as possible. She hesitated and checked her watch but then after asking him to wait she went into a room off the reception area.

After five minutes she returned and sat at her desk, drew a notepad towards her and wrote down an address and phone number.

'This is Professor Cornwall's private address in Chelsea. If it is urgent he could see you later this evening, at eight thirty.'

A meal in the station's canteen killed some of the waiting time and with still an hour to go before going to Chelsea Reid was just heading into his office when the phone rang.

'Hi, Victor, it's Andy Morgan from the National Crime Agency. I've got some info for you and believe me, it took a bit of digging so the beers are on you next time we meet up.'

'What you got, Andy?' Reid asked anxiously.

'At first I hit a dead end with Miss Polka travelling to Europe, but then I spoke with the UK Border Force who in turn liaised with the FBI. They were able to track Miss Polka from the UK to Florida, and then on to an artists' group expedition to Peru.'

'Peru?' Reid exclaimed.

'Yeah, she returned and took an internal flight to Texas, and as yet I've no further details, but if you want to let me keep going I might get further results. There's always the problem that she could have hired or bought a car.'

'Do you know if she was travelling alone?'

'I can back-track and see who sat beside her on the flights. It will take time, Vic, and the beers are now looking more like a crate of champagne.'

'Thanks but leave it for now, Andy, and I really appreciate what you've done.'

Reid hung up, in some relief that Miss Polka was obviously alive. Thinking about it, as he knew she was a keen artist, her travels made sense.

Parking in the street some way along from where Professor Cornwall lived, he walked back to the elegant property, observing that the professor obviously earned a hell of a lot more than he did. The black and white stone step was immaculate, and the freshly painted front door in a dark shade of maroon had an inlaid frosted-glass window.

The bell rang and as he waited he saw a shadow across the glass, before a very attractive young girl opened the door. She smiled and invited him in, took his coat and folded it over her arm, leading him along a thickly carpeted corridor.

'My father will be with you shortly. Please sit down, and if you would like a tea or coffee please help yourself as there are flasks on a trolley.'

'Thank you.'

She gave another polite smile and closed the door behind him. The room was sparsely furnished with wall-to-wall bookcases, a comfortable sofa and a big wingback chair in front of a large decorative fireplace. There were good Persian rugs scattered over the polished pine floor, and numerous watercolours in gilt frames on the walls. There was a low coffee table with *Country Life* magazines lined up alongside copies of the *New Statesman* and *Private Eye*. Although the room appeared to be comfortable there was a rather austere atmosphere and Reid wondered if this was where his private patients waited for their appointments.

He sat in the centre of the sofa, and it was at least

ten minutes before Professor Cornwall entered. He was dressed in a dark jacket with pinstriped trousers but had loosened his shirt collar and wore no tie. He was also wearing carpet slippers.

'Detective Reid, nice to see you again. Sorry to keep you waiting. I hope my daughter offered you tea or coffee?'

'Yes thank you, but I'm fine.'

'Probably a good thing as I think the flasks were made up a few hours ago. Perhaps a glass of whisky would be preferable?'

'Yes, it would, thank you.'

Reid watched as Professor Cornwall went to a bookshelf, which swung open to reveal a drinks cabinet. He poured two cut glasses of malt, turned to ask if he wanted water, but Reid smiled and, noticing the bottle, said he would take it neat.

'Good thinking, it's very mature and watering it down ruins the liquid gold.'

Cornwall sat in the wingback chair, placing his own glass on a small coffee table beside it.

'Right, this had better be good, I have had one hell of a day with back-to-back appointments, but now I am all ears.'

Reid opened his briefcase and removed the journal in its plastic evidence bag.

'I sincerely hope I am not wasting your time, but I need to discuss with you my feelings about the contents of Amy Fulford's journal,' he began.

'I have read it, and I can't see how I can add anything now as your investigation is over and done with – that's why I never did a full report. I was quite shocked when your DCI Jackson told me the father had murdered the daughter.'

'I just need to ask your opinion as I have concerns that the case might not have unfolded exactly as you just described it. I am also concerned about who may have written the journal.'

'Concerned?' snorted the professor. 'My diagnosis is, I believe, correct and a clear indication of someone suffering from Dissociative Identity Disorder. As you were made aware when we last met, the journal is written by someone who has multiple identities, with each one having a separate set of behaviours and memories. I referred to them as alters, if you recall.'

Reid found him a trifle overbearing, as if he enjoyed the sound of his own voice, but he knew he had to tread carefully and not insult him.

'You were told that this journal was written by Amy Fulford.'

'Yes, by you as I recall, Inspector.'

'She is or was the fifteen-year-old daughter of Lena and Marcus Fulford.'

'Sadly I am also aware of the outcome and that her father was arrested and about to be charged with her murder when he fell ill and died.'

'Yes, and unfortunately we have not as yet recovered her body, so although the investigation will continue, to hopefully bring closure, we have found no trace of her.'

'Yes, yes, I am aware of that, but I am trying to understand what you are here for and want from me.'

'What if I said that the journal was not written by Amy Fulford?'

'Pardon?' The temperature in the room seemed to drop in an instant.

527

'I know you were told that it belonged to Amy, but I need to discuss the possibility that it was actually written by her mother.'

'Her mother?'

Nervously Reid sipped the whisky and coughed before he continued.

'Amy was highly intelligent, in fact exceptionally so. This would mean that it was perfectly credible that she'd written it, even more so if you were informed that it belonged to her.'

Cornwall stared at Reid, which made him feel even more nervous, and he stuttered slightly as he continued to explain. He mentioned that Lena was diagnosed with bipolar disorder by Miss Jordan, which got a dismissive wave of the hand.

'Lena Fulford was abused by her father as a child for many years,' he went on. 'She was academically brilliant with a first-class Biological Sciences degree from Oxford, and she got a scholarship to Harvard, but due to a nervous breakdown she had to return to England with her father.' Reid had the unsettling sensation that the Persian rug was being tugged from beneath his feet as Cornwall continued to stare at him.

Cornwall drained his glass and got up to replenish it, without offering his guest a refill. Whether or not he was taking on board everything he was being told was hard to tell, as he showed no reaction.

'There is also something that we have contained throughout the investigation as we did not want to cause unnecessary panic.'

'Just a minute, please.' Cornwall held up his hand. 'I need to digest what you have been telling me about Mrs Fulford as it seems to me that you are accusing me of making the wrong diagnosis regarding Amy.'

'No, sir, I am merely asking you to consider an alternative proposition about the author of the journal. I admit to possibly misleading you into believing that the journal was written by Amy, but it was not intentional, and I also think your diagnosis is correct...'

'For Mrs Fulford, who, if I understand you, is the person you believe has DID.'

'Yes, sir.'

'Even if that is the case, from what DCI Jackson told me all the evidence points to Marcus Fulford abusing and murdering his daughter. So you see the journal may actually be immaterial, even if it was written by Mrs Fulford.'

Reid disagreed. 'If you look at it all logically there is not a shred of hard evidence, yet it has been accepted that Marcus Fulford murdered his daughter on the afternoon she went missing.'

He was eager for Cornwall to interject, to ask questions, but instead he remained silent, sipping his drink. Reid was starting to sweat under his unflinching gaze.

'My concerns are that IF it was never Amy's intention to use the poison, but was instead her mother's, then far from it being immaterial we have people still at risk, the ones named in the journal as enemies.'

At last Cornwall reacted, raising his index finger and pausing before he spoke.

'Let me get this right. You originally came to me on the suggestion of Marjory Jordan, correct?'

'Yes, sir. She read the journal and directed me to you because she didn't want to break the rules of confidentiality in respect of her patient Mrs Fulford. She'd seen you talk at a conference and said you were one of the most esteemed and experienced men in the field of forensic psychiatry.'

'But she never at any point implied that the journal was written by Mrs Fulford and not her daughter.'

'No.'

'Bloody woman, these amateurs make more trouble for our profession as they rarely if ever know what they are treating, and she should have at least wondered if her own patient was possibly the writer – it beggars belief.'

'Personally I think she saw Lena Fulford as nothing more than a good money-earner,' Reid remarked. 'She said she'd give us free help and advice, but then hit us with a bill for three thousand pounds for treating Mrs Fulford during the investigation. DCI Jackson refused to pay it and she is threatening to take us to the small claims court.' He wanted to up the ante as at last he was now getting a reaction from Cornwall.

'Right, let me have the journal.'

Cornwall put out his hand and Reid passed it to him. The professor leaned back, holding it in his hand, as if weighing up the amount of work it would now require.

'This could be a very long night, Detective Reid. I will go through it page by page and ask you relevant questions. I think we need a fresh pot of coffee and no more of my precious malt.'

Chapter 39

Cornwall was almost obsessively diligent as he carefully read and re-read each section of the journal. As none of the entries was dated, it was difficult to calculate how much time had actually elapsed between each of them. The handwriting changed so often that Cornwall began to catalogue exactly how many different identities he believed were present. At one point his daughter brought in fresh coffee and sandwiches. Reid felt his eyelids drooping at around eleven o'clock, but it was not until two a.m. that Cornwall gave a long sigh, fetched a malt whisky and downed it quickly.

'Right, you are obviously aware of my original diagnosis, but on a more in-depth read there are at least ten different identities. I have given each of them a number, and it seems to me the most dominant and controlling one is number three. She, or he, is also the most dangerous and likely to be the one who would cause physical harm.'

Reid, fighting the urge to doze off, asked why he said 'he', and Cornwall explained that an alter could actually be male or female, irrespective of the sex of the person suffering DID.

'Alter three takes over at any given opportunity, but predominantly when the other alters find themselves upset or stressed – basically whenever there is any emotional fear, it will be number three who switches in and takes control. You may recall at our last meeting I spoke about identities "switching" at any moment in time. Alter three is the dominant one, with hatred and a desire for revenge towards anyone whom the actual DID sufferer cannot cope or deal with. The different identities are also of various ages: one is a small child, another perhaps ten or twelve, and then there is the predominantly evil and obsessive "three" who is anywhere between twenty-five and forty and, I would say, female. Her writing is often of a mature style, as against some pages, which are printed, not in joined-up writing. Sometimes the handwriting is so heavy the pen almost cuts through the paper, but...' He closed his eyes.

Reid thought he'd fallen asleep, but after a long pause Cornwall continued, stressing that although there were very derogatory passages referring to Lena, she would not be aware of who she was, or that she was writing about herself.

'It is also feasible that at times Amy, or someone very similar, was an alter within Lena Fulford.'

'What makes you say that?' Reid asked.

'Some of the contents, but predominantly the fact that the front of the journal has "Amy" in-scribed on it, which makes me wonder if one of the alters actually bought it and had it personally embossed.'

'Sorry, Professor, I didn't put a photocopy of the cover in the copy of the journal I gave you last time. I also forgot to tell you that the journal was a present two Christmases ago from Marcus to Amy. My guess is that she never bothered to use it, Mrs Fulford found it and...'

'Her alters decided to use it. I would say that this

journal was compiled within that time frame.'

'I find it amazing that when an alter takes over the DID sufferer has no comprehension of it, what they are doing, or indeed have done after a switch of personality,' Reid said, rubbing his eyes.

'I had one patient who cut off all her hair when taken over by one of her alters; when she "switched" back to her normal self she couldn't recall or understand what had happened to her. In another case, a professional photographer was outraged on discovering all her best work had been slashed. She even called the police to investigate the damage, but of course it was one of her alters all along. When these multiple personalities take over and become dominant they do not usually refer to each other or even know they exist.'

Sensing that Cornwall was pontificating again, Reid reiterated his concerns that if Lena wrote the journal then the 'enemies', who had not been 'got rid of', were still in grave danger.

Cornwall said he was right to be worried, because the dominant alter three would undoubtedly want to continue and reap revenge.

'What do I do?'

'Warn them, and get them immediate protection. If alter three feels the attempted poisoning has failed I fear that other forms of physical harm may be considered and eventually used to achieve the "termination" of the "enemies".'

'Will you examine Mrs Fulford if I arrest her?'

'Most certainly. I would suggest that after her arrest you call me to the station to assess her mental condition. I will recommend that she be sectioned under the Mental Health Act, and be taken immediately to a secure medical facility as the most appropriate place to assess and treat her.'

'Thank you, Professor,' Reid said, heartfelt, 'your help and support will be appreciated as I will be up against it when I speak to DCI Jackson.'

'Well I'm perfectly happy to speak to him as well, and will be quite blunt if necessary as Lena Fulford, or rather her alter number three, is undoubtedly a continued threat and will, I feel, kill again.'

'How will you treat her?'

'If she is agreeable I will use hypnotherapy to open the Pandora's box in which her multiple personalities already reside; this will help to expedite a detailed diagnosis and treatment. Hypnosis will bring on a trance-like state and allow me to gain access to, and communicate with, her many different alters. In my opinion the poor woman is in dire need of help. The sooner she gets it, excluding what you believe her to be guilty of, the sooner we will gain answers and even give her some kind of peace of mind, as she lives in what I would describe as permanent torment.'

Reid felt very positive, even though he knew suggesting Lena Fulford was sectioned put himself in a position where he had to confront DCI Jackson and update him on the new developments. The major problem was having no physical incriminating evidence against Lena; his whole case against her was, at the present time, entirely based on the ramblings of a journal that was written by God knows who.

'I am upset with Miss Jordan's misdiagnosis of Mrs Fulford, and yet as much as it grates on me, I may need her assistance as she is on very familiar terms with Lena,' Cornwall conceded. 'The fact is, I cannot – in fact nobody can – force her to undergo hypnotherapy. Miss Jordan may be able to persuade her to do so, but the reality is, Lena has to want it, and I think truthfully, she might find it an incredible relief.'

First thing the following morning Reid, with only a few hours' sleep, went to see Jackson in his office. He was nervous, and having the bullish man glaring and swearing at him did not help, but eventually, when warned more murders could occur, the DCI sat up and listened. Jackson was an experienced officer and knew he was in a 'damned if you do, damned if you don't' position, and if he failed to let Reid arrest and section Lena Fulford he would have a lot of explaining to do.

With Jackson's approval, Reid could obtain the warrants to arrest Lena Fulford on suspicion of murder and search her house. He took with him DS Lane, DC Burrows, a team of SOCOs, and a forensic botanist to assist in the search for any poisonous mushrooms. He had also asked Marjory Jordan to be present. At first she was furious and refused to play any part in the arrest or help Cornwall, but after Reid explained Cornwall's diagnosis at length, she realized that Lena's alter three made her a very dangerous woman. Miss Jordan knew her future credibility and integrity as a therapist was in jeopardy, and it was best she agreed to persuade Lena to have the hypnotherapy treatment.

Reid had suggested that he and he alone appear at the house first, while the others waited for him to give the go-ahead. He did not want to scare Lena, but to make it as easy for her as possible, without causing undue stress. Lena looked dishevelled when she opened the door wearing a fur-lined raincoat. She smiled and said she was pleased to see him, but it was not convenient as she was just leaving for a prearranged appointment at an antiques fair at Sandown Park. He showed her the search warrant, keeping his expression relaxed but pointing out that she had no option but to permit him entry and allow the search to take place.

Her head jerked from side to side, and her eyes widened.

'You will have to come back another time,' she said sharply.

'I'm sorry, Mrs Fulford, but that will not be acceptable.'

He could feel the tension in her as she made to step back in an attempt to shut the door, but he was prepared and had his foot wedged inside.

'Why are you doing this?' Her voice was strained, as she tried again to shut the door; this time he used his arm to put pressure on it to widen the gap.

'Mrs Fulford, please don't make this more difficult. Just move away from the door.'

She seemed to jump back and the door swung open. Immediately he reached for his hand-held radio, calling for everyone to come through the gates, and asking that Miss Jordan make herself visible fast.

It was over very quickly, even though it didn't feel like it. Lena swore and cursed Reid when told she was being arrested on suspicion of the murder of her husband and Harry Dunn, but on seeing Marjory Jordan she turned her anger towards the therapist. Miss Jordan was impressive, staying calm and very reassuring. Slowly Lena backed up against a wall, asking over and over why she was there as she did not have an appointment.

Unbeknown to Lena, Barbara Burrows packed her a medium-size bag with clothing, nightwear, washbag and make-up, that was to be taken direct to the secure psychiatric unit she would later be escorted to. Marjory Jordan and two officers led Lena out to the waiting police car where a uniform officer had, as was standard procedure, wanted to handcuff her, but Reid told him that it was not appropriate in Mrs Fulford's case as it might upset her further. Her mood change was astonishing – she was smiling as they put her into the back of the car with Marjory sitting next to her. Lena didn't even glance out of the window, but sat explaining how well her new line of stuffed toys was doing.

'Have I forgotten we had an appointment, are we going to your house?'

'I have someone who wants to talk to you, Lena; he's going to help you, but first we have to go to the police station,' Marjory told her. 'You've been there before – you remember when you first went to report Amy missing. Remember how nice Detective Reid was? Well, he wants to help you again, so think of it as if we are going to his house.'

Lena never asked what 'help' she meant, she never said another word as they continued the drive to Richmond. She leant further back in the seat, her hands folded over her soft leather clutch bag, patting it with the flat of her hand. Marjory noticed that unlike her usually perfect manicure the red varnish was chipped and her nails looked dirty.

Arriving at the police station, everything went like clockwork as Reid had briefed the custody sergeant beforehand. Cornwall was waiting at the secure mental unit in Surrey, and so had arranged for a colleague to have Lena sectioned under the Mental Health Act at the station. They were back in the car and on their way to Surrey within twenty minutes; during the time at the station Lena was perfectly tranquil and never said a word, other than to give her name and address. Reid worried that it was the calm before the storm.

Marjory kept hold of Lena's hand as they walked up the path and into the secure unit, which was very clean and modern, with single bedrooms and a number of therapy treatment rooms. She seemed like a frightened child looking around, perplexed and unsure why she was there. Miss Jordan reassured her they were at a lovely new guesthouse and while they were there she could have a good rest, but Lena backed away nervously as Professor Cornwall approached with a smile.

'Mrs Fulford, I am Professor Elliot Cornwall. I have heard a lot about you, and I am delighted to meet you.'

Lena faltered, taking deep breaths, her hands still clutching her bag. His voice was soft and gentle as he took her through to the interview room, which was decorated in a serene and inviting manner with comfortable armchairs, a sofa and coffee table. Cornwall patted the seat beside him.

'Come and sit down, Mrs Fulford, I think we can have a really pleasant conversation.'

Miss Jordan looked on as Lena went obediently to sit beside him, and he lifted his eyes towards Miss Jordan to indicate for her to leave the room. As she closed the door behind her she could see Lena was starting to cry. Miss Jordan knew there was a hidden camera in the room that recorded everything and hurried to find the adjoining room to watch the treatment on a monitor.

At the antiques fair at Sandown Park, Agnes was growing anxious that she was waiting in the wrong café, which was basically a stall set up for the event. She made some enquiries and went to check a restaurant used for the races but it was closed. Returning to the stall, she rang Lena's house, but there was no reply, so she called her business line, which went straight to answer phone. Presuming that Lena must be on her way, Agnes ordered a second cup of coffee. After another half-hour, and still with no sign of Lena, she called the house again. This time the phone was answered and when she asked to speak to Mrs Fulford she was informed that she was not available. She asked rather curtly who she was speaking to, and was concerned to be told that it was DI Reid.

'Oh, sorry, I didn't recognize your voice. This is

Agnes Moors, Detective. I was expecting Mrs Fulford; we had arranged to have coffee together, but she hasn't shown up and I wondered if everything was all right.'

Reid was taken aback to hear about the arrangement, especially as he obviously knew about Agnes leaking private photographs in her unauthorised press interview. He repeated that Mrs Fulford was not available, even as he privately suspected that Lena's intention behind the meeting was to at some point administer a lethal dose of mushroom poison, and if he was correct, Miss Moors had had a very lucky escape. He asked if her daughter was well, which surprised Agnes, but she said Natalie was very well.

Eager as he was to end the call, Reid made sure to tell Agnes that she, and her daughter, still needed to be vigilant about the contents of their fridges, freezers, and also any liquids in opened bottles. Agnes asked why now liquids and what was happening with the investigation. With Lena arrested he felt more relaxed about Agnes's safety and explained that this was something they should have mentioned in the first instance, but had forgotten to do so.

'I will pass on your message to Mrs Fulford,' he said and ended the call.

The reason Reid was so sure of Lena's intentions was because the forensic botanist had discovered, in the shrubbery by the garden wall, a fresh crop of poisonous mushrooms. The area was cordoned off for the botanist to examine and take samples, but clearly visible were patches of stems, indicating that the mushroom heads had been recently removed.

The interior of the house was in disarray; dirty dishes and cutlery were stacked in the sink, along with burnt pans and discarded half-cooked meals. Empty wine bottles and dirty glasses were left in the downstairs rooms. A fire had been lit in one room, the grate piled high with burnt newspapers and the ashes spilling out onto the polished wood floor and fireside rug. It appeared that Lena had moved from one room to another downstairs; blankets and pillows were abandoned on sofas beside trays of biscuits and dirty coffee cups. The bedrooms were in the same condition; the master suite had clothes heaped across the floor; dirty bath towels, some soaking wet, were left in every bathroom, and only Amy's bedroom remained in immaculate condition. Lena's office was a mass of documents scattered over the floor and tumbling out of the wastebasket, while rotting food was left on her desk. Laundry baskets were stacked with dirty clothes and bed linen, some with blood-stains, and it seemed that the cleanliness of the entire massive house had been neglected.

A discovery in the cellar proved to be very relevant. In a small wooden crate, resting in blotting paper and wrapped in wet tissues, were more poisonous mushrooms. Close by on a small table was a granite mortar and pestle, which contained the remnants of crushed mushrooms. Aware of the danger of inhaling deadly spores in a confined space, the forensic botanist immediately had the area cordoned off and insisted no one was to go in without full protective clothing and mask.

Reid was in his office back at Richmond when Jackson stormed in, looking flustered.

'What's been happening? You should have called me, kept me updated.'

'Well I have been rather busy, sir, what with the arrest of Lena Fulford and the discovery of poisonous mushrooms growing in her garden and the cellar of her house.'

Jackson exhaled noisily. 'The original search of the house when her daughter went missing was a total cock-up. So missing the mushrooms is down to you, not me.'

'At the time, sir, I was investigating Amy as a missing person – poisoning people was not in the equation and even the sniffer dogs were looking for a possible body, not mushrooms.'

'Did she kill her daughter?' Jackson growled.

The question threw Reid and he took a moment to think about it. 'I don't know, but considering this latest outcome I have even stronger doubts that Marcus Fulford murdered his daughter, or even sexually abused her.'

'What about the fucking incriminating evidence against him? The maroon sweater, the watch, how long before she was declared missing – he could have killed her and in retrospect so could her psychotic mother. They could even have done it together and disposed of her body between them.'

Reid hated the way the bullish man's voice grated on his nerves. He did not truthfully believe that Lena would have killed her daughter, but he had to take on board what Jackson was implying and consider her aggressive alter might be responsible.

'I think, sir, we need to wait for Professor Cornwall to talk with Lena Fulford. She's at the secure unit and he is talking with her now, and will hopefully soon start the hypnotherapy sessions. Rest assured, sir, I will keep you updated.'

'Fucking brilliant, we wait for this trick cyclist to "TALK" to a woman we believe – correction, you and Cornwall believe – wrote that bloody journal. If she is suspected of murdering three people she should be interviewed at the police station and fucking charged with murder, then let a jury decide whether she is guilty or not. I suggest when Cornwall's finished farting about you bring her back here for questioning, or I will go and get her from the nuthouse myself.'

'I still think we would be wise to wait to hear from Professor Cornwall,' Reid persisted.

'I am not waiting – do you realize if this ever got leaked to the press it would create a media frenzy, far and above what we already had to deal with?'

It was at this moment Reid's desk phone rang, and he snatched it up, grateful for a reason to deflect Jackson's anger.

Professor Cornwall was on the line and Reid told him DCI Jackson was in his office and he'd put the call onto speaker.

'I've had a long talk with Mrs Fulford and she's currently resting in the therapy room, having taken a mild sedative,' the professor began.

Jackson leaned in towards the speakerphone. 'What did she say? Did she kill her daughter and–?'

'I haven't got anywhere near that far yet, DCI Jackson. I can however tell you that she understood that she may be suffering from something more than a bipolar illness, and she has agreed to undergo the hypnotherapy treatment.'

Reid felt relieved. 'Thank you, Professor, that is very positive news.'

'When will you start and how long will it take?' an impatient Jackson asked.

'When I feel she is ready,' Cornwall replied smoothly, 'and it will certainly take more than one session to uncover all of her multiple personalities. I will firstly have to attempt to take her back to the beginning of her childhood trauma and this alone will be a very highly charged and emotional session. Everything will be recorded onto a DVD and you are both welcome to watch the procedure via the large monitor in the next room.'

Jackson sucked in his breath and shook his head. 'Very well, Professor Cornwall, as long as your methods get results. What sort of time frame are we looking at? I want her back in police custody to interview and charge her.'

Cornwall sighed with disdain. 'As I just said, it's impossible to say how many treatments Mrs Fulford will require at this stage. I will let you know when I think she's ready to be interviewed by police.'

'This is a murder investigation and I make the decisions about her, not you, Professor Cornwall!'

'Let me remind you, DCI Jackson, that Lena Fulford has been sectioned and detained under the Mental Health Act and I am her appointed psychiatrist.'

'So fucking what!' Jackson bellowed, leaving Reid disgusted at the way he spoke to Cornwall, who remained totally calm.

'So that means I alone decide if and when she should be released to police custody for an interview. Now, if you don't mind, I have a patient to attend to,' he replied with an air of aloofness and ended the call.

'Who the hell does that jumped-up little prick Cornwall think he is? This bloody shambles is a waste of taxpayers' money and all your fault, Reid. Having that woman sectioned was a bad move – you should have just nicked her for murder then interviewed and charged her. The judge would have banged her up for life anyway and done us all a ruddy favour.'

Jackson slammed the door hard as he left the room. Reid smiled to himself; he didn't care what Jackson thought as he knew he'd done the right thing and Cornwall would decide when and if Lena was fit to be formally interviewed.

In the tastefully furnished therapy room Lena was sitting flicking through a *Vogue* magazine. She smiled at Cornwall as he came back in, closing the magazine and placing it neatly in line with the others on the coffee table. She frowned, tapping the edges until she was satisfied it was perfectly straight. As she turned to him, he noticed she had the most extraordinary eyes, thick lashes, and her skin was flawless – she really was a very beautiful woman. He had not tricked her, or made any promises; he had been kindly and intuitive, as he had explained that he believed he could help her, and that he knew she needed to find peace.

She said, 'Thank you very much,' adding she was tired and closed her eyes, her hands holding onto her clutch bag, like a child with a comfort toy. When she was settled, her bag would be taken from her and the contents checked and kept in a locked cabinet. Cornwall decided it would be best to let her rest for the time being and showed her the room she would be staying in while at the 'guesthouse', as Miss Jordan had put it. Lena was very appreciative and seemed to really like the room.

Cornwall knew it was going to be a long and emotional journey if the outcome of the sessions was to be positive for both Lena and the police investigation. He firmly believed that what he was going to do could relieve her torment, and he was confident that under hypnotherapy her many alters would reveal themselves. His only fear was if the dominant alter, number three, did reveal itself, then he would be seen as an enemy and the alter might try and attack him. If that were to happen, there would be no knowing how much damage the alter could inflict on him, or for that matter on Lena Fulford herself. However, he would have two female staff watch in the monitor room, just to be on the safe side.

Chapter 40

Professor Cornwall's nurses had been shocked by the amount of scars they had seen when Lena was taken to the showers.

Her inner thighs were covered in the small marks of self-abuse made by the nail scissors, some of which were still raw and scabbed. Even so, she had remained calm and appreciative of everyone. Due to his prior commitments Professor Cornwall had only been available to begin the procedure that evening. Both DCI Jackson and DI Reid were present and had been waiting in the monitor room.

Cornwall settled himself opposite Lena, who was lying on a couch dressed in her own night-dress and dressing gown. The fingers of her hands were interlinked and resting on her stomach. He took his time with her, firstly talking to her in a calm relaxing manner. His intention was to bypass her critical, logical mind, and gain access to the most powerful part of her brain, her subconscious mind, which in turn would allow him access to all her memories, habits and feelings, but most importantly her alter personalities. He needed first to get to the root of her problems and sort out the emotional baggage, so he could have a better understanding of why she suffered from DID. As Cornwall spoke softly and took her through a series of relaxation exercises, Lena looked as if she was falling into a pleasant daydream.

Jackson glanced at Reid. 'I hope he knows what he is bloody doing,' he hissed.

Reid said nothing, as he was finding it very difficult seeing how calm Lena was, especially around Cornwall. He knew Jackson wanted to arrest and interview her, but it was clearly evident she was mentally unwell and any interview might be deemed illegal and not allowed in evidence. Reid also knew that even if she was charged with multiple murders, a report from Cornwall would probably state she was unfit to plead, and result in the court sending her to a secure psychiatric institution for a nonspecific length of time, or until it was considered she was better and no longer a threat to herself or anyone else.

He knew deep down that the sweet smiling patient had administered lethal dosages of poison, and that she might also have murdered her own daughter, especially in the absence of other suspects, but Reid had no proof or witnesses to any of it. Although there were poisonous mushrooms discovered in her house and garden, he could not prove Lena grew them, and she could claim it must have been Amy, who from her schoolbooks was clearly knowledgeable on the subject. The contents of Lena's handbag had been searched and nothing incriminating was found, so even if she had intended to harm Agnes she hadn't been going to the meeting armed with poison.

Jackson sat on the edge of the low leather chair, and Reid on an identical one beside him. They were uncomfortable and by now they had been waiting for over an hour. It was another ten minutes before Cornwall signalled that Lena was now in a state of hypnosis and the two nurses could enter the room He began to speak to her very quietly, so much so that Jackson leaned ever closer to the speakers beside the large monitor.

'I can't hear him,' Jackson muttered.

'Do you recognize my voice, Lena?' Cornwall asked.

'Yes,' she whispered.

'You know who I am, don't you?'

'Yes I do.'

'You know that you can trust me, and that anything you tell me will help me to help you – does that make sense to you, Lena?'

'I suppose so.'

'What I am going to do is ask you some questions and see if you can answer and prove that you can hear me clearly, because it is important that I know you are listening. Are you listening to me, Lena?'

'Yes, I can hear you.'

'So you know that I am close, and there is no need for you to be afraid, because I am right beside you and I will not move away from you.'

Jackson sighed and pushed his fat butt further back into the chair. He glanced towards Reid with a shake of his head, and deliberately looked at his wristwatch.

Cornwall had plainly decided to take his patient to a point after the suspected abuse by her father and then regress her back through time.

'I am going to ask you about where you went to university; can you remember?'

Reid found Jackson's impatience irritating and

his constant shuffling about made it hard to hear Lena, so he turned up the volume and listened as Lena in a soft cultured voice spoke about Oxford, describing her degree course, lecturers, friends and hobbies in amazing detail. It went on for a considerable while as she was asked what appeared to be mundane questions, and she answered without appearing to be in any way distressed. It took over half an hour as Cornwall continued speaking softly and Lena replied coherently as he gradually took her further back into her childhood. Still she appeared to be relaxed and had turned to lie with her hands at her side, her head resting back on the pillow.

'I am going to ask you to go back to something that perhaps frightened you, something that maybe you have never told anyone else, something that you have never wanted to remember.'

The two detectives now became mesmerized by what was happening in front of them. Lena's body began to twist, and she started to curl up into a foetal position, and it was obvious she was becoming very distressed. Cornwall kept up the soft encouraging dialogue as he asked her to tell him what was happening. She flayed her arms, kicking out with her legs, and she began to beg and plead, saying over and over, 'No, please not in my mouth. I can't breathe, I CAN'T BREATHE.'

Cornwall calmed her before asking what was being put into her mouth. Lena spoke in a child-like voice, saying it was a dirty word, she wouldn't say the word, and when he asked her how old she was she lisped that she was eight. When he asked her where she was, she said she was in her bedroom at home.

It became painful to listen as Cornwall got her to tell him it was a 'penis', and she started sobbing and flaying her arms again as if to ward off someone; she gagged and it seemed she would vomit, as she yet again screamed for it not to be forced into her mouth.

Cornwall asked if she knew the person who was hurting her and making her feel sick, but she curled up and hid her face. It was a while before he eventually got her to tell him that she knew who it was, but she refused to identify him, and it was hideous when she turned her body over so her abuser could put his penis up her vagina and her backside. The strain of recalling the abuse made her cry out that it was hurting her; she even tried to fend off the abuser – twice the nurses had to step forward and gently restrain her from punching out at Cornwall and nearly falling from the therapy couch. She still refused to say who it was, and no matter how quietly Cornwall tried to persuade her, she would not give a name. As she was so distressed, he now moved her forward in time away from the little girl who said it always happened in the bedroom. Her body stopped writhing and twisting, and she had a different high-pitched voice, now describing how very special she was and the presents and pretty clothes and cashmere sweaters she was given because she was a good girl.

'Did you get these presents because you were just a good girl or did you have to do something for them?'

'Yes I had to do it, Monday, Wednesday and

Sunday after chapel.'

'What were you made to do?'

'Oh I can't tell you, I never can tell anyone, and it's a secret.'

'Why is it a secret?'

'Because no one must ever know or I will die, and I know this is true because he told me with my hand on the Bible.'

'Who told you?'

'Oh no, you can't trap me, I have to obey the rules.'

'How long did you have to obey the rules, Lena?'

'Mind your own business, you dirty fucking bastard, you try and trap me and I will make you sorry, you listen to me or I will cut your dick off.'

Reid sat back, his jaw open, as the voice Lena had adopted was guttural and coarse. Jackson was equally disturbed, but he refused to even acknowledge that he was suddenly hearing another one of the personalities emerge.

'Who am I talking to, Lena?'

'The Boss, you motherfucker, I am the Boss and I will not have her upset, or asked any more questions about her bastard father, you hear me? He is long dead. You had better not ask any more questions about the way he came into her room and screwed her up the arse.'

'Is this for real?' Jackson whispered and Reid declined to answer. Even though he was aware that Lena had been abused, seeing the effect on her made his whole body tense with repulsion, but what came next was even more shocking.

Cornwall had moved on to her teenage years and

another character emerged, flirtatious and sexual. She giggled, explaining in a lisping voice that she had managed to lock her father out of her bedroom and he had been weeping and crying to be allowed in, and she would make him kiss her feet and lick them clean.

'I trod in dog shit so he would have to lick it off.' She shrieked with laughter.

Cornwall laughed with her, gently encouraging her to tell him who he was now talking to, and she said that it was nobody. She suddenly sat upright and shouted that she should be careful or she would tell them about her mother.

'Don't you dare ask her about her mother!' It was the 'Boss' character again.

Lena flopped back, exhausted, as Cornwall signalled for a glass of water. He remained silent, sipping it as she began to curl her legs up and wrap her arms around her knees. He sensed, as he had anticipated, that Lena was beginning to tire and they had not even touched on the poisoning or any details about her daughter.

'Oh God, please, Daddy, don't make me do it, please...'

'What is he making you do, Lena?'

It was hard to determine which character she had become; she seemed exhausted and had started crying again. Cornwall persisted, repeating his question, and she began to make a strange motion with her hands as if washing them, and her face turned from tears into a grimace of distaste.

'Smell, she smells, horrible smell, she smells out the whole house.'

She persisted in the wringing motion, and her

face grimaced as if she were smelling something hideous.

'Who is it that is making this smell, Lena?'

'Mother, it's mother, the cancer, I have to wash her cancer out, and feed her. I hate to do it, but he refused to let anyone else take care of her because they might find out.'

The odd wringing motion took over again; she seemed to be trying to clean her hands, and her face was twisted with disgust, and then there was a low moaning and she began crying even more loudly than before. She turned over with her face buried in the pillow as she sobbed; her hands were clenched into fists as she pummelled the mattress.

'Sorry, Mummy, sorry, Mummy, sorry, Mummy.'

Cornwall leaned closer and his voice was hardly audible as he asked why she was sorry as she had been a good girl taking care of her mother. He told her there was nothing to be sorry about as her mother had been very ill.

Lena slowly turned over and once again it was the coarse voice that came out. 'I stuffed it into her mouth, you dumb bastard, I STUFFED IT INTO HER MOUTH.'

Cornwall leaned away from her, as her breathing became erratic and her chest heaved as she gasped for air. The nurses moved closer, concerned at the state of panic she was in.

'Take deep breaths, in and out, breathe in, and breathe out, that's a good girl, I am right beside you, nothing you are telling me disgusts me or makes me not care for you.'

She sighed and slowly her breathing returned to normal. He took hold of her hand and checked her pulse, then gently rinsed out a cloth and began to wipe her face.

'I am so tired,' she said quietly.

'I know, and we will stop now and you can have some nice soup and then a long sleep. You have done very well, you are a good girl.'

Cornwall told the nurses to leave them and brought Lena round from her hypnotic state. She clearly didn't remember or have a clue what had just happened in the room and told Cornwall that she felt as if she had been out on a lovely walk along a beach on a warm summer's day. Cornwall said that she had, because that was where he had taken her subconscious mind as therapy for her problems. Lena thanked him and Cornwall said he'd get a nurse to help her to her room, but she was insistent that she make her own way there.

Jackson was on his feet, angrily gesturing towards the window. 'He can't fucking stop now – he hasn't even asked her about her daughter. Jesus Christ, this is not acceptable.'

The door opened, Cornwall entered and came over to Jackson, pushing at his chest. 'She cannot continue; as I said this will require more sessions, and as you just witnessed the emotional stresses she's been through have exhausted her.'

Jackson stepped back, jerking his head from side to side.

'In the meantime, Professor Cornwall, what do you expect us to do? We suspect her of murder, multiple ones at that. Dear God, we just heard her admit to stuffing her dying mother's mouth with Christ only knows what!'

Cornwall somehow managed to maintain his dignity and control as he said that for him it had been a very positive session, and one that gave him and anyone with any sense of propriety an indication of Lena Fulford's condition. Clearly her sexual abuse for such a lengthy period, from being an eight-year-old to a teenager, had triggered the need to protect herself by forcing her mind to split into multiple identities. Added to the abuse by her father, she had also, he was certain, been encouraged to end her mother's life. The emergence of the strident identity was covering her deep guilt at what she had done.

Jackson became less aggressive, even slightly apologetic, as he said that he understood, but it still left him with unanswered questions.

'I can't bring charges against her for killing her mother – what I have to get clarification on is the reason we are here. I need to know if that poor woman did as we suspect poison innocent people. No matter how sorry I feel for her, we still have not been able to discover if she also murdered her own daughter.'

Cornwall rubbed his eyes and sighed, he was so tired.

'I will require more sessions, and will obviously allow you to be present, but I cannot at this stage say when I feel she will be able, or in my estimation well enough, to continue. I will require detailed lists of questions you wish to be answered, but as I have just said I cannot give you any confirmation that they will be answered in the near future.'

Jackson, still on edge, asked if he felt Lena could be questioned with a solicitor present. Cornwall gave a resigned sigh and abruptly reminded Jackson she was now his patient and he would not allow her to be subjected to any police interrogation until he was satisfied she was mentally capable of answering as herself.

'Detective Jackson, just what do you expect me to do? Release her into police custody when she is clearly unfit and requires treatment?'

Jackson shuffled his feet, and looked to Reid.

'Have it your way, but I will need answers. If you say she will be unfit to answer the allegations against her I will need not just your confirmation but a second medical opinion.'

Cornwall gave a brief nod and walked out, at which Jackson picked up his coat and suggested to Reid they go for a drink. Reid didn't want to spend any more time in the DCI's company, but it was impossible to refuse, and they left together.

Sitting in the Nelson's Arms, which was the nearest countryside pub, with a pint of Guinness each, they found it difficult to even talk to each other. Eventually Jackson muttered that he had never in his entire career had to deal with such a screwed-up investigation. Slurping his drink, he observed it might be easier all round if they just left the case closed, as it had been before Reid's meddling.

'But we can't do that, can we, Vic? We are just going to have to sit with our thumbs up our arse until that pompous shrink gives us the heads-up that she's not away with the fairies and calling up an army of Christ knows what in her head. It's beyond belief, and another thing we need to get clarified is who the hell is going to pay for all these sessions he's intending doing? I mean we are going to have to sort all that out and get some coherent answers for the Commander, never mind the Commissioner, and God forbid she doesn't walk out of the unit and top a few more buggers off.'

Reid still gave no answer, knowing that Jackson wouldn't listen anyway, as he appeared more interested in stuffing his mouth with the meat pie he'd ordered. He spat out bits of crust as he continued. 'It's going to be a real lesson in diplomacy getting ourselves out of this mess, never mind explaining the overspend on the budget. The way out for a quiet life is to have her deemed unfit to plead, we bury the whole fucking mess and she can rot in the nuthouse where she belongs.'

Reid downed his pint and carefully placed the glass onto the beer mat on the counter. As he had paid for the first round, and the meat pie, he felt he could now leave, but Jackson dug into his arm.

'Same again, Vic?'

'No thanks, I'll get off home. Tomorrow I'll make out a list of questions that Cornwall can use.'

'You think we'll get answers?'

Reid sighed. 'I'm not like you, sir; what I just witnessed will give me nightmares as I have never experienced anything like it.' He shook his head. 'At the same time, no matter how much I pity Lena Fulford, I also feel that her victims deserve justice, and I can't walk away from knowing what happened to her daughter. If we do get closure and discover that she poisoned Simon Boatly, Harry Dunn, and her husband, that's three murders, and it's possible Marcus Fulford was innocent.'

'They're fucking dead,' Jackson snapped.

'I cannot and will not agree to this case being put to bed. For me, burying it is nothing more than a cop-out.'

Jackson grabbed hold of his coat sleeve and pulled him closer.

'Maybe it's not just a suggestion, Vic, but an order. I am up for retirement in six months and I am not going to let this screw my pension, because I am warning you, if this whole shambolic investigation becomes public it'll be your career blown along with mine. People died because you didn't read the recipes in the back of the journal at the get-go.'

'Well, I'll just have to learn to live with that, won't I?' Reid said and eased his arm away. He brushed his coat sleeve down and walked out, leaving Jackson seething and staring into the dregs of his pint.

Back at home Reid sat up most of the night going over the entire investigation. When had Lena Fulford made the decision to poison her so-called enemies? How had she done it, and had she conspired with her husband to kill their daughter? Where was Amy's body? Buried or dismembered? He underlined this query as being the most important. By the time he was ready to go to bed, all he could think about was what he had seen at

Cornwall's hypnotherapy session with Lena and what Jackson had said about their careers being over.

He slowly ripped up the lists of questions and felt totally and utterly drained, and so tired his head ached. In the morning he would have to complete his report of the search at Lena Fulford's house. He was ashamed because although he had made a decision that he would make himself available to watch the forthcoming sessions between Professor Cornwall and Lena, in the interim he could do nothing further. It was as if the investigation was as good as over.

Chapter 41

Lena Fulford had four further sessions, in which her alter personalities were gradually brought to the surface by Cornwall. Only with their protection had she been able to exist as a child and a teenager. For years she was forced to remain under the dominant controlling influence of her sexually abusive father. She had only been released from her torment when he had begun drinking to excess. This was the first time she had started to take control of herself, aided by her 'army' of personalities, and she admitted that she had often used some of her mother's medication, which was left in the house, to doctor her father's bottles of alcohol. By making him dependent on drink, she had found a small sense of freedom.

Whilst at university she met Marcus and she had explained in detail how kind and thoughtful he was, never aggressive, but always understanding of her nervousness in having sexual intercourse.

Marcus had proved to her that she could be loved without demands and threats and she realized that for the first time in her life she was happy. Her temporary separation from him when she went to Harvard was a severely depressing time and the fact her father accompanied her to America terrified her as she feared that he was seizing the opportunity to once again abuse her. When she returned to the UK and eventually married Marcus it was as if she had finally been set free from her father.

Professor Cornwall was slowly reducing the amount of medication, so that they were able to actually have a therapeutic interaction. Lena had remained constantly sweet-natured and friendly with the staff and Cornwall found her delightful, intelligent, and keen to answer truthfully, as if wanting his encouragement to continue to help her understand herself.

She talked of her jealousy of her husband's relationship with Simon Boatly, and her attempts to dissuade Marcus from seeing him. She recalled meeting him on one particular occasion at his Mayfair flat, but said it was not productive and she behaved foolishly, which she regretted. She became uneasy when describing the birth of Amy, as it triggered feelings of despair, and she added that she had been diagnosed with 'baby blues', but nothing seemed to lift her depression.

Cornwall was interested to find out how she

had reacted to her father being around when Amy was born. Lena said it sent her on a downward spiral, during which she had become aggressive and abusive. The 'Boss' character would emerge to swear, curse and scream and it was this alter who had made her prepare the dosage of hallucinogenic mushrooms to put in her father's drink when he had visited.

She was calmer as she described the relief when he had died, because it meant Amy was safe from him. She was also safe from him ever telling anyone about their relationship and the fact she had smothered her mother with a washcloth in her mouth.

Throughout all this, Cornwall made copious notes and recordings. He observed that her mother's death brought Lena relief, as if she had rid herself of the stench of her mother and being forced to nurse her. She had therefore found it relatively easy to also get rid of her father or at the very least advance his death. The sessions after this period were often lighter as she described her joy at being with Amy. She explained it was only when it was becoming obvious that her daughter was not only beautiful, but clever, and that her husband doted on her, that the manic depression periods returned.

Lena confessed that she was not only feeling envious of her daughter's relationship with Marcus, but also his still ongoing friendship with Simon Boatly.

All at once she reverted to a hideous snarl as she grimaced that she had discovered that Boatly was homosexual, and had been in a relationship with her husband. She went into a tirade of bitter hatred against Boatly and how she had been envious of their closeness. She had forced herself to be friendly towards Simon, flirted and been eager to make Marcus jealous, but Simon only pretended to like her and was determined to break them up and have Marcus for himself. She was sitting up on the couch and wagging her index finger in anger, and her voice was high-pitched. 'I knew then, I knew I had to watch him, that he was trying to get Marcus to leave me, and Amy was behaving like a silly bitch, all hissy and moody; it felt as if all three were against me.'

She flopped back and he was stunned when the low voice whispered, 'I knew he had to go, but it was a question of when and how.'

This time Reid was in the viewing room alone, as Jackson could no longer be bothered to be present. Hour upon hour he had religiously sat listening and taking notes. He had even got used to hearing all the different voices and characters that Lena would become. It fascinated him to begin with, but now it was often quite tedious, as Cornwall never put any pressure on her. But at last she had now admitted what she intended when she had said of Simon Boatly, 'He had to go.'

Reid was shocked at the change in Lena's physical appearance; her hair was clipped back in an unflattering way, she had lost weight and looked pale and drawn. She wore woollen socks as she kept on losing her slippers, which added to her looking older and mentally unstable. Sometimes she was eager to talk, other times her voice was slurred and she seemed to find it difficult to concentrate, often repeating herself over and over, or asking for a question to be repeated as she had forgotten what Cornwall had asked.

Cornwall slowly drew from her the details of her enemies. He was able to pinpoint the time when she had begun to have severe lapses of control, which came after Marcus and Lena separated. She was repulsed by her driver, who she claimed touched her in an inappropriate manner, making her feel inadequate and incapable of being able to sack him. This was exacerbated by the suspicions that Agnes and he were in cahoots and passing information to Marcus about her business. Lena's paranoia had been moving towards a psychotic breakdown, and with Amy spending alternate weekends with Marcus, she felt that everyone was against her. As she grew increasingly incapable of dealing with the pressure, the underlying but as yet controlled DID began to take over her rational thinking. Lena was able to concentrate on her business, and even display successful financial acumen, but after the meeting with the divorce lawyers, her most controlling identity, known as alter three or the Boss, began to dominate and co-ordinate the means of getting rid of her enemies. By now she was deeply concerned about Amy's relationship with her art teacher Miss Polka, as her daughter had at some point implied that she cared for her deeply, and this was yet another sign that she was even losing her daughter's love. She had also seen the abuse directed at Amy on the web, which intimated she was having a lesbian affair with an older woman. Although she had no idea who was responsible, in her mind – by chance correctly – it had to be the nasty little Serena who was responsible and had to pay. For being unkind to Amy.

The Boss took over the story, slyly describing how she knew Amy had put a spare set of Marcus's flat keys in her kitchen drawer. She related how she had stolen into the flat many times when she knew they were out, and it was most hideous to listen to her explaining how she had used a little poison to make Amy feel unwell. Sometimes she placed a few drops in a half-drunk Coke bottle already in Amy's room, or in a meal eaten before going to her father's flat.

Cornwall gently prodded and queried how she had intended removing her 'enemies', and a previously unheard voice started to dominate the session. It was a clear, well-spoken, mature voice that often employed Latin terms. She seemed very calm and poised, using her hands very expressively, as if explaining what she was saying to someone unseen with great confidence, as if showing off.

'I worked hard to come to the best conclusions as to exactly how I should realize my theories. I thought that my optimum choice was the Common Ink Cap, *Coprinus atramentarius*, as if it is eaten in isolation it can have no ill effect. However if alcohol is consumed, a reaction will set in, even if it is taken many hours after a meal. Testing it out on my father, along with the hallucinogenic mushrooms, made the decision for me very simple; however the academic science laboratory was not available. Ergo I was thus forced to grow,

565

and cross-fertilize, the fungi in the garden and basement. I have conducted considerable research into the Death Cap mushroom and was fully aware this would cause severe liver damage. I also had to think of alternative measures, as it was imperative I was not implicated, the reasons being obvious. It had to be very cleverly administered, so I could remain undetected and ostensibly innocent, therefore I chose the slow release method as the most suitable for my desired intentions.'

Lena was sitting up with her back straight, and it seemed as if she was giving some kind of lecture. She began detailing in the same cultured voice the gastric poisons she had studied and tested in a laboratory while working in America. She was very clear about nerve poisons, especially the type that would create hallucinogenic behaviour, resulting in convulsions, irregular breathing, and often death due to heart failure. There were two types of toxins, muscarine and ibotenic acid, she found to be excellent. Her hands gesticulated gracefully as she described testing out the components to make the final decision of which exact combination she would administer.

'When you had decided this, exactly how did you go about administering it to the chosen enemies?' Cornwall asked in a relaxed manner.

In the viewing room Reid sat on the edge of his seat, listening and watching as Lena gave a long sigh, pursed her lips and wafted her hand in a dismissive gesture.

'Oh it wasn't easy, you know. My problem with Simon Boatly was how and when to get into his house at Henley to administer it. When Marcus said he had to move out from the Green Street flat and asked me to get his clothes it created the perfect opportunity, as I thought, wrongly as it turned out, that Simon was moving back in. When I went to collect the suitcases for Marcus I already knew there was an expensive brandy there from my other secret visits. I knew Simon liked expensive brandy so I decided to inject a few drops into it using a large hypodermic needle. A stroke of genius, don't you think? Tinged with a bit of good and bad luck though.'

'What do you mean?' Cornwall asked softly.

Even her soft laugh was cultured. 'That poor young man Grant I met at the flat. He had no idea he was taking poisoned brandy back to Henley.' She spread out her hands as if seeking words of approval from Cornwall.

'But Grant could have died, and Marcus died because he drank the brandy.'

'Then Grant would have been my mistake, but my plan worked because Simon did die. As for Marcus, well that was bad luck for him at the time, but looking back he deserved it as it was obvious he was abusing her.'

'Do you believe that Marcus had something to do with Amy's disappearance?'

Her face twisted in anger. 'I refuse to discuss it because it is too painful for me to even consider. The Furies came to me in continued nightmares and made me what I am.'

'Who are the Furies?' Cornwall asked.

'The three avenging goddesses of Greek mythology – they torment me because I have subverted the natural order. I killed my parents, and the punishment inflicted on me by the snake-draped Furies is the madness that constantly persecutes and controls me.'

It was difficult to know exactly what alter was controlling Lena now, as in agitation she twisted her fingers round a strand of her hair and pulled at it sharply.

'Am I talking to Lena?'

'Who the fuck do you think you are talking to? Jesus Christ, you are so stupid, I have explained to you exactly what she did, how much more do you want me to tell you. The Furies are punishing her but not me, they can't frighten me.'

It was the Boss character again and Cornwall asked if she had also intended harming Agnes and Harry, but before he could finish she dragged at her hair so roughly she pulled out several strands and held them between her fingers.

'Agnes was supposed to eat the bloody bolognese. I'd cooked it the night before the first press conference and I'm surprised the neurotic bitch never complained about the mess of dirty pots and pans in the kitchen.'

'Why didn't she eat it?'

'I put it in the freezer to give her later, but it had no sticky label describing what it was so she took it out and nearly gave it to Lena. But I was smart, see, I knew, so I told Lena to leave a note that Agnes can have it. Stupid bitch then gave it to that halfwit Harry.'

'So Harry's death was a sort of accident?'

'No, he got what he deserved as well, and as for that nosy bitch who was so ungrateful, well I haven't finished with her – selling Lena's photographs to the gutter press for money. If you hurt Lena I hurt you back tenfold.'

'What about Amy, did you pay her back tenfold?'

Slowly she lowered her head, and her shoulders shook. Reid leaned forward towards the monitor, waiting for the revealing answer, but nothing came as Lena remained silent, with a smirk on her face. It was immensely frustrating as they had gained so much this session, and he hoped it was not going to end.

'Did you really believe that Marcus would have hurt Amy?'

She shook her head and the tears rolled down her cheeks. 'He loved her more than me, but I loved her more than my life.'

It was again difficult to fathom who she was now as her tone of voice changed once more and she kept her hands over her face.

'So you don't think Marcus would have done the things the others told you about?'

'No.' She shook her head again as the tears kept trickling down, and neither Cornwall nor Reid could detect if she was now herself, or summoning up one of her army of protectors.

'Do you know anyone who harmed Amy?'

'Serena, she was very nasty to Amy.'

'How do you know that?'

Lena looked up at Cornwall with a wicked glint in her eye, then let out a loud disparaging sigh. 'Because I'm the fucking Boss so I have to know everything that goes on to maintain order. I can't have any of those other bastards inside her telling me what to do. To stay on top you need to know your enemies and that Serena was sending nasty stuff, because I saw Amy's Facebook calling her a slut, lesbian and other things.'

Cornwall realized the Boss had been playing games, luring him in with fake tears and then seeking to dominate the conversation. 'But how did you know it was Serena?'

'Because only someone close to Amy like Serena would know and make nasty comments about Lena and Marcus being separated.'

'How did you make her pay for being horrible?'

'Home-made truffles that Lena gave Amy to give to Serena as a sleepover thank-you.'

'Amy gave them to Mrs Newman, not Serena.'

Lena laughed out loud. 'Really? How funny...'

'But Serena did eat one and was very sick,' Cornwall said, deliberately pandering to the Boss's ego.

'There wasn't enough poison to really hurt Serena, but enough to teach her a lesson and make her vomit and run to the toilet. A lot of squitty poos.'

Cornwall sighed. She was retreating into a childish voice again, and he glanced towards the hidden camera in frustration, wondering if the Boss was playing games once more.

'What about Amy? Was she given anything that made her vomit?'

'I only gave her a little now and again, just enough to make her sick. If she was ill she'd want to come back home and stay with me.'

Cornwall picked up on the similarity to Serena's predicament. 'Did you give Amy chocolate truffles as well?'

Lena just stared at him and Cornwall was concerned she would retreat further before he could get the answers he sought.

'Did she eat the truffles, was there too much poison in them, did it all go horribly wrong?' he asked rapidly, desperate for an answer. He took hold of her hand. 'Tell me what's happened to Amy?'

'I don't know.' She was hardly audible as she clung to him tightly.

'You know the people that told you what they thought Marcus had done to Amy, well they need to know if you have ever done anything to harm her.'

'She ran away, she disappeared.'

'Do you know where she's gone?'

'No.'

'Did you have anything to do with Amy running away?'

'No.'

'You can tell me, I will understand.'

She withdrew her hand and covered her face and let out a wretched howl. Reid stood up, certain that she was about to admit to playing some part in Amy's disappearance, or even worse, killing her.

She screamed, flailing her arms. 'I DON'T KNOW... I DON'T KNOW... I DON'T KNOW.'

Cornwall tried to calm her and the nurses moved closer to restrain her. He knew he had to try to get an answer, even though it was obvious Lena was very distressed and becoming hysterical.

'Did you kill Amy?'

'NOOOOOOOOOOOOOOOOOOO!' she howled and began sobbing uncontrollably. He stood up and helped the nurses settle her back to lie on the couch, but she suddenly kicked out and then curled her body into a foetal position. He gestured for one of the nurses to prepare a syringe with a sedative as he leaned over her. She looked up at him, her eyes brimming with tears. She lifted her left arm towards him, and then her eyes widened as she whispered:

'You remind me of my daddy.'

Cornwall injected the sedative then checked her pulse; he asked if she could hear him, but she simply stared at the wall. There was no response, she was retreating, and it was evident as she slowly closed her eyes, totally silent, falling into a drug-induced stupor.

Reid watched as the nurses opened the door and wheeled in a gurney, gently placing her onto it, and after a while wheeled her out of the room. Cornwall remained seated. Lena's last words had affected Reid deeply and he got up to switch off the monitor.

As he did so the professor appeared through the viewing-room doorway, then came in and poured himself a cup of coffee.

'I fear that any further sessions about poisonous mushrooms, Amy, or anything to do with the investigation could be counter-productive,' he sighed, sipping from the cup in exhaustion. 'My honest opinion is I doubt she had anything to do with her daughter's disappearance and she will never be deemed fit to stand trial.'

'Do you think she was poisoning Amy?'

'Well you heard what she said about giving Amy enough to make her sick. I suspect she used exactly the same MO as on Serena with truffles or similar. If it had been going on for a while then there appears to be no intention to kill Amy, and it's highly unlikely with her knowledge of poisonous mushrooms she'd get the dosage wrong.'

Reid realized that it was indeed highly unlikely that Lena had killed Amy. To his mind it was also highly unlikely that Marcus had done so either, and it seemed more and more evident that Amy had simply run away from the maelstrom of madness surrounding her school and family life.

'So what happens now?' he asked Cornwall.

'Mrs Fulford will be treated by the resident psychiatrists from now on; they will not question her about her past as the aim will now be to teach her to control her demons. I don't think she will ever rid herself of Dissociative Identity Disorder, and she is borderline schizophrenic; her history of self-harming and suicide attempts will mean she will require round-the-clock monitoring, and it will need to be here in a secure surrounding.'

'She said at the end that you reminded her of her father.'

Cornwall pursed his lips and turned away. 'I heard it, and you have witnessed what abuse can do, and no matter what Lena has become, no matter what she has done, her father destroyed her, and I believe it will be impossible for her to survive without her army of protectors.'

Reid was left with little alternative but to drive back to the station and write up an extensive report for DCI Jackson. There was no kind of satisfaction in it; in the end the outcome was virtually as Jackson had wanted. As far as anyone knew, Marcus Fulford had murdered his daughter and disposed of her body. The case would remain on file, with the hope that one day Amy Fulford's remains would be discovered.

Try as he might, over the days and weeks that followed, Reid could not rid himself of what he had witnessed between Professor Cornwall and Lena Fulford. It was almost a relief when he was put on indefinite sick leave after being diagnosed with emotional stress by the police psychiatrist. Although Jackson had taken him to one side and said he'd keep quiet about Reid missing the poison recipes at the back of the journal, he still felt an overwhelming guilt that he was in some ways to blame for the deaths of Simon Boatly, Harry Dunn and Marcus Fulford.

He had recurring nightmares, and even social interactions with friends became difficult to handle. After two weeks he had contacted Professor Cornwall to ask if there had been any new development in Lena Fulford's condition, only to be told that she had regressed into a virtual catatonic state and remained segregated from the other patients. Considering her crimes, the professor felt it in some ways eased her existence. Reid kept his feelings to himself, and resolved to try and put the whole Fulford case behind him, but often Lena's voice would come back to haunt him. Remembering how she had lifted her arm towards Cornwall, 'You remind me of my daddy,' and the passages in the journal headed 'Daddy'.

Two months of rest made him feel more like his old self. He bought a bicycle and would spend hours cycling to parts of the country he'd never visited before and staying in small B&Bs. He did not relish the idea of returning to work and DCI Jackson had thwarted any hope of him ever working on a murder squad again. He also feared that he would never now be promoted beyond his current rank and might even be put back to uniform duties. Even if the latter wasn't the case, he was not particularly happy about the prospect of more missing persons cases. He started to look round for possible career moves, even contemplating going back to an estate agency. He surfed the web for ideas and every now and again he bought *The Times* to check out possible alternative employment advertisements...

It was noticing a small advertisement while skimming for the situations vacant pages that jolted him. It appeared that Simon Boatly's solicitors were still attempting to trace heirs to his estate. He read that anyone with information regarding the family of Simon William Henry Boatly should make contact as it could be to their benefit. Intrigued, he put in a call, only to be told they could not divulge any particulars over the phone, but if he wished for more information he could make an appointment. Against his better judgement he arranged to meet them, and without any need to hide his motives, told them immediately that he was there simply out of interest as he had worked on the investigation into Mr Boatly's death.

They informed him that there was a considerable amount of money left to Boatly's heirs and that a sum of three million pounds had initially been bequeathed to Marcus Fulford. Reid said he was aware of that fact, but was surprised to be told that Simon Boatly had stipulated Marcus only got the money if he was divorced from Mrs Fulford before he died, thus that part of the will was null and void and not even Mrs Fulford was entitled to the money, though she had rung and asked if she was. Reid was shocked at this revelation and asked if anyone else had made enquiries about the will. The lawyer said they were still trying to track down other distant relatives and friends who had been left large sums of money but without much luck, though they had recently had an enquiry that might prove positive and were waiting for further instructions.

'May I ask who made the enquiry?'

'It was a very brief call and they didn't actually give a name.'

'Did they say where they lived?'

'Mexico.'

'When was this?'

'Two weeks ago.'

Reid chewed at his lips. 'So whoever it was, you think that person is related to Simon Boatly?'

'Not necessarily; this was an enquiry regarding the monies left to Mr Fulford – perhaps I should have informed you that we are also taking care of his estate. When he came to enquire about Mr Boatly's will he asked that we handle his affairs as he was a very close friend for many years.'

Reid could feel a knot tighten in his stomach; his head was reeling as he asked if the caller was male or female.

'She was female. I said that for us to release any monies someone would have to prove they are the selfsame person as the one named in the will, and produce evidence, such as a birth certificate or passport.'

'What was her accent like?'

'English, well spoken, but don't ask me where from as I'm useless with accents.'

'But the call was definitely from Mexico?'

'Mexico City to be exact. I was curious and dialled the number back and it was a business line to a jewellery store. I speak a little Spanish and they said they had no information as to the caller. I think they were more dubious about who I was and why I was calling. Anyway, I didn't pursue the matter.'

Reid returned to his flat with the jewellery store phone number, and lost no time in ringing Agent Morgan at the National Crime Agency.

'Can you do me another big favour, Andy?'

'Tell me what it is first, Vic.'

'I'm still attempting to trace Josephine Polka and wondered if you could ask your contact in the FBI to check out if she landed or is known to be in Mexico City'

'I'll do what I can.'

'I'm getting close, Andy, I know I am. I've got a Mexico City phone number and wondered if you could get an address for it.'

'No problem. Email me everything you need and the number and I'll get straight on to it.'

Reid couldn't sleep; it could be a wild goose chase but something kept urging him to trace

Josephine Polka and he was certain she could provide him with the answers. If he was wrong, so be it, but his intuition was telling him he had finally stumbled on finding out the truth behind Amy Fulford's disappearance.

Chapter 42

San Carlos is a subdivision of the port city and municipality of Guaymas, in the northern desert state of Sonora, Mexico. A six-hour drive from the United States, and with a population of only seven thousand people, it is noted for the exceptional clarity and warmth of the ocean water in its shallow bays along the Sea of Cortez.

The vast Sonoran Desert outside San Carlos was the location used to film the 1970s movie *Catch-22*. The parts of the set that had survived were clearly visible, but what was most striking was the incredible expanse of sand. It was rumoured that the director would only film between three and six in the evening, to ensure he always had the exact same light conditions. Some people, but not many, have made the two-mile journey into the Sonoran Desert to sit, watch and experience the brilliance of the sun's glow on the mile upon mile of empty sand. The views of the sun in this desolate area were almost beyond description, the orange glow as it rose in the morning as if balanced on the horizon, then come sunset it slowly retreated beyond the horizon in azure-blue colours that created the illusion of an ocean across the soft undulating sand.

Jo Polka had first visited the Sonoran Desert years ago when she was deeply in love with her then-partner. She had watched her take hundreds of photographs, including many of her lying in the soft sand, with only the line of the vast sky to interrupt the golden desert. She had dreamed about returning, conjuring it up in her mind many times, and had even painted it from memory when she was in England. After her lover found another woman to pose and sleep with, and rejected her, she was heartbroken. Jo had never wanted to return to Sonora, or at least not until six months ago when she finally desired to see for herself the reasons why her lover had found such artistic inspiration in the desolate spot. It is true that time heals, and for her at last it had. She never believed it would be possible to form a loving and deeply committed relationship with anyone other than the woman who had in the end betrayed her. That was no longer in her thoughts, because she had found love. It was complicated when she stopped to think about her reasons for wanting to return. It was not out of hurt, but more out of a need to experience for herself the same incredible power of the Sonoran sands.

They had been together in the tiny Mexican village for six months, but choosing to remain in seclusion from the outside world they used no computers, no mobile phones and no television. They read and talked and painted and only occasionally did Jo use the ancient Land Rover to drive into the nearest town to buy any supplies they needed. They rented a stonewalled, whitewashed cottage that had long since been left empty by the previous owners and was now their home. It had become their sanctuary, their healing place, with a plentiful stock of oil paints and canvases. No electricity, just oil lamps, candles and an open-fire cooking range with a simple grid, and an old barbecue outside which was where most of the cooking was done. Fresh food was a rare treat, so they existed mostly on simple meals, of rice dishes and tortillas. They financed themselves at first from Jo's savings, but when those ran out, it became necessary to travel to Mexico City. They never travelled together, it was always Jo catching the run-down bus and spending twenty-four hours away as she carefully chose which jeweller's would be the most trustworthy. She never used the same people, calculating that the more the items were broken up the less likely they ran the risk of suspicion. She knew she was being offered low prices, but foremost in her mind was always the need to protect their safety. However, the tiara posed a real problem. They discussed it endlessly; intact, it was perfect, even though the individual stones could have fetched a good price on their own. Finally they agreed it was too beautiful to dismantle. On this occasion Jo thought it necessary to go to a more upmarket antique jeweller's, one which, judging from its window displays, dealt with finer and more costly items.

Showing the tiara to the dapper Mexican, who spoke some English, Jo explained slowly that it had been a family heirloom, and the value had to be in the region of two hundred thousand dollars.

She was taken aback that he never queried her asking price. He said the stones were of exceptional beauty and were rose diamonds, the centrepiece being an astonishing four carat which had been set in platinum with gold inlay. He asked that she leave the tiara with him so he could get his friend to look at it for a second opinion and valuation.

Jo was no fool and refused to leave it in his possession, but said she'd wait until his partner arrived. She was taken into the back room of the elegant shop, and given coffee while they waited for a José Hernandez to arrive. The back of the shop had a small yard and barred iron gates, which she stared at in the heat of the day until Hernandez drew up in a new BMW convertible. He was wearing a white suit and pale blue shirt with a flamboyant necktie; he also had a heavy gold and diamond ring on his little finger. He spoke perfect English and when his partner explained why Jo was there he was extremely eager to see the tiara. He immediately said it dated from the 1920s and then took his time with an eyeglass, inspecting every single stone. Jo found it intensely nerve-wracking, and she was sweating and beginning to think she had made a big mistake in not doing as they had done with all the other pieces and splitting the stones to sell one by one.

More coffee was served as the two men sat in a corner, carefully checking the tiara. Jo was left to wait on a plush-covered sofa with a large statue of the Virgin Mary on a coffee table beside her. There was also a copy of the *New York Times*, days old and already brownish, having been left by the window in the sun. She picked it up, trying to appear uninterested as they spoke in Spanish to each other. Hernandez left to go into the main shop, from where she could hear him talking to someone on the phone. As she turned to the back pages of the newspaper, her suspicions grew as his partner used his mobile phone to take photographs of the tiara.

The advert had a black border, and leaped out at her as she read the name of the London lawyers seeking to trace the heirs to Marcus Fulford and Simon Boatly's estates. She had not known that Marcus Fulford was dead. Without even considering the reason for the advert, she realized she had to know if this was Amy Fulford's father.

Putting the paper down and getting to her feet, she asked if it would be possible to make an urgent call to England. Hernandez, having finished his own call, hesitated then invited her to use the office phone. Jo was shaking when she finished speaking to the solicitors and could hardly take in what Hernandez said next, but gradually she forced herself to listen to him as he explained that he would require confirmation that the tiara was legally hers to sell, and if she could provide papers that proved its provenance, they would be very keen to purchase it.

She assured them that she would return the following day with the documents, and they offered to retain the tiara for safekeeping in their safe but she refused. Both men were extremely eager to persuade her to agree. Sensing they were becoming threatening, she insisted they give her back the tiara. By now she was beginning to panic, afraid that she had inadvertently created the very thing they had tried so hard to avoid. They had appeared to grow suspicious and Hernandez offered to drive her to wherever she had the legal ownership documents, but again she had refused, lying about having someone waiting for her, and by the time she had left, clutching the tiara wrapped in tissue paper in the old plastic bag, she was very frightened.

They had watched her hurry from their premises, Hernandez furious at the possibility they had just lost a big sale, but at the same time his partner was equally angry since if he hadn't queried the ownership of the piece they would have had for a quarter of the value a tiara that when broken apart would have made them a fortune in the sale of individual diamonds. The two men argued with each other, Hernandez suggesting that in his opinion it was more than likely stolen, and as such he was just protecting their good name. This had created further disagreement as they had made some very shady deals in the past, but as Hernandez pointed out, it was the Englishwoman who had approached them. He opened the pictures of the tiara on his partner's mobile and they looked with disappointment at what they believed was a golden opportunity they had just lost, and they doubted the Englishwoman would return.

Jo caught the dilapidated local bus and sat clutching the tiara; she kept on turning round, scared she might have been followed. To take extra precautions she changed bus twice, which meant a long wait in Guadalajara. To pass the agonizingly slow time she went into an internet café where she paid for half an hour and spent it checking out news items and anything on the net that was connected to Marcus Fulford's death. Eventually she got on the bus to Mazatlán after shopping in the markets for fresh provisions, the tiara hidden beneath potatoes and carrots. She had pressed her head against the dirty glass in the old dented bus, seated beside a woman with hens in a wooden crate, sweating and uncomfortable on the wooden seat. It was a long trip and she slept through the night, boarding yet another bus before she reached the nearest stop to where she had left the Land Rover on the outskirts of Mazatlán.

Jo drove for another hour before turning onto the dirt track that led to their rented cottage. She could see Anna sitting outside, breaking an old stale loaf into crumbs which she held in the palm of her hand for the hens to peck at. She was wearing a pair of faded jeans cut and frayed at the knee, and a washed-out gingham shirt tied in a knot at her waist. She had short-cropped boyish hair bleached white from the sun, and she was deeply tanned, tall and slender. Brushing the remaining crumbs from her hands, she shaded her eyes from the sun as she could see Jo approaching.

Jo remained sitting in the Land Rover as Anna gave her a wave and strolled along the small path they had lined with white seashells collected when they had visited Puerto Vallarta. Anna had such an easy way of moving, swaying lightly in her leather sandals, as she gave a smile of welcome. Her natural beauty never ceased to touch Jo, with her wide-set icy blue eyes, thick lashes, carved cheek-bones and lovely wide mouth, and the closer she came to the open window, the more Jo's heart felt as if it would explode.

'Hey there,' Anna said as she reached to open the door, and then wafted her hand, as it was hot from the sun.

Jo opened the door and jumped down, reaching into the passenger seat for the groceries and passing them out to Anna. She froze when Anna gripped her bent neck in her fingers.

'Missed you.'

She turned her arms, holding the grocery bags. Anna immediately reached for them and then stopped.

'What's the matter?'

'I'm just hot – it's been a long journey.'

Anna carried the groceries as Jo walked ahead of her and began to strip off her sweat-stained shirt. She headed to a small area beside the house they had tiled and where they'd hooked up a hosepipe from their outside tap. It was always in the shade, and so the hosepipe water, although never actually cold, was at least refreshing. She turned on the tap and ran the water over her damp hair and tilted her face to feel the spray, using her thumb to squirt the water as if from a showerhead.

Anna had already gone onto the small porch attached to the cottage with trailing fig leaf plants shaded across the wooden slats. She was sitting with the grocery bags on the table and swinging the diamond tiara round in her hand.

'So why didn't you get it sold?'

Jo kicked out a stool from beneath the table and

wiped her face with an old torn towel, and sat there soaking wet in her old jeans and bra. Looking at Anna, she knew time was running out for them.

'There was a newspaper in the jeweller's, an old *New York Times,* and there was an advert from a legal firm in London.'

Sometimes Anna's thick eyelashes acted as a shade when lowered, making it impossible to see her eyes or their expression. 'What have you done?' she whispered.

Jo broke down in tears, at which Anna quickly put her arms around her, stroking her thick curly blonde hair.

'Whatever it is, Jo, tell me – don't lie, don't ever lie to me.'

The phone ringing woke Reid and he sat bolt upright, totally disorientated. It was five in the morning and it took a few moments for him to pick up the receiver. It was a call he had never believed would happen. He had virtually given up hope, and it had been over a week since he had asked Agent Morgan at the National Crime Agency for help. The FBI Agent now speaking to him apologized for the time and said that they had traced the call to Boatly's solicitors as originating from a jewellery store in Mexico City. The FBI had spoken with a local detective who attended the store and further enquiries to the shop had resulted in a sighting that fitted the description of Josephine Polka.

Reid listened as the man went on to explain that the store was a very upmarket and respectable business in Mexico City, and the detective had spoken in person to one of the partners, a José Hernandez, who at first had been very evasive, but had eventually admitted that he had allowed a customer to use his landline in the shop. She had said it was an urgent call to England. He claimed that she had not paid for the international call, and he said that he was angry about the way she had behaved as he had considered doing business with her. He at first refused to discuss the so-called business, but then acquiesced as he wanted to make it very clear he had done nothing illegal, nor even contemplated doing so. The agent said the shop owner had been keen to prove that he was a completely legitimate honest businessman, and that he had asked the customer to provide documents of proof of ownership.

Reid was hunched over the phone listening and taking notes while he was told that the woman was trying to sell a very valuable diamond tiara. To prove yet again just how honest he was, Hernandez had forwarded from his partner's mobile a photograph taken of the piece.

Once Reid heard the description of the customer, he knew without doubt he had succeeded in tracing the last known whereabouts of Josephine Polka. It was possible that she might still be in Mexico City, but as for an address or contact number, the jewellers were unable to give any details – all they did recall was that she had brought the tiara to the shop wrapped in paper in a plastic carrier bag, which bore the logo MAZATLÁN GIFTS. Hernandez was very certain about the bag because it seemed an unlikely way to carry such valuable contents and he was concerned that she might have stolen the tiara so he paid careful attention, even more so when she decided against leaving it with them, even though they had offered to keep it in their safe.

Reid asked about Mazatlán and was told it was a very beautiful seaside resort, with golden sands, exclusive hotels and attractive markets, a popular holiday destination for tourists and wealthy Mexicans.

He lay awake for a long time, asking himself whether his obsession was now becoming farcical. He had fancied Miss Polka, admittedly, but he knew deep down it was her lesbian relationship with Amy Fulford that was feeding his interest. Eventually he got up, showered and dressed and while drinking a cup of black coffee attempted to talk himself out of purchasing an airline ticket to Mexico. He kept on telling himself that it was ridiculous as he was no longer attached to the case, in fact no longer attached to anything even connected to it. He lit a cigarette, having started smoking again, and sat interrogating himself, attempting to face the truth about his obsession, even wondering if perhaps he should make an appointment with the therapist he had been seeing. On the table was the printout of the tiara photograph, emailed to him by the FBI Agent, which he had stared at for ages, trying to jog his memory. He had eventually folded the paper so he couldn't see it, but now he drew it close as he remembered. It was at Simon Boatly's house in the bedroom, where he had seen various jewellery cases littered around the floor. He remembered

Grant Delany saying that he had not taken anything and many of the old leather boxes were empty.

He pushed his chair back and began pacing the room, puffing at his cigarette. He was pretty certain Grant had been trying to pocket some of the jewellery but then he had said a lot of the boxes had already been empty and Reid recalled them looking at the large oval-shaped case and the indentation of where a tiara had obviously been kept for years. Hastily he turned to his filing drawer and began searching through it for the notebook he used on the Fulford case.

Finding it, he sat down and lit another cigarette as he thumbed through his notebook until he found the correct page. Marcus Fulford described taking his daughter to Henley, and she had gone into the house. This had become important at the time as they were checking out the possibility of Amy taking contaminated food into Boatly's house. However, it was now clear Amy had never poisoned anyone.

Reid returned to the table and wondered if Amy had gone upstairs and stolen the tiara and other jewellery. If this was the case, it would mean that the girl was planning her disappearance for weeks and she was most probably still alive. He knew it was all conjecture, totally without any foundation, and to even contemplate reporting it to someone like Jackson would be a waste of time. That was unless Boatly's lawyers had details of the jewellery, for insurance purposes, and could identify the tiara? He was shaking when at nine a.m. he placed a call to them and explained that he was investigating the possibility that property belonging to Simon Boatly might have been stolen, specifically jewellery, and one item might have been a tiara.

It was a lengthy and frustrating call as he was transferred from one person to another as they attempted to check their files. He emailed them the picture of the tiara, but still he was kept waiting and eventually he hung up as they said it would take time to look into his queries and they would get back to him.

It was after ten thirty when they did. There was some hesitancy as the insurance certificates and photographs of the jewellery they had on record were out of date and no insurance had been renewed. They were concerned that they were unable to clarify all the items that they had not been able to locate. Reid was starting to get irritated, even wondering if Grant Delany had stolen all the jewellery after all. He was relieved when told that they did have a photograph that matched the picture of the tiara in the email, and it belonged to Mr Boatly's great-grandmother. The record they had was very precise and described the tiara as made up of matching rose diamonds, with a large centre square-cut diamond of four carats set in platinum and gold inlay. It was from the 1920s and valued at three hundred and fifty thousand pounds, but as the estimate was ten years old it was more than likely now worth a considerable amount more.

Reid could hardly believe it, but they seemed inclined to do nothing, not even to contact the police. When he told them that he had good information that the tiara had surfaced in Mexico, and as they had identified it as being the one belonging to Mr Boatly, it was therefore highly probable that it had been stolen, they didn't seem interested as it was not within their legal jurisdiction. Reid interrupted and asked whether, if the tiara could be recovered, he would be in line for a finder's percentage.

'Absolutely,' was the response, and by the time the call ended Reid rashly calculated that his plane ticket and costs for the trip would be covered. He booked a plane ticket within an hour, and he was packed and ready to leave the UK by early afternoon.

On the plane, his initial excitement palled somewhat as he went back over the call that had brought about his decision. It was possible that Miss Polka might have become scared once she learnt the value of the tiara, or saw that José Hernandez was suspicious of how she had come by it. His confidence that Amy Fulford could be with Miss Polka began to lessen and he had a sinking feeling that he had allowed his obsession to override his senses, and yet it was too late to turn back. He pulled down his tray table and began to study the maps he had bought, realizing if he was to first stop in Mexico City and question the jewellers it would mean a further delay. He decided he would rent a car, drive from Mexico City to Mazatlán and begin his enquiries from there. He had in his suitcase photographs of Amy Fulford and Josephine Polka and knew that whatever names they were using would be immaterial if he could get the pictures identified. Yet again he was certain that he was right and that Amy Fulford was alive and had engineered her disappearance with clinical and clever subterfuge. He leaned back, closing his eyes as he went over his interaction with Miss Polka at the school, how she had behaved and reacted to his questions. Had she been lying to him, was she that good an actress? Yet again a wave of scepticism swept over him, and he hoped against hope that for once he had not reached a total dead end.

Chapter 43

Anna had been sitting outside the cottage on an old wooden bench for hours. She had lit a nightlight in a lantern and the mosquitoes gathered above it like a small black cloud. Jo had looked out from the window numerous times, but could not or refused to interrupt or go and sit beside her. She had begun packing the few things they had brought, and the canvas bags for their paintings and books were ready to be put into the Land Rover. Anna's rucksack was almost full, the top left open for anything else she wanted to take.

Earlier that morning Anna had frightened Jo as she had driven off without saying a word. She had been gone for over two hours, and unbeknown to Jo, had spent the time in an internet café discovering all she could about her father and mother. She had read the newspaper coverage of her own disappearance, and had even been able to bring up the footage of a few of the programmes that had been broadcast on British network television.

Jo had not seen her cry. Her reaction had been one of utter silence when she had told her about the visit to the jewellery store in Mexico City, the phone call to London and how she had subsequently gone to the internet café. Anna had shown little reaction to the news that her father was dead. However, when she had herself read about him and that the police were no longer searching for her, and no other suspects had been arrested, she had bowed her head in shame. By the time she returned to the cottage she was aware of the consequences her disappearance had created, and was almost overwhelmed with a sense of guilt. She had not discussed with Jo the need to uproot and find somewhere else to hide. She was even uncertain that she would agree to it; for herself she had found peace and had been happy for the first time in years. She was realizing the implications and cost of what she had done, and was now contemplating returning to England, but was intelligent enough to realize that she would have to face a barrage of questions from the police and might be charged with wasting their time for not coming forward earlier. Nowhere had she read of the poisoning or the threats that had been made, so she was unaware of exactly how her father had died. The article simply stated that he had not recovered after collapsing while being questioned and the police were no longer looking for a suspect connected to his daughter's murder.

Jo heard the scrape of the bench and knew immediately that Anna had moved from the yard. It

593

was so dark outside, the small lantern the only means of light; even the moon seemed to have paled into insignificance. She stepped outside, and could see Anna standing by the hosepipe they used as a shower. She was bending down a few feet away from it, and Jo walked softly towards her.

'The new crops are coming up well – they like this damp earth and being in the shade.'

She was pointing to the old wooden crates filled with wood-chips and wet newspapers from where the growing mushrooms' white heads were beginning to sprout.

'My mother taught me how to grow the most edible ones, and how to recognize the dangerous ones, the poisonous ones. She was an authority on all the different species and helped me write an essay about the poison that possibly caused the death of the Roman Emperor–'

'We need to talk, Anna.'

'Not yet, Jo, give me a little more time.'

'We might not have it. I wish to God I had never made that call to London.'

Anna turned to stare into Jo's concerned face, and then looked away, her voice hardly audible.

'For God's sake, let me mourn for Daddy; he did not deserve to be accused of abusing and killing me. He was a stupid weak man, but not a bad one.'

'I know, dear.'

Her voice grew softer still. 'No, you don't know, you don't know at all.'

'Then talk to me, because I need to know. I am so scared I am losing you, Anna, I don't think I could bear it.'

She wanted to hold out her arms and hug Anna tightly, but was incapable of doing so because she was afraid she would be rejected. Instead she looked on hopelessly as Anna continued to press her foot down onto the trays of mushrooms. The void between them felt impossible to bridge and to stop herself from crying Jo walked into the cottage and closed the door.

The small bed of wooden planks cobbled together covered with a straw mattress was not exactly comfortable, but was just about adequate and the duvet was feather-light. Two candles lit the stone-walled room and the shutters closed out the cold night air. Jo could hear footsteps on the old wooden porch floor, the scrape of the chair, and lastly she heard the low sound of sobbing as Anna entered the cottage.

At some point in the night Jo had fallen into a restless sleep, waking before the sun rose and creeping to open the bedroom door to see into the main room of the cottage. Anna was sleeping in front of the fire she must have lit, her head resting on a quilt pillow and her long tanned legs lazily crossing each other. Her slender arms were resting in a ballet pose and her skin shone as if oiled, her white-blonde hair like a child's framing her perfect face. Placed beside her were pages and pages of her scrawled looped writing and Jo noticed that she had printed her own name on the first page. She hesitated for only a moment before she eased them away and took them back to the bedroom.

My darling Jo, I have tried to make the right decision,

and as much as I believe it is the only thing to do, it is also difficult for me to even contemplate returning to England. I know how much you love me, and love living here in our little home and find the environment perfect for your painting. However, the time has come for me to go my own way and sadly without you. I will be forever grateful for what you have done for me and you have more than likely saved my life, but I now have to face reality as I cannot continue to live in our make-believe world. I am not Anna, but Amy, and I feel a terrible guilt about what happened to my father. I suspect my mother may have brought about his death and in many ways I feel I should return home to get the answers I so desperately need. As you know, I was subjected to my mother's madness for many years, but it was when I was thirteen that things began to get really bad and she and Daddy started to argue all the time, so much so I actually hated being around them. When they decided to separate Mummy still had her mood swings, but she found solace in her work and life became a little more bearable for a short while, but I soon began to realize that every weekend I spent with Daddy was like a knife to her heart. The point came when I knew I would have to do something drastic to get away from her or I might be killed. Whether or not she intended hurting me, she did, and perhaps sometimes without even being aware of what she was doing. I often used to feel physically sick and had fevers and attacks of vomiting without realizing she was feeding me her deadly concoctions. She rarely cooked, but she sometimes made a spaghetti bolognese, which she knew was my favourite, and always just before she would drop me off to stay with Daddy. He was such a sad creature, so dominated by her, even frightened of her because he refused to acknowledge his own sexuality. He would attempt to portray himself to me as such a virile sexy man, believing his prostitutes and girlfriends were proof he was heterosexual. He so wanted and needed to know I loved him and preferred to be with him instead of Mother. I knew about his rent boys, and his love for Simon, as the way he spoke and smiled about him made it obvious. Mother would never let him go, I knew she was often outside Green Street spying on us, calling poor Daddy on his mobile, she would never leave us alone, and life with her was becoming impossible.

Daddy was so unintelligent, so incapable of being anything but a plaything for Mother, that I began to detest his weakness, and sadly found him to be a wretched failure. Every weekend I spent with Mother was an interrogation of who he was seeing, and I was forced to tell her about the peephole in the wall, his women, his wretched drawers of underwear; he kept them as some kind of trophy, I even knew he wore them and pranced in front of the wardrobe mirror, and she would insist I describe every detail. It was horrible, she was impossible and I begged her not to tell Daddy.

I am not like my father, I am not like my mother, but between them they smothered me and my life was spent constantly trying to please them. To live at home and be afraid to spark her rage if there was so much as a tissue left out of place in my bedroom was torture. She selected my clothes, she inspected my room, and my life was constantly checked for imperfections. I was made to appear as Miss Perfect. She employed Agnes, a hideous woman who would sift through my personal things, a driver who constantly tried to touch my thighs. The hope I could get away from both of them was always close to the surface, the only thing that kept me going. I behaved appallingly when I was with Daddy as I always felt so sick, and had constant bowel trouble, and I was so tired I couldn't be bothered to clean up after myself. I knew if I was to continue staying with him I would become as inept and spiritually vacant as he was.

My time with you proved that I am not wicked, that I am not incapable of loving, and if it had not been for you, my life would have continued to be unbearable. This has been a joyous and life-enhancing time and I feel I am strong enough to face whatever I need to do. I have to do it by myself, and I don't want any arguments and pleas for me to change my mind.

Amy.

Jo lay back on the pillows and the fear she had of being abandoned made her feel physically ill. She would try and persuade Amy to stay, but if necessary she would return to the UK with her and face up to her crimes and any punishment meted out by the law. They had committed a serious theft of valuable property and Jo had instigated that, and she would take the responsibility, particularly since Amy was only sixteen years old. They had celebrated her birthday together in the cottage, but nevertheless when they had begun their relationship she was underage.

Jo began to dress, putting on jeans, T-shirt and leather sandals with an old leather jerkin – although it was extremely hot in the daytime the nights could often become cold. She brushed her hair and stood staring at her reflection in a small cracked mirror on a table they used to put all their cosmetics and sun creams on. She was as deeply tanned as Amy, and her hair was also bleached almost white by the sun. Unlike Amy, her hair was very curly; she ran her fingers through it and then looked round for her old straw sunhat. She picked it up from where it lay beside the bed, looking sadly at the crumpled duvet and creased pillows. She patted them straight and stood back as the tears filled her eyes, but wiping them firmly away she refused to allow herself to become emotional. They had spent many hours curled around each other in this small roughly made bed, professing undying love, enjoying their closeness, gentle and considerate of each other's naked bodies and sensuality.

She went quietly to the door, not wanting to wake Amy if she was still sleeping. But the room was empty and panic began to rise as she ran to the small makeshift kitchen annexe, her heart beating so rapidly she gasped for breath. Pushing open the back door to the small yard where they kept the chickens, she ran to the hutch, but it was empty; the caged door left open.

Jo ran back to the cottage and, standing outside the door, called out, 'Anna!' and then, 'Amy!' but received no reply. She checked their few bags and discovered that Amy's rucksack she had packed in readiness to leave had gone. Left on the old worn chair was the empty plastic bag that had held the tiara, and all Jo could do was run this way and that, still calling out for Amy, but it was obvious that she had left.

Jo hurried out to the flattened area they had

cleared to park the Land Rover but it was still there. She hurtled down the pathway with its lines of seashells and stood in the narrow lane, shading her eyes, desperate to catch sight of Amy, but there was no sign. Berating herself for panicking, she knew she had to calm down. Amy could not have gone far on foot, and so she returned to the house to find the car keys they always left on a hook by the door. They were not there. Sobbing, she searched everywhere, trying to remember if she had brought them into the cottage. She looked for Anna's passport, but couldn't find it anywhere. All she could do was repeat, 'Oh my God, oh my God,' as, between sobbing and gasping for breath, she continued searching for the Land Rover keys, until she discovered they were still in the ignition.

Fifteen minutes later Jo was driving at a frantic pace in an attempt to catch up with Amy. The girl was not on the dusty sand track and Jo presumed she must have caught a lift from one of the locals and been driven into Mazatlán. Just as she reached the tarmac road the engine began to splutter and she closed her eyes, praying that it was not true, because the petrol gauge didn't work, but the spluttering and shuddering of the old engine signified it was empty.

There was nothing for it but to return to the cottage to get her wallet as she had simply run empty-handed from the place in the hope of catching Amy. She then had to go on foot, carrying a petrol can, on the long trek to the nearest gas station on the outskirts of town. The sun was blistering hot as Jo eventually got to the petrol station and filled the can after hitching a ride in a farmer's run-down truck. He took her back to the Land Rover and she finally drove into town. She was sweating heavily, alternating between crying and angrily cursing that she had not woken Amy sooner. She drove to the bus station and made enquiries there, and then headed for the beach in the hope of catching sight of her, but by noon, struggling beneath the overpowering heat of the midday sun, she eventually turned back towards the cottage. The hens were clucking around waiting for their feed, but she couldn't even think about tending to them as she hoped that she was wrong and Amy would come back.

Jo walked around the empty cottage, too exhausted to even cry, then lay down on the bed and tried to think what she should do next. She picked up the letter and read it again and again, and the more she read it the worse she felt. She debated returning to England by herself in the hope of seeing Amy there, but then she had to also accept the fact that she didn't have enough money for a plane ticket.

Over and over she tried to think of what Amy would be doing, and if she was heading for an airport, if she would go to Mexico City and fly from there, but she had made enquiries at the bus station and no one had seen the blonde English girl. It was depressing and frustrating, and hard to believe that after all they had been through Amy would have chosen to walk away and leave her. At some point she did acknowledge that Amy had left her parents and without any thought of the repercussions; now she had done the same to her.

She started to grow angry. She remembered her saying that Jo did not know her, and she began to think that it was true, groaning at the terrible sense of betrayal. For the second time in her life she had loved deeply and profoundly and the rejection this time felt even worse.

After a long flight on which he'd scarcely managed to sleep, DI Reid arrived in Mexico City and hired a vehicle. This had not been without its problems as the Hertz at the airport had no cars available, and so he had eventually agreed to rent a camper van, which cost more, but he was eager not to waste any more time. It had been a hair-raising few hours as he had attempted to circumnavigate the thronging mass of traffic in Mexico City. He had, with great difficulty, eventually traced the jewellers and they had confirmed when shown the photographs of Josephine Polka that it was without doubt the woman that had attempted to sell the tiara. They didn't recognize Amy Fulford as the woman had been alone. The jewellers impressed him, seeming well-established and very successful, although whether they would have paid the right price for the tiara was questionable. He had told them only that he was working for an insurance company for a 'finder's fee', and that the tiara although not stolen was part of an inheritance.

With little to go on, Reid made the journey to Mazatlán. The only clue he had was so tenuous that he hoped it wasn't going to be a fruitless costly journey. The drive was over eight hours, but he had stopped only to fill the petrol tank twice and grab a bite to eat. The heat was oppressive and he had stripped off his shirt to wear only a vest and a pair of shorts he had thrown into his case at the last minute. He had even taken his socks off, as the air conditioning in the camper van was faulty. It was getting dark by the time he eventually saw the road signs to Mazatlán, and it was with great relief that he neared the beautiful beach-side town. The air was not as stifling here and with the windows open, he was feeling less uncomfortable. He had driven through the main town, passing glorious white stucco-fronted hotels, and was on the main road when he realized he needed to fill up once more, so he pulled over to a gas station. As he picked up a six-pack of bottled water and was paying for it at the counter he casually asked if they would look at a photograph as he was there searching for some friends.

Reid returned to the camper van and opened a bottle of water; he could hardly believe that he had hit the jackpot so soon. It had taken a while for the station attendant to understand his enquiries but a twenty-dollar bill had helped. The man had drawn the directions on a scrap of paper and had managed to convey that the lady he was hoping to meet lived in a farmer's cottage on the outskirts of the main town a further twenty or more miles north. Reid was warned that the roads were not lit, and in some areas still unfinished, and when he reached the end of the main tarmac road he would need to drive carefully as the track became uneven, with gravel-filled potholes.

Reid took the wrong turn over and over again; the camper van was spluttering and the springs made each dip in the uneven road painful on his backside. Coming to a barred broken gate, he was going to carry on, but his headlights picked out small white pebbles that appeared to indicate a path. He turned in and his lights caught the parked Land Rover, and now he could see the white pebbles were seashells marking out the narrow path to a run-down cottage. The shutters were drawn, but chinks of light indicated someone was inside. He parked up and walked towards the wooden door, swearing as he twisted his ankle in the dark.

Almost at the door, he ran his hands through his hair and buttoned up his shirt, and was about to knock when it flew open. He recognized her immediately but before he could say anything she shouted at him to go away and slammed the door.

'Miss Polka, please, please LET ME TALK TO YOU.'

She inched the door open and there was no recognition on her face but rather fear as she asked what he wanted.

'Do you remember me? I came to meet you at the school in Ascot, I'm DI Reid.'

She stared dumbfounded as if unable to comprehend what he had just said. What happened next caught him completely by surprise, as she literally collapsed in front of him and he had to push the door further open to pick her up. He carried her in his arms as he looked round for a suitable place to put her down, and noticed there was a pile of cushions by the unlit fire.

'Miss Polka, Miss Polka.' He propped her head

up in the crook of his arm.

She slowly opened her eyes and he took a cushion and placed it beneath her head. She seemed to be totally incapable of speaking or acknowledging him, but just lay there, her eyes open. He glanced around to see if there was a kitchen or running water to fetch her a drink. The two candles gave only a faint light to the room and he knocked his shin on a stool before he found, in the small annexe, a plastic gallon water bottle. He poured some into a tin mug and carried it back to her.

'See if you can sit up and sip this.'

He lifted her by placing his hand under her shoulders and held the mug out for her to drink. She took a couple of sips and then rested her head against his chest.

'I'm sorry,' she murmured as he encouraged her to drink some more. It seemed to revive her, as she moved away from him, and then cradled her head in her hands.

'Do you remember me?' he asked gently.

'Yes of course I do,' she said weakly.

'I've come a long way to talk to you. I got lucky at the gas station in Mazatlán and they directed me here.'

He slowly got to his feet; after such a long drive he felt stiff all over. He walked to a low wooden carved chair with a cushion and sat down, rubbing his thighs and knees. He couldn't help but notice that she still wore the ballet shoes and her hair, which had reminded him of Marilyn Monroe's, was even more blonde and she was deeply tanned. He was slightly embarrassed that he was wearing tatty baggy shorts and lace-up shoes without socks, while he knew he must stink of body odour as he had been sweating most of the day and night.

Slowly she stared at him, then sat up further and reached for the tin mug to finish the water.

'She's not here,' she whispered.

'Are you referring to Amy?' he asked and she looked at him as if he were an idiot.

'Who do you think I am talking about? That's why you're here, isn't it?'

She turned away from him and rested both hands on the stone floor before she eased herself up.

'You have a lot of explaining to do,' he said. 'However, I've had a very long drive and I wouldn't mind taking a shower first before we talk.'

She didn't answer, but lit a candle and put it inside the small glass lantern. She went into the bedroom and returned with a cheap worn beach towel, informing him they had no shower, but a hosepipe was rigged up outside and he could wash with that. She tossed the towel to him and said there was soap and shampoo by the hose-pipe. As she led him there, she moved in the way he remembered, like a ballet dancer gliding lightly across the ground. He asked if she minded getting him a clean shirt and underwear from the camper van.

He stood like a teenager, wearing his jockey shorts and nothing else as he held the hosepipe over his head. She held up a shirt and underwear then tossed them beside the beach towel and asked if he was hungry.

'I am, in fact I've only had a sandwich since—'

She didn't listen to what he was saying and returned to the cottage. Self-consciously he realized he was standing half naked, and the gathering mosquitoes were beginning to bite the hell out of him. He dried himself off as fast as he could, got out of his wet jockey shorts and into his dry crumpled ones and then pulled on the cotton shirt that he had bought on arrival at the airport. It was typically Mexican, wide-sleeved and full, with embroidery around the collar.

Heading back into the cottage, he found she was frying up some bacon, and coffee was bubbling in a tin jug. She had set out plates and mugs on a wooden table with a lit candle in an old wine bottle.

'You said she's not here, so where is she?'

She turned with a wooden spoon in her hand. 'I don't know, Detective Reid.'

She finished frying the bacon and used the same pan for some eggs. She placed a hunk of rough home-made bread on the table and poured two mugs of coffee. Yet again he was very aware of how beautifully she moved, very light on her feet, swaying as she deftly returned to spoon out the eggs from the frying pan onto two decorative plates.

She carried both plates to the table; he had three rashers of bacon and two fried eggs. She had one egg, saying she wasn't very hungry, but she jabbed her fork into the yolk.

'I thought my hens might have run off this morning, but they are back in their hutch and these are freshly laid,' she said, as if making polite conversation.

They ate in silence; she hardly touched her food, but he was so hungry he could have eaten twice the amount. He was trying to think of how he should approach asking her the multitude of questions he needed answers to, but she took the dirty plates into the kitchen and came out with the coffee pot to top up their mugs. She crossed to the fireside and began heaping bundles of tied twigs into the grate and placing logs around them before she skilfully brought a lit taper from the candles to light the fire.

She was very adept at blowing the kindling until it caught fully alight and began to burn while he remained sitting at the table, his hands cupped around the mug of black coffee. He loved the way she moved, and she turned, catching him watching her.

'I didn't lie to you when you questioned me at the school,' she said. 'I truthfully had no idea where Amy was, and I was shocked by what you told me and was frightened that something terrible had happened to her.'

'When did you know?'

She shrugged and said that it was after she had been told to leave, and just before she had arranged to travel on a group tour with other artists to Peru for two weeks.

'She called me, and made me promise to keep silent, or she wouldn't tell me where she was, and so I agreed.'

'Where was she?'

'She'd been staying at a house in Henley as she knew the owner was abroad and where a spare key had been hidden.'

'Simon Boatly's?'

She nodded.

'But he came back to the house not long after Amy went missing?'

'I know, she told me when I saw her. It really frightened her as she had to hide in a wardrobe until late at night and then sneak out of the house.'

'Hang on a second ... if you went and saw her, where and when was this?'

'The weekend after you first spoke to me at the school. She'd gone to a youth hostel in Oxford. She knew the place a bit because her mother had taken her there before to show her round the old colleges of the university.'

'Did she see the TV and newspaper appeals about her?'

'Yes, but she'd changed her appearance with fake glasses, tied her hair up and dressed scruffily. She figured with so many students in Oxford she'd just blend in and no one would recognize her.'

'But if she saw the TV appeal and the state her parents were in, why didn't she make contact to at least say she was alive and well?'

'I tried to persuade her to get in touch with them or you, but Amy was adamant that she would not do that and refused to explain why. She only said that she wanted to go away, stay away from them forever.'

'What about money? She'd made no withdrawals from her bank.'

'Because she didn't want anyone to be able to trace her. I tried to make her change her mind, but she was very strung out and insisted that she would be able to finance herself to go abroad. I asked how, but she wouldn't tell me.'

'But she left her passport at her home?'

'I know that,' Jo snapped.

He lifted his hands in submission as she turned away and remained silent for a few moments before she continued.

'My full name is Josephine Poliakoff. I started using Polka years ago as a surname as it sort of sounded to me more like a dancer. I had a younger sister who died just before I became an art teacher at the school.'

'The girl on the beach in the picture in the hallway of your school cottage?' he recalled and she gave him an odd smile.

'Yes, you have a good memory. Her name was Anna and I still had her old passport. She was barely older than Amy.'

'I thought at the time she looked similar to Amy, but her hair was much shorter.'

'Amy cut her hair short so there was even more of a similarity between them and the passport was still valid. Then I had Miss Harrington walking into the cottage and it was just awful as she looked around and then implied that she had received some anonymous information about me – I told you. Anyway, she asked me if I was a lesbian and said that I was unsuitable for my position with the girls, blah blah, and I didn't wait to even explain anything but gave her my resignation – the relief on her face! But as to who would have written to her – God knows, probably that little bitch Serena.'

He could hardly believe it, but he didn't want to interrupt as she described booking and paying for a flight online for Amy, who downloaded and printed off the e-ticket at an internet café. Amy's flight was a one-way trip to Santa Fe and so as not to create any suspicion, she herself left for Peru and they had a tentative plan to reunite if Amy succeeded in leaving the UK.

'So when did she fly to Santa Fe?'

'About a week or two after I left the school. You have to understand that for Amy there was no going back, so she stopped reading the papers or watching the news. She genuinely didn't know about what happened to her father and mother since she ran away.'

'So how did you end up in this godforsaken place?'

'When my art tour finished I took a flight from Peru to San Francisco, bought the old Land Rover and, not even knowing if she would still be there, I drove to Santa Fe. It took me a week or so to find Amy. She was working in a restaurant, living in a commune with other kids, hippie types, junkies and runaways like herself.'

She gave a long sigh and seemed defeated as she quietly explained how they planned a trip to Mexico City and subsequently decided to keep on the move to Mazatlán. They had agreed to not use any mobile phones or even her laptop; they had wanted to be completely free of any possible contact from England.

'We found this place, and together made it habitable, and this is where we have been living since Santa Fe.'

He looked around and gave a half-smile: it was not in anyway luxurious but with the lit fire and the warm glow of the candles it was comfortable, albeit with no electricity.

'I suppose you want to know how we financed it all?'

He nodded and she continued.

'To start with, my savings, and then Amy had numerous bits and pieces of jewellery she said she had been given, and we prised out the stones and I would drive into town and sell them, but she never accompanied me. We were very careful not to create any suspicion, but had more than enough to buy the hens and the furnishings and obviously groceries, in fact everything we needed.'

She rubbed at her curls and began twisting one round and round in her forefinger. He remembered her doing the same thing when he had interviewed her in England.

'Go on,' he said quietly.

'At some point we were starting to get a bit worried as funds were low and she wanted me to use the tiara to raise cash. She wanted to prise out the stones, but it seemed to me to be too destructive as it was such a beautiful art deco design and I knew it had to be worth a lot of money undamaged.'

'Did she tell you where she got it from?'

'She said she had been left it all in a will, that it was hers to do whatever she wanted with. The other pieces had been a couple of rings, a bracelet and a pearl necklace.'

She sucked in her breath and sighed. 'Stupid, it was so stupid of me, and I ruined everything by trying to sell it in Mexico City. I had created too much interest as the men in the jewellery shop wanted me to show them something to prove I owned the tiara and I think they thought it was stolen.'

He decided to let her finish her story before telling her he suspected the jewellery was stolen from Simon Boatly, and that the use of her passport to fly out of London had been the reason he had been able to trace her. She rubbed her head, making her curls stand up on end, and then got up to place more kindling on the fire. She drew a cushion to sit beside it and told him how she had read the advert in the *New York Times* from the lawyers.

'I was even more stupid because I called them from the jewellery shop, and that was when I found out that Amy's father was dead.'

She sniffed as the tears welled up in her eyes and she used her shirt cuff to wipe them.

'Did they mention that Amy as her father's beneficiary was possibly in line to inherit three million pounds?'

She gasped. 'Three million?'

'Whether or not she would be able to claim it is doubtful because her father had been left it in Simon Boatly's will on condition that he divorced her mother. As he died before the divorce was actually agreed it is legally very questionable, but the lawyers seemed to be treating it as a possible legacy.'

'Three million? My God, she doesn't know. I am a bit confused about Simon Boatly, what happened to him?'

'He died a few days before Marcus Fulford.'

'Oh my God,' she said and drew up her knees to rest her head against them.

'I think the jewellery Amy told you was inherited belonged to Simon Boatly and she stole it.'

'Oh Christ,' she muttered, still with her head on her knees. 'She must have taken it when she was hiding out at his house in Henley.'

'Did he know she had taken it?'

Reid shook his head, saying he doubted it and that Boatly was a very wealthy man who had probably not even looked at the jewellery for many years, as he had not even bothered to renew the insurance. He was by now aching with tiredness. Although so many unanswered questions had now been ironed out, the most important one remained: where was Amy now? It was as if Jo had read his mind because she looked up and stared at him before turning back to the firelight.

'I don't know where she is. She took the tiara and left early this morning.'

She got up and walked into the bedroom, as his head dropped forward and he jolted up.

'This morning?' he said loudly, getting to his feet.

She came out with the letter.

'For Christ's sake, I took it that she had left a while ago, but this morning?'

'Yes,' Jo snapped and pushed the letter towards him. 'I have been out searching for her but no one had seen her at the bus station. I asked everyone and searched all the roads but she was nowhere to be seen. I don't know where she has gone, she could have hitched a ride. She's broken my heart, just walked out on me as if all we have been through together stands for nothing. I don't know how she could do that to me.'

He was not even listening as he stood by the lit candle reading the letter. Finishing it, he folded it and held it out for her to take.

'Well, what she has written certainly answers many of the questions I have wondered about for so long, especially over Amy's state of mind and why she ran away from her parents. Question is, do you believe everything she has written is true?' he asked.

Jo pressed the folded pages to her chest. 'How do I know if anything she has told me is the truth any more?'

'Do you remember when I saw you at the school I said that we suspected Amy was prostituting herself...?'

'Yes, I asked her about that.'

'And...?' he asked, raising his eyebrows.

'She'd seen her father with prostitutes and wanted to know why and how long he'd been seeing them, but was scared to ask him. She was confused and thought that if she dressed up in her school uniform she could get closer to the girls and talk to them. A man pulled up in a car and asked her something but she didn't hear him so she asked what he wanted and he drove away. One of the prostitutes threatened her, she was scared and ran off.'

Reid smiled ironically, realizing the actual innocence of the situation, and thought to himself how crass it was that DCS Douglas was convinced from the CCTV that Amy treated prostitution as some sort of hobby. He took a deep breath and sat down. 'Listen, I am really exhausted. I mean, part of me wants to go out and drive around to try and find her, but I think it will be more beneficial to search in daylight. I also think I need to tell you what has happened in the UK and the shock-waves her disappearance has caused.'

'Oh God, if I go back will I be arrested?'

He suddenly lost it, glaring at her. 'I should have arrested you for having a sexual relationship with an underage teenager when you told me about your lesbian affair with Amy.'

'Well why didn't you?' she snapped.

'I don't fucking know, and you have no bloody idea what this investigation has done to me.' He could keep in his anguish no longer. 'While you and that girl lived in some fantasy world of secrets and make believe, I went through a nightmare that I have been caught up in ever since. I nearly lost my mind and my job while trying to get to the bottom of it all. I believed an innocent young girl had been murdered, then wrongly accused her father of sexually abusing her and disposing of her body. You are a teacher, you're supposed to act responsibly, and now all you seem to care about is your bloody self and whether or not you might get arrested!'

The slap caught him off guard and he lost his balance; it infuriated him to such an extent he lurched forward and grabbed her by the wrists.

'Instead of bleating about the possibility of being arrested you need to realize that Amy's running away was a major factor in tipping her mother over the edge, causing her mind to become possessed by a maniac bent on revenge and poisoning anyone perceived as an enemy.'

'You can't blame Amy for that, you can see from her letter to me that her mother was already mentally disturbed.'

'Had you persuaded her to come forward at the beginning of this sordid mess, then the journal would have been exposed as being written by her mother. I could have got medical help for her, but above all three innocent men would still be alive, so yes I can in some ways blame Amy and you for that!'

Jo backed away from him, dragging her wrists free. He lifted his hands in a submissive gesture, recognizing she was genuinely frightened.

'I'm sorry, but this has obsessed me for so long, and just so you know I am not here with any connection to the police, I'm here because I needed to prove...' He couldn't find the right words and stood shaking his head because he had an overpowering feeling he was going to break down and cry. He turned from her, hating becoming over-emotional and disliking the fact she seemed scared of him.

'I was one of the casualties, believe it or not. I've lost my way and I've had to take sick leave due to the stress.'

'I don't understand.'

He held out his hand and asked her to sit with him. She truthfully did not understand and yet she held his hand as they sat in front of the fire.

'Let me start from the beginning. Lena and Marcus Fulford reported Amy missing, and it was my job to investigate her disappearance. They brought to my attention a journal purportedly written by Amy.'

'The journal, I know she told me she had been given it as a birthday present from her father. She did want to write short stories and I think had begun to write something but found that the journal had been opened so tore out the page because it was, I suppose, yet another indication that her mother pried into everything – she even said that at one time she had kept diaries but her mother read them... I think she just left it in her bedroom at her mother's house.'

'It was her mother who actually wrote in it.'

'But why?'

He kept it as brief as possible; she made no interruption and only released her hand from his to put another log on the fire. Quietly he told her about the sessions at the secure unit between Professor Cornwall and Lena Fulford and how her emotional breakdown and the appalling revelations of her abuse had affected him. Lastly he described how Lena had admitted to using poison to eliminate her so-called enemies. He made little reference to the decision by DCI Jackson to close the case, with Marcus Fulford more than implicated in abusing his daughter and disposing of her body.

'Oh my God,' she said softly.

'The most incriminating evidence against him was the discovery of the maroon sweater that Amy was last seen wearing, which was found in his rented flat. Plus the Cartier watch that had been in his car.'

'It doesn't make sense,' she said sadly.

'It did to the inquiry, because it meant that Amy had to have returned to his flat, as she was supposed to be going to see her father to collect the watch.'

Jo got up and stretched, in an attempt to detract from how she was feeling. She guiltily realized that she had unwittingly played a part in encouraging Amy to never make contact with her parents again.

'What has happened to her mother?'

Reid shrugged and explained that after the last session she had become virtually catatonic and was now held in a secure mental facility. He added that he suspected she was perhaps better off being unable to remember, and due to her condition she would be deemed unfit to plead and there would be no trial.

'Approve or not, it meant the case was closed – well it appeared that way to everyone else – but I have to live with the truth and it hurts me.'

'Why?'

He gave a long sigh and his eyes felt as if they were burning with tiredness.

'I honestly don't know, apart from the fact that I had a lot of interaction with Marcus Fulford, and he was a weak man, but I could never get my head around the accusations that he had abused Amy,' he confessed. 'He seemed genuinely distressed about her disappearance and even when all the information about him being bisexual and hiring prostitutes and rent boys started to surface he never tried to lie his way out of it, he appeared to me to want to find his daughter. I also had to deal with Lena, and not until I witnessed the sessions did I realize that she was severely mentally ill. Now in retrospect, if I play out all the numerous times I talked with her, she virtually telegraphed her different personalities. They surfaced time and time again, but I was predominantly so intent on finding her daughter I just accepted that she was behaving oddly due to stress.'

Jo was now lying on a small sofa, with one arm resting across her chest, and her eyes were closed.

'Well, now you know it all,' he said, getting to his feet.

'Do we?' she said. 'I am trying to imagine what it must have been like to live with Lena, how Amy had to become Miss Perfect, afraid to leave so much as a tissue loose in her bedroom. Then having the complete opposite when she stayed with her father, his sexual antics, and if it is true that her mother was feeding her poison to make her sick, then it's no wonder she wanted to run away.'

He yawned, stretched his arms and looked at his wristwatch. It was almost five in the morning; the sun had started to stream through the wooden blinds.

Jo shook her head. 'The way Amy had to be perfect at school, even after the times she spent with me, I am guilty of never really understanding the incredible pressure she must have been feeling. I am not excusing myself for what I did, but she told me that Serena Newman was blackmailing her, posting the disgusting comments on her Facebook page, and that she had found out that Amy had been with me in my cottage at the school, and she had wanted her Cartier watch to keep quiet about us. I am even more sure that the anonymous tip-off to Miss Harrington came from her.'

He had moved to lie on the cushions in front of the dying fire, and he was too tired to even reply as Jo went on.

'She did go to her father's that afternoon; she changed into an old hoodie and jeans and then caught the train to Henley and hid there. She told me she made the decision to run away when she got to Serena's. She'd lost her Cartier watch and thought it might be somewhere at her father's; it was expensive and she intended to sell it for cash to run away, not give it to Serena.'

She got up and went to the big bag she had put their paintings in ready for them to take when they left. She began to sort through various canvases, and then opened a big artist's sketchpad and flicked through it.

She turned as she heard him snoring, and went to pick up an embroidered Mexican rug to lay over him; he was out for the count. She carried the sketchbook into the bedroom, closing the door and opening the shutters. She intended finding the particular drawing she wanted to show him, but resting back on the pillows she couldn't keep awake.

Reid woke a few hours later. Disorientated, he sat up and then flopped back, hardly able to believe he had fallen asleep. He took a few deep breaths and got to his feet, and then wondered in panic if Jo Polka had taken off. He pushed open the shutters, but the Land Rover was still there, the hens were clucking frantically and as he opened the door to look out he discovered the sun was already blistering hot. He walked round to the hosepipe and stripped off to shower again, but paused to look into the window of the bedroom. She was fast asleep. He turned on the hose, making the most of the relative privacy.

Feeling more refreshed, but his body still aching, he went to his camper van to take out his washbag, then used the small cracked mirror in the kitchen while he shaved. He had lit the gas ring to heat up the remains of the coffee in the pot. There was no fridge, only an ancient cold box as there was no electricity. He opened the back door and noticed potted geranium plants with brilliant red flowers and, beyond, rows of fig trees and cactus plants.

Shaved and showered, he still did not attempt to wake her, but went to the hen hutch and found three freshly laid eggs. He returned to the kitchen and searched for the frying pan to make breakfast. She had left it in a bucket of water, and he wiped it dry and placed it on the Calor gas stove. The coffee was soon hot and he dried off the plates from the same bucket of water and wanted to fry the eggs, but couldn't find oil or butter. He opened a green-painted cupboard with a worn mesh door and found a small jar of honey and the remains of the loaf of bread.

He knocked on the bedroom door and, getting no response, pushed it open, but the room was empty. In panic he ran to the front door and opening it he saw her standing naked under the makeshift shower. She had the most perfect body, an all-over tan, a neat muscular frame and pert breasts with heavy dark large nipples, and he had to catch his breath because he was so aroused. He stepped back into the cottage and with embarrassment called out to her that he had made breakfast.

She came in with just a cheap threadbare towel wrapped around her body, her hair wet and her shoulders glistening as she had not bothered to dry herself.

'Well, isn't this a treat?' she said and smiled, and did her little dance steps around the table before she went into the bedroom. She re-emerged after only a few moments wearing a white cotton shift dress with embroidered flowers around the neck, barefoot and her hair still damp. She carried a large sketchpad, and placed it down on the table.

'I was looking through this last night and must have fallen asleep, but I wanted to show you something – they're some of Amy sketches, she is becoming very adept, really quite talented.'

She hesitated and bit down on her lip, then shook her head, not wanting to cry. Instead she smiled and poured herself the very stewed coffee, and prodded the rather over-cooked egg. He found her utterly endearing as she complimented him on his culinary endeavours.

'I went into the hen house,' he said boyishly.

'Well clever you, and perhaps you'd like to feed them as I didn't get around to it yesterday.'

She was trying so hard not to show how deeply unhappy she was, and he couldn't think of anything to say that would make it any easier. She constantly made him feel awkward and inadequate at small talk, so he ate his eggs and reached for the sketchpad.

'I remembered something last night,' Jo said, 'something Amy told me about a holiday she had been on with her parents to Antigua. She said that Simon Boatly had turned up in a speedboat and wanted her to go water-skiing. Her mother had got into a terrible rage and it was hideous as she had spoiled the entire holiday. Amy had overheard her parents arguing. I am not sure if she knew then about her father's relationship with Boatly, but she was forbidden to ever see him again, or go to his home in Henley, although her father used to take her sometimes on the condition she never told her mother.'

He wiped the remainder of his eggs with the bread, which was now somewhat stale.

'I saw some pictures and video of the Antigua holiday.'

Jo began to flick through the sketchpad; he leaned over and put his hand out to stop her.

'What's that one?'

'Oh that's one of mine, a sketch from the amazing desert in Sonora – it's always desolate and the sky and sand make it feel as if you are on the edge of the world. Sonora was used as a location for the movie *Catch-22*.'

He looked at a couple more of the same sketches; they were as she described, as if depicting the edge of the world.

'You get the most indescribable feeling of peace,' she went on. 'I went there when my first partner left me; it felt as if I was on the brink of despair, but then after walking mile upon mile on the incredible soft sand, and with the brilliant blue sky touching the horizon, I knew I would be able to forgive, not forget ... just forgive.'

Again he wanted to say something, but was silenced by the same inadequacy, as if his brain would not function or allow him to say what he felt.

'I loved her as I love Amy, and I still can't believe she won't be a part of my life. Have you ever loved...?' She stopped and laughed and leaned forward. 'I don't even know your Christian name.'

He flushed and said that his name was Victor, although no one ever really called him that, but mostly Vic for short.

'Victor, have you ever loved someone with a wild unexplainable passion?' she said softly and gave him the sweetest of smiles.

He had never loved anyone in the way she had described, but not wanting to answer her question, he said he would like to go to the desert while he was in Mexico.

'You should, it will open your heart.'

She sifted through the many sketches and then withdrew two and placed them side by side in front of him.

'I never met him, but that is Simon Boatly.' She tapped with her index finger.

Reid nodded and remembered meeting him, being aware of his handsomeness, his suntan, his blond bleached hair, and even recalled his ankles and feet with the soft Moroccan slippers.

'Yes, it's a very good likeness.'

She nodded and tapped the second sketch. It was a self-portrait of Amy, with a sad expression and downcast eyes. He cocked his head to one side.

'Keep looking at it, and you tell me if what I think is true.'

He looked from one sketch to the other, and then moved them closer together.

'Her mother hated him, was incandescent with rage when he turned up in Antigua, she forbade her to see him, and counted him as an enemy. I think he was Amy's father, and if she can prove she is Simon Boatly's illegitimate daughter, surely she would also be his heir. How much did you say he was worth?'

Reid was curious about the manner and tone in which she asked about Boatly's wealth. 'I don't recall mentioning an exact amount. Why do you ask, is it important?'

'Oh I see, we are back to being the detective now, are we? But what if I am right?'

He stood up and went to pick up his shoes, the good feelings he had had towards Jo now spoiled by her interest in the inheritance. She was becoming angry as she held up the sketch.

'Look at their faces, they are identical, the same eyes.'

He sat down to pull on his shoes. 'Then it would make sense for you to find her and give her the good news, maybe also fill her in on the repercussions of her actions that I spent half the night telling you about. Maybe she'd even like to apologize to Harry Dunn's grieving widow.'

'You can't blame her, for God's sake, she was driven to the brink by her mother, and if you had been a good enough detective you would have discovered at the outset Lena Fulford was insane.'

He turned on her and his face twisted with anger. 'You want to slap me again? The reason I am here is to trace that tiara, because I will be in line for a big finder's fee, which would set me up nicely and get me out of feeling that I am on the brink of fucking madness like Lena Fulford. I ate and slept months of, as you rightly say, incompetent detective work, but right now I don't give a shit if Amy is ever found – all I care about is my own self-preservation, and it seems to me that all you care about is getting your hands on your precious girlfriend's inheritance.'

It was like a red rag to a bull. Jo grabbed at one of the knives still left on the table and came at him with the blade raised to stab him in the chest. He was able to not only twist the knife from her grasp but at the same time draw her arm up behind her back, almost pulling it out of the socket. She screamed and he relaxed his hold, turning her round to face him, and pulling her close, he kissed her. She struggled and he loosened his grip to drag her head by the hair to kiss her again. She stopped attempting to get away, her body deflated, but she did not respond to his kiss, and he released her and watched as she wiped her mouth with the sleeve of her dress. She looked disgusted, yet still ferociously angry, and he felt if he even attempted to move closer she would spit in his face.

Flushed with impotent frustration, he strode past her into the kitchen, picked up his washbag and tossed his razor into it. She was still standing in the same position and he had to brush past her to collect his keys before he walked out. He was throwing his things into the camper van when she came to the front door.

'Where are you going?' she shouted.

He paid no attention and got in the van; she ran down the path and gripped hold of the van door.

'Where are you going?' she demanded.

He said nothing as he fumbled to insert the ignition key.

'You can't leave me here.' She repeatedly hit the door of the vehicle with the flat of her hand as the engine ticked over. She started crying as he put the gearshift into reverse.

'Move away,' he said angrily, and she ran to stand behind the camper van. If he reversed he would knock her over, and he turned off the engine. She came further round as he wound down the window.

'Where are you going?' she begged and started crying.

'I am sorry for what I did in there, but you should not have tried to stab me.' He was struggling to get the words out. 'And if you really want to know, I have wanted to do exactly what I did from almost the first time I met you, so I apologize, but now I just want to leave.'

'Are you going back to England?'

He shrugged, and was astonished when she asked if she could come with him.

'No, find your own way, Jo; maybe even more importantly, find Amy, then it'll be up to the pair of you to decide what's the right thing to do.'

'But what if I can't find her?'

'Not my problem.'

'But will you report back to your boss that she

is alive?'

He sighed and shook his head. In reality he was uncertain what he was going to do, and even if he did report his findings, he had no idea of what the outcome would be.

'I don't have any money to buy a ticket.'

'Sell your paintings, or the Land Rover,' he suggested.

'What about the tiara – you said you were hoping to get a finder's fee if you found it.'

'According to you, Amy has it and is the rightful heir to it. Anyway, as far as I am concerned it's over and she's probably sold it by now. Did she take your sister's passport when she left?'

'Yes, but can't you trace her now you know what name she is using?' she persisted.

'It's possible, but that will mean reporting it to the US border police as well as Interpol and London, which will also implicate you as assisting her in the possession of a false identity document and using it to travel.'

'But will you report it when you get back? I mean, will I be under arrest?'

He looked at her; yet again he found her concern for her own welfare irritating.

'Like I said, I'm not here working for the Met, and I seriously doubt I will consider returning to work for them. I just needed answers for my own peace of mind.'

She stepped back as he turned on the engine again, and stood watching him as he reversed slowly down the track, turned at the gates and drove off. Going back to the cottage, she picked up the sketches, stacked them together and placed them into the folder. She sat and counted out what money she had left, and calculated how much she might make from selling the Land Rover. She alternated between crying and feeling rejected and angry, but with most of her possessions already packed she decided she would leave – maybe she'd get a few dollars if she sold the hens. Just as Reid had said, it was over.

Reid drove for hours, aimlessly at first, but gradually he began to enjoy the freedom of having no pressure and no deadline. He decided that he would make his way to the desert and take in the atmosphere – if nothing else it was a place to go before he returned to London. He stopped by a roadside market and bought some hand-made leather sandals with thick black soles made of discarded tyres, a pair of loose white drawstring trousers and a white cheesecloth shirt. He even bought a wide-brimmed straw hat and laughed at his reflection in a parked car's window.

He headed through Culiacán, on to Guasave, and then parked alongside the road in Los Mochis, sleeping in the camper van for the night. He kept on driving the following day, in no kind of a hurry and not worried about the passing hours. Every now and again he consulted a map and ate from roadside food stalls as he passed through Navojoa and Obregón until finally he saw the signpost to Guaymas. Stopping only for gas, he drove onto the toll road 15D and then headed onto route 15N. The whole journey had taken ages, but at last he was close to his destination, the Sonoran Desert.

He parked the camper van in what appeared to be a makeshift car park, where wooden boards warned about the lack of any cover, to not go walking in the heat of the day and to carry plenty of water. There was no other vehicle around and it was as Jo had described, desolate. The one landmark was the sign pointing to the original location of *Catch-22* the film, and it was covered in windblown sand. Taking out a rolled-up straw mat and a bottle of water, he began to head towards the massive stretch of desert sand. The heat of the day was fading, but the sand even through his rubber-soled sandals was hot and made him walk with a high step. He paused frequently to take a few deep breaths. Closing his eyes he could feel the most extraordinary emotional release and a satisfying sense of calm and peace enveloped him. He continued for about an hour, hardly able to believe that there was not one other person visible and gradually, as Jo had predicted, the sand and the sky became perfectly divided as if there was a crystal ocean beyond and he belonged there.

Something sparkled as if caught by the sunlight. He blinked in uncertainty but drew his hat lower, kept up his high-step walk and then paused to drink some water. He had never experienced such an expansive feeling; every muscle seemed to relax and his eyes slowly became accustomed to the brilliance ahead, and then he saw the figure nearly a mile away in the distance.

As he got a little closer he could just about make out that there was someone under a black umbrella with their back to him. He watched as the umbrella was raised then lowered slightly, and suddenly a shaft of light appeared to reflect on something that sparkled and created a glistening white streak that shot across the horizon in front of him.

The distance was distorted like in a mirage and he was closer than he had realized, and as he moved silently nearer he felt an incredible excitement. Unable to see who was sitting beneath the umbrella, he continued, the black silk shifted sideways and again there was that shard of light, and he was within a few feet before he came to a halt, standing directly behind the umbrella. A delicate suntanned hand and arm moved out from beneath the shade and then pulled back in. He leaned forward until he could see who was beneath the umbrella.

The white-blonde hair was short and silky, the tiara was worn low and the sunlight hit the central diamond, making it appear as if an electrical current had lit it. She was wearing a white smock, her sandals lying side by side on the bright rainbow cotton rug. He was shaking and unable to speak, as she turned without any sign of surprise, rather child-like and inquisitive. Her eyes were thick-lashed and a vibrant blue, and she stared up towards him.

All the months, all the searching and wretched consequences faded into a quiet acceptance. He had found Amy Fulford, and the sense of relief was overpowering, because he knew now that it really was over.

The publishers hope that this book has given you enjoyable reading. Large Print Books are especially designed to be as easy to see and hold as possible. If you wish a complete list of our books please ask at your local library or write directly to:

Magna Large Print Books
Magna House, Long Preston,
Skipton, North Yorkshire.
BD23 4ND

This Large Print Book for the partially sighted, who cannot read normal print, is published under the auspices of

THE ULVERSCROFT FOUNDATION

Also by Aline Templeton

The DI Marjory Fleming series

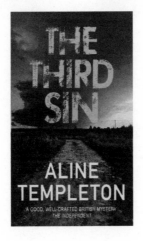